John Alexander Roche

The life of John Price Durbin

John Alexander Roche

The life of John Price Durbin

ISBN/EAN: 9783337333911

Printed in Europe, USA, Canada, Australia, Japan

Cover: Foto ©Raphael Reischuk / pixelio.de

More available books at **www.hansebooks.com**

OF

JOHN PRICE DURBIN, D.D., LL.D.,

WITH

AN ANALYSIS OF HIS HOMILETIC SKILL AND SACRED ORATORY.

BY

JOHN A. ROCHE, M.D., D.D.

WITH AN INTRODUCTION

BY

RANDOLPH S. FOSTER, D.D., LL.D.,

BISHOP OF THE METHODIST EPISCOPAL CHURCH.

"The proper study of mankind is man."—*Pope.*

"Study to show thyself approved unto God, a workman that needeth not to be ashamed, rightly dividing the word of truth."—*2 Tim.* 2. 15.

NEW YORK: PHILLIPS & HUNT.
CINCINNATI: CRANSTON & STOWE.
1889.

TO

THE YOUNG MINISTERS OF METHODISM:

IN

WHOM THE SUBJECT OF THIS BIOGRAPHY CHERISHED THE
DEEPEST INTEREST;

FOR

WHOSE ADVANCEMENT IN PULPIT POWER HE WAS EVER READY TO
EMPLOY THE BEST MEANS AT HIS COMMAND;

AND

AS AN EXPRESSION OF THE HIGH SENSE ENTERTAINED

BY

THE AUTHOR

OF THE VALUE OF KEEPING BEFORE OUR RISING MINISTRY
SO NOBLE AN EXAMPLE

OF

THE POSSIBILITIES OF THEIR HOLY CALLING:

THIS BOOK IS

RESPECTFULLY DEDICATED.

PREFACE.

IN the May number of the *Methodist Review* of 1887 there appeared an article designed to sketch the life and characterize the ministry of Dr. John P. Durbin. So deep was the interest thus awakened in the subject, that many and earnest requests came to the writer to give some larger account of this great man. The intelligence of the persons expressing this wish compelled the inquiry as to available material for a biography. Great weight was given to these private suggestions by the action of the Wilmington and the Philadelphia Conferences, which at their last session passed strong resolutions requesting the writer to prepare a life of Dr. Durbin. These two Conferences had formed but one body nearly all the time of Dr. Durbin's membership in the Philadelphia Conference, and felt a common interest in his character and services.

The New York East Conference, of which the writer is a member, passed a similar resolution. To such expression no one of sensibility could be indifferent.

But candor constrains the confession that the writer had long entertained the thought that "Homiletics and Sacred Oratory," taught with so much care and profit in text-books and by able professors, might be *impressed by example* of their most weighty and influential principles. The writer's knowledge of Dr. Durbin for forty years presented him as an illustration of the greatest number of those principles that he had met in one minister. The consideration led him to commence the writing of this book. It will be seen, therefore, that its object is twofold: 1. To narrate the life of Dr. Durbin; and, 2. To analyze his powers as a preacher.

The writer makes his grateful acknowledgments to all who have in any way contributed material that served the ends of this volume. He is under preeminent obligations to Mrs. Augusta F. Whitaker, of Philadelphia, and to Alexander C. Durbin, Esq., of Montclair, N. J., the surviving children of Dr. Durbin. They have placed at his disposal the manuscripts in their possession. From an autobiographical fragment the most accurate and comprehensive information concerning Dr. Durbin's early labors has been furnished.

The author cannot in adequate terms express his indebtedness to remaining members of the family of Christopher Smith, Esq., of Cincinnati. From and through his son-in-law, Edward Sargent, Esq., new sources of knowledge have been opened to the writer.

Cordial thanks are rendered Judge John Chambers, of Eaton, Ohio, for the minutes of a quarterly conference kept by young Durbin. A like expression is due the Rev. J. O. Roberts for his account of the early efforts of Durbin; and to a lady friend in Philadelphia who has permitted the writer use of memoranda of great value. Thanks are also due the Rev. G. W. Lybrand, of the Philadelphia Conference, for original matter as well as for numerous references; and to the Rev. G. D. Carrow, D.D., for material that was sought with care.

The writer cannot express his obligations to those who have furnished letters concerning Dr. Durbin. Among those is one who had the highest honor in the first graduating class of Dickinson College under Dr. Durbin, whom the Church now honors as its senior Bishop, Dr. Thomas Bowman.

CONTENTS.

CONTENTS.

CHAPTER IV.

CHAPTER V.

CHAPTER VI.

CHAPTER VII.

CHAPTER VIII.

CHAPTER IX.

CHAPTER X.

CHAPTER XI.

CHAPTER XII.

CHAPTER XIII.

INTRODUCTION.

BIOGRAPHICAL art is as rare as genius. Except to the stupid most biographies are stupid—mere arid recitations of matters of no interest whatever. A sufficient reason for the dullness, in a great majority of cases is no doubt that there was no reason why the life should be written. It is astonishing how few lives, even of conspicuous men in high positions—statesmen, men eminent in the professions, or who have won distinction in literature or art, or in any other way—have in them any thing deserving of commemoration after they have passed away from the earth. Immediate relatives and partial friends, unwilling to have them forgotten, seek to prevent it by publishing a biography which perhaps they read or glance through, but which no one else finds interesting unless it should be some one, or some classes, who, unacquainted with more profitable reading, derive some entertainment and possibly some profit from the recital. Where there are few books, any thing—an old almanac —is better than nothing. After all there is scarcely a poor excuse for inflicting a biography on the present age of even a more than ordinary person in his peculiar line ; if he be less than really extraordinary, or unless there be that in his character and achievements and the incidents of his life which is suggestive and inspiring, it is better that he be permitted to go quietly to rest. The age is too busy and full for commonplace. Many a man who has shone with noticeable brilliancy in the pulpit, at the bar, in the senate, and who not only won but deserved admiration, even wide fame, will not bear the strain of a biography. The attempt to dress him up for such a show is little short of abuse. He ought to live in traditions, in the glamour of affectionate memories, in the innocent exaggerations which simply rank him with sufficient indefiniteness as among the great men of the generation of giants who lived in the age just gone. The growing fables will be greatly more just to his memory than any narrative can be. The imagination will do better by him than the facts. We protest, in the interest of a class of worthy men who have well served their time and deserve to be well thought of and affectionately remembered, against their being paraded and dwarfed in the pages of dull biography.

There are occasional men who, for one reason or another, or even for many sufficient reasons, deserve to be handed down to posterity in the embalmment of a book; not necessarily greater than other men or the very greatest of all, but for some unique qualities, or possibly some accidental environments, or some inexplicable magnetism, or some triumph over peculiar and great difficulties, or some marvelous influences which emanated from them, or the conspicuous part which they played in their generation, or some incident or incidents of their history which are suggestive and helpful, especially to the young, or for other reasons.

It is a happy conjuncture when such a man finds a Boswell to enshrine him or a biographer worthy his subject; and it is not always to be deplored when, as in the case of the great essayist, the affections of the biographist render him sensitive to the finest traits of the subject, or even if the reflected image, tinted by overfondness, should possibly flatter the original. The

imagination may safely play a part. A photograph
or portrait in any style ought to be characteristically
realistic rather than ideal ; but it ought not to be com-
plained of when it gives the best expression, or even
though it should in a degree, not grossly exaggerate,
but mildly drape the form.

American Methodism rank among all her gifted and
eminent sons, in any work of official distinction or ministerial service has never had one, if we except her first
Bishop, and he only by the accidents of his position,
who more richly deserved a classic niche in her temple
of fame, or who has furnished a finer subject for the
pen of genius than John P. Durbin. If there have
been greater or more loyal sons we do not know of
them. If any have excelled him we are not able to
name them. He came on the stage in the heroic days
of the nation and of the Church, and for fifty years and
more, without a flaw or failure, stood in the public gaze
only to be honored by those whose respect is discrimi-
nated praise, and by whom to be esteemed great is
proof of real greatness. He was not simply the pride
of his own Church, but equally of all those of other
Churches, whether in pulpit or pew, and of the cultured
of no Church as well, who were capable of appreciating
sacred eloquence or admiring the charm of noble and
magnetic manhood. Modest as a child in mien and
spirit in the common intercourse of life, he was, when
at the post of duty and roused with the mighty themes
of his great commission, impassioned, fervid, irresistible as the electric flash or the great forces of
nature when stirred to their wildest fury ; but whether
in the cloister or amid the amenities of social life, or in
the pulpit careering on the storm of matchless eloquence,
alike in all places he won and swayed all hearts. No
orator ever had more complete mastery of his audi-

ences; but it was always as the ambassador of the great King that he delivered his messages and reached his loftiest climaxes. He was never forgetful of his great commission, and never compromised the dignity and glory of his adored Master.

The Church and all the admiring friends of the great Durbin have reason to congratulate themselves in his biographer. Dr. Roche brought to his chosen task the indispensable conditions of success: deep personal affection; long and intimate acquaintance; special opportunities for the observation and study of his subject; a discriminating understanding and appreciation of sacred eloquence; dramatic skill of arrangement; to which must be added spiritual sympathy. Throughout he is on fire with his theme; never wearies of it; never grows dull or vapid. He lives it over, from the boy on the Kentucky "blue-grass" farm, through all the windings of a grand and beautiful career, even to its culmination. There is nothing wanting, nothing omitted to mar the charm of the mind picture. He makes it live as he tells the story.

The rare charm of the volume, the highest stroke of biographical skill and genius, is that it is full of Durbin himself. From the first he is present with you; you see him, hear the tone of his voice, feel the charm of his sympathy; he is talking with you; drawing you to him; you are with him on the circuit; at the homes among the people where he stopped; reading the books he read; thinking his thoughts. Further on, after boyhood has widened into manhood, and early promise has grown into fruition, and study has ripened into scholarship and position, you are sitting before him in the college chapel feeling the spell of his prayers, his loving, reproving, and persuasive counsels, in the recitation-room, thrilled by his inspirations and lifted by his instructions : anon you are with him in the senate house, where his sermons and prayers hold the mighty men of the nation spell-bound ; and yet, over and over again you are hearing those wonderful sermons which, in great city pulpits and from the rude stands of the camp-ground, swayed the multitude as the tempest bends and lashes the forests.

There is so much reproduction from memory gathered from different sources, and so much from his own pen, that you seem to be listening again to the matchless orator and hearing the very tones of his voice, and find yourself crouching under those amazing gestures of his which no one who beheld can ever forget. That flash, rather shall I say glare, of his eye startles you as it did when you sat before him, that transfigured countenance, that upturned face, that wand of the uplifted hand, together with the words that made him the most magic of preachers, come to you over and over again as you read the interesting pages.

I must not detain you. Dr. Roche has nobly done his noble task. If I mistake not the book will not only be read with thrilling interest by multitudes of the present generation who knew and admired the great Doctor, not indeed in the glory of his prime, but in the toned autumn of his declining age; but it will live on as a classic of the now rapidly-vanishing mythic age of our church life ; the age amid whose shadowy outlines we discern with sufficient indistinctness to magnify their forms the heroic men who laid its foundations. "Distance lends enchantment to the view ; " but there were great men in those times. None among them all, in the best respects, excelled the hero of this story.

The young men in the ministry of the present generation, who come upon the stage with such improved equipment, entering as they do into the labors of these honored fathers will not permit their memories to perish or their laurels to fade; but coming again and again to the study of their struggles and story of their successes will strive to emulate them in spirit and power. They will continue forever to be the great legion in our traditions and in our affections.

The Church will not grow weary of the story of the past or of the men who made it illustrious. We commend Dr. Roche's book with unqualified indorsement. Let it be read by our children in the thousand homes of our Methodism in city and country. It will not fail to inspire them to a noble life as well as entertain them with the fascination of a romance. Let it find a place in every Sunday-school library for the more advanced youth it will inspire them with love for their Church.

There are hints and rules as to the use of time and habits of study and methods of preparing sermons which cannot fail to be educating in a high degree to young ministers. The book abounds with allusions to other men in all the professions, but especially the most celebrated preachers of all Churches who were the contemporaries of the subject of the memoir, so that a most valuable light is thrown upon the age itself. There is scarcely a celebrity that has not a discriminative and appreciative analysis of his peculiar powers. It is really, in the closing chapters, a treatise on sacred eloquence as well as an historical *résumé* of the men and their peculiar styles of thought and speech who in the forum and the pulpit impressed the generation just gone—as Webster, Clay, Calhoun, among statesmen ; Bascom, Olin, Maffit, among pulpiteers ; as well as the great orators of all countries and all times. The book is thus rendered rich in a remarkable degree.

I cannot close this brief Introduction without personal mention of the distinguished subject of this exceedingly interesting sketch. I feel under personal obligation to the author for doing that, and doing it so admirably well, which I had almost despaired of seeing done at all. It seemed that the man who most of all deserved a memoir was not to find a biographer. It must have been an inspiration that led Dr. Roche to undertake the work. Perhaps no other living man could have done it so well.

My recollection of the great Doctor dates back nearly fifty years, just at the time when he was in the zenith of his fame. He had just passed out of his youth into the full strength of his mature manhood. It was when Bascom and Hamline were at the height of their power. Simpson was just in the dawn of his rapidly-rising popularity. I think it is safe to say that Methodism has never since had four comparable names, and probably never will again. Circumstances have greatly to do, certainly, with the quality of men's fame; possibly with the quality of men themselves.

The country was new. The age was uncritical. The pulpit was the great throne of power. The pen and printed page were less in use. The people were eager to hear. Impassioned speech thrilled and swayed the vast expectant assemblies who rushed for miles to hear the famous orator. There was eloquence in the air. All the circumstances conspired to kindle enthusiasm. It was inevitable that, standing in the focus of such forces, the speaker should be at his best. The effect was inchoate before he began. Hungry of combustion, the assembly took fire at the first spark. On the eager flame, the orator himself more impassioned, rose and soared to the sublimest heights of inspired eloquence. The effect was often magical. It is impossible for this generation to conceive of it. The waves of feeling that rushed over the assembly were as visible as the effect of the storm on ocean or forest.   Hundreds would rise to their feet under unconscious impulse, lean forward, press toward the speaker, weeping, sobbing, or shouting, under the thrilling appeal. Many times numbers fell like the slain in battle. Under Durbin and Bascom I have repeatedly witnessed all these effects myself. It would not accord with truth to say that there are not as great men now living; but the times make it impossible that any should produce such visible signs of emotion as attended those mighty and glorious men. I must stay my pen. Read the book, and you will read it again, and will thank Dr. Roche that he has set in order his admirable words commemorative of the great life whose spell still lingers with us.

R. S. F.

PART I.

MEMOIR OF JOHN P. DURBIN, D.D., LL.D.

CHAPTER I.

Ancestry—Youth—Early Ministry.

HUMAN greatness commands the savage and the sage. It inspires the genius of the poet and is the chosen theme for eloquence. History records its results and wisdom avails itself of its benefits. In exalted reputations and influence men are "not born to die." Their lives do honor to our nature and their history is the heritage of the race. When, therefore, one has sublimely served his generation by the will of God, duty may demand that we gather up the facts that made him illustrious, and thus impress lessons of value upon those who survive. The Bible immortalizes, by name and deed, the great and good, and teaches that no man liveth to himself and no man dieth to himself. Tamerlane was accustomed to read of his progenitors, not for boasting, but to improve his virtues. The noble acts of our predecessors may lure us from paths of indolence and awaken a just ambition to imbibe their spirit and follow in their steps. Worth begets worth. As from the ashes of the phenix others rise, from great men others are produced.

Few men in any Church have ever occupied and filled with efficiency and honor so many important positions as Dr. Durbin. We may, then, be allowed to say, "As some entranced limner seizes the setting of the golden sun to sketch the landscape when lighted up with rays

still glowing, though fast fading away—as filial reverence seeks the artist's skill to portray a parent's face
while expressions of the past yet play amid the wrinkles
of age; or as the Nestor of some old philosophy en-
circles it with the last halo of enthusiasm ere yet new
theories are called to occupy the uppermost seats," so
would the writer, were it in his power, present the features of a character that remains and perpetuate the
memories that linger to enshrine the man who, while
living, achieved so much for the cause of Christ, and
who, though dead, may be to the ministry so grand an
illustration of what the conscientious application of all
our powers to our appropriate work will enable us to
accomplish.

In a record prepared by himself John Price Durbin
says: "I was born October 10, 1800, in Bourbon County,
Ky., three miles from Paris.   My paternal grandfather
was from Havre-de-Grace, Md.   My maternal grandfather was from Georgia.   Both their families settled
in Kentucky among the first who immigrated thither.
They were of industrious, plain habits, and hence made
a comfortable living approaching wealth.   My maternal
grandfather and family were among the first Methodists
in Kentucky, and continue to this day (January 28, 1830).

"My father, Hozier Durbin, married my mother,
Elizabeth Nunn, A. D. 1799.   I was their eldest child.
There were five sons of us, all living at the death of
my father. . . . My father was a generous and highly
honorable man, professing no religion.   His fortunes
were ruined by the faithlessness of friends whom he
trusted. . . . He died suddenly in March, 1813, and
left us to the protection of my mother and the clem-
ency of the world.   Fortunately, she was a woman of
extraordinary constitution, though small and delicate in
appearance, and has rarely been equaled in point of in-

dustry, perseverance, economy, and the government of her family. In the last particular she was considered by some as too severe. But she had *sons* to rule and none to help her. To her we are indebted for whatever we have of morals, industry, or a sense of honor and propriety. I can never think of her but with gratitude and wonder. Assisted in some degree by her father, she supported us by her own industry until we were old enough to be put to trades. She spun and wove the material for our clothes, and, when woven, made them with her own hands. We were raised before the simplicity of the West yielded to the extravagance of the present day."

In the *History of Methodism in Kentucky*, by Rev. A. H. Redford, D.D., Vol. I, p. 316, Dr. Durbin says, in a letter of March 5, 1868, "My mother was married to Mr. Theobold, of Grant County, Ky. A son and daughter were the fruit of that marriage. The son is dead, but the daughter, now Mrs. Sayres, of Grant County, is still living, and is the mother of a large family of children."

Again, Dr. Redford says:

"Among the distinguished women of the Methodist Church in Kentucky no one presented a brighter Christian example than Mrs. Durbin. Devoted to the Church of her choice, as well as to the common cause of Christianity, she contributed the influence of a holy life and a liberal hand to promote the great ends of religion. Endowed with an intellect of superior cast, with a heart sanctified by grace, and with an inflexible purpose to accomplish the highest aims and ends of life, whether by the bedside of affliction or in her own family circle, or pouring out the devotions of her heart around the altars of the Church, she seems every-where an angel of mercy. Through many years her house was consecrated to God, and beneath her hospitable roof the faithful minister of Christ found a welcome and a place of rest."

In a brief biography written by her pastor soon after her death, he says: "Many there are who bless God that she ever lived. Her place in the Church and family circle cannot be easily filled. In her death a pillar of Christianity has been broken and a moral guiding light extinguished. Her children and society have sustained a loss that time cannot repair. She in an eminent degree trained up her children in ' the way they should go,' and had the high satisfaction of seeing them all soundly converted and exemplary members of the Church, while two of them became eloquent ministers of the Gospel of Christ." For several years she suffered from severe affliction, yet her last attack, a disease of the throat, was brief. After a few days' illness calmly and easily she passed away.

In the record kept by Dr. Durbin, he says:

"As I advanced to manhood my mother, of course, became more infirm, and, as if by common consent, the care of the younger brothers devolved on me. As it was very evident to me that they could not expect to rank in point of inherited fortunes with their near relations I determined it was best to remove them from their native State and place them among strangers. I had two reasons for this:

" 1. For fear they might be moved by some disagreeable feeling by seeing their friends growing up in prospect of better fortunes, and to which they might, and justly too, feel they had a partial claim, which I foresaw never could be realized.

" 2. Because I had seen enough of the world to know that when one's fortune depended on his own exertion he is more successful and better sustained among strangers than among friends or relations. For if among his relations he will naturally look to them for some support, and if he does not receive it he feels grieved and injured. Moreover, when among strangers he looks for no indulgence or favors other than such as his virtues, industry, and success may authorize him to expect. He feels himself responsible to the community and dependent on himself in respect to his conduct and fortunes, and these things awaken in the heart feelings and resolutions and energies of such elevation and character as cannot be felt or formed by the person who grows up in prospect of ease and protection in the bosom of an indulgent family. From these circumstances I thought it best to remove my brothers from the house of their parents and scenes of their childhood that they might, as I have done, and expect always to do, *try their fortunes among strangers*, and make and keep friends only by their virtues and merits. Nor have I been disappointed in them yet, and feel pretty well assured that even my best wishes will be realized in regard to them.

"The same course should be pursued in reference to all youth, no matter what their prospects are. Place them in circumstances which require all their energies and make them depend on themselves. It is the only possible way to make them active, efficient, and industrious citizens, and to prevent them from being debased and useless drones, an expense to their families, and a loss to the community. The history of the brightest gems of our free and happy country will attest what I have here written."

This is rare reasoning for one of his age. The political economist who, in the maturity of his intellect and the most careful consideration of that which pertains to a State or a nation, reasons out safer conclusions than J. P. Durbin reached in relation to the best temporal

interests of his brothers and young men in general
shows a wisdom that makes him worthy of his exalted
study.

In 1868 Dr. Durbin wrote, "Myself and my brother
William (third son) are the only ones living." That
brother still lives in the State of Indiana and is a devoted member of the Church. His youngest brother,
Hozier J. Durbin, was a member of the Indiana Conference, and at the time of his death was agent of the
American Bible Society. On August 11, 1851, while
energetically prosecuting its interests, "he was killed in
a storm by the limb of a tree falling on him." Before
this he had been a member of the State Legislature in
Indiana. He was a speaker of "persuasive eloquence"
and a "powerful preacher."   .

The early life of J. P. Durbin was spent on a farm.
"His education up to his fourteenth year was of the
commonest kind of the frontier. When fourteen years
old he was apprenticed to a cabinet-maker in Paris, Ky.,
with whom he remained till he learned the trade."

He says, "About my eighteenth year I became permanently serious and was admitted a member of a class,
mainly with a design, as I afterward learned, to procure
a recommendation to the Quarterly Meeting Conference
for license to preach. The license was granted on November 19, 1818, and signed by that truly good and
great man, Alexander Cummings. . . . On Tuesday
following the grant of my license to preach I was sent
by the presiding elder, Mr. Cummings, to Limestone
Circuit, in the Kentucky Conference."

He was converted at Riddle's Mills; but "one of his
young friends was pungently convicted, struggled hard
and long, and was powerfully and suddenly converted
in his presence." Durbin assumed that *his* experience
must be of the same kind in order to be genuine; but

as it was gradual and tranquil, without violent signs, he began to distrust it, when by a gentle, yet clear impression on his mind he was convinced that "God for Christ's sake had pardoned his sins and accepted him in the Redeemer."

The Church had seen his change of life, and while he hesitated it moved. The action of the Quarterly Conference, presided over by such a man as filled the chair, and the conduct of the presiding elder in placing him immediately on a circuit, showed remarkable confidence in his character and talent, and also illustrates the care with which the Church marked its material for the highest service.

Twelve years after his entrance upon the itinerancy he thus writes: "If any one period of my life is more dear to me than another it is that in which I entered the itinerancy. I can never reflect on the incidents attending it without gratitude. The impression in regard to preaching the Gospel fastened on my mind long before I became permanently serious. This may seem strange; it is even so to myself, and yet it is true. When I was very young, hearing my father say to a friend that *he intended to make me a physician*, I asked him if a doctor could be a *preacher*. I well recollect that I concluded in my own mind if a doctor cannot be a preacher I will not be a doctor. When I found it was necessary to go to a trade, I did it cheerfully; not because I expected to get my living by it, but because I found it was the only way in which I could pass my time satisfactorily to my friends or, indeed, as things were, to myself. I therefore learned the cabinet-making trade. I followed it to some profit for a year or more; but during the last year I had but little peace, because of the strong impression resting on my mind in regard to preaching the Gospel. I often resolved with myself to go cheerfully, but as often proved faithless to my resolutions. At length I resolved when a certain engagement was out I would disclose my mind to my elder brethren for their advice. But I failed, and was on my way to a second engagement when, walking alone on my way, I felt so overcome with a sense of my obstinacy that I sat down by the way-side and wept until the sound of a horseman roused me, and I arose and went on. This engagement lasted about a month, after which I returned to the house of my grandfather, Mr. Ilai Nunn.

"I was much dejected, which he observed, and said to me, '*John, tell me the truth, do you not feel that you are called to preach the Gospel?*' I was compelled to acknowledge it with tears, perfectly astonished that he or any other being should have suspected any thing of the kind. He then gave me the following advice :

"'Go and explain your feelings and views to Mr. Lakin. He is an old Methodist traveling preacher of experience and good judgment, and he will advise you properly.'

"I took his advice and visited the Rev. Benjamin Lakin, and found him in his bed somewhat unwell, as he was then worn out by long service in the Church. He was one of the first Methodist preachers that visited Kentucky. It was his custom to preach in the dwellings of those who would give permission, and he dressed, as the people generally in those early days, in a *hunting-shirt, wrappers* (or *leggings*), *and moccasins.* He lived to see the Methodist Church numerous and respectable, and spread over the western country, and still lives, enduring patiently the frailties of old age and the infirmities brought on him by his early and continued ministerial labors. The name of Benjamin Lakin is dear to the hearts of thousands, and is consecrated in my memory as among my most endearing recollections.

"When I was shown into the room where he was resting, in the house of Mr. Lakin, of Bourbon County, Ky., the old man of God arose and sat on the side of his bed and read the letter which I brought from my grandfather with tears in his eyes. After some conversation he said, 'I advise you, first of all, imitate no person in the style and manner of your preaching; copy not their tones of voice nor gesture; study to speak in that style and manner, accompanied with such gesture, as will be perfectly natural to yourself. Let your whole performance be that of animated conversation, with such elevation of voice as will be suitable to the size of the assembly. Make choice of plain subjects, and, of course, plain texts, and endeavor rather to illustrate them perspicuously than laboriously and finely. Recollect that you should benefit the great body of your hearers and not the few. Simplicity and utility are the best traits in the composition and delivery of a sermon. These two properties will create interest and feeling; and in order to give full effect to them, without becoming incoherent and wild, you must make, either on paper or in your own mind, a draught of your discourse before you go into the pulpit, containing at least the general propositions and outlines of the subject—and, if it be a difficult one, the minor points and principal arguments in brief—and the mind will well recollect and finish them out when you come to preach. Give attention to reading also. It is a great mistake to suppose one can do his work well as an evangelist who is not studious. Study, unaccompanied by religious character and the call of God, will not qualify for the work of the ministry; neither, on the other hand, is religious character and the call of God sufficient without study. Cultivate your own language closely.   You have to use it as the medium of communication to sinners.   Cultivate biblical literature as of the first importance, but by husbanding your time you will find opportunity to cultivate every branch of literature in some useful degree.   And, recollect, every species of knowledge is, or may be, useful to a minister.   Recollect that you will find it more difficult to command your time than any thing else, because in traveling you pass into different families every day, and each will regard you as a visitor, a guest, not recollecting that you are always somewhere in the same character.   Resist this tax on your time *prudently*, and they will shortly see you inclined to improve your time and talents, and will also see the good effect of it in your ministry, and instead of complaining of you as . morose and churlish they will approve, and assist you by providing you with every convenience when you come.   This is my best advice.   Go, and the Lord go with you.'   Such is the outline of the advice which this excellent man gave me.   It is true that, as I improved by it very much, I have added a little by way of enlargement as the result of my own experience. But I am indebted to him for the nucleus around which all the minor points are associated."

From the narrative of young Durbin's anxious and painful experience concerning his duty to preach and the impression he made on those who best knew him we can judge their conduct in pressing him into the work in which, notwithstanding his convictions, he was so slow to engage.

That his grandfather, a man of commanding influence in the Church and in the community, a pioneer of Methodism in Kentucky, should have addressed to him the searching question that opened up the whole matter of his solicitude, is evidence how God, who in ancient times "revealed to his servants," still holds such access to their minds as to induce conduct that is not wholly of themselves.

The wisdom of Mr. Nunn in sending young Durbin to Mr. Lakin for aid in his perplexity may be seen in the character of the man and in the estimate placed upon his counsel by the inquirer.

Mr. Lakin was an experienced and honored minister in Methodism. He understood the demands made upon a young preacher. He knew his difficulties and his dangers, as well as his mental and moral possibilities. He had a clear intellect, and was a calm though earnest thinker. He was distinguished by conscientiousness, by self-sacrifice, by strong faith and burning zeal. He had industry and methodical habits. He seemed to be steadily governed by the rule of our Discipline, "Never be unemployed; never be triflingly employed." He was a great reader, and it was his practice to make abstracts and write an analysis of the books he studied. He thus accumulated large stores of knowledge. He was accustomed to prepare notes of his sermons, and sometimes wrote them "in full," but only to impress them perfectly upon his mind. With energy of character he was conservative. He had marked prudence, and his executive skill inspired confidence in his administration.

Such facts gave force to his advice, as his practice was an illustration of the principles he inculcated. He retired from the ministry the year that Durbin entered it, and on the same circuit. He died February 5, 1849, in the eighty-second year of his age and in the fifty-fifth of his ministry. Can we trace any resemblance between the attributes and habits of the counselor and the counseled?

These were the circumstances under which the Dur-

bin of eighteen years, in a few days after his connection
with the Church, entered upon the Limestone Circuit,
where he labored for eight months with Walter Griffith
as preacher in charge. In later life he said, "When
I look back at this period of my ministerial labors I
am astonished that the people bore with me at all. I
was young and inexperienced. My manners must have
been rude, though, I presume, artless and unpresuming.
My knowledge of divine things was very limited,
and my manner of explaining what I did know must
have been unsatisfactory to a great many, and probably
disgusting to some, as I was not acquainted with the
English grammar. My reading at this period was very
limited and desultory. I had no system for study
either in regard to books or time. Hence I learned
nothing, or very little. Yet with all these disadvantages it pleased the Lord to bless my labors in some
degree. It is still refreshing to me, and I will record
it here for the comfort of others, to recall one incident. I had been absent from the Limestone Circuit
several years. As I returned to see my friends I called
on my friend Johnston Armstrong, of Maysville, Ky.,
and dined with him. After dinner he observed, 'I have
never yet told you that you were the instrument under
God of my conversion. It is even so. I shall never
forget it. It was in August, in the old white church,
the last sermon you preached for us.' This came to
my pilgrim heart as the rain to the parched fields, and
I thought to myself, as I have a thousand times, the
minister of Jesus Christ does not, nor will he know, the
good he is doing in this world until the Lord judges the
world in righteousness. My Brother Armstrong has been
an ornament to his profession from that time until this.
I hope he may be faithful unto death and die in peace.

"In this circuit I also met with one judicious and

faithful friend, Mr. John Todd, formerly of Baltimore. He was then a journeyman in Maysville, and very remarkable for his piety. 'You are about,' said Mr. Todd to me, 'to leave our circuit. You are now young, and should seize the opportunity of improving your mind and confirming yourself in the habits of piety. I would suggest to you that possibly you have been too conversant, too much given to talk with all persons, on all subjects, and in all places. It is difficult to break our habits with old acquaintances, but recollect when you go to a new circuit you will be a stranger. Begin from the first to rule yourself down to a few words, and even this only on necessary occasions. Make a good selection of books to read and devote yourself to reading and prayer. Read one book at a time; read all of it and read it carefully. Study the English language closely, and make yourself master of a perspicuous, correct, and strong style.'

"This is about the substance of the advice which I received from this young man. It was of much service to me. Connected with a few other circumstances this advice directed my course chiefly during the next year."

The means of education that society affords to one disposed to *learn* are incalculable, and the readiness that the capable show in contributing to the worthy ends of the modest and meritorious is one of the greatest advantages of human intercourse. Durbin found friends in every place and sphere. The supply seemed equal to the demand. Where the least hope might have been cherished the most positive benefit was bestowed. He was eager to learn, and his receptivity was equal to his need. A hint was help. With him life presented not the question of ease, but of possibilities and duty. His ambition was sanctified, and his auxiliaries sustained his purpose.

How unlooked-for and yet how valuable was the counsel of his "journeyman friend!" That Mr. Todd knew so well the wise course for a young preacher to take as to conversation, reading, and style, is evidence how closely we may be criticised and how accurately we may be judged by persons who rarely approach us to tell us our faults and "show us how to mend." Nor can we fail to think, if young Durbin was ever addicted to the things named by Mr. Todd, either the remarks of his friend or his own reasoning made a complete change. His life, as we knew it, showed an utter freedom from such tendencies as here became matters of caution. How refined and judicious was the statement of the difficulty of some of the changes named, and how intelligent was his recognition of the advantages that our itinerancy affords to one who enters on a new course!

Did ever student from college or young man from the office of his preceptor more fully exhibit the impress of character or wisdom that such contact gives?

On this circuit it must have been that, from vehemence in delivery, he failed in voice and health; returning to his home with the apprehension that his ministry had ended. Another friend opportunely appeared, and advised him to visit the cabins of the colored people and talk religion to them. Again he accepted counsel and found the benefit. In six months his voice could fill the largest house, and he resumed his work.

CHAPTER II.

Greenville Circuit, Lawrenceburg, Hamilton, Zanesville, Lebanon, Cincinnati.

HE says: "I was appointed in the summer of 1819 to Greenville Circuit, which lay in the north-west part of Ohio, and was at that time a frontier settlement, and bordered on the Indians. It was my first appointment from the Conference, and I was alone, of course, in charge. From the circuit I received in all about fifty-five dollars in depreciated paper, worth about seventy-five cents on the dollar." Through the kindness of Judge J. Chambers, of Eaton, O., the writer is furnished with a transcript of the second Quarterly Conference of the year, when Walter Griffith was president and J. P. Durbin acted as secretary. The minutes are in his own hand, as now contained in the stewards' book. The members present are distinguished by capital letters opposite their names. Thus, J. P. Durbin, T. P.; William Stubbs, L. P.; James Dwiggins, C. L. The stewards are Henry Eidson, Daniel Lease. The salary of J. P. Durbin is thus rendered: "From August 1819, to August 1820, $48 62½." Mr. Durbin says: "I found about 140 members on this circuit. The country was very new, very few houses which had more than one room—log-cabins not exceeding twenty feet square. In this one room frequently a whole family, consisting of six, eight, ten, or a dozen sons and daughters, as well as myself, ate and lodged, and in the winter all the cooking was done here. This was used for chapel, parlor,

3

kitchen, dining-room, and chamber for the whole family. As would be naturally supposed, the fare was coarse. Sometimes I could not tell whether to call what I was drinking tea or coffee, nor what it was made of. To some persons this would be a gloomy prospect; but all this was counterbalanced by the cordiality with which they received me and the cheer and pleasure with which they offered me what they had." There were very few appointments except at private houses such as have been named, with all their inmates and discomforts; but he found treasures of knowledge that were to him more than homes of capacity and splendor. On this circuit was an old German who was not too poor to have Clarke's *Commentary* in numbers. These he borrowed, and slipped two numbers at a time into a tin canister about four inches in diameter and lashed it behind his saddle, and thus carried it around his circuit. As soon as preaching was over and the class dismissed he sat down in the midst of a frontier family with pen and ink to study and take notes of Clarke. His own words are, "During that year I studied English grammar considerably, and read all of Mr. Wesley's and Fletcher's Works, and Dr. Clarke's notes on the Pentateuch and New Testament, and Josephus. All these works I read closely and made abstracts in my own language from them. This exercise gave me two great advantages; namely, First, it fixed the sentiments of the authors in my mind. Second, it gave me a habit of composition, and, by consequence, a command of language. But some might be at a loss to know how I found time and means in such a circuit to read so much. I answer thus:

"1. I made it a rule to go to bed at nine and rise at five. This gave me sixteen hours for business.

"2. I made it a rule to be ready to read at six,

after having washed, said my prayers, and taken a walk.

"3. I made it a rule always to have my books, paper, pen, and ink at hand.

"4. I made it a rule immediately after preaching to sit down to read, even before dinner, or while the people were not yet all gone; and if any wished to talk with me merely out of civility or sociability, and not on necessary business, I gave them so careless an answer, continuing to read at the same time, that, after making repeated trials to converse with me without effect, they departed.

"5. When the people saw that I was bent on improving my time, instead of being offended they seemed pleased, and afforded me every facility in their power, such as the following: lent me books, provided me candles, and when this could not be done provided dry wood or bark to give light, gave me a room to myself, or, when they had no room to give, ruled the children into silence that I might have an opportunity to read.

"Under these regulations I prospered much in knowledge and piety, and came to Conference with a good report.

"While on Greenville Circuit I was compelled to study and defend the character of our Lord Jesus Christ against the Arians, called in that country New-Lights. They were numerous in that part of the country, having settled it principally from Kentucky, where the sect first took its rise among the Presbyterians of Bourbon County, in a neighborhood called Cain Ridge. There was a large sacramental meeting among them. The Lord visited them wonderfully; it insensibly and without design grew into a camp-meeting, and the people remained for seven or eight days. At this meeting began the inexplicable exercise called *jerks.* It was involuntary, and in some cases so violent that two or three strong men could not confine one female, and if they did attempt to hold her it always caused a great soreness to her. In some instances the arms would be violently thrust forward and backward alternately—that is, one arm forward, the other at the same time backward. Sometimes, and most generally, I believe, the head would be violently and quickly thrown backward and forward, moving on the shoulders (the shoulders also moving in the same direction slightly) with such velocity that the hair of females would come down, and when loose crack like a whip, and with such force as to draw the blood from the face of the by-stander if it cut it. The strongest and most wicked men were equally subject to it with the weakest and most superstitious females. It would generally come on suddenly, frequently when the person was not in any religious assembly, and sometimes when alone, engaged in ordinary employment. Some would be silent and appear sullen, some resigned, and some mortified; some would be enraged and swear profanely; all dreaded the exercise. It is said that it first seized a Presbyterian minister while preaching. It was not confined to any denomination. There was certainly no advantage in a religious point of view in being the subject of it, nor was it peculiar to the religious. Physicians examined the subjects both during the paroxysms and afterward, and in some instances gave medicine, but without effect. I have never been the subject of it, but I have witnessed it, and asked others who had been the subjects in regard to their feelings and views, but could never obtain any satisfaction. All declared it involuntary and inexplic-able and painful. Some have been known to be jerked to the ground in an instant, others have laid hold of trees and have been jerked round them until they were literally *belabored* and the tree partially lashed. These are the facts; the explanation I leave to others."

The writer has at various times and from different persons had some account of the exercise called "jerks." Some thirty-seven years ago he had a strong and strange statement from a Presbyterian minister who had been in the West and was supposed to have knowledge of what he spoke. But at no time has he had so minute, comprehensive, and graphic a narrative of the operations as that furnished by Mr. Durbin. The account comes to us, in the present instance, in a way to admit no question as to its certainty. Whatever may have been the *cause*, Mr. Durbin both witnessed the affection and inquired of those who were its subjects. A more competent witness or calmer investigator of the facts might not be found. In vain would we search for a trace of superstition or fanaticism in him. If the physicians who examined and tried to treat the cases could not by their knowledge of the human system and its liability to be operated on by external forces and influences; if from their study of physiology and psychology, or from any science, observation, or experience that they had to help them, they were unable to explain the phenomenon, and if Mr. Durbin called the affection "inexplicable," we certainly shall not attempt to do more than he or the physicians could accomplish. We may have as good a right, if we have equal intelligence, to render a judgment as to the cause as those of that day. With no more science and knowledge of the human system, and no better acquaintance with the facts, we may be alike unable to satisfy the mind.

At this same meeting five or six Presbyterian ministers took the incipient steps which led to their separation from their brethren and to the formation of a new sect called "New Lights." They were Arians in doctrine.

... these ministers all except one or two returned to the
... byterian Church. They had a considerable follow-
... in the West. Their preachers laid down these two
... great rules of action:

1. Human *creeds* are injurious to religion. Hence,

2. That they should not dwell on the controverted
points in theology in their ministrations, or but very
rarely. As a consequence of these things there was no
consistency or uniformity in their religious opinions; nor
did the people generally seem disposed to believe them.
Many of their people were not Arians in sentiment.
This state of things continued more or less for above
twenty years.

"At the time I was on Greenville Circuit," says Durbin,
"their sentiments began to assume tangible form and
the people to be sensible of the difference between the
New Lights and others. This difference became more
apparent as it regards the Methodists from the following
circumstance. I had an appointment in the court-
house in Eaton, Preble Circuit, O. At the same hour
an elderly gentleman, Mr. David P., had one in the
same place. As I had the prior appointment I proffered
to Mr. P. to preach first. He did so, and devoted two
hours and some minutes in attempting to prove that
Jesus Christ was not even the thirtieth part of a god.
This doctrine he said he had believed for twenty years,
but he had not been in the habit of proclaiming it.
During his sermon I felt alarmed, being very young
and inexperienced, and he aged and wise. But when
he said: 'Some indeed affirm that our Saviour had, and
has yet, two whole and perfect natures in his person,
namely, godhead and manhood,' and 'If this could be
proven then would I instantly give up the point and
yield to the doctrine of a trinity:' it instantly occurred
to me that the Scriptures were explicit on this point,

and the following passage, among others, came to my mind: 'Of whom, as concerning the flesh, Christ came' —here is his *humanity;* 'who is God over all, blessed for evermore'—here is his *divinity.* Instantly a flood of light burst on my mind, and I have not been embarrassed since. I rose after he had concluded and made a few remarks. Since that time I have pursued the light which I thus received, and have found, on close examination, that the Scriptures which speak of our Lord Jesus may be classed under *three* heads, by observing which the reader will find them free from confusion and contradiction :

"1. Sometimes they speak of our Lord as a *mere man,* having reference to his *human nature,* as when they say, 'he wept,' 'he hungered,' 'he knew not, but the Father,' or any other expression which implied or expressed his inferiority.

"2. Sometimes they speak of our Lord as the *true God,* as when he says of himself, 'I am the Almighty,' 'the first and the last,' 'the Alpha and Omega,' and when John says, 'The Word was God,' and when he is presented as the object of worship, etc.

"3. Sometimes they speak of our Lord as having both natures combined, as 'Who was the son of David, according to the flesh'—here is his humanity ; 'declared to be the Son of God with power according to the spirit of holiness'—here is his divinity. Again: 'Of whom, as concerning the flesh, Christ came'—here is his *humanity*; 'who is God over all, blessed for evermore'— here is his divinity. By observing these simple distinctions in the Sciptures you will discover the most perfect harmony running throughout them. I once made this statement at a camp-meeting where was one of our oldest and best local preachers, who had once been expelled the Church for his Arian opinions, but came back again and promised to be silent in regard to them, and was restored. He continued to be embarrassed with his difficulties on these points until he heard this simple analysis of the Scriptures in reference to our Lord, which I gave on that occasion. The moment he heard it his eyes overflowed, his countenance lighted up with joy, and from that hour he has been unembarrassed. The thing is so simple. The three classes of Scripture sustain the three corresponding propositions:

"1. Our Lord Jesus is really and truly *man*.

"2. Our Lord Jesus is really and truly *God*.

"3. Our Lord Jesus is really and truly *both* God and man."

In 1820 he was appointed to Lawrenceburg, Ind. He says: "My colleague this year was James Collord, a truly worthy and pious man, who entered the traveling connection a young *married man* with a growing family, and traveled *five years* without receiving $500 in that time. The consequence was he had to locate, and returned to New York and engaged in business. I recollect well the Saturday evening on which I arrived in the circuit. The first appointment was in Lawrenceburg. The sun shone on the two small steeples, one on a tavern, the other on the court-house, and gleamed at a distance on the eye of the traveler as he gazed on them from Hardentown, two miles above Lawrenceburg, on the Big Bottom. I called at the house of my much-esteemed friend, Isaac Dunn, Esq., who has long been a pillar in the church there. Himself and Mrs. Dunn were not at home, but returned in an hour or two. They received me kindly, though they had not much confidence in our religious prospects. We performed service in the court-house, having no church at that time. But before our Conference year was out we had large additions to our society, and the foundation of an excellent brick chapel was laid.

"This was a year of great prosperity and peace to us all. I was much indebted to my colleague, who was a critical English scholar, for his assistance and encouragement in the study of the English grammar. I not only attempted to *learn* the rules, so as to parse accurately, but I *endeavored*, both in composition and public speaking, to be always correct. Thus I improved my style and corrected early-contracted improprieties.

"While on this circuit I was in the habit of carrying with me always a number of religious tracts, purchased at my own expense, in order to distribute as I found occasion. Sometimes I would inclose them in a letter form, sometimes drop them in the path when I saw some one coming, and sometimes give them personally. I recollect on one occasion to have called to a young man who was plowing in the field as I rode by, and asked him if he would have a book. He answered he had no money to pay for it. I asked him if he would read one if I would give it to him. He answered he would. I gave him four tracts. This I was induced to do partly because I had seen him in class-meeting the day before and he seemed to be serious. I saw no more of the young man until some years after, when, dining in Cincinnati at a friend's house, a young man sat opposite to me and seemed to regard me very earnestly. At length he observed, 'I presume you have forgotten me, Mr. Durbin, but I have not forgotten you.' I observed I believed I had not the pleasure of recollecting him. 'Do you not,' said he, 'recollect the young man to whom you gave the tracts while plowing in the field? I am he. From that day I have sought the Lord in earnest, and have attached myself to the Methodist Episcopal Church.'"

Durbin says of Greenville and Lawrenceburg circuits: "They were comparatively new, and had few appointments except in private houses," and these such as have been described, with fare of kindred character. But then, he writes, "I have reckoned, and do still reckon, these years the best of my life. In them I made as much progress in divine things as in any other, and did as much good, apparently. I ever found it convenient to read much, notwithstanding I had no apartment to retire to. ... My manner of reading was this: I always read but *one* book at a time besides the Bible. I did not even allow myself to read a newspaper. I took care to read this one book carefully, noting down its contents briefly with my pen. ... I did not wait for an opportunity to read, but always made one. In this way I proceeded, generally reading 500 or 600 pages a week, besides the Bible.

"I am aware that many young men among us say they cannot find time and opportunity to read, write, and study. I have detailed the manner in which I found it. They could do the same, and I may add they must do the same, or they cannot do the work of the Lord as they ought to do it.

"One of the injunctions of Paul to Timothy was, 'Give attention to reading.'

' "In the fall of 1821 I was appointed to Hamilton Station, Ohio Conference. Methodism had just been planted there, and the society had built them a neat little church. We had a peaceful, prosperous year in our Zion.

"At the instance of Dr. Martin Ruter I commenced the study of the Latin grammar and language. I committed the grammar well, and immediately commenced reading Virgil's works, reciting once a day to Mr. Monfort, a Presbyterian minister. I pursued this course for some time and then declined reciting, and read and studied without assistance from any person. . . .This year I read Virgil's works and committed the Greek grammar to memory and commenced reading the Greek Testament. I read also *Newton on the Prophecies* and some other works." While at Hamilton he studied in the Miami University, and returned to his charge, a distance of twelve miles, on Friday afternoon.

"I cannot omit recording a little incident which happened this year, and in order to make it understood, I must give the proper *preface.* The society being small it was quite an effort to support their preacher. Mr. Joseph Hough, a merchant in the place, as his wife was a member, was in the habit of inviting the preacher to live with him the principal part of the year without any charge whatever. After I had been in the station some weeks he called and invited me to come and spend some time with his family. I complied. Of course I had family prayer in his house. At first, having been raised a Quaker, he would stand up very respectfully; after a little he kneeled down on *one* knee; then at last he kneeled down on both, as did the rest of us. Cold weather came on. His ice-house stood in his back yard. They were filling the house one day with ice, and Mr. Hough was in the house packing the ice away. There was a long plank from the wagon to the bottom of the ice-house, or rather to the surface of the last layer of ice, down which plank the ice was slid into the house. Some person engaged in the wagon in sliding the ice down the plank threw it against Mr. Hough's foot and injured it severely. Mr. Hough, upon receiving the injury, swore at the man profanely. But at that moment I happened to be passing the ice-house, and looking in at the door, beheld Mr. Hough without his perceiving me, and heard him swear. I said not a word, but passed on unobserved by him. On the Saturday evening following he came into my room (which he kindly afforded me, with every convenience) and sat down and engaged in conversation, during which I observed (not knowing he was accustomed to use profane language), 'Did I not hear you swear in the ice-house, Mr. Hough?' He smiled, with a little flush on his countenance, and answered, 'he thought it was probable he did, as he was in the habit of swearing without knowing at all times when he did it, and I remember I did at the ice-house, when one of the hands threw a piece of ice against my foot and hurt me. But I know it is a very unbecoming and ungentlemanly practice, and I wish I could quit it; but I am inclined to think I cannot, as I do it unconsciously from habit.' I then urged him to try. After some conversation he said, 'I will try, and will inform you next Saturday how I succeed.' Next Saturday came, and in the evening he came into my room and sat down. There was a mixture of seriousness and lightness and an inclination to smile, and he was evidently a little agitated. I said nothing on the subject of swearing, and he also was silent for some time. At length he said, 'I have come to tell you that I have sworn *twice* since I was here; but I am determined to quit it; I am more and more dissatisfied with the practice.' As he said this he seemed mortified and concerned, and I immediately replied, 'You cannot cease from profane language unless you will *pray.*' 'Pray!' said he; 'I never prayed in my life; I was never on my knees in my life but once, and that was to gratify Parson Wallace, and I then laughed the whole time.' Indeed, he seemed a little amused at the idea of *his* praying. I insisted he could not cease to swear unless he would use prayer. He became silent, and alternately thoughtful and amused. At length he said, 'I will try to pray once if you will never mention it.' 'Very good,' said I, and we parted. Two or three days afterward he came into my room, and sitting silently a few minutes, he said, smilingly, 'I told you I could not pray; I have tried *twice*, and when I kneeled down I could not utter a word. I knew I could not before.' While he was saying these things I could perceive an increased concern in his countenance; I therefore insisted on his continuing his efforts, which he did, increasing every day in earnestness, until in less than three months he was a member of the Methodist Church, and was such the last time I saw him.

"This circumstance, as well as several others, confirmed me in the opinion that the smallest beginning in religious matters should not be disregarded, but sedulously cherished, both by the subject of them and the minister of religion.

"In the fall of 1822 I was appointed at the Marietta Conference to Zanesville Station, though I shared the station with Brother B. Westlake, owing to the illness of his family. Hence I was on Zanesville Circuit half the time. I was informed that this appointment was made with design to promote the gracious work which was begun in Zanesville. The year was not so prosperous as I could have wished, notwithstanding we had precious seasons. I found in this station, as is the case in all large societies, a few turbulent spirits, and their course since is an additional proof of an almost well ascertained fact, that such never can be at peace, not even if they be first in all things. They have since withdrawn and associated themselves with the radicals of the present age of the Church. These have taken the denomination, 'Associate Methodist Society.'

"I cannot omit to record the name, services, and friendship of Brother David Young, all of which are associated with the events of this year. A good understanding well improved, and deep piety, made him a desirable acquaintance. His experience and sincerity made him a valuable friend. He admonished me of my errors in preaching, specially in manner and length; he also taught me the proper principles of the composition of a sermon, and added to his own remarks a recommendation of *Claude's Essay on the Composition of a Sermon,* which he very kindly lent me. In his house I experienced every thing which a Christian brother could ask. With him I prayed often, and for him I have and hope still to pray often. He is now one of the oldest and most valuable of the traveling preachers. He was a *pioneer* in this Western world, and continues in the work, so gloriously enlarged, which he himself assisted in planting."

After going to the West in his early ministry David Young was identified more than almost any of his contemporaries with the progress of Methodism in Ohio. He had a superior intellect. It was cultivated, disciplined, and finely furnished. " He knew theology, was well acquainted with philosophy, general history, national law, and whatever pertained to our Federal or State affairs. He was especially familiar with Church history and Methodist jurisprudence."

Bishop Morris said, "No man conducted public religious service more solemnly and impressively than he did, especially in reading the holy Scriptures or in prayer. He was deeply experienced in the work of grace."

In the pulpit he was a master. He had logic, style, and energy. "His voice enabled him to be heard at the largest camp-meetings, where he was a favorite preacher." Under one of these sermons Bishop Morris saw his sin and danger.

The Hon. John McLean, LL.D., said, " When his soul became stirred, as it sometimes did from its lowest depths, he would enchain an audience beyond almost any of his contemporaries." He died November 15, 1858. As proof of his abiding love for the ministry he left his choice library for the use of the successive pastors of South Second Street Church, Zanesville, Ohio.

Was there a man in the Church better fitted to criticise and direct the promising preacher than he ? His character gave weight to his words, and they lay on Durbin's intellect and heart.

" 1823. In the fall of this year," says Durbin, " I received an appointment to Lebanon, Ohio, a small station, but in a neighborhood remarkable for many years for the flourishing state of Methodism. In this society there is a strong proof of the importance of brotherly love. Two of the best men (as is commonly supposed) differed in the settlement of a partnership, and the simple fact of each one seeming to incline to his own interest infused suspicion into both minds, and tainted them, I fear, forever. Suspicion being attached, each, to clear himself from it, proposed to yield the claim, but each refused a settlement on principle of *gift*, or the acquisition of property when the one giving it up did not think it was proper, being offered merely for peace' sake. Their sense of independence and honor refused the adjustment of claims in this way, and as they could be adjusted in no other they remain unadjusted and still rankling in the vitals of the individuals, and gradually poisoning the existence of society.

" In this station I toiled hard, and I think faithfully and saw but little fruit of all my labors. Immediately, however, on the commencement of the next Conference year ten or twelve young men came in to brighten the hopes of the Church. During this year I applied myself closely to my classical studies in the house of my much-loved Brother Reeves. I must here record the kindness of this gentleman and his family to me. It continues mutually until this day.

"1824. In the fall of this year I was appointed to Cincinnati Station as assistant preacher to my dear Brother William H. Raper, whom I love sincerely in the Lord." This was a critical period in the history of the Methodist Episcopal Church. "The Reformers" in the West, as in the East, were seeking a radical change in the form of our government; strong men took sides with them. Prudence at such a time was a cardinal virtue. The spirit of reform showed its greatest power in some of our strongest centers. Cincinnati had its share in the excitement. Raper and Durbin were not the men for incautious action, but neither of them escaped the criticisms of adverse reasonings.

At the Chillicothe Conference a resolution was offered disapproving the course of one of its members in preaching for the "Reformers," who were organizing "Union societies." Mr. Durbin supposed this resolution would do harm, and opposed it for half a day, and finally got it laid on the table, and presented a substitute as an act of tenderness to the brother concerned. "It was merely to direct the president of the Conference to *request* the brother not to preach for the 'Reformers' *owing to the present state of excitement* in Cincinnati." This gave offense. Language of keenness was indulged when words of kindness were merited.

It is painful to see how devout and intelligent people are sometimes separated by facts which, in themselves, have no *moral quality.* Churches, like individuals, have had memories that they could wish the last trump might not awaken. Time, if not greater charity and wisdom, has effaced many of the difficulties that in earlier days divided us, and no one more certainly joyed in this than did Dr. Durbin.

His appointment to "the Queen City of the West" was a flattering testimonial to his talents. A leading member of "the Stone Church" had heard him in one of his first appointments and was charmed with his earnestness and simplicity, and saw in him the promise of a great future. He was anxious to secure his services for the charge. Then, as now, the judgment of a layman of intelligence, piety, and strength justly commanded influence with the episcopacy, and Mr. Durbin was appointed. Young as he was he "showed himself a man."

A friend of Dr. Durbin says, "His marked ability, refined and courteous manners, soon attracted the attention of prominent men in Cincinnati, among whom was General William H. Harrison, afterward President of the United States, Judge McLean, the best talent of the bar, and some of the most distinguished members of other Churches, Unitarian as well as our own people." While in this charge he resided in the family of Mr. Christopher Smith, whose house was to the close of his life his Cincinnati home. Mr. Smith was a prominent man in the Church, and was a member of the first Methodist class in Cincinnati. He knew a preacher's heart. Now Mr. Durbin had the best opportunity for study. He immediately entered the Cincinnati College, located in the city, and his people gave him six months of special devotion to his college course. But meanwhile he attended to all the duties of his station. Here was, indeed, a contrast to the embarrassments of his early studies.

At Mr. Smith's he had as real a home as if he had been a son. As his time was at his command he employed it to his mind. One of the perils of his position was like that of a man with a voracious appetite, long restrained, before whom, for the first time, a banquet is spread with liberty to eat to satisfy. Indulgence might be death. With him such was the luxury of learning that in his application to his books there was danger of impairing health and so defeating his purpose of greater usefulness. With every facility, comfort, and encouragement his efforts and progress were amazing. But as in other things, so in this, reason restrained his ambition and directed his energies. " His wonderful application and great economy of time were soon noticed by his friends; each day was systematized, each hour had its own special work." He was an early riser, and was at his studies long before the family were astir. " The house was surrounded by ample grounds, which offered many quiet spots. To one of these in pleasant weather he usually took his book, after the morning meal, to prepare for the hour of *recitation*. The after part of the day he gave to pastoral work, and study in his own room."

He seldom accepted an invitation for company, feeling his time at this period of life was too valuable to be spent otherwise than in positive duty. Yet he remembered that the bow that is constantly bent loses its elasticity, and in his own way he unstrung it. But he was careful that its fiber was not impaired or the string broken by any contact or use.

After a day of hard work he devoted the evening hour to the family circle, and his moods and manners and stories charmed the children.

His labors and experiences made their impression, and helped to form his intellectual and social habits. Years after he walked past the old home, looking at the windows where he had sat and studied, exclaiming, "Dear me, what hard work I did in that room!" This place was as real to him in its memories as Bethel was to Jacob.

Thence he went with his completed purpose of college graduation. Thence he went, with the knowledge that all his duties as a Methodist minister had been sedulously observed, that they had commanded his attention, elicited his energy, and shown their fruits. He had not done the work of the Lord deceitfully or partially, nor had he offered to God that which cost him nothing. *Study* meant *study*, whether in college or cabin, in forest or by the fireside. But he was not more certainly the "earnest student" than the attractive preacher and the faithful pastor.

In due time (1822) he was ordained deacon, and in 1824 he received elder's orders. He was graduated with honor, and as a special reward of diligence and scholarship the college at once conferred the degree of "Master of Arts."

Who can fail to honor the Providence that, after testing a man, gives him what his character deserves? As in spiritual things, "He that goeth forth weeping, bearing precious seed," comes again with rejoicing, bringing his sheaves with him, so in faithful labor the reward is certain, and the contrast between weeping and reaping may be in a short period realized.

The foundation of his future reputation in the department of education was now laid and the problem of his labor had found its solution.

The richest resources of man are in himself, and their depth and fullness are never so revealed as when under the pressure of adverse circumstances he is roused to the most vigorous and persistent effort. A great soul may show its impatience of restraint, but difficulties do not conquer conviction. Only the first man was permitted a paradise to his mind, and with him it soon

ceased. Some of the grandest achievements that history records have been performed amid embarrassments
best calculated to repress energy and forbid hope.
There are great elements in all great natures, and it is
for their possessors to determine whether difficulties
shall destroy or develop them; whether they shall be
as water to extinguish the fires of genius or as wind to
fan them to a flame. A great spirit spurns no auxiliary
to its advancement, but is ever ready to adopt the best
means for the end proposed. The wise man does not refuse the ladder to a true fame. John P. Durbin knew
that the college would advance him in the purposes of a
sanctified ambition. We speak of self-made men. All
that are really made are so made. None are great by
accident. No one receives enough from ancestry or
environment either to make him truly great or really
small.

> " Men at some time are masters of their fates;
> The fault, dear Brutus, is not in our stars,
> But in ourselves, that we are underlings."

But while we have marked the progress, admired
the courage, and rejoiced in the success of the college
student, we have had no adequate idea of his power in
the pulpit. Modesty forbade a full record of facts.
Some fruits, indeed, he has named; some trials he has
stated; and we have seen through him the theological
errors that he encountered, and that caused "the
Spirit of the Lord to begin to move upon him" for
their refutation. But the years of his close study were
years of grand, if of diverse, experience as a preacher.
In the pulpit he had his trials as well as his triumphs.

The Rev. J. A. Roberts, of Kansas, in an article in
The Christian Advocate, of New York, July 2, 1855,
says that "at a quarterly meeting held near the village
of Dayton young Durbin was put up to preach on Sat-

urday night, that being the time to *try* the boys. During the sermon the *ex-officio* presiding elder 'asked the Lord to give patience.' A brother who knew said, 'John would have preached a good sermon if he had had half a chance.'"

One of the fathers is represented as declaring he might as well go home, as there was not much in the young man. Time soon showed that there was enough in him to commend him to the notice of the world.

Mr. Roberts, who refers to his failure at the quarterly meeting named, says, "The following August, when the Methodist hosts within a radius of thirty miles were gathered at a camp-meeting, some thirty miles southwest of Dayton, on Sabbath morning, before sunrise, the Revs. John Sale and Arthur Elliott, presiding elder and preacher in charge, were in consultation touching the order of the day. Looking up just as the light was breaking from the purpling East the former exclaimed, 'Why, there comes white-headed John Durbin.' 'Yes,' said Elliott, 'and we must put him up to preach.' But Sale objected, referring to the Dayton failure. Elliott was persistent, and declared he would be responsible for costs. The presiding elder finally agreed, holding the other to the responsibility. 'But,' said he, 'we will put him up at eight o'clock, and if he fails, we will have him out of the way.' Elliott immediately ran to meet John, took him in his arms, and told him to be ready to preach at eight o'clock, leaving him at a tent for refreshment. Prompt at the hour the trumpet sounded, and to the astonishment of that great company of elect men and women, instead of greeting one of the giants present there stood before them that delicate-looking boy. His reading of the hymn was with trembling, the prayer humble, but there was a holy unction about it. The introduction of the sermon was faulty; it was slightly drawling and embarrassed; but hark! there sparkles a sentence of beauty; others follow in rapid succession of marvelous splendor, unction, and power. 'Bless the Lord,' said the presiding elder.' 'Amen! The costs won't be much,' replied the preacher in charge. Soon the vast throngs arose to their feet, crowding to the glowing orator and swaying like trees under the blast of a tornado, while the shouts of 'Glory to God in the highest!' were heard afar off."

As his ability had become known, he was requested by the presiding elder to preach at a camp-meeting near Lebanon, Ohio. The occasion was greater than he had supposed. The day came, and the preacher pondered his theme and asked God to prepare his heart. The plan was formed and his mind was filled with the subject. He returned to the preachers' tent, and was lying upon the straw, as if he had already learned one of the most important lessons in connection with pulpit preparation, namely, to allow the intellect *rest* before it makes the greatest effort. The elder, seeing him at ease, said, "John, are you ready to preach to the crowds that are pouring in to hear you?" "This," said he, in after life, "gave me the first intimation that any would come twenty miles to hear me," as he was told they were then doing. The result of that sermon is not yet forgotten. God made the place of his footsteps glorious. Preachers and people were in transports. None came too far, nor did Durbin study too long to prepare, nor rest too long to deliver that discourse. While yet in the West he was requested to preach at another camp-meeting. It was in a community where "the Trinity" and "Triune" were words regarded with disfavor. He was impressed to deliver a sermon on the deity of Christ. His mind and heart were full of the subject. It took possession of him.

Awed by his theme, and stirred by the demands of the occasion, he entered upon his duty with faith in God. He commenced the discourse with unaffected modesty, but realized his authority as a teacher of the divine word. There was nothing vague in his thoughts, nothing dubious in his language, nothing indifferent in his manner, his expressions were vigorous, his convictions profound and active. He was in a moral mood for great service. He plied them with Scripture, he pressed them with facts, he urged them by arguments. Logic was on fire. Sentence after sentence shot forth with convicting force, and the strength of every opposing argument was broken. He brought his proofs from two worlds. The infinite attributes of Jehovah, as illustrated by Christ in time, and his glories as the Son of the Highest in eternity. He showed them " God manifested in the flesh," and now seated with the Father on his throne, with the redeemed casting their crowns at his feet and saying, "Thou art worthy, O Lord, to receive glory, and honor, and power, for thou hast created all things, and for thy pleasure they are and were created." Light flashed in every direction. The divine page was illuminated, and the Saviour, as in his transfiguration, appeared with claims as pure and countenance as bright as the raiment through which his glory shone when the voice came from the cloud, " This is my beloved Son, in whom I am well pleased ; hear ye him." And they did hear him, to confess his claim, to honor his mission, and seek his power. The genius of the speaker was forgotten. The " brightness of the Father's glory filled the horizon of their vision, and the unbelieving, like Thomas, exclaimed, " My Lord and my God ! " The eye of Durbin, that in a climax seemed never equaled, revealed his soul. Truth was riveted. Looking round in the pulpit he saw a minister who had been in great perplexity on the subject, and, to use the words of Dr. Durbin, "the big tears, like bullets, were rolling down his cheeks." The work was done, the snare was broken, and he had escaped. Only in the next world can it be known how many clouds were that day dispelled, how many doubts were dissipated, and in how many cases the true faith was established. His fame spread, and the marvels of God's power that day through him have made many a thrilling narrative. The reputation then gained rested upon nothing meretricious or sensational, but upon the wise, the weighty, and the eloquent presentation of essential truth. The people who were so impressed were not strangers to able and popular preaching. It was the West of a *William Beauchamp*, from whom light broke upon the most bewildered understanding; of *Russel Bigelow*, of pure taste, ponderous thought, great emotion, intense earnestness, and in the language of Bishop Thomson, "of an eloquence of the most exalted kind;" of *Samuel Parker*, keen in perception, forcible in logic, elevated in style, with a voice that was rich, mellow, and harmonious, of whom Bishop Morris declared that before him multitudes of people melted like snow before an April sun." It was the West of *John Strange*, "one of the brightest lights of the American pulpit, formed by nature to be eloquent." "A man who could transport his hearers in one moment to the third heavens, and make it bright, glorious, present, and real to them, and the next he could bear them away to the world of woe and freeze their blood with images of terror." A man of whom Aaron Wood said, "He breathed into his sentences his own *strangeness*, which can't be imitated or described." It was the land of *James Quinn*, of *James B. Finley*, and of *John A. Waterman*, "men of mental caliber and moral might;" it was amid such ministers, and by their confession, that John P. Durbin rose and stood the acknowledged prince. Nor is it to be accounted for, except on the ground of his pre-eminence, that whenever in after years he went to the West people of all Churches and conditions flocked to his ministry and sat with rapture under his discourses.

If ever the ability of Durbin was a problem, it was solved before his habits and history had made him the scholar.

CHAPTER III.

Exalted—Character Made in Seven Years—Professor in Augusta College.

DEEDS *express character.* We have seen the youthful Durbin, and he has made his impression of energy, aptitude, and success. At the age of fourteen years, for reasons sufficient to influence a mature mind, he determined upon a trade. When eighteen he had not only acquired a knowledge of the business, but had " followed it to some profit for a year or more." By what power did he in so short a time make it available to himself? Cabinet-making requires skill, but he had *learned* and *used* the *art.* Have we felt no surprise at his accurate thinking and wise conclusions in regard to the present good and future welfare of his younger brothers? At eighteen we have seen him entering upon the work of his early taste and of his moral convictions, and then rising above the difficulties that beset his path as a student. We have seen him at the age of twenty-five the peculiarly honored graduate of college, while as a preacher he has risen to an eminence that places him in the nation's eyes.

In seven years John Price Durbin was made.

The foundation of his future was laid, the attention was directed, the confidence was inspired, and the power was evoked by which he was conducted to the positions that distinguished his after life.

1. *What was he made?*

We answer, a Methodist minister, with his sympathies,

experiences, and purposes; a herald of the cross that could be satisfied with nothing short of spiritual character, of ardent worship, of a ministry that instructed, convinced, persuaded, and was the means of saving men. The zeal that prompted him from his own meager means to purchase, carry, and distribute tracts, putting them in the path of the traveler, or seeking and with avidity supplying the plowmen from the field, reveals his spirit; such assiduity gives us insight as to his earnest wish to do all the good he could, in all the ways in his power.

While the results that crowned his efforts speak with eloquence to every one, " Be instant in season and out of season," the report that reached him years after he left the circuit on which the presiding elder placed him, showed, in addition to facts previously known, that his " labor was not in vain in the Lord," and became to his soul the *joy of success.* The conversion of his host at Hamilton may be regarded as an illustration of the influence of character and intercourse in securing access to a heart difficult to reach, and of even so conveying rebuke that it was received with welcome; and the delicacy with which he dealt with his friend shows that he had early learned that " he that winneth souls is wise." While he maintained his solicitude he would not, by *overdoing,* defeat his purpose. In this he shows a holy art that is sometimes our greatest help in bringing souls to Christ. If the important question that is sometimes so pungently put concerning a young minister, "Has he fruit?" is asked in relation to Durbin, we answer, Yes, he has fruit—real, rich, ripe, and manifest fruit.

As an orator he had commanded thousands.

But his power as a speaker was not merely in fluency of utterance, beauty of language, and force of logic; it was still more in the interest he showed, the spirit that energized, and the unction of the Holy One that the people felt.

As a scholar he was made.

His attainments in seven years caused him to be eagerly sought as Professor of Ancient Languages in the first Methodist College in the land, and to remain in highest demand in the most distinguished institutions of the Church.

2. *How was he made?*

Shall we briefly say, God made him, that he called him, sent him, sustained him, and honored his labors? Of this we have no doubt. John Newton said, "Only God can make a minister." We accept the statement; but to be more particular, how did God make John P. Durbin a preacher? We answer, by so influencing him to recognize the divine economy *in him*, the *man*, as to neglect no power, and to employ to the best purpose all the talents, time, and means at his disposal; to use every endowment, to discipline every faculty, to devote every energy that centered in him to the achievement of highest intellectual and moral results. Then God made him, by his stature and symmetry of character, a *force* in the ministry that genius alone never reaches, and that divine grace only makes perfect—a grace always at the command of him, whose "sufficiency is of God."

He gladly accepted the help of men.

He was one of the most *teachable* preachers. He knew his want, and he rejoiced in the aid of the competent. And as a man's "gift makes room for him, and brings him before great men," so the singleness of a worthy aim, the continuance of noble conduct, and the unreserved devotion to duty of all his resources, constrained those who had the ability to facilitate his advancement to make their contribution to his just ambition. Thus men helped Durbin, as they saw he deserved it, and would reward their attention.

The grandsire roused the youth to duty. Mr. Akin spoke wisely to his wants; Collord helped his grammar, Ruter incited him to linguistic knowledge; the German furnished *Clarke's Commentary* to aid the study of the Scriptures. The journeyman made the correction of faults easy. David Young gave highest criticisms and presented basis for abiding fame. When vehemence of speech had broken the voice and impaired the health, and sent him home in apprehension that his work was at an end, a plain man suggested the effective means that in six months restored his voice for any service, and secured to him in the conversational address a secret of power that philosophy never transcended, and that to his latest life showed its benefits.

It was not the day of "theological seminaries." Misled, indeed, is the young man who, having the opportunity, declines their advantages; but let us honor our fathers in the help they rendered us ere Methodism provided the schools.

When on one occasion Dr. Doddridge was commending to his theological students modern authors of merit, he paused to praise the Puritans, and said, "There were good sense and learning in our fathers' days, as well as in our own—as our grand-mothers had beauty, though their antiquated dress might disguise it in some measure."

Yes, honor to the fathers! But the stone must be of the right quality to receive the shape and take the polish that the sculptor seeks to give and that the lapidary labors to impart, or all is vain.

It is not for want of means and helpers that there are not many Durbins. Helps indeed he had ; but they did not make the scholar, the divine, or the preacher.

As we read his studies, consider his circumstances, observe his labors, and mark his devotion, we can hardly marvel that such a man should obtain any thing upon which he set his *mind* and *heart*. Will he who would attain the highest excellence consent to emulate his virtues as a student and his habits as a preacher?

May we not reverently say, as the course to the divinest riches is through a "strait gate and narrow way" of sacrifice and effort, so the most valuable and abiding wealth of the mind is through the strait gate and narrow way of the renunciation of ease and the acceptance of labor?

When a king asked Euclid, the mathematician, whether he could not explain his art to him in a more compendious manner, he answered that there was "no royal road to geometry." Might and money may seize and secure other things, but knowledge is the result of careful, if not painful, search.

1825. Mr. Durbin writes, "At the Conference of this year I was appointed professor of languages in Augusta College, Kentucky." Scarcely had he received the seal of his *alma mater* before he was invited to a chair in the first college established in the Methodist Episcopal Church. The reputation that he had made as a scholar and the distinction he had attained as a preacher justified and commended this election. His conviction of the Church's duty in higher education was a worthy motive for his acceptance of the place. It was not from indifference to the value of colleges that our fathers did not before this time have them in successful operation. In 1780 John Dickins, a fine scholar, advocated an academic institution for Methodism. In 1784, the year of our organization as a Church, our two Bishops, Coke and Asbury, were engaged in laying the foundation of a college at Abingdon, Md.

In 1787 Asbury consecrated and opened it with public ceremonies. As evidence of their *identity* with it the names of the two Bishops blended in the title of the institution. It was *Cokesbury* College. But neither name, nor purpose, nor consecration, preserved it from devouring flames. In 1795 it was destroyed by fire. A second edifice was provided in Baltimore, and this fell as the former. These adversities, following in quick succession, tempted the thought in some minds that Providence frowned on our effort, or at least that the time had not come for us to engage in *this work*. Though such reasonings for a time repressed ardor they did not extinguish the fire of the Church's zeal. The flame burned on, and in different localities a *jet* would shoot forth giving evidence of the presence of much more that would soon show itself in a broadened flame.

Asbury encouraged hope of brighter days at hand. In 1818 Dr. Samuel K. Jennings, a graduate of Rutgers College, New Jersey, and other Methodists, attempted a college in Baltimore; but this failed.

Before the admission of Kentucky as a State into the Union the Methodist Episcopal Church was in the van of other Christian denominations in inaugurating measures for the education of youth. The building of " Bethel Academy," and the noble efforts made by our fathers to sustain it, though unsuccessful, showed the vigor of their purpose and furnished ground for faith in the future. The formation of the Kentucky Conference, in 1820, placed the Church in a position to consider her resources and rise to the measure of supposed duty. Ohio, as well as Kentucky, felt the need of a college.

James B. Finley, at that time presiding elder of the Lebanon District, exerted his influence in its behalf. Aware that neither Conference alone could support such an institution, Ohio and Kentucky united in the undertaking, and the seat of the college was fixed at Augusta, Ky. It was properly chartered by the Legislature of the State, Dec. 22, 1822. The Rev. John P. Finley was appointed professor of languages in 1822 and afterward had charge as president. He died on the 8th of May, 1825.

In 1825 the college edifice was erected, and Dr. Martin Ruter was elected president, Joseph S. Tomlinson became professor of mathematics and natural philosophy, and John P. Durbin took the professorship of languages. A little later, in 1831, Henry Bascom was chosen professor of "moral science and *belles-lettres.*"

Who that reads these names and knew those ministers can fail to wonder at the early power of Methodism to raise up men for its necessities? It was a wonderful concentration and combination of mental and moral forces! It showed astonishing ability of adaptation to the Church's demand! It is difficult to think of these four men in one college, and that our first. The world has long witnessed our success in saving souls. It was our glory. To this we were trained. Nothing was ever to impair this power or disturb this purpose. On this we had fixed our thoughts and to this we had directed our spiritual energies.

Some knew, however, that with all this zeal for conversion Methodist preachers could avoid the difficulties of the itinerancy, cultivate habits of study, and make progress in learning. Among them were logicians and linguists, metaphysicians and natural philosphers, men acquainted with various sciences, well read in history and familiar with general literature. Though unaccustomed to "college shades" they made shades for themselves, and buried themselves in their depths while they explored systems, exploded errors, and solved difficult problems. "Through desire they intermeddled with all wisdom." They had in those days but small libraries, yet they knew their contents and could use them to advantage. It was not with them so much a question how many books they had upon their shelves as how much of their contents was in their memory. Their study for thought and their closet for prayer were one and the same, and after far-looking beyond the skies they often found their minds were clearer and keener to see the things at hand. Then they showed a mental acuteness that made them mighty men. They could delve as well as soar. They knew where some of the richest intellectual mines are found, and they spurned the theory of "the unprofitableness of deep mining." They obtained more than the labor cost. Some of them were not only walking concordances, but living cyclopedias.

We may glance at the men whom the Church first called to this new department of her solicitude and service.

The Rev. John P. Finley, named as first president of Augusta College, was a brother of Rev. J. B. Finley. "Under the instruction of his father he had acquired a competent knowledge of the sciences and of the Latin and Greek languages ; and of the English language Bishop Bascom pronounced him a perfect master."

The father under whom Mr. Finley studied was a student in the " College of New Jersey " under Dr. Witherspoon, and, according to the testimony of the son, James B., he passed through the regular college course at Princeton, though for some unknown reason his name does not appear on the list of graduates.—*Sprague's Annals of the American Methodist Pulpit.*

The first President of Augusta College was "an amiable and highly gifted man, an excellent teacher, and an earnest and impressive preacher."

Dr. Martin Ruter was one of the earliest men in Methodism to receive the degree of doctor of divinity. This honor was conferred by the Transylvania University, Kentucky, in 1822. It was at a time when the degree meant more than honor. In 1801 he was admitted on trial in the New York Conference and filled stations of high responsibility. In 1818 he was placed in charge of the New Market Wesleyan Academy, under the patronage of the New England Conference. This afterward became the "Wilbraham Academy." From 1820 to 1828 he had charge of the Western Book Concern at Cincinnati. Thence he was called to the presidency of Augusta College, which he accepted, and remained there till 1832.

His heart was in the regular work of the ministry, and he longed to return to that service. This he did in the Pittsburg Conference, and was stationed in that city. There he remained till 1837, when Bishop Hedding appointed him Superintendent of the Texas Mission. To this field Littleton Fowler and Robert Armstrong accompanied him, and in Texas he laid the foundation of a splendid superstructure. He had just entered upon his work with consuming zeal and implicit faith when the Master said, "Well done." He died in Washington, Texas, May 16, 1838. All *Methodism mourned!* He sleeps in a missionary grave on the banks of the Brazos, in Texas. The fine scholar, the trained teacher, the early friend of John P. Durbin, who so encouraged him in his classical studies when on the circuit, served as president of Augusta when Durbin was professor. As a writer his name has found an abiding place in his work on "Church History," so long a text-book in the Conference course of study.

John Smith Tomlinson, after an apprenticeship at the saddlery business, entered Transylvania University, and for his support depended principally upon his trade, to which he devoted his spare time. He graduated with honor and was called to Augusta College, and there at various times filled the professorships of languages, mathematics, natural science, moral philosophy and *belles-lettres*. In scholarship and in brilliancy of intellect, as a conversationalist, a debater and preacher, he was one of the rare men of Methodism. After serving as professor he was at last chosen president, and remained in that office till 1849. He died at Neville, Ohio, on the 4th of June, 1853. Art, science and religion mourned his untimely end.

Henry Bidleman Bascom, who filled the chair of moral science and *belles-lettres*, was one of the most remarkable ministers in Methodist history. He had no advantages of early education, and the need of his family demanded his utmost energy and care as a boy. But he entered our itinerancy in his seventeenth year, and through incredible difficulties and painful prejudices made his way to the very front of the American pulpit. So great was the influence of his eloquence upon Henry Clay that, through his advocacy, in 1823 he was elected chaplain to the lower House of Congress. In 1827 he was elected president of Madison College, Pa. He filled in succession the most distinguished positions in the Church, and in 1850 was made Bishop of the Methodist Episcopal Church, South. On September 8, of the same year, he died at Louisville, Ky., in the fifty-fourth year of his age.

In this college, distinguished by the talents, virtues, and labors of these men, John P. Durbin began his life as an educator. There he showed his ability to simplify truth, to communicate thought, to impress principles, and to impart to young men the noble sense of their responsibility, their duty, and their hope. Here he so explained the difficult that the least receptive imbibed knowledge, and the dullest intellect could not say "the subject is dark." Here he added to his already remarkable ability in judging men.

Will they who recall those days of their college-life at Augusta ever forget them? Will they forget these honored teachers, these sublime preachers? Will they ever forget their massive and eloquent sermons, the eagerness with which they heard them, the miles they sometimes walked to listen to the discourses—when they preached at distant points—that must ever abide?

Will the writer be pardoned for expressing the belief that never on this continent has any college had more able and eloquent and overpowering discourses than those delivered by the men of that faculty in this our first college?

The desirableness of Methodist colleges, and the fruits of this one now established at Augusta, were soon seen in the students that entered it from Methodist families at even remote points, and the position in society that they took after their return from this institution. The writer well remembers on one of his first circuits—Accomack County, Va.—two young men who went to Augusta, and on return cherished happy memories of the college, and showed in their wider spheres the advantages of their course. Robert J. Poulson, son of Major Poulson, of Onancock, in a short time represented his county in the Legislature of Virginia, and Albert Melvin, son of a devout widow near Hearntown, graduated to the bar in Drummondtown, of his native county.

From New York went one son of the Rev. Samuel Merwin, the present Rev. John B. Merwin, D.D., long an honored member and now the oldest effective minister in the New York East Conference. Nor can the Church forget what she has received through two of the early students of Augusta still with us, Bishop Randolph S. Foster, D.D., LL.D., and the Rev. John Miley, D.D., Professor of Dogmatic Theology in "the Drew Theological Seminary."

One of the first cares of Professor Durbin was to obtain funds for the college, and he spent the year 1825 in the South and East making collections in money and books for the school, and he says, "I collected about $4,000 in money and 1,000 books." This result might astonish us at this time when colleges receive such princely donations. It might be supposed that this was only *gleaning.* No, it was *reaping;* and that when the sickle was in a skillful hand. If John P. Durbin did not know how to appeal to the intelligent and strong men of the Church and to collect for a college, then the writer, who had evidence of his labors, is at a loss to find the man who does. Yet, with all his ability, one year gave him only $4,000 in money. It is not easy for those who live sixty years after those days to judge the facts. Our country in 1825 was rich in territory, in talent, in patriotism and virtue, but not in money. The population was sparse and there were few men of wealth among us. Methodists were not rich, and to them chiefly was the appeal.

The writer remembers when, for the raising of $1,000 at the dedication of one of our ablest churches, the fact was heralded as an illustration of what great things Methodists can do when they *fully set themselves about it.* Nor has he forgotten that when in a borough of 8,000 people he undertook to build a church it was assumed if we could get the strongest man in the society to give $100 we should accomplish the work which, from the lack of such liberality in former times, had in repeated trials caused failure. The $100 was given by the man, and $50 was afterward added. The walls rose and the church was dedicated, and still stands, and is crowned with honor. It was $100 for *their own purposes* that was asked.

Nor must it be forgotten that $4,000 then would go as far, perhaps, as four times that sum now.

1826. Professor Durbin writes: "Nothing of great consequence occurred this year except my acquaintance with my wife, and this is not of much consequence to any but myself." On entering the ministry he adopted for his motto Job xxxi. 1: "I made a covenant with mine eyes; why then should I think upon a maid?" It might excite no wonder that with his experience of less than $50 a year, and with the fact before him that his devout and educated colleague in five years had not received more than $500 or $600, and then had to leave the ministry and go into business, one might justly ask, Why should I think upon a maid? Surely not to take *care of her*, and he might not wish her to take care of him. In the days of early Methodism many ministers had to leave the itinerancy when they married, as they could not obtain support. It was a grief to Bishop Asbury, who never felt that he was in a position to take proper care of a wife up to 1836. The Discipline required a young preacher to remain single four years, or at least till admitted to the Conference.

But a weighty reason for Mr. Durbin's making this covenant was, that he wished to give himself wholly to study till he had compassed his end and made a character. But now the seven years were passed, the conditions of the covenant had been kept, and he allowed himself to think upon a companion, and on the 6th of September, 1827, he was married to Miss Frances B. Cook, daughter of Alexander Cook, Esq., of Philadelphia, and in his noble companion God showed him how in a wife he can honor him who first seeks the divine honor.

In 1828 he writes, "I have anticipated 1827." This was in his marriage. He says: "We spent a pleasant year with Mrs. Sarah Armstrong, with whom we boarded, and who is one of the excellent of the earth. On the 16th day of December of this year our first child was born, a daughter named Augusta, after our college, and Ann, after her grandmother Cook." . . . No change of relation or domestic cares relaxed his energy in the work of God.

In 1829 he says: "In the fall of this year we visited Philadelphia to see our friends." But he spent the year in making collections for the college. The winter was passed chiefly in Washington City, endeavoring to get a bill passed giving the college a township of land. He says: "I got it reported, passed to a second reading, and then it was laid on the table in the Senate." Here, as in every place, we see the man in purpose, in his resources, in his perseverance. He put himself into whatever he undertook, so as to secure all that earnestness and effort made possible. Had he been successful in his proposition to Congress a future would have been secured to the institution that the innovations of time might not have harmed.

In 1829 he was nominated to the chaplaincy of the United States Senate. There was a tie vote, and John C. Calhoun, President of the Senate, gave the casting vote against him. On receiving additional information he regretted his action and sent for Mr. Durbin and apologized, and some of the political friends of Calhoun told him he had made the mistake of his life. Mr. Calhoun assured Mr. Durbin he voted for the other candidate only because he was a minister of the same church to which his mother belonged.

In 1830 he says: "I sent to London for some apparatus for Augusta College."

The Rev. D. Stevenson, of Barbourville, Ky., writes: "The only piece of apparatus of any value that still remains in the old college building is a telescope secured to the college by the labors of Dr. Durbin."

Professor Durbin says: "On the 16th of November, 1830, our second child, a daughter, was born in Augusta, Ky., whom we called Margaret, after her aunt Margaret Cook." This daughter was the late Mrs. Fletcher Harper, Jr., an honor to her sex, and a benefactress in society. Of 1830 Professor Durbin says: "This was a year of a good deal of anxiety and some perplexity which I need not describe ; but losing a little confidence in the institution's prospects, especially pecuniary, and not seeing how to remedy it, I determined to resign, and did so August 6, 1831." He adds: "Upon my resignation at the commencement of the college information from Philadelphia of the dangerous illness of Mrs. Cook arrived. Myself and family set out for Philadelphia August 8." They reached the city through many difficulties from modes of conveyance and the sickness of Miss Margaret Cook, who had been stopping with them in Augusta. They accomplished their journey in time to see Mrs. Cook pass from the cares of earth to her reward in heaven. September 25 he writes : "At the invitation of preacher and trustees of the church in Baltimore I spent a quarter of a year with them. It was a season of great peace to my own heart and of some good, I hope, to the church. I generally spoke publicly three times a week, and as I did not like preaching at night I preached at 3 o'clock P. M."

Professor Durbin had done his utmost for the interests of Augusta College. Much of his time had been given to the raising of means to sustain the efforts, meet the expenses, and maintain the reputation of the institution. But all who read the history of our colleges know that while a few are richly endowed, many, with the best men at their head, and planted when the demand seemed imperative, have languished and expired. Dickinson College came into our hands after having in its trustees some of the greatest men in America and in its faculty some of the ablest scholars and preachers, and that when the locality made so strong an appeal and Presbyterian prestige was back of it. So, alas! after long and painful struggles to sustain itself, in 1849 Augusta College, with all the hopes that it had inspired, and with all the good it had accomplished, broke down from the withdrawal of the patronage of the Kentucky Conference and the repeal of the charter by the legislature of the State.

Of the deep devotion of Professor Durbin to this college we have most eloquent proof in the name of his *first born*, now Mrs. Augusta A. Whitaker of Philadelphia. Though the college has ceased she lives, and we trust will long live to perpetuate the virtues of her parents and the name of the institution that was a demonstration of the zeal of Methodism in higher education, that received so much of her father's sympathy, support, and wisdom, and that for nearly a generation was so highly honored in the men it graduated.

While the extinction of such a light in Kentucky leaves gloom in the community it is the Church's joy that there are now twenty-six universities and colleges, fourteen female colleges, and sixty-one seminaries and academies, all of them denominational institutions, under the immediate patronage and control of the Methodist Episcopal Church. To these are to be added three well-appointed and well-endowed theological schools. The buildings and grounds belonging to these institutions are valued at $8,000,000. Their endowment funds amount to near $6,000,000, and their annual income is not far from $800,000.

For the cause of education the Church now makes such an exhibition as justifies exultation. If the first light in Kentucky ceased, a hundred others blaze over the land, and Methodist education shines all through the republic.

In the department of education a wide door was quickly opened for Professor Durbin, as in 1831 he was appointed professor of natural science in the Wesleyan University, at Middletown, Conn. He had evidently cherished fondness for this department of study. His first appearance of which we have knowledge in the way of authorship is in an improved edition of the *Mosaic History of the Creation of the World,* by Thomas Wood, A. M.

The original work, by Mr. Wood, shows research and learning. The later, of Professor Durbin, greatly broadens and advances it in the more modern discoveries of science. The introduction, written by him, is brief, direct, and intelligent. The Notes through the book are many, ample, and weighty. They show an acuteness and discipline of mind that are an honor to an author of thirty-one years. About this time he also edited for J. & J. Harper *Lyell's Geology.*

These Notes of Professor Durbin, in their scope, design, and influence are largely of the character of the Bridgewater Treatises, showing the power, wisdom, and goodness of God. They also antagonize the theological teachings of Dr. Priestley.

CHAPTER IV.

Chaplain to the United States Senate.

WE have seen that in 1829 Professor Durbin failed of election to this chaplaincy on a tie vote, in which John C. Calhoun, as president of the Senate, through misapprehension, gave the casting vote for another.

But on the 19th of December, 1831, writes Professor Durbin : "This day I left Baltimore for Philadelphia, where my family is. Next day I received intelligence from Washington City that I was elected chaplain to the Senate of the United States. This was very unexpected news indeed. I had not solicited the place ; I had not been to Washington for nearly two years; I did not know that any such project was intended until the fact was announced to me in Philadelphia. The election was made on the day I left Baltimore. As I had already accepted the appointment of professor of natural science in the Wesleyan University at Middletown, Conn, I hesitated about accepting the appointment of the Senate. Finally, upon weighing the whole subject, with advice from friends and consent of the president of the university, I accepted, and arrived in Washington, January 3, 1832."

In the following papers he gives his reasoning as to the acceptance of the honor, the responsibility it involves, and clearly shows the spirit with which he entered upon the duties and strove to discharge the obligations of the place, while he justly conceived and forcibly expressed the possibilities of usefulness in one who properly filled the office.

We have the reasonings of a clear mind and the aspirations of a devout heart as he withstood those prejudices that statements of the difficulties of the place would have created.

It is to the honor of those whom he served, and a commendation of the discretion, the dignity, the Christian devotion, and the eloquence of the man, that as chaplain he had encouragements and supports that probably transcended his strongest faith. He says:

"I undertook this duty with fear and trembling; and do earnestly pray I may prove the means of comfort and good to those to whom I minister.

"I preached in the hall of the House of Representatives, January 8, 1832, from ' *Christ was once offered for sin, the just for the unjust, that he might bring us to God,*' and again on the 23d, from ' *Fight the good fight of faith,*' etc.

"Judging from the deep and almost breathless attention, and other indications, I have presumed to hope some good was done in the immense assembly. Indeed, I have since seen some little fruit of it. On the 24th of January I received a letter signed 'a young man,' expressing his great distress, and wishing my prayers; and this day (January 24) one of the members (Mr. Howard, of Baltimore) requested me to call and see Mrs. Howard, at her earnest request. He seemed concerned that I should call, and observed his wife was a Presbyterian, belonging to Mr. Nevins's church, Baltimore, but hoped that would not prevent my calling. Surely not; and I promised to call. . . .

THE SENATE.

"Previously to my serving in the capacity of chaplain I had supposed that the Senate and House of Representatives showed very little respect for religion or religious services. I had taken up this opinion from the remarks of some who had served, and others also. Rev. Mr. B. told me he resigned because of the irreverence of the members. But I must here do justice to both Houses, and say I have not seen them deficient or disrespectful in regard to religious services either in the ordinary morning services or those of the Sabbath. I cannot hope to say prayers for a more respectful body, and I am sure I cannot desire to preach to a more respectful and attentive assembly. Some, no doubt, will dissent from this. I cannot help it ; I speak and write what I see and know.

"I do not intend to say that the members are religious when I say they are respectful to religion ; but let religion approach them as she ought and she does not meet with a rude repulse.

1832. WASHINGTON CITY.

"*Employment of Time.*—As the winter had already set in before I left Philadelphia Mrs. Durbin did not accompany me, and I am here alone, boarding in the family of a worthy friend, Mr. Enoch Tucker. I have a delightful room in the third story (the second being parlors, and the lower kitchen and dining-room), well furnished and completely retired. My windows look to the south, a little east. I leave one window-curtain drawn aside that I may see when 'jocund day stands tiptoe on the misty mountain's top.' I usually rise then, sometimes before, shave with cold water, dress, say my prayers, and, if the morning be favorable, take a walk, or rather a run, throwing my hands about and lifting up my arms as high as I can, in order to stretch my limbs and dilate the chest, etc.

"I find this good exercise, and return to read a portion in the Old, and one in the New Testament, before proceeding to the morning reading, which is now geology. If I find any thing curious or doubtful in my Scripture lessons I consult some commentary as a help.

"I shall not say any thing of my scientific reading *here*, except to mention the authors. I have just finished Bakenelly's Geology, having made extracts and memoranda of it in a book for that purpose.

"I generally go to the Capitol, when it is my week to serve, at half past eleven A. M.; when it is not my week to serve, I go up between eleven and twelve o'clock, and devote the time to miscellaneous reading in the splendid library saloon, which is well furnished with books, chairs, tables, ink, pens, paper, etc., and kept well-manned.

"The chaplains generally serve alternately for a week and preach in the hall of the House of Representatives alternately on Sabbath morning. We serve the House first; go into the hall five or ten minutes before the time; when the Speaker comes in he knocks on the clerk's desk with his knife, and all rise and stand during prayer, which occupies about one and a half or two minutes; which should generally be ended with the Lord's Prayer, as some of the members requested a chaplain before me, and which is certainly proper. The chaplain then immediately repairs to the Senate chamber and performs prayers in a similar manner. Both houses are generally very respectful to the services.

"I am convinced many ministers misjudge the manner in which religious services should be performed here. I make them as simple and devout as I can in morning prayers, varying occasionally with grateful reference to the providence of God in giving us independence and liberty, filling our land with peace and plenty, and to the necessity of wisdom and heavenly guidance in order to be able to do the duties of legislators for a great nation, *and to the necessity we are under* (for I identify myself in prayer with the members) *of commending our families to the paternal guardianship of Heaven.* In preaching, select plain and important subjects—important because they present some grand leading point in the salvation of men. Discuss them calmly, clearly, and forcibly, with a mixture of argument, reflection, and (if judiciously done) anecdote rarely, and apply the whole at every opportunity, and, in conclusion, with as great earnestness and power as you possibly can.

"I have not the presumption to hope I shall be the instrument of great immediate good to the members, as their political employments and associations stand greatly in the way. But I do hope for three great advantages:

"1. To elevate and impress the national mind favorably to religion by the uniform and profound respect which our national Congress evinces toward its institutions and ordinances.

"2. By this same respect, to cause religion to find a lodgment in their minds which shall shut out infidelity.

"3. To make good impressions on individual minds which may awake to life in after years and under better circumstances, and bear the fruit of salvation.

"I will simply record my opinion here of the great advantage to any Church to have an efficient and able minister as chaplain to Congress. It brings that Church more before the eye of the world. The vast concourse of strangers as well as members, from every part of the country, then hear the words of life occasionally from a Methodist minister who had been in the habit of supposing no such minister could be fit to preach. A favorable impression is thus made, and tolerance and even liberality of feeling, which is often improved into goodwill and respect, grow from these occasions. Our

friends should not contend improperly for the place, but
should take any reasonable and proper means of having
it filled efficiently.

"*Saturday, Jan.* 28.—Saturday and Sabbath I generally devote to religious and moral reading, and I must
here say by 'miscellaneous reading' in the library I do
not mean strolling from alcove to alcove, and from chapter to chapter, and from book to book; but I select a
book and read it through, or read throughout the subject I have selected in it.

"I have hitherto appropriated my miscellaneous reading to Germany. It is an interesting country, and not
generally well known. I have read the papers in the
American Quarterly Review on ' *German Literature.*'
They are very good, and would bear a reperusal. I
read the first volume of *Hodgskin's Travels.* This is
good in order to get an insight into German manners
and customs in the lower walks of life. He was a pe-
destrian traveler. His second volume is devoted exclusively, or nearly so, to Hanover, its government and
statistics of every description, and to German literature
and universities. Of these I did not think him a competent judge, and therefore have commenced reading
Russell's Travels in Germany. His volume is a very
good one, though it is deeply tinctured with irreverence
for religion, if not actual hostility to it.

"I felt, of course, more interested in the schools and
literature of Germany. Scarcely a century since Germany could be said to have a national literature.
Wieland, Klopstock, Schiller, Goethe, Herder, etc., laid
the foundation of German literature. All of these, except Klopstock, were collected at the court of Weimar,
and chiefly around Amelia the duchess. Hence Weimar
may be said to have taken the lead in the higher literature. It is very probable we have not yet correct and

full ideas of the extent and excellence of German literature.

"Their universities are founded on the same general plan; namely, a small fixed salary, with privilege of lecturing on any subject they please, besides the one committed to them by their appointment. Hence there is great, and in some cases unpleasant, competition, as one professor may invade the province of another, and there is no remedy but superior talents and popularity.

"They do not generally have university and college buildings, as other European universities. For instance, at Göttingen the number of rooms registered for the accommodation of students was above 1,000 in various parts of the town. Each student selects his own room and *restauretum*, or boarding-house, from those registered, and he is registered on the books of the university accordingly. If he change, the change must be registered. The students are allowed to attend such lectures as they may choose. There are from 800 to 1,200 students generally at Göttingen, and above seventy professors. Such were the facts of that period.

"Their recitation rooms are provided by the professors. The library is the first great concern of the university, and its general fixtures, collections, etc., in which there is much more attention to utility than to splendor. Hence the *means* of education are at Göttingen more abundant and probably superior to any other university.

"Notwithstanding the reputation of this university and its professors they can scarcely provide suitably for their families if they should die. Hence there is a widows' fund attached to the university, partly given by the Government, partly by private donations, partly by the professors, for the support of their widows and orphans in case of their death.

6

"Prussia is said to be very careful of the interests of education. Education and religion are joined and are committed to a proper minister of the crown, resident at Berlin, who has charge of the whole interest. The ministers of the Church are made to serve an apprenticeship to school teaching before they take charge pastoral. The minister of education and religion directs the department by means of the consistorium in the several districts of the several circles of the Government. Education is said to be more generally diffused in Prussia than in any country in the world.

"Austria, capital Vienna, 300,000 population—very luxurious and very licentious. No liberty of speech because of the secret police, no liberty of press because of the censorship. In a population of 23,000,000 of souls about thirty newspapers. Austria has very little sea-coast; Trieste her only sea-port, properly speaking. But she has an ample and fertile territory, and some of the noblest rivers in the world.

"There are districts of great interest to the mineralogist and geologist. The salt mines, not far from Cracow, in Poland, and the quicksilver mines in Idria, in the mountains at the head of the Sare.

"Austria is justly considered the most despotic and intolerant government in Europe. She does not encourage liberal education, but rather takes every means to keep her people in ignorance. Prussia, in this respect, has set Austria a noble example. Under the administration of Stein and Hardenberg she created the peasantry real and independent land-holders, and instituted universities, and supports them liberally. Yet the great mass of the population in Austria is as contented as in Prussia, except her Italian subjects. But they are contented on different principles; namely, the enjoyment of a great majority of the political arrangements which benefit a country. The Austrian population is happy because it is devoted to pleasure, and the fertility of the soil is such as to prevent actual want; and they are not concerned about the administration of the government, in which they have no part.

"From these circumstances the Austrians are fond of the fine arts and exhibitions which impart pleasure, but can scarcely boast a single Austrian author of celebrity. They are passionately fond of music, operas, dancing, theaters, etc.; but they have no native composers or performers of merit; and though all play on many or even most instruments of music, they are chiefly imitators, and perform well from practice.

"1832. *Monday, Jan.* 30.—Yesterday morning I preached in Georgetown to a good audience and saw some of my old friends.

"*Tuesday, Jan.* 31.—Went to Alexandria to assist in a missionary meeting of the Methodist Episcopal Church. A pleasant meeting.

"*Wednesday, Feb.* 1.—Called to see Bishop McKendree at Mr. McKenney's, Georgetown, and found him quite unwell. He is a venerable old man, full of days and good fruits, and his end doubtless will be peace. May it indeed be so."

He Gives His Estimate of Clay and Webster.

"*Thursday and Friday, Feb.* 2, 3.—Mr. Clay. I have heard this gentleman on the great question of the American System, in the Senate of the United States. It is allowed on all hands it was his master effort. I have heard him with deep interest, and after careful reflection I must say he is not a *finished orator* according to the rules. He has not the elegance, grace, and dignity of action and speech which become his years, his rank (senator), and the place in which he was speaking.

Yet he is eloquent, very eloquent; he has the power of arresting the attention forcibly and detaining it irresistibly, and this must be eloquence. He is very vehement at times: frequently pleasant, and sometimes too low in his style, evidently evincing a disposition to make himself agreeable to the superficial when he should win the judgment of the profound. Upon the whole he is a good parliamentary speaker, and well calculated to be a leader of a party. He is a powerful man, a strong intellect, but he has not the intellectual resources and power of Webster. He has too much volatility to make commanding and permanent impressions.

"As it regards Mr. Clay's policy in the American System, I must think his general principles correct; their details in the present tariff may be injudicious."

UNITED STATES SENATE, FEB. 6, 1832.

"I heard Mr. Clay nearly three hours to-day on his motion to reduce the revenue by taking off the duties on imported articles. He did not excel himself to-day, though he was able. I have no doubt but his policy is the true interest of this country; yet he does not advocate it always with becoming dignity. In speaking of his willingness to reduce the revenue as low as any gentleman of the United States, he said: 'They shall not out-*brag* me.' His references to sacred Scripture and sacred subjects were not always happy nor always correct—sometimes savored of profanity. For instance, he said he would 'take his oath *on the holy evangelists of Almighty God* that General Smith (of Maryland) was an enemy to the American System.' But the termination of the session was a personal altercation between himself and Mr. Smith. Mr. Smith rose and said he could unfold something, but would not be personal. Mr. Clay called to him to *speak out.* Mr. Smith repeated the expression, *he could but would* not. Mr. Clay, with a great deal of vehemence, said to him across the Senate chamber: 'I dare you! I dare you!' 'Order! order!' from several parts of the Chamber and from the Chair. Senate immediately adjourned."

DANIEL WEBSTER.

"I called on Mr. Webster this morning. He was affable, yet dignified. As my call was merely respectful, our conversation was promiscuous and diversified.

"There is something *sui generis* indeed in Mr. Webster, and he does not seem to be insensible to it, as I heard one of his friends remark that he (Mr. W.) on being asked why his card was simply *Mr. Webster*, and not Daniel Webster, in order to distinguish himself from others of the name of Webster, answered: '*I am Mr. Webster.*' Others, of course, might put their given names on their cards; he need not. Mr. Adams's card is simply 'Mr. Adams' also, and probably for the same reason.

"Several opportunities of hearing Mr. Webster and of observing him have confirmed the opinion I had taken up two years since; namely, that he is the most perfectly full and ripe man of this country. You cannot hear him speak or be in his presence without feeling that he is a superior intellect, every way exceeding his fellows in strength and majesty of mind.

"Yet Heaven gives not every thing excellent to one being. It was Mr. Webster's political fault or misfortune to be too closely allied to the measures of the opposition in New England to the last war; and this gave his enemies a great advantage over him.

"Mr. Webster is justly considered the great bulwark of our Federal Constitution, and I think it probable that he may be more serviceable to the country in time to come than any man in it. I believe he is held in great respect even by his political enemies, and every stranger feels a curiosity to see Mr. Webster, and all who can call on him. I could not but observe the great number of visiting-cards stuck in his mantel glass of the most distinguished personages in the country. The number and respectability of visiting-cards which collect in one's drawing-room may not be an incorrect measure of the consideration in which he is held. I observed that Chief Justice Marshall used no *printed cards, but wrote his name with a pen.*

"*Feb.* 22, 1832.—To-day was one of the proudest days of America. One hundred years have rolled away since the birth of that greatest of men, George Washington. To celebrate this day in an appropriate manner seemed to be the desire of the whole nation. A joint committee from both Houses of our National Legislature for the purpose of making arrangements for its celebration directed divine service to be performed in the Capitol. This was well done—wisely done; it will be grateful to the nation; we owed it to that God whose special superintending providence guided and supported us through our Revolutionary struggle. The performance of the service was left to the two chaplains. It fell to my lot to preach. It was a heavy lot indeed. Yet I determined to speak in honor of my Master. I knew the rulers of the land would be there, and the Supreme Court, and the bar; indeed, I never expect again to see such an assembly; I therefore determined to present the worship of God as a national obligation."

We copy the following from a paper of the period:

OUTLINES OF A DISCOURSE,

delivered at the request of both Houses of Congress, in the hall of the House of Representatives of the United

States, on the Centennial Birthday of George Washington, by the Rev. John P. Durbin.

"Thou art worthy, O Lord, to receive glory and honor and power: for thou hast created all things, and for thy pleasure they are and were created." Rev. iv. 11.

The subject which the text presents immediately to our consideration is the worship of God; and our appearance in this hall, by a joint resolution of both Houses of our National Legislature, for the purpose of divine service, clearly indicates how deeply the national mind is impressed with its obligations to Heaven. Our obligations to worship Jehovah are founded, mainly, on his infinite excellence, our relations to him as his creatures, and his benefits to us.

It is fairly to be inferred that the present service was intended to recall, in some degree, our national obligations to God for his beneficent providence toward us as exhibited in the events connected more or less intimately with the person and actions of George Washington, whom we rightly call, under God, the father of our country.

It certainly was not intended that the present services should partake in any degree of the nature of funeral obsequies or of a eulogium on that illustrious man; but rather an offering of thanksgiving to our common Lord for our chief national blessings, the possession of which is so clearly referred to his agency by all who bestow a moment's reflection on our history.

It would be a pleasing and profitable employment, and might well consume an hour, to contemplate the blessings we have received from God, in all their bearings, as a cause of worship and gratitude to him. In such an exercise each individual heart should burn with devotion, which would be abundantly increased by contemplating the innumerable benefits to mankind by the wide diffusion and firm establishment of the light and institutions of religion.

But as this is a national jubilee, I propose to contemplate a few of those national blessings which are of national interest, and which ought to inspire the national mind with a sincere and permanent devotion to God. It is scarcely possible to mention one of those which may not, by a very little effort of faith, be referred either prospectively or directly to that great man whose centennial birthday we celebrate.

1. The settlement of a transatlantic population from Europe on the shores of North America has commanded the astonishment and awakened the admiration of the whole civilized world. The causes which drove the pilgrims from their homes in the Old World, the strongly-marked providences which directed them to the New, the unearthly fortitude with which they encountered and endured the unparalleled perils and difficulties of their novel situation, the high, holy, and apostolic piety which marked their general character, all point out a superintending, paternal, and almighty hand.

2. Passing over a wide chasm of time, from the landing of the pilgrims to the commencement of the difficulties between the colonies and the mother country, it is impossible to contemplate the ascendant spirit of that period without perfect astonishment and the deepest conviction that it was awakened and sustained by the special agency of our heavenly Father. This is a fact of vast importance to virtue, to religion, and to our country, and has been too generally overlooked.

It is impossible to account for the deep and ardent spirit of liberty and patriotism which agitated every American bosom at that period, from any existing principles or elements, either on this side the Atlantic or the other.

We can indeed readily find the immediate cause which set fire to the match; but we cannot find the origin of those principles which oppression in the mother country forced into action, except we look to the special agency of Providence.

In other countries oppressions were felt more severe and intolerable than those which pressed upon our fathers, and occasional patriots, or bands of patriots, appeared and struck for their country; but the spirit of virtuous freedom and well-regulated patriotism had not gone through the land to sustain those friends of mankind. In this respect the history of America is without a parallel. The world has never seen, possibly may never see again, so many distinct colonial governments lying through so many degrees, from Massachusetts to Georgia, having so many various interests, all awake with such simultaneous impulse and resolution to resist encroachments upon their liberties.

The uniformity and energy of this spirit of freedom I could not even shadow forth, much less illustrate. The only correct picture ever drawn or that can be drawn is composed of the unexampled fortitude, heroism, and devotion of the army and country.

3. The unexampled diversity of talent which was associated in the direction of the action of the spirit of liberty at that period must also be referred to a special providential agency, which prepared in anticipation the materials for this astonishing revolution. It would not require an American mind to be convinced, nor an American tongue to declare, that the sun never shone before nor since on such an association of patriotic talent.

But amid all these elements which were engaged for the civil redemption of mankind, and which had made their first unconnected and unconcerted efforts, there was one necessary agent wanting still—a master spirit which could command the confidence of the whole, concentrate their forces, or distribute them at pleasure. All felt that this superior spirit was wanting, and all looked around to discover him. Without management, without the machinery of modern political decisions, as if by revelation from Heaven, George Washington stood forth that spirit. Nearly six thousand years had rolled away, and no such man, with such peculiar destiny, had appeared. One hundred years have passed away since, and such has not appeared a second time.

It is not so much my province to-day to illustrate his personal excellencies as to show that he was the peculiar gift of Heaven to us; the instrument by which God gave us our national liberty and blessings. He is not, therefore, so much an occasion of boasting or exultation as of gratitude to God, who raised him up and preserved him, and guided him through all that eventful era of our national parturition and infancy. From this view of his character and destination by Heaven his political sentiments and example should be held but little less, if indeed less, than sacred by all American citizens.

That he was the peculiar gift of God to us, and his special servant, his history and actions sufficiently show; that he was the special care of Heaven, insomuch that we may say, in the language of a great man on another occasion, *he was immortal until his work was done,* his almost miraculous preservations attest.

4. His own mind seems to have been deeply impressed with the same view of this subject ; so much so that all his public papers, general orders, and private letters during this period have constant and frequent reference to a special superintending providence over himself and our affairs.

His orders on the day after the surrender of Yorktown closed as follows : "Divine service shall be performed to-morrow in the different brigades and divisions. The commander-in-chief recommends that all the troops that are not upon duty do assist at it with a serious deportment and that sensibility of heart which the recollection of the surprising and particular interposition of Providence in our favor claims."

In his address to the governors of the different States at the close of the war reference to a superintending Providence is made no less than eight times. It closes in these words: "It remains then to be my final and only request that your Excellency will communicate these sentiments to your Legislature at their next meeting, and that they may be considered as the legacy of one who has ardently wished, on all occasions, to be useful to his country, and who, even in the shade of retirement, will not fail to implore the Divine benediction upon it.

"I now make it my earnest prayer that God would have you and the State over which you preside in his holy protection ; that he would incline the hearts of the citizens to cultivate a spirit of subordination and obedience to government; to entertain a brotherly affection and love for one another; for their fellow-citizens of the United States at large, and particularly for their brethren who have served in the field; and, finally, that he would most graciously be pleased to dispose us all to do justice, to love mercy, and to demean ourselves with that charity, humility, and pacific temper of mind which were the characteristics of the divine Author of our blessed religion, without an humble imitation of whose example in these things we can never hope to be a happy nation."

In his address which accompanied the resignation of his command of the armies of the United States, which took place at Annapolis, there is one paragraph which cannot be read by an American without the deepest emotion. It is this: "I consider it as an indispensable duty to close this last solemn act of my official life by commending the interests of our dearest country to the protection of Almighty God, and those who have the superintendence of them to his holy keeping."

Many instances of his devout and religious feeling could be given; but surely these are sufficient to show all American statesmen and patriots that the father of our country always carried with him a profound respect for the Christian religion, and considered a deep and permanent sense of religious obligation a necessary principle in every good citizen's character. These quotations also will answer the anxious inquiries of many hearts in regard to Washington's religious sentiments and feelings, and will place the recollection of him and his deeds, if not in a higher, at least in a holier shrine in the memory of his country.

5. As was to have been expected, the fruits of his patriotism and that of his compatriots and countrymen, under the special governance of God, have been indeed national blessings.

They have been so abundant there is danger that our hearts may become proud and forget the God of our fathers. Yet scarcely are the fruits begun to be gathered. The harvest is not ours only; the world is reaping, and shall reap largely from it. Our success under

God has given a powerful impulse to the spirit of freedom and sent it abroad into the Old World. Nothing can enchain it or lay it to rest but our political degradation and fall. If we stand the world is free.

6. The stability of our civil and political institutions is desired by all the country. The all-absorbing inquiry is, How can it be insured? A glance at this question will close our discourse.

It is neither my will nor my province to allude to those political measures which may affect our stability as a nation. No; I have to refer to a higher and ulterior cause, namely, *the respect we pay as a nation to the reasonable service and worship of God.*

The theocracy and history of the Jews as developed in the Old Testament completely establish one fact: that a nation may fill up the measure of its iniquity as well as an individual, and then God visits it with national calamities. The history of all the nations of the earth which have fallen by great and dreadful evils is a luminous commentary on this fundamental principle.

The national morals, therefore, is a subject of vastly more importance than particular political measures. Because when these are sound no measures can be absolutely fatal. But when the degradation of these passes the limits of the forbearance of Jehovah, no measures can save us from national ruin.

7. Finally, I hail the services of this day as an auspicious omen, to which the rulers of our land will do well to take heed. They should recollect, also, that in this, as in all other countries, the public morals take more or less their complexion from the morals of the government and rulers of the land. The subject of good morals, which can be based on a proper influence of religion only, should be ever in their thoughts—should occupy the thoughts of every good citizen. Let it engage our earnest and constant prayers; so shall the blessings of Heaven rest upon our country. The light of our institutions shall illumine the political world, and our national happiness become an irresistible example to awaken the patriotism of all countries and bring to

the nations- that state of national liberty which is to precede the universal establishment of the kingdom of peace.

Thus writes Professor Durbin in relation to this effort :

"Surely a whole life-time will not be sufficient for me to express my gratitude to God for the special and unexampled aid he gave me on this occasion. Undismayed, because I trusted in the living God to be able to glorify him on this great occasion ; calm, collected, and earnest, because I felt full conviction of the greatness and goodness of my cause, I chose the subject which would give me occasion to present these two great truths: 1. A special superintending Providence prepared the materials of our national existence and independence, and made George Washington a special gift to us, and his peculiar servant to accomplish this great work. 2. That our stability as a nation depends ultimately on our national morals, which are intimately connected with the reasonable and constant service of God.

"Never did I see a more profoundly attentive assembly. I hope the effort will not be without its fruits. I ask the blessing of Heaven upon it."

Yielding to the demand of this memorable occasion, we have from Professor Durbin's own pen what seem to be *words of the heart* upon entering upon the duty, his forceful expressions on the delivery of the discourse, his evident conviction of the presence of a higher power that gave calmness to his spirit and control to his thoughts and energies, while he glows with gratitude for the manifest results.

As we consider the outline of this discourse we honor him in the choice of his theme, we admire the train of his thought, commend the logical coherence of the parts, and mark the progress of his subject, and clearly see what a climax the orator could secure. Who feels not the force of his appeal to the mighty men before him?

But vain is any attempt to reproduce the power of his culmination. He was one of the last of men to be judged by the words he employed. There was so much in his utterances besides the language used that his sentences were inadequate as a *conveyance.* And we can as readily paint the vivid lightning's flash when it dazes, or show the rending bolt from the artillery of heaven when it sunders the gnarled oak of a century or shivers the massive tower that has stood for ages, as to hope for any complete exhibition of the eloquence of Durbin at a time like that, when patriotism made its strongest appeal—when before him sat the mightiest statesmen of the republic listening to a discourse that they had invited on the man "first in peace, first in war, and first in the hearts of his countrymen." Sense of duty woke the mind and set the speaker's heart on fire, when the heart threw its brightening flame on the intellect, and love of God, more powerful than even that of country, constrained the just recognition of the Providence that, through our immortal Washington, gave us our territory and our triumphs. None may wonder that when he was at his intellectual and moral height his magnetic eloquence awed and transported that vast assembly. At the close of the discourse John C. Calhoun approached him, shook his hand, and said, "I advise you never to preach again," as this, he assumed, could never be reproduced. The same statement is made by Governor Wickliffe, of Kentucky.

CHAPTER V.

The Persistent Student in Baltimore and Washington.

IS it not proof of the greatness and the essential energy of a human mind when by no progress in knowledge or achievement of skill it can be long satisfied, but is ever reaching out for something beyond? Is it not evidence that that which is done is unequal to the mind that did it, as "he that built the house is greater than the house." God, that made the worlds, is greater than the worlds he made. Nor can we conceive of him as unemployed. And has it not been a fact, through all the ages, that however long the life and multiplied and brilliant its successes, the light of all *great minds* has gone out in death while yet there remained some work of supposed importance to be accomplished? Thus death is a perpetual *nonplus.* He who is profoundest in wisdom,

"Dying, sighs to see how little he has learned."

Why is this? Why these *undying* aspirations? Why such fruitfulness in devising and ingenuity in employing means for a higher end? Shall we call it mental instinct? Intellectual intuition? Is it that the mind can find no proper *rest* but in labor? Is it that man, made in the likeness of God, retains in his intellect so much of the original impress that he still feels the stirrings of that which is only less than the infinite?

Does the Author of our being thus speak within us in relation to our faculties, as he does without us in regard to moral investments, saying, "Occupy till I come?"

As in our *graces*, so in all our *endowments*, we are to "go on to perfection." This is the law of our being, and He only may not obey it who is a law to himself as the eternally perfect One. G. W. Hervey, Esq., related to the writer a fact of which he avails himself as illustrative of the experience of one distinguished in his art. "Soon after Thorwaldsen, the great Danish sculptor, had finished his celebrated colossal statue of Christ for a church in Copenhagen, a friend called at his studio to see it. During the visit the sculptor remarked: 'I think my faculties are failing.' 'Why do you so judge?' asked the friend. 'Because,' replied Thorwaldsen, 'with this statue I am *satisfied*. I can find no fault with it. From this state of mind I infer my ideal of perfection is decaying, for never before have I been able to satisfy its demands.'" With the great artist the *creation* is not equal to the *conception*.

The achievement that relaxes energy by the satisfaction that it has given must always be regarded as a misfortune for the future reputation. It prevents progress and precludes what was the possible; but he who studies our complex nature sees that even the greatest minds are liable to impulses and habits that interfere with the noblest designs and throw the intellect off its guard. There are susceptibilities that war with each other—as Paul found in his moral nature the good and the bad, that made strife. There is in him who has grand purposes the inert as well as the vital—passion as truly as reason. Success may enervate or energize. Powers from without exert themselves to exalt or depress. Adversity may dispirit, criticism impair, adulation puff up, and wind may take the place of nerve and muscle. There is no "pressing toward the mark." The eye is taken off. The ardor is cooled. Such can now "sacrifice unto their net and burn incense unto their drag." Apathy, in its silent encroachments, closes the keen vision of the intellect. Mental obliquity has carried the man from the straight line of duty upon which he entered, and when the diversion is discovered the innovation has gone so far as to set effort for recovery at defiance. If indolence enter the mind it is a foe difficult to dispossess. It is a strong man armed with logic and proneness to self-indulgence. *Of the facts so presented*, the ministry, as well as others, have felt the influence. Candor makes the confession and intelligence deplores the results. That praise or blame should quench the ardor of a flaming herald of the cross, that any thing should suppress the vigor of one called of God to preach, might excite amazement. But history is vocal. He who ceases effort at advancement, at accomplishing more in mind and heart and ministry, either from reputation gained or from apprehension that success is not within reach, makes a mistake that is little less than a sin against his nature and his calling. He immolates his greatest self, or the most of himself, in his undeveloped powers, upon an altar whose sacrifices God always spurns. What follows? Character is fixed. Improvement is at an end. Satisfaction in what he has done, or faithlessness in his endowments, has induced rest; but it is rest on the edge of an anguish that future results will awaken. He that does not advance declines. Were it only a rocket none could expect more than that, when it exploded in mid-air, by a law of gravitation what remained would descend. But there are forces and fires in man that remain to act as long as they are possessed. He is

7

kindled as a light to shine brighter and brighter to the perfect day—that is, when all the beams of the intellect give forth their effulgence.

When from any cause one concludes the acme is reached, whether it is high or low, we look in vain for close application. In five, ten, fifteen, twenty years, are comprehended the mental labor of one who in age reaches fifty or seventy years. It is soon remarked that freshness of thought is gone and there is no fruit of present study. The observant say, "He has gone to seed." Has it not been seen that some who promised most have never risen above the reputation of the first five years of their ministry? Why is this? Is it so in secular professions? Is it so with a live lawyer— with the worthy physician? Does not the scientist grow? Is it not of the nature of the mind to reveal its powers when encouraged? Is not advancement a normal result of exercise? Shall the lines of Ovid apply to the minister whose reputation is soon made:

> "Succeeding years thy early fame destroy;
> Thou who began'st a man, will end a boy?"

This is not God's order. We grow from boys to men, not from men to boys. It is as if the sun rose with meridian splendor and at noon gave only the early dawn.

Dr. Samuel Johnson has said that "the advance of the human mind toward any object of laudable pursuit may be compared to the progress of a body driven by a blow. It moves for a time with great velocity and vigor, but the force of the first impulse is perpetually decreasing, and though it should encounter no obstacle capable of quelling it by a sudden stop the resistance of the medium through which it passes . . . will in a short time . . . wholly overcome it. Some hinderances will be found in every road of life, but he that fixes his eye upon any thing at a distance necessarily loses sight of all that fills up the intermediate space, and therefore sets forward with alacrity and confidence, nor suspects a thousand obstacles by which he afterward finds his passage embarrassed or obstructed."

It was remarked of Hannibal that he wanted nothing to the completeness of his martial virtues, but "that when he gained a victory he should know how to use it." Nor is it less necessary to a great general that he should be superior to a defeat. Commanders that are immortal have snatched victory from the hand that had conquered. He is the great soldier whose courage rises and whose skill improves from the adverse issue, and achieves, by greater skill, the purpose of the conflict. Thus, too, the faithful preacher who has left the pulpit for the day with a sunken spirit has returned to witness the grandest moral conquest.

If early success in learning or in preaching would impair his energy, few men have had such temptation as we have seen in J. P. Durbin. He early rose to favor; but it may be a question whether he was ever a more persistent student or a more assiduous minister than when the positions that he filled were best calculated to satisfy a different nature. He resembled the general who would deem nothing done while there remained any thing undone.

That he had been invited by the pastor and trustees of the Methodist church in Baltimore to spend three months with them, preaching the word, was one of the most convincing proofs of their estimate of his ability. In no city of this land might Methodism boast a more intelligent membership or a more efficient ministry. He went there, not as an evangelist or revivalist, but as an edifying and eloquent preacher who could build up the Church and extend its influence. Three times during the week, as well as on the Sabbath, he delivered his powerful discourses. The numbers who crowded to hear the word were immense, and the Lord helped him mightily.

But the biographer who should overlook the use that he made of his time while in Baltimore and Washington would fail in seizing facts essential to the integrity of the narrative. With work of such magnitude and responsibility as that which engaged him in Baltimore, with services in which the mind and heart took so deep an interest, with successes such as crowned his efforts, with the attentions and hospitalities that continually forced themselves upon him from a people famed for their entertainment of preachers, it might be supposed he would be perfectly absorbed, and that any thing outside such interests and engagements could not be allowed. But his record shows that he found time to increase his scientific knowledge and to improve his mind. Thus he writes: "I attended lectures, or some of them, in the University of Maryland medical department, also mineralogical lectures in the department of science." He adds : "I must here record my grateful recognition of the gentlemanly professors who so kindly proffered me their tickets gratuitously, but must be more particular with regard to Dr. Cohen. He was not only so kind as to admit me to his lectures, but to his collection of minerals daily, and offered me his aid in familiar and personal explanations. I can never forget his friendly and gentlemanly conduct toward *me*, and I felt this all the more acutely because he was a Jew—a child of Abraham in whom I have always felt especial interest. He came once to hear me preach the Lord Jesus Christ. I do sincerely hope that he may yet find him to be the Hope of Israel."

Elsewhere Durbin says : "About this time I commenced reading Ure's Geology a second time. I think him a man of great research—self-taught. His language is strong, rather imperious, and sometimes severe."

Professor Durbin was no sciolist. The superficial did not satisfy him, and dogmatism passed for no more than its worth. His mind delved, grasped, and utilized. As he had opportunity, he sought the reason of things. When his own mental penetration and breadth were unequal to the inquiry he bowed to a superior intelligence. He could not brook the imperious of men, or think of being " wise above what is written." He would illustrate the fact that mental culture, moral growth, and spiritual usefulness may co-exist and co-operate in the aggregated influences of him who pleads for God and souls.

But if possible, we are more deeply impressed by the tenacity with which, while in Washington, he adhered to his habits of study and the success with which he prosecuted his purpose to increase his knowledge in science and literature. He who reads his convictions of the possibilities of usefulness in the chaplaincy, and observes his solicitude to accomplish all that was in his power for the spiritual benefit of those who had chosen him, will know that he neglected nothing that would be profitable to them. He brought beaten oil that would afford the best light to those he would guide. No time was too long that this required. His sermons before the great men of the nation were not perfunctory deliverances. They were of vital thought—were living words—often as " goads and as nails fastened." They had sentences that were " swords piercing to the dividing asunder of soul and spirit." Sermons they were with facts and force which the most rebellious and obdurate might not readily resist. Of this an illustration is furnished in the desire of the member from Baltimore. Cases of conscience might be submitted to him by men in public life—cases requiring great skill and much thought for their adjustment. He who keeps in mind what there is in the national metropolis during Congress to distract and dissipate the mind—the demands of etiquette, the calls of friends, the visits of persons from a distance, the courtesies expected from him by ministers of his own Church and of other Churches, the appeals made for services in various places—these required the devotion on his part of much time, and often awakened deep sympathies which made sad inroads on his nervous system, and demanded rest. Then a man of his capacity and taste would often feel a deep interest in attending Congress to hear great arguments and witness the effects. It was, as we have seen, the days of Henry Clay, of Daniel Webster, of John C. Calhoun. Besides these greater lights there were other stars of acknowledged brilliancy. He would naturally desire to see and enjoy their beams. Of the care with which he heard the mightiest of them, and the candor with which he judged of mind, of character, and of eloquence we may form some idea in the expressions he gives of his estimate of Clay and of the result of his call on Webster, and of the impression that intercourse and hearing produced. *He was not more really a student of subjects than of men.*

With such duties as we have named to engage a chaplain, besides many of which we have no knowledge, we would naturally say study outside his chaplaincy was impossible. Desultory reading must satisfy him. We would be inclined to say "the thieves of time" are too many, too active and artful, to allow more than this. He did not permit them to invade the precinct of conscience and rob it of its dictates. It told him to "redeem the time." He did it. He that had learned to study by the backwoodsman's fire, that secured mental serenity in the

room of the log-cabin with six or twelve of various ages
about him, with as much difference in the matter of discipline as there was in age, he who could under such circumstances reveal his intellectual and moral manhood
would not yield to the diversions and difficulties of study
in the city of Washington during a Congressional session.
He rose early, took exercise, attended to his devotions,
entered upon the public work of the day at half past
eleven o'clock, went to the duties of chaplain, then entered the library of the Capitol, not to go from alcove
to alcove, from chapter to chapter, not from book to
book to open and shut it, to examine the table of contents, and then assume knowledge of the author. But
he selected his book, and then, if necessary for his purpose, read it " from end to end," or as much of it as his
reason for studying it induced. He was there as the
close, consecutive thinker, making progress in science,
broadening his acquaintance with the best English literature in the lines that he perused. The record he
left speaks for the man. He did not, according to the
figure of Dr. Johnson, allow the " blow " that the mind
had received to send it " toward its object," to spend
its force till the end for which it was given was reached.
That *end* was his highest improvement and greatest
efficiency. He measured the distance, considered the
force, adopted the means, reached the end. In Washington he was the chaplain and the student. He secured
honor in both relations.

CHAPTER VI.

Editor of the " Christian Advocate and Journal."

ON the 26th of May, 1832, Professor Durbin was elected by the General Conference editor of the *Christian Advocate and Journal* and *Zion's Herald, Youth's Instructor, Child's Magazine*, and of Tracts and Sunday-school Books. This was a remarkable evidence of the confidence reposed in his literary ability and adaptation to the place. He was not then, nor had he ever been, a member of the General Conference. He was but thirty-two years old. He entered upon his labors with a promptness and intellectual vigor that showed his deep conviction of the importance of the duties that his place imposed, and with a manifest purpose to exert the proper influence of this great denominational office.

July 27, 1832. In an article on the design and progress of the Chartered Fund he urges the duty of the people to save the pastor from perplexing care and the obligation of the preacher to give himself wholly to his work. He is to " give himself to reading that his profiting may appear," as says the apostle ; and the Discipline says the minister *should give the morning to reading*, at least five hours in the day. If all preachers would do this how differently would their performances appear in the pulpit ! How clear, well arranged, and refreshing would be their discourses, and consequently how their power and influence would be elevated and extended in the community for good! Then he urges upon the people the importance of the fact that a studious man must have a *study*, must have many and various books, and says, "few have the means." Then, as through all his life, he considered the duty of the minister to seek by all the means in his power the culture in mind, as well as grace in heart, to make him the greatest power among his people. On Sept. 6, 1833, he writes upon a subject and expresses a judgment that is pleasant to recall—the first Commencement of Wesleyan University at Middletown, which took place August 28, 1833. He says : " We were struck with the absence of that excess of pomp and splendor, both in diction and gesture, of the speakers, which is too common on such occasions. Most of the sentiments in the compositions were elevated and just, and many of the paragraphs were elegant and chaste. Their gesture was sometimes very fine, often appropriate, rarely excessive. President Fisk presided to the entire satisfaction, perhaps I ought to say to the admiration, of the whole assembly, and Professor Whedon's inaugural address was very good, abounding with some new thoughts, many new combinations of thought, and excellent reflections and inferences. Finally, we are assured that this first Commencement of the Wesleyan University is, or ought to be, a new era in its progress to complete success."

On October 4, 1833, he records another fact that goes with our history. This is the first visit of the *Christian Advocate and Journal* to its subscribers from the new building erected in Mulberry Street, between Broome and Spring streets, New York, for the accommodation of the General Book Concern. He gives its history in the issue of October 4, 1833.

December 6, 1833, he writes of the morality of the

theater, and says in his editorial, "The theater represents the highway to destruction, degradation, and ruin, especially to youth."

The Sunday-school of the Church became an early and a constant care, and he discussed the system of rewards and methods of instruction with a clearness and candor that showed the attention he had given to the work. He made weighty suggestions for its increase, intelligence, and efficiency. Early in his editorship he projected the publication of the Sunday-school Library, and edited many of its earlier volumes. "This," says Dr. Longking, "was a favorite enterprise with him."

He gave the closest attention to our doctrines, economy, peculiarities, and, as far as need suggested, to our administration.

The deep reverence that Dr. Durbin associated with public worship, and the proprieties to be observed in regard to attendance, show his exalted moral sense. Nor are his suggestions to the preacher as to the proper spirit of reproof to the people for delay and irreverence of less value to him who is striving to do good, but who by incaution may do harm.

He says: "There are those who seem to think that the power of public religious services to do good was considered too generally to rest almost wholly with the preacher. Congregations calculate and prepare but very little, it is to be feared, to enter into and sustain the spirit and forms of public services. Hence but few are serious, fewer still join reverently, devoutly, and uniformly in the public prayers, and many, at least too many, make very little account of reaching the church in time, and often leave it as soon as the service is closed. Their object seems to be simply to hear the sermon. They do not appear to enter themselves into public services and take a suitable part in the worship and praise of God. The deficiency can be remedied, measurably, at least, by the prudent, firm, and affectionate conduct of the ministry. If they will on all suitable occasions insist in proper manner, in a spirit of kindness and respect, not of scolding or satire, upon the people's being all quietly seated in the church before the time of commencing the services, and in the same affectionate manner upon their remaining until dismissed, these important points can be carried effectually."

In editorials of the *Christian Advocate and Journal* of September 13, 1833, and October 25, 1833, we have a calm, clear, and vigorous setting forth of the doctrine of the " Witness of the Spirit " to our conversion, in reply to an article in the *Evangelist* on " Premature Hopes," in which the writer says, " The settlement of our controversy with God is a business which respects our whole past life." Dr. Durbin replies, " Surely, it is unspeakably important that our hope be built upon a rock, and that we have an assurance of an interest in his favor; our holiness as well as happiness is so connected with it that neither can be stable or flourish without it." He sees the mind confused from the substitution of the word "hope" for "assurance." He says, " The inspired writers never employ the word hope for what is matter of experience and present possession. . . . We see or know the things that are freely given to us of God. Here substitution of the word 'hope' for the word 'assurance' in relation to Christian experience is not a matter of small moment; it has the effect to lower the standard of Christian experience; to bring into the Church a host of merely awakened sinners and to weaken the springs and motives of holy obedience. It is difficult to see how the fruits of the spirit, love, joy, peace, long-suffering, gentleness, goodness, faith, can subsist in the soul without the 'Witness of the Spirit.' "

In an editorial on "The Building up of the Church" he remarks :

"Next to the conversion of souls the leading on of the Church to the *perfection of holiness* should be the object of the ministers of Christ. The honor of Christ, the prosperity of the Church, and the happiness of individuals all require them to pursue this course.

"And here we may inquire why so little has been done in reference to this object? It cannot be that the necessity is not apparent. Look which way you will, lukewarmness and the love of the world are prevailing evils among Christians. From the evil roots which remain in them every evil practice may spring up, to the wounding of the cause of Christ, the grief of the few truly pious, and the exultation of enemies. All of which evils would be prevented by the perfection of *holiness.*

"Why, then, we ask, has so little been done to *perfect* the saints? To this we may answer, that little comparatively has been done to set the subject fully before the Christian. The evils growing out of this neglect are frequently felt, and almost as frequently palliated by saying, 'That is human nature;' 'We do not expect perfection here,' or something to the same effect.

"Sometimes, indeed, the duty of perfecting holiness is asserted, but to little effect, while Christians are given to understand that they cannot be perfectly holy in this life (we speak only of moral holiness); nay, that they can never rise above being *carnal ;* sold under sin while they remain in the body.

"Now we cannot think that the minister of the Gospel does his duty while he asserts the duty of holiness but offers no encouragement to expect it. Holiness can only be obtained by faith. If, therefore, we repress expectation, we repress faith, or rather cut it up root and branch, and induce a state of lukewarmness as the natural result of our erroneous instruction.

"To such teachers we would put the following questions: Is not God infinitely well pleased that his rational creatures should possess *perfect moral* holiness? If this be his will is he not able to effect it? Has he not made provision in the Gospel for this very thing? Is not the blood of Christ efficient to cleanse from all sin? And is not the Holy Spirit able perfectly to renew us in the spirit and temper of our minds? Would it not be for the glory of God thus to renew and save us? Indeed, we want but two points yielded (neither of which can be denied) to enable us to infer this, the possibility of holiness, with the utmost certainty; namely, that it is his will that we should be practically and perfectly holy, and that he has made provision for this in the Gospel. But our present object is not so much to prove the assertion as to ascertain why those who believe it make so little use of it. One branch, at least, of the Christian Church has been highly famed for the last half century in having the doctrine of holiness, both in precept and in promises relating to it, clearly set before them. The great and good men whom God has raised up among them have clearly explained and powerfully proved the doctrine of Christian perfection or complete moral holiness. They have not only shown this to be the doctrine of the Bible, but they have shown also that the thing is attainable. Many have believed the divine testimony and entered into the enjoyment of this, the greatest of all blessings. A considerable number at the present day can testify 'truly that they have fellowship with the Father and with his Son Jesus Christ,' and that 'the blood of Christ cleanseth from all sin.'

"But it is a serious question whether the number of these bear a fair proportion to the instances of conversion among us at the present day—that is, whether these are increasing in the same ratio as conversions are. In truth we must say they are not. . . .

"The standard of Christian holiness is not to be taken from the creeds and writings of men, but from the word of God. That commands us to love the Lord our God with all the heart, soul, mind and strength, and our neighbor as ourselves. Did we fulfill the former of these commands we should devote ourselves, our whole selves, our life and health, time and substance, to the service of God; not in profession merely, but in deed and and in truth. . . .

"Did we fulfill the latter there would be no war, no oppression, no defaming or slandering one another, no strife of tongues or angry disputations, nor any of those passions which embroil society. . . .

"The views which the Scriptures give us of the perfection of holiness lead to the conclusion that it is a distinct thing from what is commonly understood by regeneration; distinct, not in nature, but in degree and in its completeness. This being the case, all who obtain regeneration should be taught to seek that high moral state of evangelical righteousness which the Scriptures describe as the perfection of holiness. And if they seek it with all their heart they shall obtain it. For, 'if we *confess our sins*, he is faithful and just to forgive us our sins, and to cleanse us from all unrighteousness.'

"But how can this succeed without the aid of the ministers? These must show the 'household of faith' what is in this respect the hope of their calling, what the length and breadth of the commandment, what is implied in the provisions of the Gospel, and what the character of the *covenant of promise.* Let a conviction of remaining depths of depravity in the nature be deeply fixed in their consciences, and let an earnest desire after a full conformity to the will of God be produced within them. This will enable the minister to point out the course and to 'lead them like a flock.' He must be as attentive to this branch of his work as to that which goes before it; and never till this is the case will this work revive with power and appear in all its glory.

"Here is the great responsibility of the ministers of Christ; and yet here they most frequently fail, not, indeed, in respect to preaching this doctrine occasionally, but in following it up in private as well as in public, in introducing it into prayer-meetings, class-meetings, and love-feasts. And here let me mention one thing more which deserves the most serious attention of all ministers, and that is the institution of meetings expressly for this object. Till this is done little will be done toward filling the earth with righteousness and peace. While it is impossible for a number of Christians, however small, to meet together for this object without being benefited, on the other hand, if no meetings are instituted, this work, when it occasionally revives, will be greatly limited and decline. Brethren, let us think on these things."

As an exhibition of his desire to advance our ministry in learning and pulpit power we have an editorial of July 18, 1834, giving his views on "An Educated Ministry," and approving a "Theological Seminary." And this at a time when even Bishop Hedding could go no further than recommend a "Biblical Institute." This was a long step, and at first a staggering one; others soon followed of greater steadiness.

Dr. Durbin says: "It is hoped the reader will not be alarmed at the words which stand at the head of the

article. They are intended simply to open a very grave
and weighty question for the consideration of the
Church. It is not intended to decide the question in
its details, but to present it for calm and prayerful examination. This is done the more cheerfully, and in
some degree in the discharge of our duty, because our
correspondence, conversations, and observations made
exclusively clearly develop the interesting fact that the
question of an educated ministry among us is occupy-
ing the thoughts, eliciting the attention of many of the
wisest, best, and most experienced both among the
preachers and the people. . . . In order to consider
this question fairly it is necessary to divest ourselves
of our prejudices against theological seminaries as we
have been accustomed to see and understand them.
There was a time when these seminaries were chiefly
employed in educating young men for the ministry
merely as a profession, without proper regard to their
morals and evangelical piety. The profession was too
much a matter of calculation for subsistence, as the law
or medicine. But, in our opinion, most of these institutions have rapidly approximated the true and tenable
genius of an educated ministry, the grounds which we
ought to occupy if, upon calm reflection throughout the
Church and free exchange of opinions privately and
publicly, it should be deemed advisable to act in the
case. The grounds are these:

"1. Let none be educated in view of the ministry but
such as are called of God to this work and approved by
the proper authorities.

"2. Let the education be solid and useful, directly in
view of the work they are called to do.

"3. Let its extent and time consumed depend very
much upon the demand for laborers in the work and the
progress they have made."

Among the advantages he gives are these:

" 1. It would advance and establish the young minister's personal piety and deep rational devotion.

" 2. It would impart a moral and intellectual power which cannot be derived in any other way. This is the general rule; of course there will be *exceptions.*

" 3. Such an education would enable the ministry to perform its pastoral duties much more successfully, to fill our churches and retain our families—they go elsewhere."

While editor, Durbin's literary taste, mental furniture, Christian spirit, denominational loyalty, just perceptions, and sound judgment made the paper a means of intellectual and moral culture to the Church, and a power in building up Christ's kingdom in the world.

The *Advocate* was like eyes to the Church to overlook her territory, to discover her opportunities, to reveal her resources, to awaken her energy, to encourage her hope, to broaden her sense of obligation, and to inspire the purest ambition for the grandest future.

Never were the doctrines and institutions of Methodism more sedulously guarded or vital piety more consistently enforced. Dr. Durbin resigned this place to fill the presidency of Dickinson College; duty seemed to demand such action.

8

CHAPTER VII.

Presidency of Dickinson College.

THE war of the Revolution had hardly closed and our independence been established before great men in the nation, looking to the future of the country, saw we had need of all the advantages that education could give to enable us to meet the high demands of the Providence that had strangely set us free.

The Pilgrim Fathers, with their religion, had sought to establish education on the best basis. Harvard was organized and did its work. Yale's influence was commanding. William and Mary gave advantages to the youth; and Princeton, known as the "Log College," had entered the field for needed service. But now that independence was established several gentlemen of high character determined to have a college west of the Susquehanna River. Among these men were the Hon. John Dickinson, whose name the college bears, and who was then Governor of Pennsylvania; Dr. Benjamin Rush, William Brigham, and others noted for their public spirit and benevolence. A charter having been obtained from the State the first meeting of the Board of Trustees was held on the 15th of September, 1783. "The attention of the board was probably directed to Dr. Nisbet, as a suitable person to lay the foundation of the college, by Dr. Rush, who is believed to have made his acquaintance during his residence in Scotland." Dr. Nisbet was accordingly elected president of Dickinson College on the 8th of April, 1784.

The prospects of the college were gloomy enough, except in the glowing imagination of its projectors. A report was made to the board at the very time of Dr. Nisbet's election which stated the total amount of the funds of the college, including money, stocks, and lands, to be £2,839, 12s. and 6d., Pennsylvania currency, the productive portion of which yielded only £130 per annum. The trustees relied for increase of the funds upon the liberality of the public and of the State Legislature, and yet they offered Dr. Nisbet a salary of £250 sterling, a house rent free, and the payment of his expenses from Scotland to Carlisle. Dr. Rush wrote to him repeatedly in pressing terms, making the most unqualified promises, indulging the most sanguine prophecies of success, and pledging the honor and estates of the trustees for the payment of the obligations. . . . Dr. Nisbet finally yielded. On the 23d of April, 1785, he sailed from Greenock with his family and landed in Philadelphia on the 9th of June following. He reached Carlisle on the 4th of July and was received with highest marks of respect. On the next day he took the oath of office as president of Dickinson College, and commenced his duties at once. . . . "It was a period of unvaried labors, constant anxiety, and mortifying disappointments on his part." . . . Promises failed, assurances of success did not avail. The country languished for years after the close of the exhausting and protracted war. The derangement of the commerce and currency, and the prevailing scarcity, presented difficulties for which the trustees were not responsible. They who were disposed to be liberal toward the college found themselves so embarrassed that they could neither give money to its aid nor educate their sons in its halls. Dr. Nisbet was grieved, depressed, and humiliated in seeing the failure of the trustees and the people to support the institution as had been promised. He resigned the presidency. It was not from apathy. It was that they had been incautious in the steps they had taken, and had raised false hopes in one who did not so well know the condition of the country as they who invited him were supposed to know it.

Dr. Nisbet was a man of exalted reputation. He had graduated in the ministry at Edinburgh, had remained six years in Divinity Hall, and had filled positions of high responsibility as a preacher. In 1767 Dr. Witherspoon applied to him to permit his name to be presented among the candidates for the presidency of Princeton College. He was regarded as among the most learned men in Scotland. He was a hard student, and was called the "walking library," and his memory bordered on the prodigious. The late Dr. Samuel Miller, of Princeton, says, "He was one of the most learned men of his day." After Dr. Nisbet, in 1804, Dr. Robert Davidson was elected. Then followed, in the order named, Dr. Jeremiah Atwater, Dr. John McKnight, Dr. John M. Mason, Dr. William Neil, and Dr. Samuel B. How.

President after president came to the chair, and every one to witness the failure of his hopes. The institution did grand work for those who entered it. It graduated some of the first men of the country. There James Buchanan, late President of the United States, graduated, and it was the *Alma Mater* of Chief Justice Taney.

In December, 1821, Dickinson, that had entirely suspended for several years, received as its president that princely preacher, Dr. John M. Mason. As a scholar, teacher, and divine he had great influence among the first men of the nation. He had been the intimate friend of Alexander Hamilton, and delivered a famous address at his funeral. On going to Carlisle, Dr. Mason took with him as students some of the most promising young men of the country, among whom were the late Dr. George W. Bethune, Drs. John Knox, William C. Brownell, J. M. Mathews, and Dr. Thomas De Witt.

He had an able faculty, and the college enjoyed the labors of that brilliant genius and eloquent · preacher, Dr. Alexander McClelland. Despite the erudition and eloquence of Dr. Mason, despite his reputation as a great preacher and the encouraging patronage that his presidency secured, despite the cherished hopes, distinguished talent, and earnest effort of the faculty, the institution failed, and in 1824 Dr. Mason resigned his place. The trustees elected as his successor Dr. William Neil, of Philadelphia. Dr. Mason congratulated them in procuring "a gentleman of such standing." For eight years Dr. Neil filled his position with scholarship and personal dignity; but, failing in his purposes and plans, he resigned his place.

Under such circumstances and with such a history of the college, Dickinson was offered to the Methodist Episcopal Church. Bishop Emory was residing within the bounds of the Baltimore Conference, and he, with the Rev. Alfred Griffith, took such steps as resulted in the acceptance of the offer. To the memory of Bishop Emory the Church and the ministry owe a debt of gratitude that time may not repay; himself a very scholarly man in Methodism, it was his effort to raise the standard of ministerial qualifications, and afford to the Church the advantages of college education. On reaching the episcopacy, at the early age of forty-four, he turned his attention to preparing a Course of Study for Candidates to the Ministry. He soon after issued a small volume, entitled *One Hundred Questions on the Bible,* a work which necessitated research, and burned its way into the memory of many a man, and of which the writer has a vivid recollection. In the future of Dickinson and of Dr. Durbin we see his hand and feel his power. In the brief space of four years in the episcopate he left his intellectual *impress*, never to be effaced.

In the *Christian Advocate and Journal* of November 15, 1833, Dr. Durbin wrote of Dickinson College, "This is the oldest college in the State except the university at Philadelphia, and has received liberal appropriations from the legislature at different times. From various causes the board found it necessary to close the institution and the faculty was dissolved. The building is an extensive and durable stone edifice, with ten acres of ground, situated in one of the healthiest and most beautiful towns of Pennsylvania, with a population of three thousand persons, the morals, manners, and intelligence of whom are very favorable to a literary institution. The Baltimore and Philadelphia Conferences propose to endow the college with permanent funds for its benefit." Dr. Durbin and Dr. Holdich were appointed to prepare an address in behalf of Dickinson College. They saw "no insurmountable difficulty to its prosperity" in the fact that Middletown University was commenced; "no reason why a college should not flourish at Carlisle."

Again he writes of Dickinson College in the *Christian Advocate and Journal*, April 4, 1834, "In one hour in the Baltimore Conference there was subscribed $12,000. This is an indication of vast importance. It is characteristic of the true spirit and enterprise of Methodist preachers in any cause which they think contributes to the glory of God and the conversion of the world. There is scarcely such a body on the earth as a Methodist Conference. Dr. Durbin was present, Bishop Andrew presided, and Bishop Emory was with him. The entire subscription in favor of Dickinson College in both Conferences amounted to about $30,000. About as much more is wanted in order to meet the resolution on which the college is to be opened."

The following is an interesting and eloquent record of the strong men in Methodism associated with Dickinson College when it came under our control. The Board of Trustees were:

Hon. John McLean, Judge Supreme Court, United States.
Rev. John Emory, D.D., Bishop Methodist Episcopal Church.

Ex officio.

Rev. S. G. Roszel, Baltimore.
Rev. Joseph Lybrand, Wilmington.
Rev. Alfred Griffith, Baltimore.
Rev. Job Guest, Carlisle.
Dr. Theodore Myers, Carlisle.
Dr. Samuel Baker, M.D., Professor Materia Med. University, Md.
John Phillips, Carlisle.
Dr. Ira Day, Mechanicsburg.
Dr. Thomas Sewall, Professor Columbian College, Washington.
Sam'l Harvey, Esq., Germantown.
Henry Antez, Esq., Harrisburg.
Dr. J. M. Keagy, Philadelphia.
John Davies, Esq., Harrisburg.
Dr. Matthew Anderson, Philadelphia.
Richard Benson, Esq., Phi'adelphia.
Henry Hicks, Esq., Wilmington.
George W. Noble, Esq., Attorney-at-Law, Baltimore.

Dr. S. H. Higgins, Wilmington.
Charles A. Warfield, Williamsport, Md.
Dr. James Roberts, Harrisburg.
James Dunlop, Esq., Chambersburg.
Benjamin Matthias, Esq., Philadelphia.
Charles McClure, Esq., Attorney, Carlisle.
Samuel Parker, A.M., Esq., Philadelphia.
William M. Biddle, Esq., Attorney, Carlisle.
Thomas A. Budd, Esq., Attorney, Philadelphia.
Dr. Thomas E. Bond, Baltimore, and J. B. Longacre, Esq., Philadelphia.
Rev. J. P. Durbin, A.M.
Hon. John Read, Law Professor, Carlisle.

Under this organization of the college Dr. John P. Durbin was, by a "unanimous and enthusiastic vote," elected president.

On July 18, 1834, Dr. Durbin resigned the editorship of the *Christian Advocate and Journal* to fill the presidency of the college, being profoundly impressed with the need of the institution to Methodism. It is just to history to remark, that as editor his salary was only $1,200, and Dr. Durbin said he was unable to live on it. When complaint is made of the high salaries of some of our most distinguished preachers and officers in the Church, it were well to ask if any in our ministry lose more financially than do those whose talents elsewhere would secure them double the support they receive.

If it is instructive and salutary to watch the progress of mind in its struggle upward to the goal, it should not yield less interest and pleasure to witness its achievements when it has attained the place for the full exhibition of its powers and skill: to know that past efforts are rewarded by the greatness of present results.

Dr. Durbin was now in a most responsible, not to say critical, position. He was but thirty-four years old. Dickinson was among the earliest of our colleges. With us they had not been popular. This institution, with ablest men, had failed under the great Presbyterian body. Dr. Durbin, though a graduate, was a Methodist preacher; his training had been in the itinerancy, and for such a man under the circumstances to expect success shows no little faith and determination. It required a great heart and uncommon capabilities to engage with wisdom in this work. But he at once showed himself master of the situation. He was remarkable for his knowledge of men, as is shown by the character of those whom he secured for the various chairs of the institution.

At the beginning of his presidency Robert Emory was elected professor of ancient languages. He had graduated at Columbia College, New York, with the first honors, and perhaps no man of his age in our history was of greater weight and worth than this honored son of Bishop Emory. He was elected president when Dr. Durbin resigned. Rev. John McClintock, who was a graduate of the University of Pennsylvania, was elected professor of mathematics, and it was said his education fitted him for any chair in the college. William H. Allen, graduate of Bowdoin, who was subsequently and for many years the distinguished president of Girard College, was called to the chair of chemistry and natural history. Merritt Caldwell, also a graduate of Bowdoin, was professor of metaphysics and political economy. He was also a most successful teacher of elocution. Who will wonder that with such a faculty Dickinson College at once obtained influence and support? The sagacity of the president was as manifest in the conduct of the institution as in the selection of men. By his prudence and suavity he maintained discipline, as he imparted to the students a self-respect that was a glory to Dickinson. Sympathy on the part of the patronizing Conferences induced many of the ministers to subscribe for its pecuniary needs, and in every way the president sought the improvement of its finances.

Notwithstanding the prejudice existing in many minds at that day against colleges Dr. Durbin obtained an annual collection throughout the patronizing Conferences, and secured the appointment of Charles Pitman and Edmund S. Janes as agents for the Philadelphia, and Stephen G. Roszel and John A. Collins for the Baltimore Conference, to travel through the bounds of the Conferences and obtain subscriptions to aid the rejuvenated institution. Ministers of the best talent and in great demand by the strongest churches were secured to help the college. To do this required no little influence on the part of the president. He appealed to the legislature of Pennsylvania and received from year to year an appropriation of $1,000. Members of Conference sometimes said the president of Dickinson did not know their trials. Once he replied, "If the brother thinks I know nothing of the difficulties of his life I shall be pleased to exchange notes with him on ministerial privations." To Dickinson College Dr. Durbin gave eleven of what he called the best years of his life; and while through its entire history it has done noble work for the Church its friends fail not to recall the days of his connection with it as a palmy period.

Some of the first scholars and most eloquent ministers of our Church came from Dickinson during Durbin's administration. Not to name laymen that have made their impress at the bar or on the bench, in the American Congress, in different professions and positions, the Church can boast in the pulpit the names of Rev. T. V. Moore; of Bishop Bowman; of the late Bishop Cummins, of the Reformed Episcopal Church; of Dr. Charles F. Deems, and Dr. George R. Crooks. After eight years of confinement to college duties Dr. Durbin deemed it desirable to have relief from his cares, and also leisure to increase the stores of his knowledge by travel.

While president of Dickinson College Dr. Durbin had the great sorrow of burying his wife, the mother of all his children. She was a lady of great modesty and merit.

To those who have long felt so deep an interest in Dickinson College, and who made contributions to its meager means in its earliest struggles, it affords no common delight to know that within the last few years, besides raising the standard of education and sending forth some of the largest classes in its history, it has made so great an advance in its material means and increased its facilities to the high purpose of its origin. Within the last sixteen years, under the presidency of

Rev. J. A. McCauley, D.D., there have been added three new buildings:

Memorial Library Hall, Scientific Building and Gymnasium	$120,550	75
Repair of old buildings	17,871	81
	$138,422	56
Increase of Permanent Endowment from 1872–1888 about	103,000	00
Total additions	$241,422	56

The Church may justly felicitate herself in the fact that Dickinson College, though starting with means so limited, received such an impulse and inspiration as well as character under the young Durbin that for more than fifty-four years it has been accomplishing its appropriate work. That our first colleges should have been so distinguished by the men placed over them might well awaken wonder. We have noted the remarkable faculty of Augusta in the South. In the North, Wesleyan University had Wilbur Fisk as first president, who deserved, as he received, the highest honors. To Dickinson was given John P. Durbin, who filled the presidency with an efficiency and success that might be a marvel. When Fisk died came Stephen Olin for the Wesleyan, and when Durbin resigned Robert Emory took his place. If in our first efforts at higher education it seemed as though Providence frowned on our purpose, allowing our property once and again to be destroyed; now once and again, and again at a later period, it looked as if Providence was full of benignity in giving us the men that were equal to their high responsibility.

The following are the presidents of Dickinson since the college came into the hands of the Methodist Episcopal Church:

Dr. John P. Durbin in 1833; Dr. Robert Emory in 1845; Dr. Jesse T. Peck in 1848; Dr. Charles Collins in 1852; Dr. Heman M. Johnson in 1860; Dr. Robert L. Dashiell in 1868; Dr. James A. McCauley in 1872. Dr. McCauley served a longer term than any of his predecessors.

CHAPTER VIII.

Travels in Europe and the East.

AFTER filling the presidency of Dickinson College for about eight years Dr. Durbin indulged the wish that he had long cherished, to go abroad. The period of his service in Dickinson had been marked by care and labor that no one not familiar with the facts can adequately judge. His attractions as a preacher caused him to be sought on great occasions and in every direction. The sermons that he then preached were a heavy tax upon his nervous system; while to increase the financial resources of the college, to extend its patronage, and to secure the most exalted reputation to the institution were his perpetual ambition and effort. His vacations could hardly be called seasons of rest. Then, as at other times, he was devising means and executing plans to accomplish the high purpose of the Church in this, one of her first colleges. No power that he possessed, no time that he could command, was withheld from this service.

For years he suffered from his throat in such a way as to demand daily attention. A desire of relaxation was both natural and proper. But, apart from the need of rest and recuperation, he had a wish to increase his knowledge through the observation and intercourse of foreign travel. As a tourist he went not merely for pleasure and health, but for intellectual profit. And in this, as in other matters in which he engaged, he applied himself to the end he sought. He was as really the student abroad as at home; the difference was in the direction of his faculties. The customs, civilizations, governments, systems of education and religion, the fine arts, sciences, the spirit, the manners of the people where he traveled, all entered into his calculations when he went abroad. Alexander was accustomed to say, "He had discovered more with his eyes than other kings comprehended in their thoughts." Thus he spoke of his travels. Lord Bacon remarks: "When a traveler returneth home, let him not leave the countries where he has traveled altogether behind him."

In 1844 Dr. Durbin published his *Observations in Europe*, principally in France and Great Britain (2 vols. 12mo). Shortly after this he gave to the press his *Observations in the East, in Egypt, Palestine, Syria, and Asia Minor* (2 vols., 12mo). The Harper Brothers were his publishers.

No fitter title could have been chosen for these works. They were emphatically and pre-eminently "observations" on what he saw, on what he studied, and on what impressed him. They are the "observations" of a man of fine culture and in mature life; of one who in every place was accustomed to *observe*. They are also the "observations" of a man of calmness, candor, and sagacity; of a tourist who takes nothing on trust where his opportunity and capability enable him to judge for himself; one who will dare to differ from any supposed authority when his own investigation leads to an adverse conclusion.

Such are the works of travels that an inquiring mind should seek. It will be found that, while in these volumes much is brought before the reader that others have presented, it is sometimes in aspects and with reasonings that give him a claim to special attention.

In these works there is an excellence of style, a fascination of narration, a philosophic breadth and vigor of statement that commend them to the inquiring and intelligent reader.

On leaving the country Dr. Durbin writes: "At two o'clock on the afternoon of April 27, 1842, we cast off the cables of our steam-tug in the Narrows and spread all our canvas to a stiff breeze. In a few hours our noble ship, *Ville de Lyon,* was plunging her bows into the waves looking directly toward beautiful France. The city of New York had vanished in the distance; the Highlands of Navesink disappeared with the setting sun; and at this last glimpse of my country I awoke to the assurance that I was about to accomplish my ardent and long cherished desire of visiting the Old World, whose history had inspired my young heart with a restless longing to behold the scenes of so many great achievements.

"We sat down to our first dinner at sea full of life and gayety. I need not tell the reader what a change came over the spirit of our company when our gallant vessel began to mount the waves and descend from their crests into depths from which the inexperienced passenger felt an involuntary apprehension she could never rise again. Laughing eyes became mournful enough, and jolly faces were lengthened into dolorous visages as one by one my companions sought the sides of the ship and looked wistfully into the sea. Inexorable Neptune demanded his accustomed tribute. One of my young friends obeyed at one gangway, while Professor L—— answered at the other. My time came late, but alas! when once arrived it never departed. I shall never make a sailor. There was a little coterie of Frenchmen and women aboard whose mercurial temperament was proof against seasickness, and expended itself in laughing, dancing, and every form of merry-making. I envied them most heartily."

After this vivid and facetious sketch of some of his experiences in the voyage he lands at Havre on the 19th of May. We soon find him in the magnificent cathedral at Rouen, and have his graphic description of its interior. "Let us enter the gloomy Gothic pile. Our sensations are indescribable. It is not admiration; it is not the religious sentiment, but a strange astonishment, not unmingled with awe, yet certainly not akin to reverence. The long ranges of lofty pillars; the countless sharp Gothic arches; the numerous chapels on either side, adorned with pictures and statuary, frequently with candles burning before the image of the Virgin with the infant Jesus in her arms, all seen in a flood of light poured into the church through more than a hundred windows, whose glass is stained with every shade of color, from fiery red to the soft tints fading into white, until nave, and choir, and aisles seem magically illuminated; the silence that reigns in the vast space, broken only by the occasional footfall of a priest, in his long black robe, flitting along the nave, or entering one of the numerous confessionals followed by a penitent; with here and there the form of an aged and decrepit female kneeling in superstitious reverence before some favorite image; all taken together overpower the eye and the mind of the Protestant traveler unaccustomed to such scenes with strange impressions and oppressive feelings; and he retires from his first visit confused and astonished."

But the æsthetic taste that here shows itself makes not so strong an appeal to our admiration as the tenderness of his spirit when respecting the request of a bereaved heart. He says: "When I was leaving home a widowed friend had requested me to find out the grave of her youthful husband, who died a stranger in Paris, and bring her back a rose, a flower, or a spire of grass from his resting-place. I promised her to do so; and looked for the English quarter of the cemetery, naturally supposing that I should find the tomb of the American stranger among those of his fatherland. There were many noble English names, but none of historical celebrity, and we passed them rapidly by, until at last one of my companions cast his eye upon a group of neat, plain tombs, and saw 'Baltimore,' 'Philadelphia,' 'New Jersey.' Here I soon found the tomb for which I had been in search, by the inscription, 'W—— W. M——, counselor and advocate at the bar of New Jersey in the United States of America, died in Paris, July 24, 1825, aged twenty-nine years.' A vigorous maple is springing at the head of the tomb and will completely overshadow it. I plucked some tender leaves and spires of grass (no rose or flower was there) to convey to his widow and orphans at home; wreathed round the urn with my own hands a rich green garland from the boughs which shaded it ; went on my way with sadness and returned from this city of the dead to the busy abodes of the living within the walls of Paris." What could better show the man of sensibility? He offers remarks also on the battle of Waterloo so minute, comprehensive and forcible as to suggest a war critic. He noticed the facts of Methodism in England and Ireland; and his descriptions show that he felt the disabilities under which it then labored.

Geneva was to him full of interest and suggestion. He dwells upon its history in a "religious point of view," and deplores the moral decline that it had long shown, but extols the work of Mr. Robert Haldane about the year 1816, when he invited a number of students of the theological seminary to meet him at his rooms in the hotel. . . . "About a dozen of the young men were awakened, enlightened, and turned to God with all their hearts. Among these were Dr. Malan, Felix-Neff, Mr. Henry Pyt, and Dr. Merle d'Aubigné. This was the commencement of the second Reformation in Geneva." He says : "It bears some resemblance to the origin of Methodism in the Church of England, and has the same object in view—that is, a revival of piety and sound doctrine in the State Church of Geneva, among the Protestants of France, Belgium, and Holland, and a more general diffusion of vital Protestant Christianity. Like Mr. Wesley and his associates, these first children of the second Reformation became children of Providence, and followed its openings. Part of them formed themselves into an evangelical society to labor for the advancement of the kingdom of God,

"1. By teaching theology, for which purpose they have instituted a theological seminary at Montauban, in France. 2. By popular exposition of Scripture, for which ministers, but particularly traveling evangelists, are employed. 3. For the distribution of the Scriptures and of tracts and religious books, either by gift, loan, or sale. This society was instituted in 1831."

Dr. Durbin was not less an American for his tour in England. Nor does he fail to charge upon *Alison's History of Europe* the injustice done us in his chapter on our country. But he sees in the true sentiment of the intelligent in both Europe and our own land that which justly binds us closely together.

Dr. Durbin as a tourist in the East had much to engage his talent for observation and to gratify his taste as a Bible student. He went as a Christian minister, and devotion mingled with inquiry. An intelligent tourist in Palestine on his return to this country said : "The Holy Land was to him like a fifth gospel." Not less did it impart added power to Dr. Durbin. There were "sermons in stones, and good in every thing."

We may give a short description of his approach to Alexandria : "On the morning of the 5th of January, as the sun struggled up through the clouds which pressed down heavily on the sea, the low coast of Egypt showed its sand swells to the east of the Pharos, or lighthouse of Alexandria, and in the course of an hour the fort and indented sand coast became visible to the West. The sea was exceedingly high, and the pilot-boat had much difficulty in getting to windward so as to give us the direction of the narrow channel between the shore and the breakers which extend westward from the light-house. But having once got our bearings our gallant steamer moved into the deep, safe harbor, and took her station amid the fleet of merchantmen and Egyptian ships of war."

We see him at the pyramids. "But what a sight is that from the top of Cheops! The world has nothing like it. To the east is the Arabian desert, boundless and desolate like a sea ; while westward stretches that of Libya, without a green spot, far away to the horizon's verge ; in the south appears the valley of the Nile, like a thread of green earth lying on an ocean of sand, and the pyramids of Abukir, Sakkara, and Dashur towering up in succession to the skies. Turning northward your eye rests upon the widespread Delta in the distance, and nearer, in the north-east, upon the lone obelisk of Heliopolis. Immediately before you rise the precipitous heights of Mount Mokkatam, crowned with the citadel of Cairo, under which lies the ancient city enveloped in a thin vapor which just suffices to hide the deformities of the place, while a thousand domes and minarets of graceful proportions, their gilded crescents glittering in the sunbeams, rise up to complete the vision of beauty. I turned from gazing on it to look upon the rocky plain immediately around the pyramid. There, deeply buried in the rock now covered with sand and rubbish, lie the dead of four thousand years ago. It is, indeed, a vast necropolis. It seemed as though I were among the earliest born of men. From the plains before me had gone forth the elements of science, art, and wisdom, to Greece, to Europe, to America. I felt as a child, born after unnumbered generations, returned to the home of his ancestors, and behold! it was all desolate."

Not less impressive is his language concerning Sinai. "It was three miles from our position on Jebel Musa to the summit of Sufsafeh (Sinai on the map) which overlooks the plain Er-Rahah. It took us three hours, with great fatigue and some danger, to reach it. No one who has not seen them can conceive the ruggedness of these vast piles of granite rocks, rent into chasms, rounded into smooth summits, or splintered into countless peaks, all in the wildest confusion as they appear to the eye of an observer from any of the heights. But when we did arrive at the summit of Es Sufsafeh and cast our eyes over the wide plain, we were more than repaid for all our toil. One glance was enough. We were satisfied that here, and here only, could the wondrous displays of Sinai have been visible to the assembled host of Israel; that here the Lord spoke with Moses; that here was the mount that trembled and smoked in presence of its manifested Creator! We gazed for some time in silence, and when we spoke it was with a reverence that even the most thoughtless of our company could not shake off. I read on the very spot, with what feelings I need not say, the passage in Exodus which relates the wonders of which this mountain was the theater. We felt its truth, and could al-

most see the lightnings and hear the thunders, and the
' trumpet waxing loud.'

"I had stood upon the Alps in the middle of July and
looked abroad upon their snowy empire. I had stood
upon the Apennines and gazed upon the plains of beautiful Italy. I had stood upon the Albanian Mount and
beheld the scene of the Æneid from the Circean prom-
ontory, over the Campagna to the Eternal City and the
mountains of Tivoli. I had sat down upon the Pyramids of Egypt, and cast my eyes over the sacred city
of Heliopolis, the land of Goshen, the fields of Jewish
bondage, and the ancient Memphis, where Moses and
Aaron, on the part of God and his people, contended
with Pharaoh and his servants, the death of whose
' first-born of man and beast in one night' filled the land
with wailing; but I had never set my feet on any spot
from whence was visible so much stern, gloomy grandeur, heightened by the silence and solitude that reign
around, but infinitely more by the awful and sacred
associations of the first great revelation in form from
God to man. I felt oppressed with the spirit that
seemed to inhabit the holy place. I shall never sit
down upon the summit of Sinai again, and look upon
the silent and empty plains at its feet; but I went down
from that mount a better man, determined so to live as to
escape the terrible thunders at the last day, which once
reverberated through these mountains, but have long
since given way to the gospel of peace. I could scarcely
tear myself away from the hallowed summit, and wished
that I *too* could linger here forty days in converse with
the Lord."

His remarks on the "Reputed Sepulcher" of the
Lord are of high interest. He says: "To visit this spot
had been one of the earliest dreams of my youth. The
impression which a perusal of Chateaubriand at that early

period made upon my mind followed me through successive years. A subsequent reading of the journals of less ardent and less credulous travelers should perhaps have corrected these impressions, but they did not; my judgment was convinced for the time being, but the earlier visions of the imagination always triumphed over the convictions of reason. It remained for the painful revelations of a personal visit to the reputed sepulcher, the monstrous absurdities of an unreasoning tradition, the frauds and impositions of a corrupted religion, the degradation and debasement of credulous pilgrims, the strifes between contending factions all professing Christianity, and all unworthy of the name, to banish forever the dreams of my youth, and to correct whatever tendency to superstition might have existed in my imagination." He discusses the restoration of the Jews to Palestine, and anticipates its accomplishment. There is real sublimity in his remarks on the seven Churches of Asia. "Ephesus affords one of the most striking instances of the mutability of human affairs, and perhaps of the fulfillment of divine predictions, that can be found in history. The wealth in the old pagan times rivaled, if it did not exceed, that of any of the Grecian cities of Asia; in the arts her name was connected with the renown of Parrhasius and Apelles; in architecture she far outstripped all her rivals. Her splendid temple, which required the wealth of Asia collected for centuries for its creation, was the wonder of the world, and around its sacred inclosures the Persian, the Lydian, the Greek, and the Roman in turn bowed as worshippers. Nowhere in the world did the old idolatry display so much pomp and magnificence. Nowhere did it press into its service with so much success the highest powers of human art. But it was not only in the palmy days of paganism that Ephesus was glorious.

The visits of Paul, the preaching of Apollos, the ministry of Timothy, the faith and patience of the first converts to Christianity—these, and a thousand other recollections make the early Christian days of Ephesus glorious in the annals of the Church. And even after the lessons of Paul and Timothy had been forgotten, and the 'first love' of the Ephesian Church had waned, the city was still the seat of Christianity and the chosen place of assembly for her bishops, her synods, and her councils.

"But all this glory has departed. 'Unto the angel of the Church of Ephesus write,' was the message of Christ by his servant John. 'Remember, therefore, from whence thou art fallen, and repent, and do the first works, or else I will come unto thee quickly and will remove thy candlestick out of his place, unless thou repent.' It was not long before the candlestick was removed. For a few centuries the Church of Ephesus was powerful, but in that period error and superstition on the part of the people, combined with and fostered by worldly-mindedness and ambition on the part of the lordly prelates who sat in the place of Timothy, Onesimus, and John, prepared the way for its destruction. The Christian history of Ephesus may be said to have ended with the sixth century; since that period it can hardly be said that the Church has existed there at all; and now there is neither angel nor candlestick in the once flourishing city. From the ruins of her theater, the scene of noble martyrdoms, from the broken columns and scattered sculpture of her temples, from the desolation of her once peopled plain and terraced hills, a voice, audible enough to those who will listen, proclaims, 'He that hath an ear, let him hear what the Spirit saith unto the Churches.'

"The promise of divine interposition in the hour of

temptation is the distinguishing feature in the letter of Jesus to the Philadelphians; and wonderfully has it been fulfilled for the last eighteen hundred years. The candlestick has never been removed; the angel of the Church has always been there. The altar of Jesus has been often shaken, both by the imperial pagan power when Philadelphia supplied eleven martyrs as companions to Polycarp in the flames at Smyrna, and by the arms of the false prophet when Bajazet and Tamerlane swept over Asia Minor like an inundation; yet it has never been overthrown. The crumbling walls of twenty ruined churches, and the swelling domes and towering minarets of a dozen mosques, attest the hours of fiery temptation; yet three thousand Christian Greeks, and a half a dozen churches still kept in repair, and still vocal with praise to Jesus, attest that he has been faithful to his promise, 'I also will keep thee from the hour of temptation, which shall come upon all the world, to try them that dwell upon the earth.' Ephesus is desolate, and without a Christian temple or altar; Laodicea is without inhabitants, except the foxes and jackals that prowl amid her circus and her theaters; Sardis is represented by one Turkish and one Greek hut; a handful of downtrodden Greek Christians worship in a subterranean chapel at Pergamos; but, in the language of Gibbon, 'Philadelphia alone has been saved by prophecy or courage. At a distance from the sea, forgotten by the emperor, encompassed on all sides by the Turks, *she* only among the Greek colonies and churches of Asia is still erect—a column in a scene of ruins.'" Christianity in the East is considered with solicitude and faith, as he knows the efforts of missionaries doing their appropriate work, and regards them as the highest hope of the Oriental world.

A beautiful illustration of the vein of sentiment, of

the delicate and almost feminine susceptibility which pervaded Dr. Durbin's character, and appeared in fine contrast to stronger qualities, is afforded by the neatly-arranged volume in which he preserved floral mementos of various points of interest in his extended tour through Europe and the East in 1842.

Here are roses from the soil over Pompeii, then undisturbed by the excavator's pick, and a cluster of maiden-hair from the fountain of the nymph Egeria. These leaves are from the lofty galleries of the Coliseum, and these from the walks in the gardens of Cicero. On other pages are suggestive reminders of the tombs of Luther and Marshal Ney, and palaces of Frederick the Great at Potsdam, and Mehemet Ali at Cairo.

As a means of the most definite instruction, Dr. Durbin had a map of the Holy Land prepared which was used in our Sabbath schools as a help to the study of the Scripture.

Dr. Durbin had knowledge and grace enough on leaving his native land to return a wiser and better man. He had a broader education, and such verification of Scriptural history as prepared him to present Bible truths with greater realization and effect. Few men knew so well how to render all that they gain available to the highest purposes of evangelical instruction. Not only in books but in the pulpit the results of his travels won their way to the minds, and became the means of reaching the hearts of those among whom he moved, or to whom he ministered. To him knowledge was power. His intellectual store had no dead stock. What he had was *usable*, and he used it.

CHAPTER IX.

The General Conference of 1844.

DR. DURBIN led the delegation of the Philadelphia Conference in the memorable General Conference of 1844. No fact of his history is more worthy of notice and commendation than his heroic conduct in that great crisis. The marriage of Bishop J. O. Andrew to a lady in the South owning slaves had precipitated upon the Church a difficulty that it had not anticipated, as it could not allow slave-holding in the episcopacy. For successive weeks this was the burning question of the body. The strongest ministers delivered their greatest speeches in the debate. The writer was present when Bishop Soule gave such expression to the proposed action as showed his desire. He charged them to "beware what they did," adding, "the civilian, the jurist, will examine your action and judge you by this book," holding the Discipline of the Church in his hand. He then asked, "Where do you find authority in this book to depose Bishop Andrew, or to do what is proposed?" It was all the South could ask: it was enough for the Church to deplore. Bishop Soule, though originally of the North, had performed less of his episcopal labors there than in the South. He was a preacher of great ability and was remarkable for personal dignity. When Robert Newton, as delegate from the Wesleyan body, attended the General Conference in Baltimore in 1840, and delivered his farewell words, he expressed the wish that we would send Bishop Soule to England as fraternal delegate.

The General Conference appointed him, and he selected the late Dr. T. B. Sargent as his traveling companion. In 1842 Bishop Soule went to England in this official character. His preaching received great commendation. In person and manners he was compared to the Duke of Wellington. He was the first Bishop sent in this relation. The high honor rendered him at home and abroad would naturally add to the influence of his office and give weight to his deliverances.

It is impossible to tell the strength or weakness of a nation till some great crisis reveals its resources in men and means, or what it lacks in one or both of these. Let war rise, and patriotism speaks as never before; military prowess displays itself; diplomacy achieves its grand results; and coffers yield a wealth never suspected. Others now see, admire, and commend. Greatness is confessed. If wanting in those things that give distinction the conflict stamps the cause with weakness.

Thus it is in a deliberative body. It is never fully known what talent is in it till some subject or occasion makes an appeal that rouses thought, quickens intellect, and taxes the forces at command.

This statement has its illustration in the contrast between two General Conferences, the one in Brooklyn, in 1872, the other in New York, in 1888. In Brooklyn there was next to no discussion. Yet in that assembly were some of the strongest laymen and ablest ministers of the Church. There was nothing to call them out, and they were not soldiers on parade. In New York city there probably was not, in proportion to numbers, more talent than had been in Brooklyn, but there was a vast difference in the evidence furnished. At the very beginning the question of the eligibility of "women as lay delegates," became the absorbing theme. Scores, not to say hundreds, were anxious to "show their reason." For five consecutive days there seemed no abatement of interest or decline of eloquence. The warmth was maintained, and hardly a spark of the fire was quenched till the vote decided it in the negative.

The size of the "Metropolitan Opera House," where they met, and the difficulty of being heard by the chair, induced almost a scream by those eager to obtain the floor. This added to the seeming earnestness, that might half exhaust a speaker before he began his address.

From first to last it was an exciting scene. At no General Conference were there ever so many questions as to rules of order raised—so many of equal breadth, diversity, and novel aspect—so many of privilege. Never were questions submitted to the chair answered with greater promptness and precision, and all this when hands were shooting up all over the house like the bayonets of an army.

But, able and eloquent as were the debates of 1888, greater talent never showed itself in any General Conference than was called out in 1844. The most tremendous issues were trembling in the scale. The fact faced the speakers. Every mind was awake; every nerve was tense. And there was no heart not ready to pour out its fullness. The coloring of the thought was of the graver hue. There was some sharpness, but great depth of feeling. For twenty days the cloud hung upon the horizon. Day after day but deepened the gloom and intensified the sadness that fear awoke. In ability of speech the South was not behind the North. Dr. Channing once said of it, "Here eloquence is most at home, as seen in Marshall, Madison, Patrick Henry, and John Randolph."

As an orator Henry B. Bascom had a national fame. Though not accustomed to discussing questions on the floor, he was a brilliant and powerful writer. He was therefore selected by the Southern delegates to prepare the "Protest" against the action of the majority of the Conference. In 1828 Dr. William Capers, of South Carolina, was appointed the representative of the Methodist Episcopal Church to the British Wesleyan Conference, where his eloquence won him high honor. In 1844 he still had a smooth voice, a fine address, and was distinguished for a steady flow of language and for silvery eloquence. Such was his reputation in the South that he was invited to be the successor of Dr. Henry Kollock, of the Presbyterian church in Savannah, where the salary was $4,500; supposed to be the highest at that time in the country. Dr. Kollock was one of the finest preachers in the American pulpit. Dr. Capers was deemed worthy to follow him. *But he was strongest in debate.*

Dr. Lovick Pierce was a princely man. He made no set speech on the case of Bishop Andrew, but was unyielding in his support. His son, George F., late Bishop of the Methodist Episcopal Church, South, was a bold and brilliant speaker. As his father was by some considered our best preacher in the South, so the son was deemed by many its greatest orator on the platform. Though one of the youngest members of the General Conference, he indulged in the most defiant utterances.

William Winans ranked among the ablest preachers and most skillful debaters of the South. He had mental grasp and tenacity of purpose. In person he was tall, slender, and almost haggard. But that casket contained a precious jewel. He had a strong voice, and his temperament and determination forbade its restraint in this discussion. He did not obey Bishop Soule in using "soft words;" but he did his best to give "hard arguments," as the Bishop had suggested.

Dr. William A. Smith was a frequent and fluent speaker. To him the floor had no terrors. He had a quickness and aptness in discussion and repartee that showed him to advantage; but he sometimes did more with an off-hand shot than by deliberate aim.

A. L. P. Green was remarkable for his colloquial style, easy address, and, as a *preacher*, for his naturalness and magnetism.

Rev. B. M. Drake was in an agony of apprehension for results that he was anxious to avert. In the estimate of judges no man from the South was his superior in polish and moral beauty.

The Rev. A. B. Longstreet, usually addressed as "Judge," enjoyed the highest confidence. He well knew the power of language, and his words lacked neither vigor nor sharpness.

The Rev. Dr. John Early, afterward Bishop in the Church South, was a strong character. There was a show of *hauteur* in his manners. His speeches were brief and his utterances oracular. He had the skill of a leader, and he swayed men.

Dr. Robert Paine, afterward one of the Bishops of the Southern Church, was deliberate, firm, and influential. He was modest, quiet, and well poised. Men looked to him for safety. These were men to be weighed, as well as counted. Others there were that we would gladly name.

From the North came George Pickering, after Jesse Lee the most honored pioneer of Methodism in New England. Stephen Olin, an intellectual and moral colossus. Nathan Bangs, the historian of the Church. George Peck, one of the most honored ministers of his day; he was calm, clear, and strong. James Porter, a man of conviction and prompt action.

Jesse T. Peck, though one of the young members,

never more distinguished himself than in his reply to George F. Pierce, who in his flaming speech had said, "Let New England go." Peck was full of force and fire, but took care of his logic and rhetoric. When he closed Mr. Pierce rose and, with amiability and wit, acknowledged he might owe an apology for his unfortunate expression about "New England," but added, "if my speech has shocked the nerves of Brother Peck, my explanation will not ruffle a hair upon the crown of his head." This was a stroke that gravity could not resist, and there was a burst of laughter. Then, as in later life, the "crown of his head" was as destitute of hair, and about as round and bright, *as a new silver dollar.*

From the West came Peter Akers, the erudite, the far-seeing, and the weighty. Charles Elliott, in patristic lore the scholar of the Church. James B. Finley, whose age, ability, and influence suggested him as the proper person to offer a resolution in Bishop Andrew's case. Though much younger in years the character and position of J. M. Trimble made him a worthy seconder of the motion. He still lives, as one of the few survivors of that General Conference. Peter Cartwright, whose eccentricities and style diverted thought, was also distinguished for hard sense. Thence also came E. R. Ames, Edward Thomson, L. L. Hamlin, and Matthew Simpson. For astuteness, logical force, rhetorical beauty, sublimity of thought and pathetic eloquence, these were men that cannot die while history lives. They were all exalted to the episcopate.

The border Conferences sent men that would be distinguished in any body. Baltimore gave Alfred Griffith and John Davis. The one was the seconder of the resolution that the other offered. These were mentally stalwart men. From the same Conference, more uniformly prominent in debate, came John A. Collins, the parliamentarian and orator.

To name no more from the Philadelphia Conference, in the midst of that assemblage of the mighty men of the Church stood John Price Durbin. The North, the West, and the border Conferences, as well as the South, were honored in their delegates, who were not more distinguished by their talents than by their devotion. It was a tremendous conflict. It was like a battle among the gods of mythology.

Bishop Soule took what he called a favorable moment to offer to the Conference a few remarks . . . before final action . . . on the subject pending before the Conference. His remarks were neither few nor feeble. They were multiplied and vigorous. Dr. Durbin rose to reply, and expressed the embarrassment of the hour, but stood in the serene dignity of conscious right. His mien was modest, but his courage was commensurate with his convictions, and no dignity of office or weight of character on the part of an opponent deterred him from duty. He was a native of Kentucky, and was in a position to judge both of the North and the South, being from a Conference that contained slave-holding territory. He was president of a college that thence derived much of its patronage. Four out of the six delegates of the Conference that he represented were with the South. He and the late Bishop Scott stood alone. It was a "border Conference," the whole of the State of Delaware, the eastern shore of Maryland and of Virginia being included within its bounds. No harder battles were fought in the division of the Church than on that ground. But he was intent on his purpose. Though one of the most prudent men he squarely met the issue with Bishop Soule. He knew the trouble of the Church in the secession of

1828. He was in its midst, saw its influence, felt its power, and deplored its results. It was like the iron going afresh into his soul. He said:

The first remark that I have to offer is in regard to a statement of Judge Longstreet, that in the early Church the aggression of popery had always been resisted by "a pure and steadfast minority." What was the application of this remark? Did the brother mean to say that the action of the Methodist Episcopal Church in regard to slavery in any way resembled the growth of popery? Or did he mean to say in this age of the world and in this country that the interests of society, whether civil or religious, are safer in the hands of the minority than of the majority? Sir, the voice of history does not say so. The institutions of our country do not say so. The brother will not go before the world and say so.

The brother has also stated very broadly that the legislation of the Methodist Episcopal Church on the subject of slavery has always done harm! So, then, the objection is not so much against our action in this case as against the uniform action of Methodism on the general subject. Sir, I wish I could go before the world and to the bar of God with as clear a conscience and as firm a trust in regard to every other part of our legislation as in regard to our action on slavery. But we are told, again and again, that we are called here to judge of the laws of sovereign States; that in the case of Harding, and in every similar case, we must be judges of law—a business with which we have nothing to do. Nay, more, sir; we are told that in the vote on Harding's case this body not only acted above the law of the land, but above the law of Methodism—that we voted to sustain not the Discipline of the Church, but simply the *usage* of the Baltimore Conference. I have heard this repeatedly on this floor, and have seen it repeatedly in print, and fear that the public mind has really been misled by these statements so confidently reiterated. But, sir, I deny the whole statement. It is utterly groundless. It is unjust, both with regard to the Baltimore Conference and this General Conference. The sole question we had to judge of in Harding's case was, whether it was practicable for him to emancipate his slaves. We found, sir, that it was practicable. It is to-day practicable. On *that* ground, and on that ground only, in full conformity with the provisions of the Discipline, we voted against the motion to reverse the decision of the Baltimore Conference. We could not do otherwise, sir, with the Discipline in our hands. I *did not* vote, nor, I believe, did my brethren in the majority, to sustain the usage of the Baltimore Conference, but to sustain the laws of Methodism.

We of the North have been repeatedly taunted on this floor with our differences of opinion on the subject of slavery. Sir, whatever other differences of opinion there may be among us, on one point there is none. Our minds and hearts and feelings are all united on this *one* point at least—that the episcopacy of the Methodist Episcopal Church ought not to be trammeled with slavery. On this point, sir, our minds are as the mind of one man, and the brethren of the South will find it so. Nor is this any sudden purpose. It is the ground we have always held, and we shall be found standing up for it, shoulder to shoulder, to the end of the battle. We have also been told, sir, that the early Methodists, in their protest against slavery, went further than Christ and his apostles had done. Nay, sir, we have had arguments to-day drawn from the Bible to sustain slavery. What do brethren mean, sir? Is it their *intention* to plead the word of God in defense of slavery? Do they really believe with the brother from South Carolina, who spoke this morning, that the system of slavery is to find its authority in the Decalogue, written by God's own hand? Sir, they cannot mean this; they will not affirm this. And yet we were gravely told that because the commandment speaks of the ox and the ass, and the man-servant and maid-servant in the same connection, that therefore the right of property was assumed on the same ground for the latter as for the former. As well go a little further and assume that the wife too was a chattel, according to the intent of the commandment. O, sir, I hope we shall never be compelled to hear the Bible, the record of God's truth, the charter of human freedom and human rights, appealed to in support of American slavery.

We have had some strange statements here in regard to the legislation of the Church on the subject of slavery. Brethren have tried to make the impression, to use one of their own figures, that the North has been putting the screws on the South, and continually pressing them harder, until at last the compression can be endured no longer. Sir, the facts in the case are just the reverse of all this. The history of the Church shows this point indisputably: that the highest ground that has ever been held upon the subject was taken at the very organization of the Church, and that concessions have been made by the Church continually, from that time to this, in view of the necessities of the South; that, while the antislavery principle has never been abandoned, our rules have been made less and less stringent, and our language less and less severe, because experience has shown it to be absolutely necessary for the welfare of the Church in the South; and these concessions have been made, too, while the power of the Church has been continually passing from the slave-holding to the non-slave-holding States. I trust brethren will bear this in mind. Without laying stress upon Mr. Wesley's denunciations of slavery, what was the declaration of the Church in 1780? "We pass our disapprobation on all our friends who keep slaves, and advise their freedom." The language of 1784, when the Church was organized, was equally bold. All private members were required to emancipate their slaves in those States where the laws allowed of manumission. The action taken was too strong, sir, and in six months it was suspended—in accordance with the genius of Methodism, which does not all the good she would, but all she can. The Church then made a concession to the South on the score of necessity. Even the language of the question on slavery was mitigated. In 1796 it was, "What regulations shall be made for the extirpation of the crying evil of African slavery?"

In 1804 it was, "What shall be done for the extirpation of the evil of slavery?" In 1808 all that relates to slave-holding among private members was stricken out, and no rule on the subject has existed since. I might advert to other points to show the truth of my position, that the Church has gradually made concessions to the necessities of slave-holding States until our brethren from the South say they stand firmly on the ground of Discipline. But I forbear; it will not be denied by any who are conversant with the history of the Church. Is it necessary to make still another concession, and allow slavery to connect itself with our episcopacy?

Now, sir, I do not mean to say that these concessions ought not to have been made. Our fathers wisely made them on the ground of necessity. The Methodist Church could not have existed at all in the South without them. This should be a rebuke to our abolition brethren every-where who would urge this question to extremities. I take my stand on the conservative ground of the Discipline, as far from extreme opinions in the North as in the South. I have no sympathy with either. I would not, dare not, urge on our Southern brethren to a position where they cannot stand. The Discipline has placed the Church in the proper relation to slavery in the South. She does not propose to distrust the relations of our Southern brethren on the question of slavery in the South, but to leave them free to contend with the evil in the best manner they can under the laws of their several States. But while I stand up firmly for their rights and privileges, and shall be ever ready to lend what weight I can to protect them if assaulted, I must beg our brethren of the South not to turn the question of slavery upon the North in connection with our general superintendency. This is the real question: Shall slavery be connected with our episcopacy, which is common to all parts of our Church, the North as well as the South, and thus cause the Church to give her example in favor of the "great evil of slavery" in a form which will be pleaded as decisive of her judgment in the general question, and in those parts of the country where no necessity exists for such a declaration, and where it will fearfully agitate our societies? There is no necessity in the South for any one of our Bishops to hold slaves in order to do his work there. This is admitted on all hands, while it is as readily admitted, even by the South, that there are many Conferences "in which his connection with slavery would render his services unacceptable."

I come now, sir, with as much delicacy as possible, to examine the question of the power of the General Conference over the Bishops. It has been maintained here, sir, that the General Conference has no power to remove a Bishop or to suspend the exercise of his functions unless by impeachment and trial in regular form, for some offense regularly charged. If this be true, sir, I have greatly misunderstood the nature of our episcopacy. From whence is its power derived? Do we place it upon the ground of divine right? Surely not, sir; you do not plead any such doctrine. Whence, then, is it derived? Solely, sir, from the suffrages of the General Conference. There, and there only, is the source of episcopal power in our Church. And the same power that conferred the authority can remove it, if they see it necessary. Nor is this a new doctrine, sir. The Minutes of 1785 declare that at the organization of the Church "the episcopal office was made elective, and the elected Superintendent or Bishop amenable to the body of ministers and preachers." The Notes to the Discipline assert that the Bishops are '*perfectly subject* to the General Conference; their power, their usefulness, themselves, are entirely at the mercy' of that body. Again, sir, I bring you the authority of a witness sanctioned by the Conference of 1792 and by Bishop Asbury, and whose doctrine on this subject is indorsed by our late beloved Bishop Emory. I do not mention those venerated names for the mere purpose of awaking the feelings of brethren.

I would not call the sleeping dead from their honored graves, as some have done on this floor. No, sir; they are escaped from all our strifes and warfare. Let them rest, sir; let them rest. They never saw the Methodist Church threatened with so fearful a storm as that which now hangs over us. I know not what they would say or do were they with us now. But hear my witness: Rev. John Dickins, the most intimate friend of Bishop Asbury, in a pamphlet published in 1792, as already stated, with the sanction of the General Conference, thus answered a question put by Mr. Hammett in reference to this very point: "Now, who ever said the superiority of the Bishops was by virtue of a separate ordination? If this gave them their superiority how came they to be removable by the Conference? We all know Mr. Asbury derived his official power from the Conference, and, therefore, his office is at their disposal." "Mr. Asbury was thus chosen by the Conference, both before and after he was ordained a Bishop; and he is still considered as the person of their choice by being responsible to the Conference, who have power to remove him and to fill his place with another, if they see it necessary. And as he is liable every year to be removed he may be considered their annual choice." Bishop Emory states that this may be considered as expressing the views of "Bishop Asbury in relation to the true original character of Methodist episcopacy," and gives it the sanction of his own authority by quoting and using it in the twelfth section of the *Defense of Our Fathers*.

I have thus, sir, expressed. and I trust maintained, my views of the authority of the General Conference in regard to the episcopal office. I am sorry, sir, that this opinion differs somewhat from your own (if I may be permitted to address you personally), knowing, as I do, that my judgment, thrown into the opposite scale to yours, is but a feather against a thousand pounds' weight. Still, sir, I must hold my opinion.

A few words now in regard to the application of this power in the present instance. The action that is proposed to be taken in the case of Bishop Andrew is contained in the substitute now before us. We are told that it is in fact a proposition to *depose* Bishop Andrew. Sir, we do not so regard it. The venerable man who moved it does not so regard it. I am sure he does not. I know him well; he has called me "John," sir, from my boyhood, and on the day when he offered this substitute he called to me across the pews, "John, explain this for me." Understanding his views of the substitute I now propose to explain it, having the opportunity of doing so for the first time. It reads:

"*Whereas*, The Discipline of our Church forbids the doing of any thing calculated to destroy our itinerant general superintendency; and *whereas*, Bishop Andrew has become connected with slavery by marriage and otherwise, and this act having drawn after it circumstances which, in the estimation of the General Conference, will greatly embarrass the exercise of his office as general superintendent, if not in some places entirely prevent it; therefore,

"*Resolved*, That it is the sense of this General Conference that he desist from the exercise of his office so long as this impediment remains."

Now, sir, this action is not contemplated without cause. The preamble states the ground of the action clearly and distinctly in a statement of undisputed and indisputable facts. And what does the resolution propose? Expulsion? No, sir. Deposition? No. If I am pressed to a decision of this case in its present form I shall vote for that substitute, and so will many others; but if, after we have voted for it, any man should come and tell us personally that we have voted to *depose* Bishop Andrew, we should consider it a personal—shall I say insult, sir? The substitute proposes only to express the sense of this Conference in regard to a matter which it cannot, in duty and conscience, pass by without suitable expression; and, having made the solemn expression, it leaves Bishop Andrew to act as *his* sense of duty shall dictate. Will any of the brethren on the other side of the house tell us that if such is our deliberate sense, and we deem it our duty to the Church to say so, we ought to suppress it? One brother answers, "Yes." I will not take that brother's answer for the answer of the South. There is too much magnanimity among the brethren of that region of chivalry to allow of such an answer from them. In passing this substitute—if we do pass it—we make a clear declaration against the connection of slavery with our episcopacy, a declaration which we cannot avoid making if we would, and ought not if we could; a declaration, sir, which the world will approve. I will take the excellent advice which you gave us this morning, sir, and not appeal to the passions of this Conference, nor to the audience in the gallery; but if an appeal must be made, sir, to any tribunal out of this body, we are willing to abide by the verdict of the world, sir, and by the decision of a far higher tribunal. There, sir, we shall fear no reversal of our action in this case.

O sir, when we were left to infer this morning, from the remarks of the Chair, that the passage of this substitute would affect not only Bishop Andrew, but perhaps others of our Bishops, I could not but feel that a momentary cloud gathered before my eyes to dim the clearness of my vision. The feelings which that remark excited were not calculated to give greater freedom to the action of my reason or greater precision to my judgment. But, strong as were and are those feelings, they cannot stifle my conscience or darken my understanding. I have read in the public reports of the proceedings during my absence some things that gave me great pain. Mention has been made here of proceedings at law—of the possibility of obtaining an "injunction" upon the Book Concern, and stopping our presses. I am sorry such words have been uttered here. Perhaps such an injunction might be issued. I do not know but a judge or chancellor might be found (though I do not believe it) wicked enough to rejoice in our difficulties and exult over our strife. Ah, sir, wicked men would indeed exult in it! Satan would exult in it. Perhaps, I say, such an injunction might be obtained; but what then? You may lay an injunction upon types and presses and newspapers, but, thank God! no injunction can be laid upon an honest conscience and an upright mind. The Book Concern! There is no man here, I am sure, whose soul is so mean and paltry as to be influenced by such a motive. Sir, that Book Concern was burned down *once,* and I grieved over its destruction; but gladly would I see it destroyed again this night—gladly would I welcome the first flash of light that might burst into that window, even though in the conflagration buildings, types, presses, paper, plates, and all, were this night to be destroyed—if it could place the Church back where she was only six months ago.

Before I sit down I desire to call the attention of the Conference to a proposition made by the brethren from the South in the Committee of Pacification. The language of part of that proposition was, "that Bishop Andrew should not be required to preside in any annual Conference in which his connection with slavery would render his services unacceptable." Now, sir, here was a clear admission of the fact that Bishop Andrew's position did render him unacceptable to many of the Conferences, and a proposition founded upon it. Keeping the admission in mind, and recollecting that we are forbidden by the constitution to do any thing that shall impair our itinerant general superintendency, I beg the Conference to look at the bearing of this proposition, and of similar ones that have been made here from time to time. It is wrong to do that for one of the Bishops which, if done for all, would be destructive to the system. Now, sir, suppose that you should become an Abolitionist, and on that account you could not go to the South; for the same reasons precisely a resolution might be brought here to confine your services to the East. Suppose some similar contingency to continue another Bishop in the North and another in the West—is not our itinerant general superintendency effectually destroyed? Assuredly it is, and it seems to me that we cannot take the first step toward such a result without violating the constitution as it now stands.

I am free to declare that I do not wish to come to a direct vote on this momentous question. I have looked long and earnestly for some way to escape. I have hoped our brethren of the South could agree to say to this Conference, "Brethren, we have been very unexpectedly and unintentionally the occasion, in the person of our beloved bishop, of bringing the Church into great danger; we had not apprehended such a cloud as now covers our Zion; we have stood up for what we believed to be our rights and the interests of the Church in the South; we have heard you feelingly and plainly declare the certain danger which threatens you in the North. The sacrifice of the peace and unity of the Church is too costly a sacrifice to be made almost by accident; postpone all proceedings in this unfortunate case and we will see that the Church suffer no harm." Such an announcement as this would come upon the Conference and the Church like a message from heaven; and no man would ask you how, when, or where you are going to deal with the case. This Conference and the Church would trust your word and your religion in the case, and ask no questions. I will conclude, sir, by saying, a few days ago Brother Early, from Virginia, threw out a suggestion at the close of the session—namely, "*might not this matter be referred back to the Church or the Conferences?*" This course was distinctly advised by yourself, sir, this morning in your address to the Conference. These weighty facts led me to believe that the North would meet the South on the following resolution, which I would willingly offer if I had the least intimation that our brethren from the South would meet us on it—namely:

"*Resolved,* That the case of Bishop Andrew be referred to the Church, and that the judgment of the next General Conference be deemed and taken to be the voice of the Church, whether Bishop Andrew shall continue to exercise his functions as a general superintendent in the Methodist Episcopal Church while he sustains the relation to slavery as stated in his communication to the Conference, as reported to the Conference by the Committee on the Episcopacy. "

In the speech of Dr. Durbin the *orator* as well as the logician appeared. No one can tell the energy, the pathos, and the moral majesty of the man when, drawing to a close of his weighty address, he exclaimed, "O!

sir, we were left to infer this morning," etc. As he spoke of the predicted result of the passage of the resolution, and of a remark that had been indulged not calculated to "give greater freedom to the action of his reason or greater precision to his judgment," yet declaring that strong as were those feelings they could not stifle his convictions or darken his understanding; and when the apprehension was expressed that an injunction might be secured upon the Book Concern—an event that would cause Satan to exult: yet even the *conflagration* that might destroy building, types, presses, paper, plates, would be a slight matter to him if it could place the Church back where it was six months before—with an emotion that imagination may never reproduce he showed the power of speech when pervaded by the deepest sympathy, the profoundest conviction, and the intensest grief.

Afterward, as chairman of the committee consisting of J. P. Durbin, George Peck, and Charles Elliott, to reply to the protest from the South by their committee through Dr. Bascom as chairman, Dr. Durbin declares, the doctrine advocated in the "Protest" is "novel and dangerous in the Methodist Church, that such difficulties cannot be corrected unless the person objected to be personally arraigned under some specific law to be found in the concise code of the Discipline—doctrine not the less dangerous because it is applied where 'objections, unimportant in others might be productive of the most dangerous consequences.'"

The speech of Dr. Durbin, and the answer to the "Protest," together with that most powerful and convincing speech of the late Bishop Hamlin, have gone into our history as the most intelligent vindication of our economy and of the inflexible purpose of the denomination to keep its episcopacy clear from the evil of

American slavery, though at so great a cost as the division of the body.

The Methodist Episcopal Church has passed through three periods of great perplexity and peril. In 1792, when James O'Kelly made a schism: in 1828, when the conflict resulted in the organization of the Methodist Protestant Church: and in 1844, when the Church divided between North and South. It was our comfort in 1792 to have John Dickins as a power to *sustain.* It was our joy that in 1828 Dr. John Emory and Dr. Thomas E. Bond were equal to her defense. Nor can the time ever come when the Church will forget the service rendered her in 1844 by L. L. Hamlin and J. P. Durbin. The difficulty of 1792 was a *burning fever;* the secession of 1828 was a *lancinating pain;* but Bishop Andrew's case in 1844 *rent the body and covered the Church with enervating gloom.* But Drs. Hamlin and Durbin then threw around our economy a breastwork of argument that the heaviest artillery failed to impair.

That Dr. Durbin, then only forty-four years old, should have had the position of chairman of the most important committee of the General Conference, though the first General Conference of which he ever was a member, is strong evidence of the confidence reposed in his wisdom. That he performed his part with such ability did honor to the choice.

CHAPTER X.

His Pastorate and Presiding Eldership in Philadelphia.

IN 1845, having resigned the presidency of Dickinson College, he returned, after the absence of twenty-five years, to the pastorate, and was stationed at the Union Church, Philadelphia. Some believed that for his reputation this was a mistake. He had been in great demand on special occasions, and these exerted their greatest power through the commanding influence of his presence and ministry. His sermons, addresses, and lectures had made him a peerless preacher. It was thought impossible for him to sustain himself with his two sermons every Sabbath. He had said that no man should be expected to preach more than once a day to the same congregation. Two such as he preached on extra occasions no man could deliver. They were often an hour and a quarter, or possibly an hour and a half, and even two hours in length, and with a physical expenditure as well as mental tax that would break down the strongest man. On entering upon this charge he displayed the practical wisdom that distinguished him in every place. It was shown in the disposition of his time, in the devotion of his talents, and the direction of his resources to the best results. There was a ready recognition of all departments of his work, and he addressed himself to every duty with an interest and energy that made efficacy inevitable. From the beginning to the end he commanded a congregation that filled and thronged the church, and his sermons were regarded as incomparable in excellence and power.

He was a faithful and edifying pastor. As in Cincinnati, so in Philadelphia, he showed the importance he attached to this duty. Here, where the preacher is seen in his sympathy, solicitude, and spiritual qualifications as he can nowhere else appear, he conversed with the sick, the sorrowing, the tempted, and such as might be disturbed by questions of conscience, and imparted the instruction and cheer that were the highest commendation of his holy labor. His visits to his people were neither formal nor perfunctory, and they secured the end he sought.

The late John Whiteman, Esq., who was a member of his charge, and one of the most intelligent Methodists in Philadelphia, and who from his relation to Dr. Durbin as trustee of Dickinson College and otherwise knew him perhaps as well as any man in the city, said to the writer, we "knew when Dr. Durbin came to our charge that we were receiving a great preacher, but we did not know what experience has shown us—that in him we have also one of the best pastors."

He would have necessary time for his studies, and if disturbed would appear and stand, and, if no business was expressed, asked, "Is there any thing I can do for you?" If there was no duty in the call there was one in his study, and he resumed it. To be able to deliver two sermons to please and profit the people, as well as to dispose with judgment his material, he cut his sermons down to fifty minutes and divided one day *into two.* He retired after the morning sermon just as he did at night, and took such rest as nature demanded, that he might come to his work at night with the freshness of the morning. These sermons were listened to by many students of the university and medical colleges, as well as by his own people, with delight and profit. He delivered special discourses to young men, and was honored in seeing many of them come into the Church, of whom quite a number entered the ministry. An extensive revival followed his preaching, and he was loved as well as honored.

He was full of work. His character as a preacher was maintained, while as a student he was constantly making valuable accessions to the stores of his knowledge. He kept himself up in the literature of the day, and in all his reading was the thinker and the critic. He read to judge. It was for assimilation or rejection. And as " aliment is changed to vital blood," so he was becoming more and more the man of power. Thirty years ago the writer said, on the physiologist's theory that the human body so changes in every seven years as to present a new one, so Dr. Durbin gained enough knowledge every seven years to make another great man. The first seven years of his ministry raised the uneducated youth to the professor of languages; other sevens were appropriated with equal judgment. He could not live without work, and he knew how to do it with advantage. It was as if, with an ancient philosopher, he made it a practice " to do some difficult thing every day," or as if his motto was, " no day without its line," or, still stronger,

> " Deem that day *lost* whose low descending sun,
> Sees from thy hand no *worthy service done*."

He gave a week-night lecture on " Bible lands." His tour and studies in the East " furnished necessary material." These discourses were sought with eagerness and heard with delight. The writer has recently seen a lady in Philadelphia who was drawn to his church by the interest that these awakened. From her youth

she had not only been a reader but even a student of
the Scriptures. These lectures met her wish. She
was charmed by the richness of the matter, the famil-
iarity of the style, and the directness of the address.
She then attended his Sabbath sermons, and though of
another denomination she felt she owed it to her
highest good that she join his Charge, which she
did, and to this day she continues a devoted member
of the Methodist Episcopal Church. Wishing to retain as much as she might of the sermons that
yielded her so much profit she took ample notes.
These she retains, and prizes for the memories they revive and as choice treasures of the mind and heart.
To these the writer has been permitted access. They
show the spirit of the man and the care with which he
presented doctrinal, practical and experimental religion.
They have a wide range but a close application. They
instruct, encourage, and exalt. In this Dr. Durbin
showed the pastor after God's own heart. "Repentance," "conversion," "secret seeking after God," "justification by faith," "death," "the punishment of the
wicked."

Scriptural biography was made a powerful means of
enforcing truth. With what skill did he present the
case of Esau; the sad condition of Balaam; the lessons
of Lot's wife and the moral grandeur of Christian
heroism in the "death of Stephen." So simple, direct
and impressive were the sermons of Dr. Durbin notwithstanding his reputation of a great preacher, that
children could understand. The wife of the Rev.
A. II. Ames, D.D., of the Des Moines Conference, when
a child of nine years, on hearing a sermon from Dr.
Durbin on "the harvest is past and the summer is
ended, and we are not saved," says she was so impressed that she felt that she could not delay giving

her heart to God, and at that early age was converted.

It was no uncommon thing for Dr. Durbin to preach a series of sermons upon a theme or a history. He had one on "the life of Christ;" another on "Christ under the old dispensation," another on the "kingdom of Christ." With the beatitudes he spent several Sabbaths. On a week night he delivered a series of lectures on the epistle to the Hebrews, and dwelt particularly on the "priesthood of Christ."

It clearly appears from the notes how full were his thoughts of the glory of Christ's character; of the grandeur of his dominion; of the righteousness of his claim and of the blessings he brought to men. Nor did he fail to show "the priesthood of Christ," in language of assurance, of exaltation, and of divine power.

In the administration of the "Lord's Supper," in the address he made and in the spirit that pervaded the service, it is said communion was an occasion of rare manifestations of grace, and that after the benediction was pronounced the people would linger as at the gate of heaven and ready to enter.

Full as Dr. Durbin was of the work of a pastor while in Philadelphia, he nevertheless cherished a desire to help young ministers in the study of sacred eloquence. To this end he formed a class to which he gave the observation and experience of his life. The writer was permitted a place with the favored few that formed it, and he can never forget some of the important lessons that he strove to impress. To three of these we may give some notice :

1. As to the length of a sermon.

In a pastoral charge it should not as a rule transcend forty-five or fifty minutes. But he supposed a preacher might say, "I am not through my plan, and some of

11

my best matter is yet to come." To this his prompt reply was : "The people do not know what you have in store, and can feel no privation from your withholding it. Keep it for another occasion, and know the value of husbanding your material. You have had time enough to feed them with knowledge. They will receive it better when they are hungry for the word." Surfeiting sickens.

2. Take texts that have the Gospel in them.

Here he related his experience as given by the Rev. Mr. Roberts. He selected the passage, " The trees of the Lord are full of sap." With some, analogical sermons were popular. Dr. Adam Clarke notices the possibility of going too far in such efforts. Keech on the *Metaphors* is a fruitful source of such discourse, and it has its use. Bunyan showed its power in " Solomon's Temple Spiritualized." But young Durbin did not have a good time. The venerable Solomon Sharp said, in such cases "the preacher got in the bushes." Well, it is a very embarrassing position, especially if the bushes are in the mire. It is worse than a tangle. "The Boy Preacher " got into " the tree," and though it was one of the trees of the Lord he did not find it so easy and expeditious a thing to get down as Zaccheus did. He talked about "trees," "trees," "trees," till for a time he would have been glad if he could have just been a "tree " and no preacher. He talked about "sap," "sap," "sap," till he felt too *sapient*. For such aspiration in preaching Durbin was ready to say,

" I charge thee, fling away ambition."

3. As a general preparation for preaching he urged storing the memory with the best passages of literature, whether in poetry or prose. They were to be so at the command of the preacher that if they came appositely

the memory would throw them off, in the order of extemporaneous speech, and so add force to the sermon. Any one familiar with the "sermons and plans of Joseph Benson," one of the best theologians and ablest preachers in early Wesleyan Methodism, will see what use he made of the best poets.

Ganganelli, who had given so much time to sermonizing, when writing to an abbé in relation to the "Soul of Christian Eloquence" urges upon him better acquaintance with the "Fathers of the Church." He says, "They are like the fertile trees, which ornament gardens while they enrich them." He compares the genius of Tertullian to iron, which breaks the hardest bodies and will not bend; Athanasius to the diamond, which can neither be deprived of luster nor solidity; Cyprian to steel, which cuts to the quick; Chrysostom to gold, whose value is equal to its beauty; . . . Jerome to brass, which neither dreads swords nor arrows; Ambrose to silver, which is solid and shining; Gregory to a mirror, in which every one sees himself.

The advantage of a judicious use of such resources may be judged by the high authorities whence they issue and observation as to the effect.

When his aid was asked by a young minister with regard to helps in his pursuit of necessary knowledge, he gave the following "What and How to Study." In this he expresses his views of what ought to constitute a young minister's library after completing his Conference course. He writes:

PHILADELPHIA, *July* 12, 1847.

DEAR BROTHER: I have not neglected your letter of June 13. I have been busy and absent, and it requires some time to give you a judicious answer. Below you have such books as I suppose would be suitable to be read in addition to your Conference course. Perhaps

I., IV., and V. might be read together, then II. and III., and then VI. and VII. You should have an Index Rerum to insert references, and a commonplace blank-book in which to copy any sentence or to write any remarks of your own as you read; also a blank-book in which to insert texts for sermons as they occur in your reading, and such subordinate divisions under each head as may occur to you at the time. Thus you will collect a magazine of material for use in the pulpit. If you were with me an hour in my own study I could show you much more readily and clearly how to proceed. If you are in the city call and see me. It will give pleasure to aid you.

I. Profane History.
    1. Tyler's Universal History.
    2. Gibbon's Decline and Fall of the Roman Empire.
    3. Hallam's Middle Ages.
    4. Russell's Modern Europe.

II. Church History.
    1. Ruter's.
    2. Mosheim's.
    3. Gieseler's, 3 vols. (very good.)
    4. Neander's.
    5. Milman's History of Christianity.
    6. Neander's Planting and Training.

III. Theology.
    1. Schruncher's or Stockhouse's Body of Divinity.
    2. Dwight's Theology.
    3. Storrs's and Flatt's Theology.
    4. Knapp's Theology.

IV. Interpretation of the Scriptures.
    1. Ernesti on Interpretation.
    2. Clarke's Commentary.
    3. Benson's Commentary.
    4. D'Oyly and Mant's Notes.
    5. South and Patrick's Commentary.

V. Helps to Interpretation.
    1. John's Hebrew Commonwealth.
    2. John's Biblical Archæology.

VI. Doctrines and Interpretation.
    1. Burnet on the Thirty-nine Articles.
    2. Pearson on the Creed.

VII. Scripture Geography and History.
    1. Robinson and Smith's Palestine.
    2. Horne's three volumes, late edition.

VIII. Homiletics.
1. Porter's Lectures on Homiletics.
2. Preachers' Manual.
3. Claude's Essay on Composition of a Sermon.
IX. Townsend's Bible, arranged chronologically, should be used in daily reading, with at least two commentaries at hand to consult when necessary, as well as biblical dictionaries and other books of reference.

The desire of Dr. Durbin that young ministers should have every facility for their improvement, was clearly brought out in the days of his editorship, as appears in various articles from his pen. So far did he go, as we have seen in his editorial of July 18, 1834, as to advocate a "Theological Seminary."

In all young men he had a deep interest as the hope of the country as of the Church. He felt the importance of impressing them with sound principles of morality, of broadening their intelligence, and of adding weight to character by the lessons of wisdom that they should carefully study.

While pastor in Philadelphia he wrote an introduction to Burgh's *Rules for the Conduct of Life*, as a means of inculcating correct conduct. We quote his language:

The instructions and rules contained in this unpretending volume are not applicable only or chiefly to the emergencies which may arise in our affairs, but also to the ordinary business and relations of life. Success in these respects depends chiefly on some settled plan, and a few sound maxims by which we are steadily guided. President Edwards owed much of his greatness to seventy-five rules which he drew up for his daily conduct; and although they are not so generally applicable to the ordinary affairs of life as those in this work, yet I have deemed it proper to present them to the reader in the form of an appendix.

It is impossible to ascertain the prominent characters and instances of extraordinary success in life which have resulted from the sound maxims that Dr. Franklin published on the margin of his Almanac, under the sobriquet of "Poor Richard." I happen to know that the most extensive publishing house in this, or, perhaps, in any country, was produced by its elder partner adopting while he was an apprentice, and practicing steadily afterward, one of the maxims of Poor Richard.

He says, "As the slightest touch will defile a clean garment, which cannot be cleaned again without a great deal of trouble, so the conversation of the wicked and the debauched will in a very short time defile the mind of an innocent person in a manner that will give him great trouble to recover his former purity. You may therefore more safely venture into company with a person infected with the plague than with a vicious man; for the worst consequence of the first is death, but of the last the hazard of a worse destruction. For vicious people generally have a peculiar ambition to draw in the innocent to their party, and many of them are furnished with artifices and allurements but too effectual for ensnaring."

The advice to those who are just commencing business for themselves, particularly with regard to the strictest integrity and patience, and overtrading and expensive living, is exceedingly judicious. The methods recommended in order to penetrate the characters and motives of those with whom we have to deal are just and honorable. The following remark is worthy to be remembered. It will save us a great deal of that trouble which holds out no prospect of profit. "There are six sorts of people at whose hands you need not expect much kindness: The sordid and narrow-minded think of nobody but themselves. The lazy will not take the trouble to serve you. The busy have not time to think of you. The overgrown rich man is above minding any one that needs his assistance. The poor and unhappy have neither spirit nor ability. The good-natured fool, however willing, is not capable of serving you."

The rules laid down for conducting the affairs of courtship and marriage will be read with pleasure and profit even by those who have already entered prudently

into the marriage relation. The instruction to parents
on the proper management of children, and advice with
respect to aiding their early settlement in life are excellent. I conclude by expressing my opinion that a
more suitable book could not be placed in the hands of
youth of both sexes, particularly when they are about
to enter into the world and assume at least some of the
important relations in society, and come into contact
not only with liberal and right-minded persons and
favorable opportunities, but also with ill-natured people, untoward circumstances, and eager competition in
business.

Again, in the introduction to *Edmondson's Short
Sermons*, he makes an extract as most salutary counsel
to young men.

There is scarcely a condition in life that will not find
a sermon in this volume appropriate to it, in which judicious advice is given to guide the conduct in the case.
The two sermons to young men are an invaluable treas-
ure. They are not so much an appeal to them on the
subject of religion as a manual to direct them in the
affairs of life. I select two passages as specimens of the
matter and manner of the discourses on the various
conditions and duties of life. The first is a word to
young men on going into business ; the second, on their
duties to their parents:

"Many young men have entered on business at the
wrong end, and have made a figure in the world without a sufficient capital to support it ; but their thoughtless extravagance has soon dashed them down to the
lowest degradation. They would be gentlemen at first,
and, before they knew on what ground they stood,
involved themselves in debt, robbed their creditors,
disgraced themselves, and in their folly sunk into
poverty and want. That you may avoid these fatal
rocks, 'let your moderation be known unto all men.'
Be attentive to business ; keep correct accounts ; deal
in good articles ; aim at a moderate and fair profit ;
be punctual to all your engagements ; be kind to your

servants; live rather below your income; and resolve to be fair traders and honest men."

"Have you parents? Let them be dear to you. Remember who hath said, 'Honor thy father and thy mother, that thy days may be long upon the land which the Lord thy God giveth thee.' Obey them in all things lawful, and if they be poor supply their wants. They have done more for you than you can do for them, and the time may come when you may need the help of your children. Conceal as much as possible the faults of your parents; bear with their growing weaknesses and infirmities, and cheer their drooping spirits. He who is unkind to his parents under any pretense is unworthy of a place in the Church of God."

But in all this work there was proper care of his pulpit duties. No day was so cold and no storm so heavy as to prevent his preaching sermons that filled the people with rapture. The same wisdom of conduct and grace of intercourse that had distinguished him in college relations marked his intercourse with the people. His plans were accepted as his ministry was commended and sought. Having served the Union the full period he was appointed to Trinity Church in Philadelphia. Here he sustained the same reputation. In the outer world he was known by his eloquence in the pulpit, on the platform, and wherever he appeared. Besides the studies for the improvement and better furnishing of his own mind he was in his own house as a professor to his children, training them in their studies and giving them the results of his observation and skill. During his pastorate in the city, amid the pulpits of Albert Barnes, Dr. S. H. Tyng, Dr. G. W. Bethune, and of Dr. T. H. Stockton he was an ascendant attraction. Among such popular lecturers as Judge Conrad, Morton McMichael, and Joseph R. Chandler he commanded the most eminent place. His pastorate in Philadelphia did not impair his reputation as a man of mental and theological resources, nor was his eloquence in less repute.

While in this city there was a Sabbath Convention held in the Musical Fund Hall, then the popular place for great assemblies. The Convention was to petition the Legislature for a law in regard to the sanctity of the Sabbath. It was a large and intelligent body of laymen and ministers. Among those who spoke was the late Governor Alexander Cummings, at that time the editor of the *Evening Bulletin.* His speech was prompt, direct, incisive. The Rev. Thomas Brainard, with his accustomed wit and brilliancy, had delivered an address with fine effect. Rev. Dr. G. W. Bethune, at the height of his fame as a pulpit orator, had spoken with an eloquence transcending any thing the writer had ever heard from him. He declared that he belonged to a church whose faith is that Christ's kingdom is not of this world in the means by which it is advanced, that her appeal is to God and not to legislators. His attitude, gesture, and manner, suggested George Whitefield as no other speaker had ever done. With uplifted and extended arms he exclaimed, "Christianity has cost us mountains of wealth, and rivers of blood, and ages of suffering, but the repose of the saints is in the Saviour who is strong to deliver; he still walks in the midst of the seven golden candlesticks and holds the seven stars in his right hand." The audience was at fever heat. This was not the time for a like exhibition, but for all the weight that wisdom gives to words. Dr. Durbin rose. There was universal stillness. He was calm, clear, conciliatory and convincing. There was no passion; it was all logic. At the close of his remarks the Rev. Mr. Longmore, of Manayunk, a Presbyterian minister lately from Ireland, full of enthusiasm, said: "I have listened to the last speaker with the greatest admiration, as I have thought how forcible are right words. How valuable is good common sense!"

At the end of his pastorate at Trinity, having been in the city four years, he was compelled by the law of the Church at that time to leave. In this brief period he had done a work that only eternity will fully disclose. He had brought many to Methodism who had not known its character, and made an impression upon our Church that abides.

He was then appointed presiding elder on the North Philadelphia District. Though there but one year it is spoken of as a period of thorough supervision, and as furnishing a brilliant episode in the history of the district. The position was not pleasant to him, but his great sermons were an untold power. One on the resurrection, preached at the Attleborough camp-meeting, is still spoken of as overwhelming in its effects.

A short time after his appointment he made an official visit to Bristol, Pa., and preached on Sabbath morning. His congregation was very large. Among those present was the Rev. S. H. Smith, now and long a member of the New York East Conference, but at that time a resident of Burlington, N. J., just across the Delaware from Bristol. Mr. Smith says he was accompanied by a very intelligent member of Saint Mary's Protestant Episcopal Church, Burlington, then under the rectorship of Bishop Doane.

The preacher conducted the introductory services in a very quiet manner, and then announced his text, Heb. iv, 14–16, presenting as his theme the priesthood of Jesus.

There was nothing particularly impressive in the first few sentences of his discourse, but soon he uttered something which seemed slightly paradoxical, which immediately arrested the attention of all hearers. They

soon saw from lucid statements that though at first apparently doubtful it was entirely legitimate to the subject in hand. From that moment onward to the close
of the sermon he not only held the attention, but evidently enraptured his congregation. The whole scene
of priestly offering and intercession as known to the
Levitical dispensation was so graphically depicted, and
the superiority and effectiveness of Christ's mediatorial
office so powerfully shown, that every one seemed to
see and feel that remission of sins had been clearly
provided for in God's great method of atonement. It
was interesting to watch the effect upon the hearers, as
seen from the close attention given, and expression of
deepest interest upon every face. Mr. Smith says:
"The friend who accompanied me at first seemed disappointed, but soon he became fixed, and then transfixed,
and with the spell of that marvelous sermon upon him
declared, as he mingled with the returning throng, that
it was the greatest religious discourse he ever heard."

While in Philadelphia it was well understood he
had a most tempting offer of a pastorate in the city
from another denomination, when the weightiest arguments were brought to bear to induce his acceptance.
This, too, was at a time when he keenly felt the law that
compelled his removal from the pastorate of the Methodist church after a service of four consecutive years in
the city. Besides, he was filling the presiding elder's
office, which was one that he did not desire.

CHAPTER XI.

The Missionary Secretaryship.

IN 1850, on the failure of the health of Dr. Pitman, Secretary of the Missionary Society, the Bishops unanimously called Dr. Durbin to fill the vacancy.

The General Conference of 1852 elected him to this office, and successive General Conferences continued him there till 1872, when bodily infirmities induced his resignation. To this position Dr. Durbin came in his physical vigor, his mental strength, and in the full knowledge and discipline of all his powers. His executive ability, superior judgment of men, as well as his remarkable eloquence, commended him to the Church as a most suitable person for this high office. By travel in foreign lands he had added to his intellectual resources and become familiar with the moral wants of the world. The place was most congenial to his tastes. He entered upon his work with the force of conviction and the inspiration of hope. He formed his plans, adopted his policy, and as far as possible reduced every thing to system. He called to his support competent men, and exercised a supervision at once general and minute. His alertness was equal to any exigency. His oversight often seemed like prescience. He impressed pastors with the obligation of enlightening and inspiring our people. For this he urged monthly missionary concerts for prayer and the diffusion of appropriate literature. He insisted that with such zeal and effort the people would be educated to giving. He guarded against spasmodic action as sure to react. He discouraged collections at the Annual Conferences, exhorting the preachers to give with their people, that their charges might have both the inspiration and credit of their offerings. He assured the pastors that he reposed more upon their skill than upon his own efforts. He organized auxiliary societies and directed contributions to the proper treasury.

In the public anniversaries he made it a study to put the greatest amount of matter in the smallest space and to render it the most vital. The addresses on these occasions were such as gave the broadest views and the brightest prospect. They increased liberality and awoke a higher ambition. Who that was present on the occasion can ever forget the anniversary at Steinway Hall, when Bishop Thomson, on his return from abroad, delivered his mighty address on India? Did we ever so see the country and its peoples? Did we ever so see the learning we have to meet, the logical skill and powerful prejudice we have to encounter? He studied every question of the foreign work in its relation to country, government, and race. He considered the obstacles and inducements to missionary service. With the statesman he was the statesman ecclesiastic, wisely presenting the condition, showing the triumphs, and securing the protection that the comity of nations demands. In the monthly meetings of the board of managers, and in the committees on various mission fields, he showed his perfect grasp of all detail and knowledge of the cases to be considered. Himself the center of intelligence, he threw light on every subject. His reports to the board were so clear and just as to allow little discussion, as they carried with them the force of a logical statement and of an inevitable conclusion. In the board were business men and ministers accustomed to independent thought and expression; but it was difficult to make an issue with the secretary. He had discernment, foresight, address without cunning; and if he managed men it was not because he was a manager. If the world ever saw greater harmony than pervaded that board, the writer has not lived long enough or gone far enough to see it. But who can tell his service to the Church in his keen discrimination of character, his ready perception of the qualification of candidates for the diverse fields, the education demanded, the abilities possessed, the grace enjoyed, and the subjection to discipline required. His correspondence with them in the work, his recognition of their cares, his estimate of their difficulties, his generous judgment of their mistakes, the sympathy he expressed in their sorrows, his words of cheer in their successes, and his perpetual anxiety to succor and strengthen them are beyond the power of words, while loyalty to the interest that he was to guard and direct compelled a strictness that is the offspring of inflexible integrity.

With a heart so full of the cause it was natural that he should wish to visit the missions, that he might better understand their needs. The society approved his proposition. He went and made such observation and reached such conclusions as were of permanent profit. He lived, he wrote, he gave addresses, preached sermons, and kindled his own ardors in hearts as cold as icebergs. Parsimony unlocked its coffers, and mines of unknown wealth were discovered. Many a saint nearing the celestial city remembered in his will the cause that would "bring many sons unto glory." Churches felt their dignity increased by the munificence of their offerings, and the Philadelphia Conference, of which he was a member, was and continues to be in its collections the banner Conference.

What character, what church, what Conference could be cold when he showed the "signs of the times?" Will the spectacle ever vanish? Will the reasons ever cease to operate? Under his administration the "Woman's Foreign Missionary Society" was organized, and received his sanction and support. When Dr. Durbin became Missionary Secretary the Methodist Episcopal Church had but two small foreign missions: one in South America, one in Liberia; one just being formed in China. Under him its missions were extended in China, into India, Germany, Switzerland, Sweden, Norway, Denmark, and Bulgaria. When he took his place as secretary the receipts of the society were one hundred thousand dollars per year; but before he retired they amounted to seven hundred thousand dollars a year.

In 1866, the centennial year of American Methodism, appropriations were made on the basis of one million for the missionary cause. Within the last year a million dollars has been raised. To this sublime work Dr. Durbin gave twenty-two of the best years of his life. If ever his unreserved powers were given to an interest they were to this. When, in 1852, much was said about making him Bishop, he expressed his conviction that he had a work of superior claim on his energies, and one that he preferred.

The following is from the pen of the late Bishop Wiley when editor of the *Ladies' Repository*, January, 1872:

Dr. Durbin cannot be called the father of Methodist Missions, for our society had a history of thirty years before he came to its head; yet in very important senses he is the creator of the society in its present form and magnitude, and deserves and will receive the undying gratitude of the Church as the chief in-

strument in the wonderful development of our missionary work during the past score of years.

In 1850, when Dr. Durbin entered the office as secretary, the missionary appropriation was $100,000. Of
this sum $23,400 were appropriated to "domestic mis-
sions," $38,300 to "foreign populations in our own coun-
try," $37,300 to "foreign missions." Our only foreign
missions were Africa, China, and South America. The
African Mission was a pet, and received $21,000. South
America took care of itself, the missionary being supported by American and English residents. The China
Mission was in its infancy, having just secured its loca-
tion at Foochow, and receiving an appropriation of
$7,000. California and Oregon were reckoned, in some
sense, foreign missions, two missionaries having just
been sent to the former and seven operating in Oregon.
The collection for the preceding year was $106,196 09,
being an average of $16\frac{3}{10}$ per member. From that
time to the present there has been a steady increase in
appropriations and receipts, except a seeming decrease
since 1865 and 1866. The highest point reached in
these appropriations was $1,000,000 for 1866. The
highest point reached in receipts was in the same year,
$671,090 66, being an average of 77 cents per member.

In accepting this post Dr. Durbin knew the care it
would cost, the wisdom that it would require, the labor
that must be performed. He could conceive the solicitude that the demands of the work and the needs of
the treasury might compel. He knew that to him the
Church would look as inspiration to men, as argument
for increased liberality, as judgment for foreign fields.
He was not unmindful of the wear that would be upon
body and mind. He knew that Conferences would expect his presence and ask his knowledge, and individuals might tax his faith and try his patience.

But no knowledge of facts, however weighty and
difficult, kept him from a proper study of his duty and
the acceptance of what the Church imposed.

When the Rev. Elias Cornelius, D.D., was appointed Corresponding Secretary of the American Board of Commissioners for Foreign Missions he said, in writing to a friend some weeks after his election, " Hitherto I have felt more like *praying* than either writing or conversing. The most I can or dare say at present is, and that with my eyes turned to Heaven, and death and the judgment before me, I am trying to ask, 'Lord, what wilt thou have me to do?' Next I desire to have my ears open to every thing which is likely to make known his will. . . . I beg you to remember me in your prayers."

Thus felt the man of God when contemplating the duties that his position involved. Dr. Durbin had as full a realization of his responsibility when he became the " Corresponding Secretary of the Missionary Society of the Methodist Episcopal Church." But he loved the cause, and he welcomed the work when he saw the " finger of God." He was converted about the time that our Missionary Society was organized. In his early ministry he was permitted to see this work among the Indians in the West, and it was his delight to narrate the conversion of John Steward, a colored man, who had some experience among the Indians in what was then the far West; of his remarkable solicitude for the red men of the forest; of his determination to go among them and tell them of the Saviour that he had found; and how God honored the labors of this earnest laborer in one of our first mission fields, in the days when James B. Finley, by his devotion to their good, was honored by being made a " chief." The cases of Jason Lee, of Joshua Spaulding, the condition of the " Flat Head Indians," and of the anxious inquiry about the work of the Great Spirit—these men and facts had taken hold of his heart and produced and deepened

12

sympathy. Such also was the case with regard to Melville B. Cox and his African work.

He saw the world lying in wickedness. He saw millions of his race "without God and without hope in the world." He saw peoples of every color and clime bowing down to gods of wood and stone. In human souls he saw no discriminating hues excepting those that are moral. He knew the Gospel would save them. The Methodist Church had it in its power to send it. For this it had organized the Missionary Society, and he believed that what might not be accomplished by individuals could be effected by the combined effort of many. He knew that the voluntary association of good men for advancing the kingdom of Christ could accomplish wonders. He believed that there is no object to which this power cannot adapt itself, no resources which it may not ultimately command, and "that a few individuals, if the public mind be gradually prepared to favor them, can lay the foundations of undertakings which would have baffled the might of those who reared the Pyramids." Has not this bold statement been justified in the cause of missions?

Early in the history of our missionary efforts as a Church Rev. Stephen G. Roszel, of the Baltimore Conference, a man of exalted character and of strong faith, had the holy daring to predict that the day would yet dawn when his Conference would raise as much as $1,000 a year ! Let us not be severe on his judgment : it was a day of small things.

Of John P. Durbin we may say the cause of missions commanded his confidence, inspired his heroism, and furnished a basis of the highest and holiest hope.

When the Macedonian cry fell on his ear, " Come over and help us," his response was, " I am a debtor both to the Greeks and to the Barbarians, both to the wise and to the unwise."

His faith saw the sword converted into a plowshare and the spear into a pruning hook ; saw idols going to the moles and to the bats; saw the "wilderness and the solitary place" becoming glad, and the desert blossoming "as the rose."

Such thoughts, such faith, such appeal, made him willing, anxious, to give his powers to this department of the Church's service. Study had trained him, education had honored him, the pastorate had roused his moral as well as intellectual powers : the editorship in the Church had given him a wide view of the world's want, and now the missionary cause absorbed him.

Others might be discouraged; he borrowed faith from emergency. While others stood still and speculated he went forward and demonstrated. Pressure did not crush him, for love was mighty in his support. To him every cloud had its "silver lining," and when the sun of the hopes of others was going down his rose full orbed on the moral horizon—the clouds gave way, and the sun tinged what he touched. The deep silence or stirring statement of an empty treasury made him ring out as the battle-cry, "Can ye not discern the signs of the times ?" Who can tell the value of such a man? What a spirit did he inspire ! What self-abnegation did he induce ! What possibilities did he make manifest !

When he resigned his place as Corresponding Secretary of the Missionary Society, the General Conference, in appreciation of his services and to retain his counsel, elected him Honorary Secretary of the Missionary Society. Then he, whose life had been so full of labor and whose labor had been so full of grand results, withdrew from the active services that had been his delight.

It is reported of Queen Mary, when about to die, that she said, "If her body was opened 'Calais' would be found written on her heart." If mind could so imprint itself on matter, and the affections show themselves on human tissues, the examination of the heart of this great Secretary would show "The Missionary Society of the Methodist Episcopal Church." The writer has not been accustomed to think that a human intellect wears out by use; but if he has ever been tempted to this, it is in the case of John P. Durbin.

CHAPTER XII.

Sermons on Special Occasions.

NO thoughtful person knowing the diverse and responsible positions which J. P. Durbin filled for so long a period with so much success can doubt that, irrespective of his pre-eminence as a speaker, he was a man of remarkable endowments and skill; for fifty years the name of John P. Durbin was before the country as a synonym of inimitable eloquence.

Though the writer may not literally reproduce the great sermons that Dr. Durbin delivered allusion is allowed to some of those discourses that will never die in the memory of those who heard them.

We have seen that while Dr. Durbin was pastor in Philadelphia his themes had adaptation, and that there were variety and popular power. For these his method of preparation was uniform. But his sermons on special occasions, in subject and treatment, respected the facts before him. For any thing else he seemed not to have the slightest concern. He would preach from the same text any number of times or in different places though near together. The writer heard him preach at the seat of the Conference in Eastern Maryland in 1848 from the text: " I have written unto you, young men, because ye are strong, and the word of God abideth in you, and ye have overcome the wicked one." The Sabbath before he preached it in Baltimore. Easton was just across the Chesapeake Bay. He was not deterred by the fact that Dr. Bond and others from Baltimore had heard it. At the dedication of the church at Cambridge that week he took "I have written unto you, young men." There may have been a score of people at Cambridge that heard him on both the former occasions. He knew the advantage of having a sermon fully at his command. Dr. Southey commended Whitefield in his habit of often preaching the same subjects, because he could thus learn the points of power—what to leave off, how to add, or to modify. Dr. Franklin said he could tell when Whitefield had a new subject by its lack of maturity. No one could tell how often Dr. Durbin preached from his chosen themes. Frequent preaching from the same text was one of the advantages of our fathers when they traveled circuits or filled the office of presiding elder. Dr. Durbin once said in the Preachers' Meeting of Philadelphia, "I am like the old Roman, I never throw away a sword while it will cut." If rusty, he rubbed it up.

BALAAM.

Among the interesting and impressive *biographical sermons* that Dr. Durbin preached while pastor of the Union was one on Balaam. A friend has told the writer that when he announced his text "tears were in his eyes." If the history of the subject gave him such pathos at the start we might naturally suppose the sermon would not be wanting in emotion. It was not. It was as if the heart of the preacher ached in the contemplation of such a false character, a man of such contradictions in himself : a man of such exalted conceptions of God and such sublime utterances of this power and grace, of such knowledge as suggested the true prophet, and yet with a conduct to show how perfectly a strong man may be lured by love of lucre ; and in the face of the most instructive facts in the history of God's people daring to desire their defeat and reprobation, yet uttering language that would indicate divine inspiration; cherishing desires to die the death of the righteous, and willing, if he might be permitted, even to curse the people of God. When once refused, again applying, and after such answer as allowed to his *mind* the liberty that he sought, hasting to the house of the messengers of the king to inform them of the gratifying answer given. Arriving at the place Dr. Durbin represents Balaam as eagerly rapping at the door, and, "suiting the action to the word," with the dramatic power that he possessed, made three raps upon the pulpit that sounded as if eternity was making its terrific charges upon the ears of guilt.

We may not now give the moral word-painting of Dr. Durbin. Word-painting, was it? Did he not rather sculpture character? If in ordinary thought he presented the *thing* can we wonder that this strange compound of good and evil, of prophecy and profanation, of orthodox faith and heterodox practice—two men in one, two natures struggling one against the other—which Balaam presented, should command his great power in the delineation of character? Shall we say that he was

> " To hell and heaven equal bent,
> While both a devil and a saint ? "

For lucid exhibition, for forcible reasoning, for analysis of human nature, for profound pathos, for stirring appeal, for facts to induce moral introspection, the writer must not be expected to give a just impression.

NAAMAN.

Dr. Durbin had a sermon of great eloquence upon Naaman. In this was the best exhibition of the beauty and force of his familiar style, a power to any one who understands its use.

Lord Brougham, writing of Bushe, said: "His merit as a speaker was of the highest order, and his power of narrative has not perhaps been equaled." He assumes that the narrative of Livy himself does not surpass in the great effect of his orator. He names perfect simplicity, but mingled with elegance; a lucid arrangement and unbroken connection of all the facts and constant introduction of the most picturesque expressions, but never as ornaments. These, the great qualities of narrative, accomplish its end and purpose. They place the story and the scene before the hearer and the reader as if he had witnessed the reality.

Dr. Durbin's vividness in moral word-painting was one of the most striking features in the composition of this sermon. Narrative had large place. Who has not seen this in Dr. Durbin? Was it not this that gave such effect to his statements of the claim, condition and prospects of the missionary cause? Perhaps there was no power that Dr. Durbin possessed of which he was so conscious as this. While commending narrative in preaching, on one occasion in the Philadelphia Preachers' Meeting, he said: "This ability I owe to my mother's habit of telling me stories when I was a small boy. I would lie on the floor as she walked to and fro drawing out her yarn with a large spinning-wheel, so common in those days, and she would tell me some story and fill me with delight, and, looking up from the floor into her face, I would say, 'Mother, tell me more.' And more she gave." Dear mother and woman of God! how little did she think when spinning yarn for the clothing of her household and telling stories to amuse her son that she was imparting a taste for narrative that would cause him to thrill vast congregations; that

she was teaching him to weave a net to catch the ear
and win the heart of many a sinner !

In his sermon on Naaman Dr. Durbin showed his
homiletic skill in the use of the facts of Scripture history
and his ability to derive from them, and present to the
congregation, lessons of profoundest wisdom, and to
render practical, in the highest sense, portions of the
word which, though familiar, are rarely seen in their
deep moral significance.

Pride was made odious, and human power unavailable to the great necessity of human salvation. The
altar of God on the camp-ground or in the church, the
bread and wine at the Lord's Supper, were seen to have
a claim that had been denied them, even as the Jordan
was a means that Abana and Pharpar could not reach.
Now, in the full swell and sweep of his voice, he would
urge the dying sinner to forget all but his disease and
God's cure, and to believe, after all our reasoning, that
God is wiser than man, and with an earnestness that
only the peril of the sinner justified he urged the spiritual lepers to come to the "fountain opened in the
house of David for sin and uncleanness," and so have
a new nature. In the Hebrew maid he saw the missionary for Christ. All Christians were to show what
they could do in any sphere where Providence places
them. Thus the sermon was *practical* in the highest
sense.

DEDICATION OF TRINITY.

In the use of choice literature Dr. Durbin did as he
advised others to do. The climax of his sermon at the
dedication of "Trinity," Philadelphia, in 1841, was in a
quotation. The service was on a week-day. It is
doubtful whether we ever had such a congregation as
at this time. Men of all professions were there. Ministers of various churches were present in great numbers.

When the preacher had so far shown the sins of men
and the word of grace—when the audience had hung on
his words though in profound silence—he gave vent
to the strongest emotion and the most burning passion
in what the writer regarded as familiar language from
Cowper :

> "O! for a lodge in some vast wilderness,
> Some boundless contiguity of shade,
> Where rumor of oppression and deceit,
> Of unsuccessful or successful war,
> Might never reach me more. My ear is pained,
> My soul is sick, with every day's report
> Of wrong and outrage with which earth is filled."

It is impossible to tell the power of that passage,
unless it was heard from Durbin's lips and with his impulse and emotion. When he laid his emphasis on "my
ear is pained" we felt disgusted at wickedness. When
he pronounced "wrong and outrage" we knew not how
to meet the enormity. With the first it was as if a
shingle started; when he uttered "outrage" as if the
roof rose. It was as if a stone spoke out of the wall
and a beam out of the timber answered it—as if
material things were shocked at such unexampled sin ;
as if the very temple became vocal with accusations and
filled with revolt, while virtuous Nature sought sanctuary from sin in the lodge of "some vast wilderness,"
in "boundless contiguity of shade." Beside the writer
sat Dr. George B. Ide, the brilliant preacher of the First
Baptist Church. He said, as we separated, "parts were
inimitable." We had often heard that poetry *quoted*,
never before *rendered.* It was not the quotation ; it
was not the words, but Durbin in them.

RESURRECTION.

Conception can hardly transcend the influence of his
quotation from Dr. Young when preaching on the

" Resurrection of Christ." The didactic and expository had had their place, reasoning had exerted its greatest power, and for a time logic seemed to predominate in the discourse ; but when the moment came to be relieved from severe mental process—when the proof presented had accomplished its end, the soul took wings and mounted from the earth and seemed sublimed by the subject. The fact made its full appeal ; some wept, others shouted ; all were absorbed. Then in the fullness of a triumph never more manifest in any moral demonstration, he exclaimed :

" And did he rise?

Hear, O ye nations, hear it, O ye dead!
He rose! he rose! he burst the bars of death.
Lift up your heads, ye everlasting gates!
And give the King of glory to come in.
Who is the King of glory? He who left
His throne of glory for the pangs of death.
Lift up your heads, ye everlasting gates!
And give the king of glory to come in.
Who is the King of glory? He who slew
The ravenous foe that gorged all human race.
The King of glory He. whose glory filled
Heaven with amazement at his love to man,
And with divine complacency beheld
Powers most illumined 'wilder'd in the theme.

The theme, the joy, how then shall man sustain?
O the burst gates! crushed sting! demolished throne!
Last gasp of vanquished death! shout, earth and heaven,
This sum of good to man, whose nature thou
Took wing and mounted with him from the tomb.
Then, then I rose! Then first humanity
Triumphant passed the crystal ports of light
(Stupendous guest) and seized eternal youth.
Seized in our name. *E'er since 'tis blasphemous*
To call man mortal. Man's mortality
Was then transferred to death ; and Heaven's duration

> Unalienably sealed to this frail frame,
> This child of dust! *Man, all immortal, hail!*
> *Hail! Heaven,* all lavish of strange gifts to man,
> *Thine all the glory,* MAN'S the BOUNDLESS BLISS."

No one can wonder that the sermon at the Attleborough camp-meeting that contained this passage is remembered and spoken of as one of such stupendous power. He had no need to go to others for either elegance, elevation, or eloquence; but he did it to support the grand truths that he presented.

BASCOM WITH COLERIDGE'S LAY SERMON.

The passage that we have heard quoted from Bascom more than any other is from S. T. Coleridge. Speaking of Christianity he asks, "But whence did this happy organization first come? Was it a tree transplanted from Paradise, with all its branches in full fruitage? Or was it sowed in sunshine? Was it in vernal breezes and gentle rains that it fixed its roots and grew and strengthened? Let history answer these questions! With blood was it planted; it was rocked in tempests; the goat, the ass and the stag gnawed it; the wild boar has whetted his tusk on its bark. The deep scars are still extant on its trunk, and the path of the lightning may be traced among its higher branches. And even after its full growth, in the season of its strength, when its height reached to the heaven and the sight thereof to all the earth, the whirlwind has more than once forced its stately top to touch the ground : it has been bent like a bow, and sprang back like a shaft."

The readiness of Dr. Durbin to utilize important material in a way consistent with high intellectual capacity extended, in one case, certainly, even to the *plan* of a sermon. In *The Christian Advocate* of No-

vember 13, 1884, there is a very copious outline of a
sermon on the text, Hosea ii, 8, 9, "For she did not
ˌknow that I gave her corn, and wine, and oil, and multiplied her silver and gold, which they prepared for
Baal. Therefore will I return, and take away my corn
in the time thereof, and my wine in the season thereof,
and will recover my wool and my flax, given to cover
her nakedness." No one on reading Jay's sermon and
Durbin's sketch can deny the close conformity, and
there is no doubt that the outline was derived from Jay.
But even in the three main propositions there is a verbal
and real difference. The themes *are different.* The introduction of Dr. Durbin as given, no doubt about its
full length as preached, is entirely unlike that of Mr.
Jay. Then, in the progress of thought, it is seen how
Durbin extended, illustrated, and impressed truth in his
own way. Besides these differences in the most weighty
part of the discourse which the Doctor presents as the
peroration, we have the following points not recognized
in Jay:

1st. Let us be continually impressed with the constant agency of God in all our affairs.

2d. Let us make all our plans conform to his will,
that they may receive his blessing.

3d. Let us remember that all the instances of God's
goodness lead us to repentance.

4th. But if, through all these, we go down to hell,
how terrible will be our damnation !

Moreover, the Doctor's sermon is about three times
as long as that of Jay. His fruitfulness of thought, his
verbal affluence, and the mental independence that distinguished Dr. Durbin, together with the dissimilarity
of style, preclude thought of culpable plagiary.

The Lamb of God.

Among the great doctrinal discourses of Dr. Durbin, was one on the text, "Behold the Lamb of God, that taketh away the sin of the world." The *Atonement was his theme.* With what clearness, fullness, and force did he present the sin of *the world*, real, aggravated, damning; the sin of the heart and the life; the sin of unbelief and of rebellion; the sin, not of a color or clime, of a nation, but of a race; the sin that has run through the ages, and that as a tide surges in the streets and avenues of our cities, and that sometimes as really inundates the homes of the refined as the huts of the rude. This called Christ from heaven. He came to be led as a lamb to the slaughter. The paschal lamb had its significance and exerted a power; the sacrifices by the priests under the Levitical law impressed their moral lessons. But through the "Lamb of God" we have "eternal redemption." By his death on the cross he has made the pardon of sin a possibility. And no sin, however atrocious—no iniquity, however long indulged—no depravity, however deep and dire—is too great for the merit and might of Calvary.

Then, as a means of our saving benefits through the atonement made, he bade us "Behold the Lamb of God." Attempt nothing impossible; repose in no way upon the merit of good works, but with the soul concentered in his eye, "behold," not Moses, not Abraham, not the prophets, but Christ. To him look as the Author and Finisher of our faith. Though there is *sin*, and the *Lamb* that taketh it away, it is only by *looking* to this Lamb that the sin of our hearts and lives is removed. But as it is hunger that prompts the effort for food, as it is thirst that induces approach to the fountain, as it was peril that caused the man-slayer to flee to the city of refuge, so it is the felt need of Christ that makes beholding him of any avail.

But Dr. Durbin did not show the Lamb without the law. "The law was our school-master to bring us to Christ." He knew whence the law issued. Therefore to Sinai he took us. We heard its angry thunders mutter. We saw its lurid lightnings glare, the smoke was upon its summit, and even a Moses quaked with fear. But when he did this it was in sight of Calvary. Long centuries intervene between the convulsing of the one and the crimsoning of the other. But as a star may suddenly shoot athwart the midnight of gloom so in a moment the splendors of noonday may break from the darkest moral horizon, and we may be "all light in the Lord."

Fidelity to his calling constrained him to utter the fact, "God is angry with the wicked every day." But it was to induce the transgressor to lay hold of the hope set before him in the Gospel. Promises he brought to revive the spirit of the contrite ones. But whenever he entered the Bible, as a garden of the Lord, every rose that he plucked, every flower that he culled, every garland that he wove, was to deck the brow of Him whom malignity crowned with thorns. He understood his place. Sinai should only blaze that Calvary might bless; and such was the relation in which he placed us to each, that from the rending height of the one we beheld the bloody summit of the other, assured that a visit to Calvary would accomplish nothing without a sight of the mount that flashed and flamed. With such a beholding of the Lamb of God, in intensity of desire, in depth of penitence, in implicit faith, the brow that care had wrinkled was smooth, the heart that guilt had tortured found peace, and the spirit that had been ready to sink into the depths of despair rose in divinest rapture to the very bosom of God. Then did we so "behold the Lamb of God" that all other objects passed from our vision. We saw the meaning of *the atonement* and the function of faith. People were swayed like the trees of the forest before a mighty tempest. Men wept and praised, and it was as if God would now show something of what Isaiah saw when he said, "The posts of the door moved at the voice of him that cried, and the house was filled with smoke." The Rev. B. F. Crary, D.D., told the writer of the great grace that rested upon the people as Dr. Durbin preached from this text before the Illinois Conference, held at Paris, about 1853. During its delivery attention was fixed; interest was manifest and profound; but silence reigned except as the preacher's voice filled the place. It seemed as if the thoughts of others could almost be heard. There was a majesty in the man, there was a grandeur in the theme, and there was the conscious presence of the Holy Ghost in the assembly. The feeling that prevailed was like,

> "The speechless awe that dared not move,
> And all the silent heaven of love."

But who shall tell the effect at the close, when Dr. Durbin broke forth in his climax and quoted from Cowper, in his own matchless manner,

> " There is a fountain filled with blood
>   Drawn from Immanuel's veins ;
> And sinners, plunged beneath that flood,
>   Lose all their guilty stains.

> "The dying thief rejoiced to see
>   That fountain in his day ;
> And there may I, though vile as he,
>   Wash all my sins away ! "

He gave the entire hymn. The whole congregation, as they rose to sing, seemed full of the sense of the presence of the Holy Ghost. They took each other by the hand, and with gushing tears, and glowing hearts, and many almost speechless, stood on the verge of heaven. Bishop Ames, Peter Cartwright, and Peter Akers seemed as profoundly moved as any of the assembly.

Hope the Anchor.

To exhibit Dr. Durbin's claim to the highest style of eloquence, we name a sermon, the first the writer heard from him, delivered in the "Union," Philadelphia, on Sabbath morning, April 12, 1836, during the Conference. This church had a short time before been built on the site of the old "Academy" of Whitefield. Dr. Holdich had filled it as pastor. He had been succeeded by Charles Pitman. Both were at the height of their reputation. They were followed by the Rev. Samuel Kepler, transferred from the Baltimore Conference. It was the period and place of his greatest success. The edifice was in size and style unequaled in the Conference. In architecture and furniture it was such an advance upon any other Methodist "meeting house" in the Conference that some wondered if it was not a departure from our simplicity.

The pulpit was broad and of mahogany. It had a platform that was covered with Brussels carpet. Only a few years had elapsed since ingrain carpet on the pulpit steps of another of our churches had given offense. Of the Union Church Dr. Durbin, while editor of the *Christian Advocate and Journal,* thus writes, April 25, 1834: "It is certainly the most superb and convenient church I have seen among us. All the materials are select." The choir was sustained by the skill in singing

of James Harmstead and Samuel Ashmead, leading
members of the charge. The house was usually filled
with one of the most quiet and intelligent congregations in Methodism. As the seat of the Conference it
was now thronged by people and preachers anxious to
hear Dr. Durbin. It was a question whether we could
obtain a seat. How far the æsthetic taste of the
preacher exalted his thoughts in a temple of such attraction and associations, how much such an assembly
roused him, others may as well judge as the writer.
This we may say: the place, the occasion, the audience,
the theme, were well calculated to awaken every energy
of mind and heart.

The text was one of the grandest in the Bible, Heb.
6. 17–20: "Wherein God, willing more abundantly to
show unto the heirs of promise the immutability of his
counsel, confirmed it by an oath: that by two immutable
things, in which it was impossible for God to lie, we·
might have a strong consolation, who have fled for refuge
to lay hold upon the hope set before us: which hope we
have as an anchor of the soul, both sure and steadfast,
and which entereth into that within the vail." Difficult
as it now is to write of that sermon, it was then more
difficult to speak of it. The people heard it with attention, delight, and transport. The preacher showed that
the Christian has real, strong, everlasting consolation in
Christ. That we are in the world as the ship is in the
sea; that we as really need an anchor for the soul and
that we as truly have it. Storms arise, dangers threaten.
Satan allows "no sea of glass" in the present state.
Our anchor is hope. Its ground, the promise and the
oath of God. It is cast within the vail of the upper
temple, and as the anchor holds the ship so this holds
the soul. This shown, the preacher seized the anchor of
our hope as if it were of iron, and flesh were equal to

spirit.   Like a Samson of strength, with gesture and posture answering to his purpose, he gave one tremendous heave and shouted, "Brethren, it is within the vail!"   Judging from the accuracy of the aim, the impulse it received, the direction that it took and our own feeling, with the appearance of the preacher, we accepted his word.   Then he declared, "The ground is good and there is no dragging of the anchor."   He began to draw on the cable, the people joined him.   It was as if every one in the congregation would lay hold.   The preacher was more than himself.   His eyes like orbs of light rolled and flashed as if kindled by celestial fire. His countenance radiated.   Every feature spoke.   Every fiber of his frame seemed charged with an electrifying power.   Had Vinet been there he might have quoted this as one of the most perfect demonstrations of the power of "dramatismia" in the pulpit.   In that sermon was there lacking a single element of the sublime given by Longinus?   Was there not "grandeur in the thoughts;" "the pathetic;" "skillful application of figures;" "graceful manner of expression;" "and the structure or composition of all the periods in all possible dignity and grandeur?"   There is a lady in Philadelphia who, when we meet, speaks of that sermon as the joy of her life.

CHAPTER XIII.

Correspondence Concerning Dr. Durbin.

TO aid in conveying the best idea of Dr. Durbin's power as a preacher, as an educator, missionary secretary, etc., we present the reader with the following letters prepared for his biography.

The first we offer is from the Rev. John B. Merwin, D.D., the oldest effective minister in the New York East Conference. His father, the Rev. Samuel Merwin, was one of the distinguished Methodist ministers of his day. He availed himself of our first college for the education of his son.

The nation and Church were awakened, interested, and expectant by reason of the eloquence that distinguished the bar, the senate, and the pulpit. Webster, Clay, and their confreres were gratifying and training the taste of the public. In the Church the seraphic and sainted Summerfield had drawn together and fused into one assembly people of all denominations. Henry B. Bascom, grand in appearance, and by grandeur of oratory and argument, drew crowds that overflowed the largest churches. Among the attendants were found in large numbers lawyers and students of all professions. In the air there is borne a rumor of the equal of any of them, in the person of a young professor of Augusta College, Ky. In the summer of 1829, in Philadelphia, it is circulated that John P. Durbin is to preach in the Academy (the Union) on a Sunday morning. A member of its Sabbath-school, I occupied a front seat in the gallery, commanding a good view of pulpit and congregation. The house was filled. Unnoticed in his coming in, a quiet, neat, unpretentious man appeared in the pulpit. In every mind the question is, "Can this be he?" The hymns and Scripture were read, prayer offered with low and monotonous tones and peculiar cadence. The text was Heb. xi, 24, 25, "By faith Moses, when he was come to years, refused to be called the son of Pharaoh's daughter; choosing rather to suffer affliction with the people of God, than to enjoy the pleasures of sin for a season," was read more measuredly and in more drawling tones than his former readings, and ended with the rising inflection, and an instant full opening of the eyes. For half an hour, with voice and manner little changed, his statements were clear, his thoughts a chain of appropriateness, his expressions often of marked aptness and condensation, but all in language so plain and accurate that to mistake or misunderstand were impossible. The audience listened eagerly and inquiringly at first, then restfully and expectantly. A few concluded it was a disappointment, and here and there one and another left. Soon he stood erect, his voice took on strength, his eyes flashed with emotions—preacher and audience were transformed. In some way the attraction was felt in the street, and the seats were filled, and in the space between the pews and doors the people stood. After that when it was known he was to preach the throng came from every direction.

At this time commenced that acquaintance of Dr. Durbin with my father and family that became intimate.

In 1830 Dr. Durbin and family had been on a visit to Philadelphia. I had come home from Wilbraham, and arrangements were made for me to accompany him on his return to Augusta and enter the college there. In June Dr. Durbin and his wife, her sister, with a young lady of Augusta, who had graduated in a ladies' school in Philadelphia, and myself, started together from New York. By steamer we went to Albany. From there by stage to Schenectady, where we took boat on the Erie Canal to Buffalo. From Buffalo by steamer on Lake Erie to Painesville, and from Painesville across the State by stage to Millville on the Ohio, where we took boat for Augusta, which we reached in a little less ·

than a fortnight from New York. Our journey was so arranged as to avoid traveling on the Sabbath. We spent one day at Niagara, so the days of actual travel were about ten days and nights. The faculty took their turn in preaching. Once in about five weeks we heard Dr. Durbin. None were willing to lose their opportunity of hearing him. His statements and propositions were so lucid and manifest as to captivate assent. His manner disarmed your criticism, and you were left fully under his power as his imagination took wing, or he enforced the conclusion of his argument. The prevalent feeling left was, we ought and must be better, and we will.

If to know people we must travel with them, the opportunity was most perfectly furnished by the time and mode of this journey. The considerateness, genialness and affability, the playfulness and instructiveness in conversation of Dr. Durbin leave an impression unmarred and indeficient.

In a few days Joseph Longworth, of Cincinnati, Alexander Crawford, Mrs. Durbin's nephew, and myself were installed members of his family. As such we were treated and made to feel. Dr. Durbin was at that time editing Sir Charles Lyell's *Principles of Geology*, for J. & J. Harper, and we became participants of what was striking and special in this new science of wonderful disclosures, and in ways so easy and natural that it seemed like talking of the news that the daily papers furnished. Each was allured without embarrassment to express opinions or thought on any subject introduced, and to add from their own stock of reading, gossip, or invention.

The family devotions after breakfast completed the bond of home feeling and the kindliness that was enkindled and kept alive gave proof of its benediction. As professor and member of the faculty no feeling was entertained for him but the fullest respect. He regarded and treated the students as gentlemen. The spirit of mischief and fun that overflows in pranks of ringing the college bell in the night and introducing animals or effigies in the chapel, and such like, could never make him the object of its diversion. To do so would only be to have it return and plague themselves.

In the recitation room no intimation was given of his suspicions or intentional shrewdness when a passage was given to this one or that, or one was selected for the burden of the lesson, but it came to be felt that it was wise for each to be fully prepared. He favored a liberal translation in the reading of the Classics, but kept us to the grammatical construction, or secured proof that we knew how the sentence was to be parsed. There was a freshness and interest in the lesson that made the impression that he was both teacher and learner ; that we were pursuing the subject together, with this advantage to us: that he had mastered the subject, and was ready with the aid that we needed. Sometimes an incidental conversation and debate would elaborate itself into a lecture exhaustive of some point or fact. He was observant and thoughtful of the moral and spiritual interest of the young men, and for his kindly and timely counsel, unobtrusively given, many will hold him in grateful esteem more than for all things else.

Rev. Mr. Hebberd.

The following letter of the Rev. E. S. Hebberd, of the New York East Conference, gives an account of the earliest appearance of Professor Durbin in New York city :

I first saw and heard John P. Durbin about fifty-six years ago; he was then called Professor Durbin. The first time that I heard him was at a missionary meeting in the old Greene Street Church, New York. There were three speakers who addressed the meeting. The first was the Rev. J. Holdich, who made a very fine speech—clear, chaste, beautiful. The next was Rev. F. Hodgson. I thought those speeches were the best I had ever heard. Professor Durbin was announced, whom I did not then know even by reputation. He commenced his speech in a very tame, uninteresting manner. I pitied him, and wondered why they should put up so poor a speaker after the congregation had listened to such eloquent speeches. But as he proceeded, in a little time his face became radiant with intelligence, his eyes sparkled, and his words glowed with fire. I was entranced; such eloquence I had never heard before. The congregation was aroused with enthusiasm, and showed their appreciation of the orator by hearty old-fashioned Methodist shouts.

I heard James Harper, who afterward became mayor of the city of New York, describe his impressions the first time he heard Dr. Durbin. Mr. Harper was then a member of the old John Street Church. He said one Sabbath afternoon, after Rev. Peter P. Sanford had preached, he called upon a man whom he had never seen before to conclude the services. It was announced that Professor Durbin would preach this evening, who, he learned upon inquiry, had just dismissed the congregation. Mr. Harper said, "I made up my mind I would stay at home that evening. But before the service my friend, the Rev. Mr. Collord, who was then foreman of the printing department in the Book-room, called on me, and invited me to go with him and hear a great preacher. I said, "Although I had made up my mind to stay at home this evening, I will go with you to hear a great preacher. But where does he preach?" My friend replied, "In John Street." I said, "I beg you will have me excused. A dry college professor is going to preach there to-night; I heard him read and pray this afternoon." "Come along!" said Mr. Collord, "and after you have heard him if you do not pronounce him a great preacher you may charge the disappointment to me." I went and heard him, and during the first few minutes of his sermon I said to myself, "If he is Collord's great man I do not know where he will find his small men," when suddenly a flash of eloquence startled me. It seemed like a sky-rocket blazing in the heavens, and I said, "That is fine." Then he fell back for a few moments into his calm manner, and then came another sky-rocket, and ever and anon another, until the church became illuminated with brilliant thoughts and glowing eloquence, and as he concluded I said, "A great man indeed."

When, in 1832, the cholera was raging so terribly in many places and had not yet visited any part of New York State, the Governor of the State appointed a day of fasting and prayer, and called the people together in their several churches to pray that the cholera might be averted from our shores. A meeting was appointed in the Greene Street Church, and Rev. P. P. Sanford preached. After his sermon Professor Durbin exhorted; and such an exhortation! After dwelling on the dreadful ravages with thrilling power and showing that the victims were largely among the intemperate, he said with great earnestness: "But should the scourge visit us it would be one of the greatest auxiliaries the temperance cause has ever had, and were it not for the consideration that men have immortal souls I would say, "Good Lord, let it come." The effect of this speech on the congregation was thrilling, and sobs and crying were heard throughout the church.

I heard him about this time deliver one of his inimitable missionary speeches in New York. He announced his theme, "The Missionary Society the crowning theme of the nineteenth century." I can only say that that speech was the crowning glory of all the brilliant and eloquent missionary speeches that I ever heard, before or since.

I heard the Doctor deliver a Missionary speech before the New York East Conference in its session at Bridgeport in 1856. He dwelt in that speech largely upon the success of our missions among the American Indians. He said that in the early part of his ministry he was very much prejudiced against the Indians. He thought they were a cruel and treacherous race. He said that when very young in the ministry he was invited by a missionary, who was going to visit and preach to a tribe of Indians, to go with him. He accepted the invitation. He said: "As I sat in the stand, when the missionary was preaching, I fixed my eye upon a large, rough, hard-featured Indian, and when the missionary was dwelling upon the coil of sin and its consequences the Indian looked ugly and ferocious, and I said to myself, 'He is an ugly fellow; why preach the Gospel to such?' But when the missionary passed on to speak of the sufferings of Christ for sinful men, of redemption through his blood, the Indian's countenance changed, the tears started in his eyes and ran copiously down his cheeks, and he sighed audibly. I then looked around and saw others affected in a similar manner. I saw then that the red man had a heart that could feel the power of the Gospel of Christ, and ever since I have been a particular friend of the poor Indian." There were heard on that occasion, when the Doctor was delivering his eloquent speech before the Conference, loud amens and enthusiastic hallelujahs.

I heard the Doctor preach his great sermon on John i, 29, "Behold the Lamb of God, which taketh away the sin of the world," during the session of the New York East Conference in Hartford, Conn., in 1852. The sermon was preached in the largest Congregational church in the city. The church was crowded to its utmost capacity; the Governor of the State of Connecticut and many distinguished citizens were there. It was a great occasion, and the Doctor was in his happiest mood. The Rev. J. J. Matthias was present, and he was a precise man every way; of the strictest school of orthodoxy, and ever wakeful against the approach of heterodoxy. He sat in a chair near the pulpit, and as his eloquent brother would soar away in his brilliant flight he would move forward in his chair, as though he feared he would go beyond the bounds of orthodoxy, and then he would fall back with a look of satisfaction, as much as to say, "all right."

It seems to me that John P. Durbin, without going beyond the bounds of orthodoxy, was fifty years ago further advanced in progressive thought than any of the Methodist preachers with whom I am acquainted at the present day.

Again I was impressed with the fact that, while he ranked among the greatest pulpit orators of the world, there was a power in his moods of simplicity that all great orators do not have. In my youth I used to hear Bascom quite frequently. While he stood as high in the sublime flights of oratory, he could not descend with Durbin to what St. Paul calls " the simplicity that is in Christ." Bascom would not condescend to tell an anecdote in his sermons, he called those preachers who would "anecdote mongers." Durbin was not only grand and sublime, but was also beautiful and sometimes overwhelming in his simplicity.

I heard him in one of his grand missionary speeches in New York, in speaking of the folly of heathen worship, say, " If I had before me on this table some of the gods that the heathen worship, little, ugly, impy things, and should say 'These are the gods that made heaven and earth,' I do not ask what this intelligent congregation would say; but that little girl whose eye has been so steadily fixed on me during my speech would say, ' No, these are not the gods that made the heaven and the earth; for my mother and my Sunday-school teacher taught me the Lord God omnipotent made the heaven and the earth.' "

In a sermon delivered in New Haven during the session of the New York East Conference in that city, in 1859, I heard him relate his experience on his conversion. He said for some weeks he was under deep conviction for sin. In a protracted meeting at that time there was a young lady named Miss Prince converted; she was brought into the liberty of the Gospel so clearly, and told her experience so sweetly, that I thought I would like to be converted just in that way, and I prayed that the Lord would convert me just as he had converted Miss Prince; but the blessing did not come in that way. One day, as I was kneeling at the altar, I heard a man next to me say, ' Praise the Lord!' and I repeated it, ' Praise the Lord!' and then the blessing came, and I shouted, ' Glory to God!' and I found that I was not converted in Miss Prince's way, but in the Lord Jesus Christ's way." And there was no part of that great sermon that melted the hearers as that simple relation of his conversion. The experience of that great and good man was a great help to me in revival services, and I helped penitents into the kingdom by telling them how God converted John P. Durbin.

In regard to Dr. Durbin's gift in prayer, I remember that James Harper received a poor opinion of the doctor's talent after hearing him pray and before he heard him preach. My opinion is, that there were times when his prayers did not show a marked ability; but at other times in prayer he would have " the unction of the Holy One," and his prayers were attended with great power. I heard him pray previous to a sermon that I heard him preach in New Haven, and it was one of the most impressive prayers I ever heard. Although forty years ago, I remember some of the phrases of that prayer. He prayed with much fervor that nothing might occur to militate against the sacredness of that hour; that there might be no unusual noise, no alarming fire, but that we might quietly and without disturbance wait on the Lord. It seemed a prayer like those of Cornelius that came up for a memorial before God. The Rev. Otis Helland, of the Norwegian and Danish Conference, told me that he heard Dr. Durbin pray during the session of the General Conference of 1844, and, although nearly a half a century has past, he remembers that prayer. How earnestly and eloquently, in that day of her peril, he prayed for her union, her prosperity, her future welfare and usefulness!

One thing more I remember, nearly allied to this: Dr. Durbin's regard for the *pure* worship of God. I was present some years ago at the preachers' meeting in New York when the question was discussed of the impropriety of allowing some notices of secular character to be read from the pulpit. Dr. Durbin said when he was pastor he never read any notices in connection with the worship of God. The first thing he did when he entered the pulpit was to read the notices, and then say, " We will now commence the worship of God."

Another thing I observed in this brilliant and eloquent man was his impulsive extemporizing; his readiness to turn passing events to account. I heard him preach a Thanksgiving sermon on Thanksgiving afternoon, in the old Mulberry Street church. Toward the conclusion of his sermon a cloud came over the sky and brought twilight earlier than usual. He seized upon the departing light as a figure of the passing away of life's short journey, and poured forth a burst of the most charming eloquence I ever listened to. At another time I heard him deliver in New York one of his incomparable missionary speeches. He announced two propositions, and then said, "Allow me to digress a moment. A fresh thought strikes me;" and he continued uttering fresh and inspiring thoughts until he had consumed his time, and as he sat down he remarked he would at some future time deliver the speech he had prepared for that evening.

I did not in my former communication give an account of a sermon that I heard Dr. Durbin preach, on the Prodigal Son, in the Seventh Street Church in New York, in 1834. The discourse was very eloquent and produced a great effect upon the congregation; but I have a more distinct recollection of the application than any other part of that wonderful sermon. I remember how earnestly he pleaded with sinners to leave the land of famine and come home to their Father's house. He impressed upon them the *necessity of coming home now*, and quoting from our hymn-book; and who could recite Charles Wesley's poetry with such force and effect? The effect produced upon the audience when he, in his best style and with the unction of his peerless eloquence, quoted

> " All things are ready, come away:
> Ready the Father is to own
> And kiss his late-returning son ;
> Ready your loving Saviour stands,
> And spreads for you his bleeding hands.
> Ready for you the angels wait,
> To triumph in your blest estate."

And then he said, " Sinner, Gabriel is here now, waiting for your decision. What do you say, wanderer; will you come home? And then he bent forward in the attitude of a listener, as if waiting for the prodigal's answer; and then, changing his position and looking up, he cried in a tone of sadness, " O, Gabriel, the sinner says, 'No;' he will not come home." And, after a short pause, he said, "O, thou messenger of heaven, write not 'No' on the docket of eternity! Wait, angel of God, the sinner relents. I see the tear in his eye. Gabriel, the sinner says 'Yes;' the prodigal is coming home." Then, with expressive gesture and appropriate words, he represents God's angel as flying through the heavens and entering the pearly gates of glory to announce the good tidings. And then the eloquent preacher cried aloud, "Lift up your heads, O ye gates, and be ye lifted up, ye everlasting doors, that we may behold the joy of the happy hosts of glory, and hear the joyful notes of the heavenly choir singing, 'The dead is alive, the lost is found;'" and then, amid the sobs of penitents and the shouts of the redeemed, he sat down. It seemed as if we could look through the gates and see the happy immortals and hear their songs of rejoicing.

George Whitefield said something like this; Durbin might have taken some grain from his garner, but the kernels went through Durbin's mill and came out with his brand upon them; the voice, the action, the manner, the whole thing, was Durbinian.

Professor Durbin made his first appearance in New York as an eloquent and popular preacher about the time of my conversion, and from the first I took to him. His voice, his manner, his words charmed me, and helped me very much in my early Christian life. I once heard him address young men, and, with the much excellent advice which he gave them, he said, "Young men, lay up in youth a stock of useful knowledge. What I learned last week I have to learn over this week, but what I learned in my youth comes to me with the freshness of the morning. So, young men, what you learn now becomes part and parcel of yourself, and when you become old it will not depart from you." So I pondered over and cherished and laid up in my memory many of the sayings of this great and good man. I observed as closely as I was capable his doctrine, manner of life, purpose, faith, charity. This I observed also: that as a pastor, college professor, president, or missionary secretary, he always could say to all, with the apostle, "I am an ambassador for Christ: as though God did beseech you by me, I pray you in Christ's stead be ye reconciled to God." I observed, farther, in all his great missionary speeches that I was privileged to hear he loved to dwell upon the power of the Gospel in the conversion of the heathen. He would shame into repentance the impenitent living in Christendom by showing them the greater contrition of the heathen with inferior privileges. His eloquence and zeal were calculated to move the lukewarm professor to diligence by considering the work of grace and salvation going on in the regions beyond them. He showed his hearers that while they were feeling for and praying for the salvation of the pagan, and giving of their means to send the Gospel to them, their prayers and bounty would return to their own bosoms. Under the charm of his evangelical eloquence his hearers were made to feel (to borrow the language of an eminent divine) that while the love of distant nations glows in our hearts it melts us all down into love to each other, and burns up all jealousies and strife, and makes us workers together with Him who, though he was rich, yet for our sakes became poor, that we through his poverty might be rich.

Rev. S. A. Seaman.

Men fight their way to fame. The reputation of the young preacher from the West might not satisfy a New York audience, and we see in Rev. S. A. Seaman's letter the reasoning of strong men.

On Sabbath morning Rev. S. Merwin entered the church followed by a stranger of gentlemanly appearance, who occupied the pulpit. In reading the hymn and first Scripture lesson there was considerable apparent hesitation, and a disagreeable twang in his voice. The prayer, however, though marred by the same defects, abounded in rich thought and melting pathos. His text was the Song of Solomon iii, 2–4. As he proceeded his manner changed, he suddenly seemed to grasp a great thought, and in a moment was another man. The disagreeable twang disappeared, his voice rose, his eyes glowed, and his gestures were easy and natural. For nearly an hour he held his hearers enchained, and closed with an address to young Christians in which he referred to his own experience and the teaching and example of a godly grandfather. No one who remembers the Rev. J. P. Durbin will need be told that he was the preacher. My father used to tell of his going to John Street, one Sunday morning, and being told when he got there that a very able preacher was to occupy the pulpit. When the services began, however, there was such a drawl and twang in the preacher's voice, that he concluded the expected preacher had not come, and this was some raw backwoodsman who had been put in his place. But when the sermon was fairly begun my father was convinced that he was *the preacher*. This sermon of which my father speaks must have been among the first, if not *the* first, which Dr. Durbin preached in New York.

The following letter is from Rev. Thomas Bowman, D.D., LL.D., senior Bishop of the Methodist Episcopal Church. He was a member of the class of 1837, which was the first that graduated after Dickinson College came into our hands, and by the vote of the faculty was the valedictorian.

In personal appearance Dr. Durbin was not specially attractive. He was a little below the average in height, and his limbs were not well proportioned. His features were somewhat irregular, and when in a quiet mood were not very expressive. When, however, he became engaged in conversation or in a public address the whole man became entirely changed.

He was always approachable, and in a few minutes the fear excited by his prominence and reputation would disappear, and one would feel entirely at home in his presence. In his own house the visitor was made to feel at ease, and abroad he was always a welcome guest. After my first acquaintance with him I never felt any special restraint in his presence anywhere.

As a teacher I have never known his superior. He had a wonderful ability to communicate his ideas in plain, simple language, and in a most interesting and attractive manner. In the recitation-room we frequently started questions suggested by something in the lesson, sometimes, perhaps, to have a hard lesson laid over for another day, but generally for the information needed and desired. Before we were aware of it the hour would be gone, and as we retired to our rooms such expressions as these would be heard from every member of the class: "Wasn't that interesting!" "Worth a dozen recitations!" "Delightful!" "What a wonderful man!" I do not think that I ever heard a student complain of a dull hour in Dr. Durbin's room.

As president of the college, both in his administration and governing power the Doctor was fully up to the demands in the case. The institution was in its beginning with us, and every thing was in a formative state. It had failed thrice in the hands of other denominations, and our church in Carlisle was comparatively weak. The students were of a mixed character, representing various grades of society north and south. Indeed, every thing was in a crude state. But the wise and prudent president managed all the affairs with marked success. It is true he had a noble faculty, composed of Professors Caldwell, Emory, Roszel, Allen, and McClintock, whose equals are rarely found. But he secured and retained their confidence, respect, and love to such an extent that there was no division among them, and he had their hearty support to the end. He was equally successful in winning the confidence and respect of the students. He had a high sense of manliness and honor, and both by precept and example he imparted these to his students. He was firm and decided, yet kind and tender, and none but the most wayward were inclined to disobey him. On one occasion there was quite a rebellion among the boys. Under the leadership of a tall, courageous fellow, they marched into the campus, and after a fiery speech or two were ready for any thing. The president, having become aware of the trouble, came out of his office and made his way into the midst

14

of the enraged crowd. He spoke kindly but firmly of the impropriety of the course they were taking, and, having suggested a wiser and more honorable way, he asked them to retire to their rooms. In less than five minutes the campus was clear and we heard no more of war. A little incident in this writer's college history will illustrate the manly, honorable spirit of President Durbin.

My father having business in Harrisburg, and not having time to make me a visit, requested that I should be permitted to spend a couple of days with him. Leave of absence was obtained; but my father detained me a day or two beyond the time specified in my leave of absence. On my return late in the afternoon I sought the president in his office and at his home, to hand him father's letter of explanation. But I could not find him. Soon the evening prayer-bell rang, and I went to prayers, intending to hand him the letter at the close. Unfortunately, however, two or three students had been before the faculty for the violation of the rules during my absence. Immediately at the close of the service the president announced the penalty awarded those students, and added, "the case of Mr. Bowman has been laid over for further consideration." I was terribly mortified, and, handing him my father's letter, with explanations for not having given it sooner, I retired to my room, determined to pack up my books and go home. My chum and other students tried to dissuade me. But I said, "I cannot stay here under this open disgrace." In the evening the president, as he was passing through the building, called at my room and found me packing my things. "Why," said he, "what are you doing?" I frankly told him, and he said, "You had better take a little more time for reflection," and retired. This rather added to my grief. But the next morning after prayers he said: "Young gentlemen, I wish your attention for a moment. Last night I thoughtlessly committed a mistake which I wish as publicly to correct. I did injustice to Mr. Bowman, and I ask his pardon." This settled the whole matter. If he had said any thing like it even privately I would have been satisfied. As we retired from the chapel the students gathered around me and said, "You cannot go after such a manly and honorable apology." I felt so too, and Dr. Durbin stood higher in my respect and admiration and in the confidence of all the students.

But it was in the pulpit and on the platform that Dr. Durbin reigned supreme. During a period of nearly forty years I heard him speak in public under greatly varying conditions. I heard him in the country village, in the large towns and cities, at the camp-meeting, at the Conference, and at great public anniversaries; and I never heard him when he did not give me valuable instruction, move my emotional nature, and leave a lasting impress on my heart.

It is always difficult to analyze the elements of an eloquent speaker's power. In Dr. Durbin's case there seemed to be a wonderful combination of elements, no one of which could be positively said to be *the* source of his marvelous power over an audience. His discourses abounded in strong, practical thoughts, presented in clear, plain, pure English. In the beginning his voice was somewhat heavy and drawling, and his general delivery a little repulsive. After a little all that disappeared. His voice became clear and full, his action animated, his face radiant, his eyes enlarged, and his entire person almost transfigured. He was happy in illustration and had a wonderful power of description. I once heard him describe the destruction of Sodom in such a vivid manner that the whole scene seemed to be a living reality, and I a part of it. The great audience seemed to be similarly affected. One bright young skeptic, sitting just in front of me, became so powerfully affected that he could hardly contain himself. And yet, as I afterward heard him say, he went to the church fully determined that the great preacher should not move him.

The doctor's elocutionary powers were quite superior. His voice was rich, full, and melodious. His gesticulations were easy and natural. His features were remarkably variable and expressive. Indeed, the outward man was in full harmony with the inward, and both,

without any discord, combined to impress and inspire
the hearer.

Usually the introductory portions of his discourses
were considered rather dull and heavy. But they
were full of excellent expositions of Scripture and fine
thoughts bearing on the questions in hand, and always
preparatory for the eloquent descriptions and applica-
tions that were to follow. The disappointment of the
hearers in the beginning was largely attributable to the
fact that he rarely threw himself into his subject until
he had briefly stated the line of thought he intended to
present. But when the great questions that were in
the mind of the speaker were clearly and fully given
to the minds of the people, they were prepared to appreciate and enjoy the wonderful bursts of eloquence
that would follow like flashes of lightning across the sky.

His sermons, though not written, were thoroughly
prepared, and the leading thoughts were clearly and
impressively presented to his hearers. While preaching he looked at the people and talked as naturally as
he would with a company of friends in his parlor, or
with his class in the recitation room. Hence he measurably read their thoughts and knew where their minds
and hearts were. Thus the speaker and hearers were in
hearty sympathy with each other; and when his mind
and heart were full of the inspiration of his theme, they
were ready to receive the electric currents as they
flowed out from him. I never heard a speaker who
thrilled me as did Dr. Durbin, or left upon my mind
and heart so many clear, solid, and abiding impressions.

A few incidents will show how others regarded his
power as a public speaker.

In his early ministry he was sent to a prominent town
in Indiana. On his arrival he was entertained by one
of the leading families of our Church. Soon after his
introduction to his hostess her husband found her in an
adjoining room weeping. "Why," said the husband,
"what is the matter?" "O," said she, "to think
that I have been for weeks praying that the Lord
would send us a good preacher that we might have a
precious revival, and now to see what a man has

come!" On Sabbath, however, the unpromising young man swept every thing before him, and the good lady, with the rest of the audience, had a glorious hour. As she left the church she exclaimed, "Glory to God! He knew better than we what kind of a man to send us."

About the time the doctor was retiring from the college I heard him preach in one of the large towns of Pennsylvania, where I had on former occasions heard two of the most eloquent preachers of that day. The next day I met a prominent lawyer, afterward one of the supreme judges of the State, whom I had seen at church on Sabbath, and whom I had seen present also when the other two preachers were heard. I said to him, "How did you like Durbin's sermon yesterday?" "O!" said he, "it was magnificent!" I said, "I think you heard two other distinguished preachers"—naming them. "Which do you think is the greatest preacher?" "All three of them," said he. "You cannot compare them. Each is greatest in his line. Durbin, I think, has the greatest moving power."

Some time after this, while the doctor was the pastor in Union Church, Philadelphia, this same lawyer spent a Sabbath in the city. He invited a prominent lawyer friend from another part of the State to go with him to hear Dr. Durbin. After the friend had heard the doctor talk a few minutes he wished to retire, saying, "We will get nothing specially interesting here." But he was persuaded to remain. In a little while he was seen leaning forward, his hands grasping the seat before him, his eyes and mouth open, and he almost upon his feet. At the close of the sermon he settled back upon his seat, and whispered to his companion, "I never heard the like of that!"

On one occasion, at a camp-meeting in the Cumberland Valley, I heard the doctor preach a sermon of marvelous power. As in a few other instances, his discourse was intensely interesting and attractive from the beginning. Although it was about two hours long there was not the slightest sign of uneasiness or weariness in the great congregation. About the middle of the sermon the mass of the people unconsciously rose to

their feet, pressed around the pulpit, and stood spell-
bound to the end. At one time, while he was describ-
ing the condition of the lost, an intelligent, well-edu-
cated lawyer standing near me grasped a tree against
which he was leaning and began to climb it. Three
times I had to pull him down, and after the close of
the services he could not be made to realize the condition through which he had passed.

On the platform as well as in the pulpit the doctor
was rarely equaled, and never, I think, excelled. His
Sunday lectures in the college always drew a crowd of
citizens and students, and they seldom retired without
feeling that their fullest expectations had been realized.

On several occasions at missionary anniversaries I
heard the doctor speak in connection with several of
the most distinguished platform speakers of the day,
and, in every instance I think the general judgment was
that his address was fully equal to the best.

The following letter from a distinguished layman of
New York city may justly follow that of Bishop Bowman, as it shows a like spirit to that which so affected the
young Bowman:

An illustration of his wisdom as well as kindness in
compassing his ends in the government of a college was
furnished by a gentleman of Mississippi, well known for
his genial hospitality, charming manners, and literary
culture, who used to tell how, as a boy and through life,
he had cause to love Dr. Durbin most gratefully for his
wise counsel, kind forbearance, and discreet use of authority. While a student at Augusta College in Kentucky he was inclined to show more devotion to fishing
and shooting than to study. Professor Durbin, who
was then acting as president of the institution, had
vainly endeavored to lead him to a better observance
of academic rules, but the young gentleman, in the ex-
uberance of health and spirits, continued to be careless
of discipline until one day, while engaged in some
sports on the grounds, he heard a window raised and
himself summoned, in the peculiarly mild but firm

and controlling voice of the professor, to come to his room. Professor Durbin there read to him a letter which he had carefully prepared for the young man's father, setting forth clearly and with affectionate regret the shortcomings of the pupil, and advising that the boy should return to his home and remain there until he was better prepared for the discipline and steady work of earnest school-life. The young man was asked if there was any thing in the letter which was not just. "No!" he frankly answered, "the letter is just and fair in every way, Professor Durbin ; all I ask is, that you will withhold it for one month, and give me the opportunity to redeem myself in your eyes and save my dear father from the pain which such a letter would inflict upon him." The wise and kind professor never had occasion to send the letter or to again remonstrate with his young friend, whose devotion to his books soon equaled his devotion to sports. He was graduated with distinction at a northern university, and became well and widely known as an honored and useful citizen of his State.

Doubtless during the many years that Dr. Durbin was a teacher he had many such cases to manage ; and doubtless, too, he managed them with wisdom, discretion, forbearance, and tact, and, above all, with that kindness united with firmness so characteristic of his administration of many enterprises better known to the world, perhaps, but surely not more useful and important than the training of the young and the development of manly character.

The following letter is from one of the early graduates of Dickinson College, the Rev. C. F. Deems, D.D., pastor of the Church of the Strangers, New York. It was prepared for the biography of Dr. Durbin, though published in *The Christian Advocate:*

My father was a local preacher in the Methodist Episcopal Church. It was natural that he should send me to the new Methodist college under the great preacher, that I might receive my education. I was

five years in Carlisle—one in the preparatory department and four in the college—and therefore came in
sight of Dr. Durbin and under his influence when he
was in the prime of his power. Wonderful were the
advantages of the boys who lived in that college town
at that period. Apart from the scholastic advantages
there were the immense church privileges.

Dr. George Duffield was at the Presbyterian church,
a man of rare learning and great skill in preaching.
Dr. McGill, since of Princeton College, was preaching
to a small congregation, I believe of Covenanters.
Young as I was, I was struck with the contrast between
the smallness of his congregations and the massiveness
of his discourses. Two years of the time the Methodist pastor was the Rev. George G. Cookman, one of the
most thrillingly eloquent preachers of his denomination.
In the college were Drs. McClintock and Emory, two
young, gifted, and accomplished professors, who had
the stimulus of alternating with such men as Durbin
and Cookman. No mortal man in any age of Christianity, I am persuaded, ever enjoyed superior church
privileges, so far as preaching was concerned, to those
at the command of students in Carlisle from 1834 to
1839.

The chief of these pulpit princes, by great odds, was
the Rev. Dr. Durbin. I have never studied any man
so closely to find out his methods as Dr. Durbin; and
yet, putting together all I have thought through the
nearly half-century since I first knew him, I find it
difficult to give a satisfactory analysis. His physique
was not at all impressive. An orator should be large.
Indeed, size in a man counts every-where. In public men
the lack of the last half foot can be compensated only by
doubling the brain-power. Dr. Durbin was small. He
did not have that brow which is supposed to be the throne
of thought. He lacked the great nose by which Napoleon set great store. His eye was very pleasant, but not
striking, when he was in repose. His manner was a
little finical, his voice was not very musical, and his
utterances at the beginnings of his discourses were
made with a drawl. Yet, being a man like that, he

would begin his sermons in an elocution which is a cross between a Quaker intonation and the hard-shell Baptist whine, and succeed in almost immediately arresting the attention of his hearer by making the appearance of a cat-like approach upon his intellect. The hearer would watch to see what was coming next, and felt very much like a mouse that knew that the distance between the cat and himself had diminished, but was afraid to run lest any motion should provoke the dreaded sudden spring.

Then there came a period in which the attacking party moved from side to side, apparently, and did not make much additional approach. Then there was a moment of stillness, and then there was a bound, not as of a cat on a mouse, but as of a tiger on some nobler game, producing a thrill that made all the vegetation of the jungle tremble.

I can think of no other figure to describe my remembrance of the style of this remarkable man. So sudden and so prodigious would be those shocks that I have seen whole congregations swayed by them. Twice in my junior years I sat and watched the approach, and just as it came sprang to my feet to meet it. The word magnetic is sometimes used about men, generally very loosely, I think. I have met only two men who to me were magnetic; namely, Henry Clay and John P. Durbin. In my boyhood I could never see Mr. Clay rise from his seat to speak without having a nervous chill, although I heard him only in his declining years. So John P. Durbin drew me, thrilled me, filled me, and in a large measure formed me. I am sure he could not have done this merely through the great kindness which he always showed me in the class-room, in his own study, in his home, and when I began to preach, if there had not been behind it all a remarkable force of intellect. I could not call that intellect profound. It was searching, analytic, practical, forceful. He was a student of books and a student of men. He was a man of affairs as well as a man of pious offices. Rarely do men who had his oratorical powers succeed in business matters as Dr. Durbin I know succeeded in the presidency of the college, and, as I think his Church believes, as he succeeded as a great missionary secretary.

I cannot conceive how any printed sermon of his would give any adequate impression of his genius as an orator to one who had not heard him. His most powerful passages were really like claps of thunder out of a clear sky. Men have set themselves to watch him, but have found themselves like hunters who were so absorbed in the rush of the deer that they forgot to fire the rifle.

I remember that on one of the hottest days I ever felt in Philadelphia I saw a congregation actually almost asleep during his introduction, who all seemed to wake up and turn to him with brightened eyes at the first explosion of his oratorical battery. It is much easier to describe phenomena than to assign causes or explain methods.

Dr. Durbin prepared his sermons carefully, ordinarily spoke from a brief, and largely engaged himself in tracing the soundness of what he had learned from books by his application thereof to his current knowledge of human nature, which he had seen under many phases. I have gazed upon most of the constellations of pulpit oratory in America and in Europe. To this day, in memory and imagination, John P. Durbin stands as the one particular star, divinely bright, always beaming with something of the radiance of that glory of God which shines in the face of Jesus.

I do not think that this estimate of him is greatly exaggerated by my affection, since we met very seldom in the last forty years of his life. If I spoke of him as a teacher I should pronounce his distinguishing characteristic to be the power of stimulating the intellects of his students. The moment he found one of the class interested in the question he would drop every thing else, and perhaps lose the whole recitation, in order to discuss that question with him. Having discovered that, and having found that I was particularly able somehow to get into a metaphysical discussion with the doctor, our class in its senior year put me forward two or three times when their preparations were not very complete, to start a question with the doctor and argue with him by the space of ten minutes. That was all that was necessary. The rest of the hour was spent in a thrilling, glowing discussion of the question in hand. I ought to say, perhaps, that my occasional deficiency of preparation to be questioned increased my zeal in these questioning exercises.

At last one day Dr. Durbin said to me, with his peculiar intonations which must be supplied by those who heard him :

"Mr. Deems, do you not think that you and I may be a little selfish? I have noticed now for several mornings that you and I have taken up the whole hour in discussions in which we both were very much interested, but it had the result of cheating the class out of recitation. If you will come to my room after recitation we will discuss this question which you have just asked, but we must not take up another hour with *our* little debating society."

And then he went in on me and the other fellows through the rest of the recitation, absolutely refusing to explain any thing, and demanding that we should explain every thing.

I need not tell any student in psychology that that treatment cured me of my little trick, which will probably be pardoned, as it was almost the only mischief of my college course—a course without a single lark, a single hair-breadth escape, a single dramatic or picturesque situation; a course which was probably as barren of mischief as any ever passed in collegiate walls.

It gives me pleasure at this late date to lay this humble tribute on the grave of my old master.

Some recollections of J. P. Durbin, from Rev. W. Lee Spottswood, D.D. Dr. Spottswood was one of the early graduates of Dickinson, under Dr. Durbin:

How carefully we keep the recollections of departed friends! Such recollections are rich treasures. It is a pleasure at fitting times to bring them from their storehouse and show them.

Dr. Durbin was chargeable with artifice; but like the cunning of St. Paul, when he wrote to the Corinthians, "Being crafty, I caught you with guile," it was sinless. When he had prepared a sermon he knew that he had something worthy of being said, and he desired very properly to say it to as many hearers as possible. So he had—for students, at least—a notification of his being booked to preach somewhere. It was this: the wearing at Sunday morning prayers in the college chapel of a white cravat, never worn under any other circumstances. The students knew the sign, and asked, "Where does the president preach to-day?" And they always flocked to the church indicated to hear him.

He could in a public assembly, with well-trained skill, seize a circumstance and make it tell with great effect. In the Eutaw Street Church of Baltimore, many years ago, he spoke on a platform to a crowded congregation met in the interests of the Tract Society. In the very torrent, tempest, and, as I may say, whirlwind of his passion, he cried out, "I would rather, Mr. President, that a young man would read novels than never read at all." Bishop Waugh said, "Doctor, I have been told of your making that remark before, and I thought that if I had been present I would have rebuked you. Now I am here, and I have heard you for myself, and I rebuke you." When the Bishop took his seat up sprang Dr. Durbin and excitedly replied, "What I want, Mr. President, is to give the mind a start; it is then in the wrong direction, to be sure, but I hope to head it off and turn it back and press it into the right course." His reply brought down the house.

He was an interesting teacher. His lecture-room was not a place to suffer a burden, but one to enjoy a real pleasure. He was a shrewd instructor as well. In the spirit of students, every-where and in all times, who will go to more trouble to avoid a lesson than to learn it, our class, in order to escape a recitation, used to provoke a controversy on some point suggested by the author studied. Dr. Durbin would take the bait readily, enter the arena of debate with a will and keep up, with keen

jest and great vigor, the wrangle till the ringing of
the college-bell told the wranglers that the hour for
recitation in his room had ended. Then the president,
with that peculiar smile of his, almost an agreeable
grin, showing all his front teeth, would blandly say,
"Gentlemen, if you please, get to day's lesson over,
with so much in addition." And we, green students as
we were, would leave, chuckling in the belief that by
trickery we had foiled our teacher. But now, after
more than one third of a century in pondering the
matter, we know full well that he was not foiled a whit.
The wise president knew what he was about; he was
aware that such a discussion, awakening thought and
making it all alive, requiring intellectual skill, demanding the application of knowledge, and calling every
mental gift into exercise, was far better than any mere
recitation from a text-book.

He was an accomplished declaimer. The writer has
heard him at a church-meeting, where several exercises
were in progress, declaim with the correctness and action
of a true elocutionist, and with the fire of religious emotion burning in his heart, the whole hymn commencing

> "Sinners, turn; why will ye die?
> God, your maker, asks you why!"

The effect of his declamation was profound. He was a
genuine orator. In his oratory, however, was reversed
the usual order of things, often named, "After a storm
there is a great calm." His order was, After a great
calm a storm. One of the young men who accompanied
him on his European tour used to tell of the doctor's
first sermon in England. The preacher lingered so long
in his uninteresting way that his fellow-tourists began
to fear that he would linger in that way to the end, as
he sometimes did, and that his sermon in consequence
would be a marked failure. But no; the sign was given,
up went the right arm, crossed over to the other side,
and struck hardly the palm of its hand upon the left
breast. Then burst the oratory suddenly, and rolled on
continuously, to the wonder and rapture of all his
hearers. Forty years ago, when a mere lad, the writer

heard Dr. Durbin, then in his prime, preaching at a camp-meeting. His text was, "That at the name of Jesus every knee should bow, of things in heaven, and things in earth, and things under the earth; and that every tongue should confess that Jesus Christ is Lord, to the glory of God the Father." The impression made upon the relater, especially by the concluding portion of that sermon, can never be effaced. It is as clear to-day as it was in the long ago. On that Sabbath morning the orator's voice very soon lost its drawl, monotone, and tameness, and then reaching the richest tones it rang out rapidly, clearly, and in the fullest volume. His eloquence came "like the outbreaking of a fountain from the earth, or the bursting forth of volcanic fires, with spontaneous, native, original force." And his peroration was a picture inspired by a vivid imagination, and so graphically word-painted by the aid of superior descriptive talent in its best estate that it seemed a picture of terribleness, real and present to the sight, and the writer remembers that a tremor passed all over him, as it did, no doubt, over others also. . . . Longfellow, in *Morituri Salutamus,* says:

> "The great Italian poet, when he made
> His dreadful journey to the realms of shade,
> Met there the old instructor of his youth,
> And cried in tones of pity and of ruth,
> 'O never, from the memory of my heart,
> Your dear, paternal image shall depart:
> Who while on earth, ere yet by death surprised,
> Taught me how mortals are immortalized:
> How grateful am I for your patient care
> All my life long my language shall declare.'"

And the author of this simple *In Memoriam* repeats, as all other pupils of Rev. John P. Durbin, D.D., at the mention of his name, will also repeat:

> "To-day we make the poet's words our own,
> And utter them in plaintive undertone."

The following is from the Rev. J. H. Hargis, D.D., of the Philadelphia Conference:

On the occasion of his last visit to Carlisle, during the last session preceding the Wilmington division of the old Philadelphia Conference, convened in Harrisburg, March, 1866, Dr. Durbin, as a member of the Conference and first president of the college under the Methodist *régime*, came from Harrisburg, an hour's ride to Carlisle, to fill his appointment for the Sunday-morning sermon in Emory Chapel. It was largely descriptive of the Tabernacle, delivered distinctly, with deliberation suited to his time of life, and in a narrative style. The remarkable feature of the discourse was the facial expression of the preacher when he reached the climacteric description of the Shekinah. His eyes dilated and illuminated with a light that never was seen on sea or land. His face was transfigured and "did shine as the light," and the congregation was entranced with the shining splendor of his person until the venerable form, with closed eyes, was bowed in the final prayer.

The following is from Rev. Thomas H. Burch, D.D., member of the New York East Conference :

Residing for a term of years in New York, he often officiated in the pulpits of that city and its vicinity. I heard him frequently—in fact, whenever it was practicable. But of these eagerly coveted opportunities two left a deep and lasting impression on my memory because of certain extraordinary features which I want briefly to describe.

The first of these sermons was delivered at the dedication of a church in Brooklyn. It was a bright and balmy Sunday morning in June. The congregation filled the audience-room; even the aisles were crowded with the occupants of chairs and camp-stools, while a considerable number were obliged to be content with standing-space about the doors. Several clergymen were present, some of whom conducted the preliminary exercises. Then Dr. Durbin announced his text: "Behold the Lamb of God, which taketh away the sin of world!" He began with the characteristic drawl, though much abridged, however, in this instance, and soon

passing into various vivacious tones. The earlier part
of the discourse was largely taken up with references to
Old Testament scriptures, familiar to most hearers, yet
so put as to fix attention and excite growing interest.
Perhaps he was never more animated: form erect, face
flushed, eyes rolling in a way peculiar to him in higher
moods of thought and expression; in short, each tone
and movement betokened rapt absorption in his theme
as he advanced from one period to another with telling
force. At length the turning-point was reached, in effectiveness at least, when the preacher introduced a
touching narrative, quite simple in its materials, but
used with masterly skill. In substance it was this:

Some years ago while in Cincinnati he had been
asked to visit a dying man, a stranger in the city, cut
off from Christian association and sympathy. Agreeably
to this request, at midnight the visitor climbed seven
flights of stairs to the top floor of a high building,
where he found the sick man, obviously in the last
stages of mortal disease. Although religiously educated he was much disturbed concerning the great
hereafter; for, having been caught in the meshes of the
Calvinistic theory, not daring to count himself among
the elect he could see no room for hope. His visitor
made no attempt to reason away these gloomy impressions other than by citing pertinent Scripture passages,
especially the words, "Forasmuch as the children are
partakers of flesh and blood he also himself likewise
took part of the same." I remember asking myself
at the time whether that was the most felicitous quotation
to be used in the circumstances; but as it was repeated
slowly, and then the question put more than once with
most persuasive emphasis, "Are not *you* a partaker of
flesh and blood?" all doubt vanished. Assuredly that
was the exact passage demanded. The dying man caught
the meaning, and clinging to it, lost his fears in blissful
confidence, affirming that he could fearlessly trust himself to his Saviour. The effect of this recital was
electrical. Sitting where I could see the whole congregation, there seemed not so much a wave of emotion
sweeping gradually over it as a down-rush of feeling

simultaneously touching and melting every person in the house. For so wonderfully vivid and graphic was the picture that each felt himself a witness of the scene ; each looked into the face of the dying man, heard him cough, listened to the fervid words of his counselor, saw the troubled expression change into one of sweet tranquillity; in short, realized the whole at once. As also when the preacher added that, going the next morning to the stranger's room, he found him dead, but on his face a smile of a soul that had entered into rest, every one *saw that smile.*

Thereafter the speaker swayed the audience at his will. The merit of the sermon was sustained to the end ; but had it fallen off, or had the discourse been greatly lengthened, not one would have become impatient It was a rare triumph of oratory.

When the people were dismissed, a brother, then assistant pastor of the dedicated church, but since serving with distinction in another denomination, a man of considerable phlegm, and strong self-control, came up to me, his eyes swollen with weeping, and exclaimed, " What a wonderfully effective discourse ! "

That was the first occasion. The second, following an interval of not more than six weeks or two months, differed very widely from the former. Indeed, the strange and strong contrast of the one with the other has chiefly prompted this letter.

About the time referred to some persons in the city of New York united in an effort to promote a larger attendance at public worship, particularly among non-church goers. For this purpose several churches in the lower part of the city were induced to open their doors for Sunday-afternoon services, and eminent preachers were sought for to insure the success of the project. Dr. Durbin preached to one, if not more, of these afternoon congregations; for then I heard the second of the two sermons I am writing about. As said above, this was strikingly unlike the first. One point of resemblance, however, was noticeable at the outset; namely, the text, which was the exact language used before. The opening sentences, too, suggested

15

that the sermon to follow might be similar. To me that was no disappointment. On the contrary, a repetition of what he esteemed the most powerful discourse he had ever heard would afford a young minister, eager to learn all the mysteries of the sacred art, a more favorable opportunity to penetrate the secret of the great preacher's power. Well, the sermon proved to be the very same, and yet how different! Identical in structure, in agreement, in illustration, in diction, in every literary aspect, nevertheless, it fell so far short of the mighty utterance first heard as to be altogether another and vastly inferior thing. Possibly there were verbal differences, perhaps even minor changes in illustration, but I did not perceive them; most assuredly the same in substance, but by comparison how tame, and stale, and dull! There came, too, in due order, the story of the dying man, identical in *form*, but all the pathos and power lacking. Nobody seemed moved by it; even the preacher appeared to have no special interest in it. Yet there it stood in the right place, a mere memory, a sort of ghost! So to the end—except that in the first sermon some concluding sentences were especially conformed to the dedicatory character of that service—to the end the second was a reproduction of the first in every particular, so far as I was able to note, save *effectiveness*. The man sitting next to me drowsily nodded from time to time. In seats to the front several persons were asleep. Sheer amazement at the contrast between the two deliverances of the same message, if nothing else, kept one hearer wide awake.

I left the church thoroughly puzzled. Of course, due allowance ought to be made, on the one hand, for the greater inspiration of the first event, and, on the other, for the less favorable time of day when the second discourse was delivered. So, too, it might be surmised that the physical condition of the preacher was not good, though of that there was no sign.

But after every concession the strange discrepancy still remained perplexing. Even now I cannot solve the problem with any satisfaction to myself. Can you?

The following is from the Rev. L. F. Morgan, D.D., member of the Baltimore Conference, and one who had known Dr. Durbin from the time of his entering upon the presidency of Dickinson College:

I regard Dr. Durbin as the extraordinary man of the extraordinary men of his time; the greatest orator and organizer the Church has produced. I have heard almost every preacher and statesman who has risen to eminence in the country for the last fifty years. Durbin was the first to measure up to my conception of the power of eloquence in a sermon preached at the Baltimore Conference, in the city of Winchester, Va., in the spring of 1835. I never lost an opportunity of hearing him afterward. My admiration made me seek to know him in the early years of my ministry. I was honored with his friendship, and frequently had his services in the pastoral charges I served. When I was stationed in the city of Washington he preached for me in the Foundry Church. The building had recently undergone repairs. An immense audience crowded the place of worship. The girder of the end gallery broke with a crash, which produced the wildest consternation. Almost every one left the house; but when they saw from the outside that the walls and roof were all right they crowded in again, and were soon made to forget every thing but the "Lamb of God, which taketh away the sin of the world." Contrary to his usual rather prosy opening, he seemed at the very outset to catch the inspiration for which he was remarkable in reaching his climaxes, which were often overwhelming to his audiences.

As an organizer of church-work he excelled as much as he did in pulpit eloquence. The great missionary scheme for the conversion of the world to Christ operated by the Methodist Episcopal Church is a monument to his genius. For generations to come he will be recognized as the great missionary secretary. It is no disparagement to those who have filled the office since he vacated it to say that he has not had an equal, and he of the future who shall rival him must be blessed with the opportunity of developing agencies now unknown to the work of evangelization.

The Rev. Benjamin F. Price, of the Wilmington Conference, a minister of more than fifty years, thus writes of Dr. Durbin:

In him simplicity, courtesy, and dignity of manners seemed to find perfect exemplification. In the gallery of great men I look upon Dr. J. P. Durbin as the highest portrait. And I am willing to be criticised, if any have the temerity to do it, when I say that as a preacher, if he had any equal among his contemporaries, none surpassed him. And in all the qualities that give efficiency to manhood he abounded and excelled. In nothing, it would seem, was his life a failure; he honored every post he filled. As college professor and president, as editorial journalist, as missionary secretary, as representative in church councils, as presiding elder, and as pastor and preacher, simplicity, clearness, grandeur, and power, were elements that made his eloquence the wonder of his hearers. If he did sometimes speculate in the pulpit it was never in a way to mystify the subject; he was always sure to make his meaning plain, and even if you disagreed with him, which was seldom the case, you were at no loss to understand him, and you were fascinated by his ingenious methods of illustration and argumentation. His eloquence in the pulpit was like a gale full of odors; the stars flashed and the electric chords made music as the current passed. On the Conference floor he was the statesman and philosopher. When a question seem tangled and tied in knots, and it was necessary to understand the situation, Dr. Durbin would calmly rise, and by his wonder-working analysis not only unravel the web, but present its various phases with such skill of exposition that the perplexity would cease and the end of the debate was reached; the vote was taken without dissent, and while the older men would smile with satisfaction, the younger ones wondered in admiration. He has disappeared from our midst, but the trail of a comet will radiate the moral firmament for half a century.

The following letter is from the Rev. O. H. Tiffany, D.D. Few ministers had stood in so close a relation to Dr. Durbin as the writer of this letter:

Once on paying a visit to Chambersburg, Pa., Mr. Seibert, a venerable member of our Church residing there, took me to see the *physical proofs* of Dr. Durbin's eloquence. We went to the old brick church, then standing, and he pointed out to me the sockets of the outside fastenings of the shutters: they were many of them deprived of the irons which they formerly held, and some of them gave clear and unmistakable evidences of force and violence used in their removal. Mr. Seibert then told me the following story. He said that Dr. Durbin preached there one bright and sunny Sabbath, when the windows were all raised on account of the heat, and the blinds all closed on account of the sunshine. The doctor preached on "the coming of the day of judgment," and drew a vivid picture of the consternation wrought on a city full of people; he then passed to note the effect on a village hamlet, and depicted with rare skill the coming just at the moment when an aged man was holding family prayer, and pleading for an only son far away from home; then, turning suddenly, he exclaimed, "Where is that wandering boy?" and traced an imaginary journey, till at last he found him on a ship at sea, keeping his watch alone on deck. As the young man looks up to the stars suddenly the heavens are parted as a scroll; the audience heard the tearing, ripping, of the skies as a piece of parchment cracks when it is torn, and became violently agitated. No one knew whether a passing cloud momentarily obscured the sun or not; but the whole assembly rose as one man and rushed to get out of the building, paying no regard to the doors, but pressing against the closed shutters, which were wrenched off from their fastenings by the hurrying crowd; the utmost consternation prevailed, and many persons were more or less injured, but none seriously. I once asked Dr. Durbin about it,

but he would say nothing except that " there was some
excitement."

When Dr. Durbin returned from his trip to the East
there was a great desire on the part of the college and the
citizens of Carlisle to make some fitting demonstration
in his honor. I was then a student there, and had the
proud distinction, as I then felt it to be, to be placed
on the committee of reception. I was on the sub-com-
mittee of illumination, and we succeeded in placing
a lighted candle at each window-pane in all the
windows of the college buildings. The town was
alive with excitement, and on the arrival of the
Doctor, in the forepart of the day, after he had
been seen by the members of his family, he was told
something of the plans for the celebration. He at once
sent for me and forbade the illumination, on the ground
of the danger to which the buildings would be exposed
in case of fire. I pleaded with him not to disappoint
us in our cherished plans, told him all the money had
been already spent for candles and necessary fixtures,
and said the disappointment would be intense. For a
long time he would not yield, but finally consented, on
condition that some person should be placed at each
window with a bucket of water, and not to leave the
place until all the lights were out. Very many of the
students were thus deprived of the chance to greet the
Doctor in the reception, and grumbled accordingly;
but we had the illumination and counted it a great
success. This will suggest the extreme diligence of the
Doctor in looking after details. No man was ever more
scrupulous in his attention to the little things which go
to make up more conspicuous results, and no man more
sincerely in earnest in carrying out his plans to success.

Little details sometimes help to depict a man. He
always dressed in the morning for the principal event of
the day; would put on his best suit at breakfast-time if
he was to wear it to an evening entertainment. So on
Sundays if he was to preach anywhere during the day
he would appear at morning prayers in the chapel in a
white cravat. On such occasions there would be an
immense rush of students to discover where he was en-

gaged, and to secure permission (necessary in those days) to attend. Closely watching him I discovered that if he was to preach in the morning his cravat would be nicely folded and securely tied so as to conceal the knot, but if he was not to preach until evening he would have it carelessly wound about his neck in less fastidious fashion. I made use of my observation, and seldom made the mistake that others constantly made in attempts to hear him. As I became familiar with him, by being employed to transcribe his journals when he was preparing them for publication, he once, when I asked for the customary permission to attend some other than my own church, said to me, "Tiffany, how do you always manage to find out when and where I am to preach? I wish you would tell me, for I try not to have it published." I said to him : "Doctor, you always tell me *when* you are to preach, and it is easy to discover *where*." "I tell you!" he exclaimed, with astonishment, "I tell you! Why, I never told you in my life, and yet every-where I go I always find you there." Then I told him about his always wearing a white cravat on preaching Sundays instead of the usual black one; and when he pushed me about how I knew the fact of his evening and morning sermons, "because," he said, "you never make the mistakes the others do," I told him about the tie of his cravat. He refused to credit me until Mrs. Durbin, being summoned to the study, confirmed my statement. He merely said, "Young man, I'll fix you yet." And so one Sunday I did miss hearing him, for he purposely wore and preached in a black handkerchief. When he gleefully informed me of it afterward I ventured to say to him that I probably did not miss much, as the sermon was preached on false pretenses and with the intention to deceive. He laughed, and said I was probably correct.

He had a curious way of preparing his great sermons. The Annual Conferences which he was called to attend all met in the spring; the Baltimore Conference usually in March, and the others following about as they now do. Some time in January he would begin his preparation by going out some Sunday morning to a neighboring town and preaching quietly, developing some one idea; the next Sunday he would go somewhere else, and add another thought to the one previously discussed, and so he would complete the round of ideas with a round of separate sermons; then on the Sunday before Conference he would arrange all the effective parts of these separate sermons into one logical order and preach them in Carlisle; the whole sermon of the future would be there, but only in outline. The altar was arranged, the sticks all laid for the fire, but there was little if any heat; but those who heard him the next Sunday at the Conference would scarcely be able to contain the tremendous electric shocks of discharged power with which the matured sermon was preached. Those who never heard him will probably never hear his like, for the day of such magnificent display of moving, melting, persuasive power would seem to have passed. He would present the simplest truth as if it were a startling novelty, and so clothe it with a new force and distinctiveness that the hearer would wonder why he never had thought of it before in such relations. He had a marvelous power also in prayer.

I remember that once in the absence of the stationed preacher I was appointed to conduct a series of protracted meetings in the church, which had been begun with some indications of good results, and on one Thursday evening about twenty persons were forward at the altar, as penitents, for prayers; the meeting seemed to have passed the crisis of power, and I was very fearful that there would be no conversions that night, and felt terribly moved at the prospect. I explained my apprehension to Dr. Durbin, and asked him to pray. We all knelt inside the chancel-rail, and he began in the low, subdued tone so habitual to him, to intercede for those seeking forgiveness. Soon his words came more and more calmly, but with more and more power; slower and slower he prayed; but there came such a divine presence that it seemed tangible. Heaven and earth seemed coming together. I felt oppressed as with a weight, and prostrated myself more and more in the altar until the prayer closed, when I was prone on my face on the floor. But during that prayer every soul forward was powerfully converted, and the whole congregation was moved as I never since have known people to be moved. The meeting was dismissed and we all went out silently. I do not think that there was any interchange of words except the hearty greeting of joy we gave the new-born. Every one was awe-struck and kept silence.

His hearty sympathy with young men kept him always fresh, and his earnest way of putting the evils of dissipation before them saved many a one from destruction. He would approach a man in such a side-way—so unexpectedly—as to disarm intended concealment. I remember that four friends had been guilty of some violation of rules, and were to be "hauled up" before the faculty, as they supposed, but bound themselves by the most solemn compact to stand by each other and not reveal the delinquents. I was with them at the compact, and also at the time when one of them was summoned to the presence. He was the one of all the number in whose bravery and persistence we had the greatest confidence, and we waited hopefully for his return. He was not long gone from us, but when he returned all bathed in tears he said, "Boys, it's no use; the old man got it all out of me in the first five minutes." Durbin had first asked him some side question which, though wisely planned, had no seeming relation to the case on hand, and then suddenly turned on him with a remark so unexpected and astounding as to throw him off his guard and complete his discomfiture. As an administrator of discipline I have never heard of his equal. And however severe his decisions every body loved him, and no fault was found with him even by those most intimately affected by the issues. He was a most masterful college president.

The following letter is from Rev. J. A. McCauley, D. D., who resigned the presidency of Dickinson last June, after serving for sixteen years.

It is with diffidence I venture on personal impressions of Dr. Durbin as a college president. The conditions essential to discerning judgment, competence and opportunity, were not, perhaps, during my college residence sufficiently mine to warrant confidence in such impressions. The first year of my college life happened to fall in the last of his connection with the college, affording thus but a single year for personal impression ; and as, in the distribution of work obtaining then, first-year men had but an hour a week with him, it was the year of least avail for lecture room impression, affording but the minimum for testing the touch of the great teacher. For the rest—aims and methods of administration, executive ability, disciplinary tact—a freshman's estimate would hardly pass for that of a competent judge; were little apt, indeed, to be discerning or just. Hence to reminiscences of him, or of his performance, having ground no more assuring than the inexperienced and inopportune conditions of this association, little value could attach. The occupance, however, through sixteen years, of the position he so ably filled has had the effect largely to supplement these deficiencies—to interpret and verify reminiscence—has ministered opportunities for noting his impression on the organism of the college, and, as I may claim, a measure of competence to estimate the work which has won for him enduring place among the greatest educators of his time. The tradition of him which lingers here as the ideal president has assuredly less of exaggeration than commonly attaches to traditions. As this judgment can derive warrant only from his work, these lines have the aim of tracing these memories in the sobering light of experiences and responsibilities similar to his.

Had it been his part, on coming to Carlisle, to lay new foundations—to plan as well as build—that marvelous organizing faculty from which the Church in after years so greatly profited would doubtless have had earlier exhibition. As it was, the college had been half a century in operation at his accession to the presidency. Charter and statutes both were old. Around it, moreover, had grown a net-work of custom and tradition more intractable, as more exacting and imperious, than written codes. The question, then, that fronted him was not of working as he wished, but as, under this environment, he might. Inheriting the labors of distinguished predecessors, and girt about with influences of inveterate prescription, it was unavoidable that this environment should largely influence, if not determine, the course he must pursue. The task imposed by his office was, therefore, to modify and judiciously adapt existing provisions to the altered conditions created by the transfer of the college to its new control. That the Conferences assuming its patronage were fortunate in having this work committed to him is unquestionable. With a distinct perception and a thorough comprehension of the problem demanding solution, he gave himself thereto with a single purpose and a practical wisdom rarely excelled. With strong views of prerogative the founders of Dickinson had, by charter provision, reserved to themselves ultimate authority in all that related to its management, including even the penalties of discipline. Untold evil had come of this. At times in the history of the college friction and collision between the boards of instruction and of control had led to crimination and recrimination, not only subversive of college order, but even sometimes of the peace of the community. One of the first cares of the new president was, therefore, to secure by legislative enactment the remedy of this evil. The amended charter vests discipline wholly in the faculty, reserving to trustees appellate jurisdiction in cases only of expulsion. The cure was complete and final. The bitter stream was dried at once, and its existence even has ceased to be remembered.

When Durbin came to organize the new venture, that knowledge of men for which he was famed stood him in as good stead as in any need of his after career. In the constitution of the faculty which so grandly wrought with him this intuitive discernment of men was especially conspicuous. Were his penetration without other witness, his discovery and selection, one by one, of the notable men who took the chairs at Dickinson render it incapable of question. Composed of men mostly young, with reputations yet to make, and,

though dissimilar, without exception able, and growing
with their work, they proved a teaching and disciplinary force of unsurpassed ability. Under their impulse
the college speedily advanced to a reputation for scholarship and efficiency which stirred the admiration of
the Church, and gathered to it the enthusiastic interest
of its patronizing territory. Memory lingers fondly
around these dear names, from which the lapse of years
has taken nothing of youthful admiration. Though
asked for reminiscences of the president alone, so large
was their ministry to his success that mention at least
with him is always their due; all, now, among the
crowned! Merritt Caldwell, oldest in years and least
a novice in teaching, of balanced faculties, imperturbable composure, a very Rhadamanthus in equity, was a
careful, patient, and successful teacher. Robert Emory,
himself just from college, and but twenty years of age,
took the chair of languages, and, except a brief period
of pastoral service, gave the whole of his working life
to Dickinson—the closing years in guiding the helm.
Of faculties, analytic and synthetic, marvelously keen
and strong, of executive ability versatile and great,
there was in every sphere in which he wrought the
demonstration of ability entitling him to foremost rank
in each. When Dr. Durbin left there was unanimity in
thinking him the fittest man to take his place. At the
early age of thirty-four he passed away, with the impression widely made that, if he left an equal, he left
no superior in the Church. John McClintock and
William Henry Allen, the remaining two, of whom only
I venture a word, though in the main contrasted men
were yet in much alike. Both were men of genial,
kindly nature, urbane, complaisant, and of aptitudes
and requisites for easy and effective teaching. Perhaps no single statement would better describe what
then seemed most notable in Professor McClintock than
to say that he united almost electrical celerity of mental action with exceptional power of continuous application. He could study hard and long, and with matchless rapidity. Hence, though but in youth, his acquisi-
tions were extensive and minute, and thoroughly pos-

sessed. Of all the faculty he was, perhaps, the most magnetic and inspiring. If as an instructor there was in him any thing, I will not say to fault, but to wish different, it was that his own intellectual quickness, coupled with a nature bordering on the impulsive, rendered him, under special provocation, a trifle impatient with those whom indolence or lack of aptitude caused to grope or stumble. For myself it is a pleasure to record that, while consciously a debtor to all the noble men composing that faculty, the best fruits of college life were gained through his assistance. Professor Allen, in his early prime enthusiastic, keeping himself abreast with current achievement in every branch of natural science, was an equal master in his department.

Such were the men who, under their great chief, made the opening era of the new *régime* illustrious. It was, indeed, a bright day for the college. In the dawn of a new alliance, ardent friends pressing to its side, the pulsing of new life where late was the languor of decline, able men in all its chairs, and at its head the prince without a peer, it is not without reason that people reckon that the " golden age " of Dickinson.

But, returning to the president : Dr. Durbin brought to the office some experience in the work of instruction, having been professor in Augusta College, Lexington, Ky. The picture of him which rises to me through the mists of more than forty intervening years is of an alert, solicitous, enthusiastic teacher ; of one whose primal purpose was to draw out—*educe* —what students knew of the matter in hand ; to assure himself how thoroughly it had been grasped ; one in whose presence deficiency or inattention were certain of detection ; whose rare power of concise and lucid statement, of apt and facile expression, and of abounding illustration, served admirably for dispelling mists and for making the recitation-hour rich in interest and instruction. While it was his custom to explain freely, and to gather illustrations from wide fields, he never lost control of the situation. Alert, shrewd, discerning, he never, perhaps, was lured to wasting time by any of the artifices to which, in emergency, students sometimes resort to evade the testing of orderly recitation. While for myself I would have to say that, in power to inspire—that contagion of activity which contact imparts—he was excelled by at least two members of the faculty, he yet had this power in high degree, and had I gone with him, as afterward with them, through abstruser realms, I would not, perchance, have this to say.

As executive, it is conceded that through the twelve years of his presidency he administered the affairs of the college with exceptional ability and with marvelous success. Vigilant, forbearing, firm, he knew how to exercise effective discipline with the smallest measure of severity. Prudent, discerning, wise in measure, and fertile in resource, and of energy that rested only with success, he was peculiarly fitted to grapple with the difficulties that lay around the college in its second infancy. Reference was made to his early removal of the organic bar to harmony between the boards. It is not known that, during his protracted term, a shadow of dissension came between himself and those with whom he wrought. The felicity was theirs of spending all their strength in promotion of the interest supreme in their regard.

But the most availing force which the new president brought to his office undoubtedly was that wondrous eloquence, of which the fame already filled the Church; and, in the newness and urgency of the enterprise, it hardly admits of doubt that the most availing service rendered it by him was his devotion of this gift to the pleading of its cause. So greatly did this force minister to the success of his presidency and to the enduring weal of the college that, while attempting no adequate analysis or description of it, a word respecting it seems called for.

Any just account of Dr. Durbin's power in the pulpit or on the platform would need to credit much to his knowledge of human nature. He was familiar with the easiest approaches to mind and heart. His faculties, moreover, were of a kind peculiarly suited to make this knowledge serve the purpose of conviction

and persuasion. His manner of conceiving and presenting truth was uncommonly felicitous. Quick perception,
nice discernment, skillful distribution, taken with a
singular felicity of language and of appropriate illustration, enabled him so to shape and clothe the truth he
was presenting that pleased attention and impression
were the uniform result. The *dictum* of the ancients
demanding emotion in the speaker—*si me vis flere,
flendum est tibi primum*—was instanced in him. At
times his deep emotion, flashing from look and trembling in tone, stirred and thrilled vast assemblies. In
the earlier stages of discourse there was little in his
manner to please or impress. His voice, of tenuous
tone and of movement slow almost to drawling, was apt
to cause a feeling of disappointment in those who were
hearing him for the first time ; but, exercised awhile,
that wondrous voice acquired a power little short of
fascination. His style was mainly conversational, but
when he wished to emphasize some truth, or to vent some
emotion with which his whole being seemed aglow, he
rose from the colloquial to the highest order of impassioned speech. At such times voice and eye and attitude were eloquent in a way peculiar to himself.
Masses swayed under it like trees in the wind. Certain
sermons of his early prime are yet, after the lapse of
more than fifty years, spoken of as instances of trans-
porting and overmastering power, with which memory
yields nothing to compare. This great force he
wielded to the utmost for the college. From platform
and pulpit it sounded in strains of convincing and persuasive speech, and with marvelous effect. Churches
and communities were stirred. Preachers were moved
to zealous advocacy. At family altars, as in social and
public worship, prayer was made in its behalf ; and it
was not long till in the great commanding centers of its
territory there was earnest practical co-operation in the
common work of nurturing to strength this new agency
which the Church was preparing to assure its future.
Along with these benign results bright minds in every
community were stricken with desire to receive the
training of the college. Though of the things we can-

not know, there yet is reason to believe that no achievement of this honored servant of the Church will, in the
final showing, transcend that wrought by him for the
institution whose infancy it was his mission to nurture.

As Dr. George R. Crooks found himself unable to
write a letter for this biography, as he had intended, he
kindly sent his Centennial Oration on Dickinson College, delivered in 1883. From this we select for our
use the following eloquent tribute to his honored professors, and pre-eminently to Dr. Durbin as the president:

Come to me, ye memories of long past years! and
bring before me again those beloved, those idolized
men, the members of our first faculty. I see Emory,
the picture of manly vigor, walking up the chapel aisle
and taking the oath of office administered by Judge
Reed. Durbin, whose large, lustrous eyes fascinate the
beholder, reads once more with slow and measured
accent the morning lesson from the chapel pulpit and
offers the simple prayer of childlike faith and trust.
Caldwell, the Christian Aristides, tender and just, sits
again in his chair and with slow and hesitating speech
unfolds the intricacies of mathematics or clears up a
dark point in psychology. McClintock, as radiant as
Apollo, and as swift, too, as a beam of light, amazes us
by the energy with which he quickens our minds.
Allen, massive in form and solid as his own New England granite, moves among us to show us how transcendent power can be blended and interfused with a
sunny temper. But what shall I say of him, the man
of genius of that brotherhood, whose lips had been
touched with celestial fire—orator, administrator—the
matchless John P. Durbin? In the class room his conversation was more brilliant than the text which he explained. His fertile and suggestive mind wandered
from point to point, and we sat exhilarated as new
vistas of truth, one after the other, opened before us.
Or it is Sabbath morning, and he occupies his throne,
the pulpit. The text is, " Wherefore God also hath

highly exalted him, and given him a name which is above every name;" the theme, the humiliation and exaltation of Christ. The first propositions are so simple that they seem to be truisms, the first manner is so didactic that but for the composure of the speaker you would resent the attempt to fix your attention by such methods. Statements are made so obviously convincing that you wonder you had never thought of them before. He holds you, and you cannot choose but listen. All the time the enchanter is weaving his spell about you and preparing for the triumphant assertion of his power. Suddenly, as suddenly as the lightning flash, his vehemence and passion burst upon you. The torrents of feeling which he had until now sternly repressed flow forth with irresistible force. He has made no mistake; he has calculated to a nicety his possession of your sympathy, and you are borne along by him whithersoever he will. His port and bearing have changed; his manner is that of one fully conscious of mastery over the hearts of his fellows, and his voice, vibrant with emotion, searches all the recesses of the soul. You are absorbed, captured, and when all is over you are aware that for a time you had wholly lost consciousness of yourself.

It abates nothing from these facts that Dr. Durbin's power as an orator declined after he had committed himself wholly to administrative tasks. In his later years he lived among us less as an orator and more as a statesman:

> "With shoulders fit to bear
> The weight of mightiest monarchies."

He himself never grieved over the change, and welcomed the men who increased in public favor while he decreased; for he was careless of fame, solicitous only to do his appointed work thoroughly well.

16

PART II.

HOMILETICS AND SACRED ORATORY.

CHAPTER XIV.

His Eloquence.

THE life of Dr. Durbin is not to be merely *narrated*. It should be *construed*. We can derive from it the best lessons only by an analysis of that power that gave him such distinction. He who would adequately render this service should be the philosopher, the moralist, and the divine.

As in the study of the human system the physiologist inquires into the origin and laws of animal life and learns the functions of the tissues and organs, as the anatomist gives detail and description of whatever enters into the system, so to find out what there is in the physical, mental, or moral constitution that distinguishes one man from another may justify the greatest effort of the understanding. If there be underlying or interpenetrating facts we should search for them as for essential knowledge.

In the interest of homiletics and sacred eloquence we may justly inquire after the elements of Dr. Durbin's strength. From its origin Methodism had been distinguished for the ability and popularity of some of its preachers. But in the first quarter of this century three ministers arose who may be denominated the triumvirate of eloquence in the Methodist Episcopal Church—Henry B. Bascom, born in 1796; John Summerfield, born in 1798, and John P. Durbin, born in 1800.

Of Bascom's preaching the talented but erratic John N. Maffit said: "The model of his sermons is not found in the libraries of the Old or New World. He is a pure original; his shining dims no other star; he is the solitary star that fills with a flood of effulgence the skies of his own creation." There was majesty in his manner; there was depth and richness in his voice. His diction dazed and his utterance awed men. No one who heard him in his prime could fail to feel that he was an amazing speaker—in his way peerless. But his eloquence allowed no relief in the progress of his discourse. His address may have seemed rather to the imagination than to the conscience. In the kind, diversity, and accumulation of his figures the hearer might sometimes be confused if not confounded. There would have been less to perplex had the composition presented more unity of idea, better articulations of thought, and a more easily-recognized logical coherence. A more conscious "touch of nature" would have added to the effect.

Of John Summerfield we may speak in the language that Izaak Walton employed to describe Dr. Donne. "He was a preacher in earnest—weeping sometimes *for* his auditors, sometimes *with* them, always preaching to himself; like an angel, *from* a cloud but *in* none; carrying some, as St. Paul was, to heaven in holy raptures; here picturing a vice so as to make it ugly to those that practiced it, or a virtue so as to make it beloved even by those who loved it not; and all this, with a most particular grace and an inexpressible addition of comeliness. His life was a shining light."

Summerfield blazed on the world as if by the light of his example God would show young men what they may be in the pulpit with a consecrated intellect, a sanctified spirit, and a soul in profoundest sympathy with His work. Rev. Dr. G. W. Bethune writes "of the charm of his seraphic eloquence," and says, "He was the most persuasive preacher I ever heard." James W. Alexander regarded William Wirt as one of the most classical and brilliant extemporaneous orators in America, but declares "John Summerfield was a greater orator than he." He asserts that "he was the most enchanting speaker he ever heard;" and adds, "The charm of his brilliant and pathetic discourses will never be forgotten by those who heard him." He had a genius for eloquence. His heart was in his genius for divine subjects, and God filled and ruled his heart.

Bishop Bedell, in his admirable work, *The Pastor*, p. 304, says of Summerfield: "The tradition of his holy humility, his loving, earnest, quickening utterances of the Gospel, his soul, wrapt in the power of his theme, thrilling and swaying and melting into passionate tears whole masses of almost breathless auditors, will live as one of the choicest memorials of the brightest days of the Methodist Church."

Bishop Bascom lived till the resources of his genius were fully furnished to the Church—till its highest honors crowned him. He died at fifty-three.

Dr. Durbin was spared to us till his seventy-sixth year. He had time which he grandly improved in revealing those abilities which so eminently fitted him for the exalted spheres which he was called to fill, and in his protracted life conferred upon the Church the benefits of his wisdom and worth that only eternity will fully disclose.

Between Bascom and Summerfield there was great contrast. Bascom had grandeur and vehemence. Summerfield had simplicity, pathos, and a flowing stream of silvery eloquence. Durbin was unlike them both, but had some of the elements of each. What was said by the English poet Dryden in reference to Milton, as compared with Homer and Virgil, might be asserted of Durbin as associated with Bascom and Summerfield:

> "The force of Nature could no further go;
> To make the third she joined the former two."

If we speak of Dr. Durbin in the pulpit as he seemed we should say he attempted nothing in the way of eloquence; that his single object was to present with simplicity, directness, and persuasive power the message that he had received from God. In the progress of his discourse we should be profoundly impressed with the belief that nothing less than the salvation of men would satisfy him. To obtain or retain reputation was no part of his care. As he began to address the people there was no show of physical earnestness; but at no time was he aimless.

An old writer says, "A good orator should *pierce the ear, allure the eye, and invade the mind of the hearer.*" All these Dr. Durbin did. His commencement was calm and undemonstrative. His first utterances were measured and seemed sluggish, but his sentences were fraught with meaning, his paragraphs showed progress, and when he reached his theme the subject was opened. He could be heard in all parts of the house, and for simplicity and precision of language could be understood by all. Though there was no display there was something assuring in speech and manner. His conceptions were clear, and in a little time what seemed sluggish disappeared. Thought deepened and broadened. Genius began to flash; a novel idea made its appearance. The hand was drawn from the bosom; the soul was tender. Style was diversified; a beautiful figure was employed, and there was no lack of vivacity. He was felt to be a fine *teacher*, and his resources entertained. He had *pierced* the ear, so it was all attention. *He allured the eye.* His audience saw in him more than an instructor; he pleased. His voice, manner, spirit, showed he was becoming more exalted by his theme. It was as if the hearts and minds of all who heard were in his power, to be taken where he would. Now he painted a picture or described a fact. It was life-like; he awakened sympathy and was a magnet that drew. There was a charm in his address. He kept his purpose in view, himself out of sight.

He allured the eye, and it was well taken; no fitter object could engage it. The eye is an opening to the heart. He invaded the *mind of the hearer.* He considered human passions and well understood the avenues to the soul. He comprehended his duty and performed it. *Attention* was fixed by *instruction.* Interest was awakened by the *force of truth. Impression* was made by the *power of appeal.* Every thing contributed to the end sought. He *invaded* the mind; he removed the doubts that filled it—conquered the prejudices that there struggled; found way to the heart. It was as if the "house" was being "set in order." He offered arguments that could not be answered. He presented facts that were readily confessed. He showed conclusions that candor pronounced just. The subject that filled the speaker possessed the hearer. From the flaming tongue shot a strong sentence that like a bolt went crashing through a coat of mail and pierced a mind that was thought invulnerable. So did Dr. Durbin "*invade* the mind," assailing it with the heaviest weapons that logic can forge, assaulting the heart with facts that no power could repel. There was a breaking down of moral resistance, and there was no sanctuary but in surrender. He was full of his theme. His wife was before him—by the pulpit. He did not see her. He saw nothing but subject and souls. In such *concentration* and *intensity* eloquence *always resides.* If he saw the congregation was under the influence of the word he would not lose his hold. He repeated; he emphasized; he said "one more thought"—now a "last word"—and it was the longest in the language. He was like Queen Esther,

who ventured her own life for her people, saying, "If I
perish, I perish." Then with an earnestness that breathed
her soul she said, "We are *sold to be destroyed*—to be
slain—to *perish!*" Why this triplication? Was not one
word, one expression, enough? No, one word would not
express what her soul felt. Now redundancy is a merit.
It gives force. It is not enough to say, "*he will kill us.*"
The thought is ground into her soul, and she will grind it
into the soul of the sovereign. Noble woman! she had
an orator's spirit. The finest expressions of poetry, the
most eloquent utterances of patriotism, the noblest
achievements of human skill, and the most convincing
demonstrations of philanthropy and Christian devotion
are found in association with self-abnegation. St. Paul
counted not his life dear unto him.

Quintilian says: "The orator must do all not only in
the best manner but with the greatest ease; for the utmost power of eloquence will deserve no admiration if
unhappy anxiety perpetually attends it and harasses
and wears out the orator. He that has reached the
summit ceases to struggle up the steep." Vol. ii, 450.

Ganganelli (Pope Clement XIV) says: "There are
certain moments when great orators seem neither to have
style nor words, lest the sublimity should be altered
by studied phrases. There are people who put themselves into an *alembic* to be eloquent, and nothing issues
from the operation but forced conceits and bombastic
phrases. Whereas, if they would give themselves up
to the energy of their hearts they would have golden
tongues." He adds, "I find nothing but elegance in
almost all the writings of the times, and yet they are
very far from being eloquent." Quintilian supposes of
one that "his greatest excellence is that he has no
faults, and his greatest fault is that he has no excellence.
Elegance pleases, but eloquence captivates, and when it

is natural it amalgamates itself with all the beauties of
nature and genius to show them in all their luster and
according to truth."

Dr. Durbin was now the inspired orator. Nature,
under the divinest influences, pressed into the service
every power tributary to the result. Gesture came
without call—came to assist or to impress when words
sought an auxiliary. We should say he *made* no gestures; *they made themselves.* At first they were few
and modest, and came with such ease and stealth
as hardly to be recognized. They expressed emotion
as words conveyed thought. In the periods of his
highest excitement and grandest achievement all his
powers were vocal. The body was full of tongues,
and gesture was the rival of speech. The finger, the
hand, the arm, the attitude, as well as the eye, communicated, but each in unity with the other, and the
hand could not say to the foot, "I have no need of
thee." Abbé Besplas declares, "Sweetness, with noble
simplicity, should form the constant character of declamation." Pascal believed that in gesture the motion
of the body or its members should help to *paint the
thoughts of the soul,* and that the *painting* ought to be
exact.

Gesture, with Dr. Durbin, was unaffected, appropriate, inspired, and therefore necessitated. When thus influenced, all his faculties waited on him. Memory came
as purveyor of the soul and promptly yielded her treasures. Invention revealed its fruitfulness, passion flamed,
but left reason unharmed. Logic took fire and burned
its way through the whole realm of thought; every
faculty was alert, every force at command. We saw
the man in all the fullness of his mental resources. The
late Dr. Nadal, after hearing Dr. Durbin in one of his
grandest efforts to " preach the word," said, "The spell

of his eloquence remained on me, and the very air was full of the figures that he used, and they gleamed and glowed with their brightness." The cyclone is not more unlike the ordinary currents of the air; the earthquake is not more dissimilar from the uniform operation of physical laws; the ocean, when the tempest sweeps it and the mountain billows break upon the shore, presents no greater contrast to the serene surface when it tempts children to sport upon its waters, than does the orator under his high afflatus to the same speaker when no pressure is on him.

His eloquence was the soul in its intellectual culmination. It was the high-water mark of the emotional nature. It was the tidal wave of influence that carries every thing in its course. Rev. Joseph Castle, D.D., a classic and a critic, expressed the belief that Demosthenes was not more eloquent than, in particular passages, was Dr. Durbin.

Between Dr. Durbin's earliest and later ministry there was *difference in manner*. We have seen that at the commencement of his labors his vehemence broke him down in six months; that as professor in Augusta College failure of health required respite from his duties. On coming East he made it a study to husband his strength in the opening of his discourses. The conversational speech that he had learned in the cabins of the colored people now availed him, and he acted on the principle that the conservation of his forces was essential to culminating effect. His eloquence, therefore, became less *pervasive* and more *concentrated*. His greatest power might not be found in more than two or three passages. Here, in his grandest moments, it was surpassing eloquence. At such time he was a law to himself.

It was a remark of Dr. Lawson, that "he who is animated all the time is not animated at all." However these statements may apply to certain styles it is true of that which distinguished Dr. Durbin.

Dr. Nott, of Union College, in his day one of the grandest pulpit orators of this land, laid it down as a fact not to be disputed, that "No man can be eloquent for more than five minutes at a time." We argue this as a philosophical necessity. "All high emotions are of short duration." The influence upon the speaker or hearer is not sustained for a longer period; like violent diseases, they cannot be both acute and protracted.

For pungency or power a well-couched sentence cannot be too brief. For pathos and moral grandeur what verse in the Bible makes such an appeal as that which is shortest—"Jesus wept?"

It is, however, a mistake to suppose that, while the effect of Dr. Durbin's eloquence was in a short passage, it derived none of its *influence* from that which preceded it. As in painting there is needed light and shade, so the mind of the hearer is prepared for the greatest effect by that which went before.

There was eloquence in stilling the thoughts, in holding the mind, in insinuating the truth, and in keeping the soul in a state of moral *receptivity*. The *result* recognized was the work of a moment, but not the *preparation*.

For long years General Newton, acting under the authority of the United States Government, was working on a reef of rocks at the entrance of the New York harbor. What he did was out of sight. Many were skeptical as to his opening the passage. The conception was formed; the engineering was done; the labor was over. When all was ready the hour was fixed, and at the touch of an infant's finger there was the explosion that shivered and scattered the rocks, shook two cities, and opened " Hell Gate." It was the work of a moment, and commerce exulted in the achievement. But for this grand result preparation was an imperative demand.

Dr. Archibald Alexander's Life, by his own son, Dr. J. W. Alexander, gives an account of his wish to know more of the eloquence of Patrick Henry. He says : " When a young man in Virginia I was anxious to ascertain the true secret of his power. One thing I had particularly desired to have decided; namely, whether, like a player, he merely assumed the appearance of feeling, or whether it was real. Understanding that Mr. Henry was to appear in the defense of three men charged with murder I determined to seize the opportunity of observing for myself the eloquence of this extraordinary orator. I obtained a place in the court-room. The examination of the witnesses closed. It was at the twilight of evening. Candles were brought into the court-house. The judges put it to the option of the bar whether they would go on with the argument or adjourn until the next day. The attorney of the State, a man of uncommon dignity and an accomplished lawyer, professed his willingness to proceed immediately, while the testimony was fresh in the minds of all. Now, for the first time, I heard Henry. He began with declaring his willingness to proceed with the trial, but added, ' My heart is so oppressed with the weight of responsibility which rests upon me, having the lives of three fellow-citizens depending probably on the exertions that I may be able to make in their behalf (here turning to the prisoners behind him), that I do not feel able to proceed to-night. I hope the court will indulge me and postpone the trial till the morning.'" Dr. Alexander remarks, " the impression made by these few words was such as I assure myself no one can ever conceive by seeing them in print. In the countenance, action, and intonation of the speaker there was expressed such an intensity of feeling that all my doubts were dispelled. Never again did I question whether Henry felt or only acted as feeling." He continues, "I experienced instantaneous sympathy with him in the emotions which he expressed, and had no doubt the same sympathy was felt by every hearer." The proceedings were deferred till the next morning. He declares, "The speech that he made was ingenious; his appeals were overwhelming." In spite of his better judgment Alexander confesses he was swayed, though he could counteract the impression by a moment's reflection. The illusion of his eloquence was complete, but nothing that he ever heard so convinced him of Henry's powers as the speech of five minutes which he made when he requested that the trial might be adjourned till the next day. E. G. Parker, biographer of Rufus Choate, said, "Daniel Webster once in a sentence and a look crushed an hour's argument" of an adversary.

But Dr. Durbin was the sacred orator, and felt that the Gospel is the great commission. The object that he sought, the spirit he possessed, and the effort that he made showed that his eloquence was a "virtue." No sermon that he published, however grand the theme, or excellent the plan, or appropriate the diction, or logical the reasoning; nothing that he ever wrote or that others can ever write of him, will give his voice or exhibit his spirit. Eloquence cannot be printed. Like the soul, it is never found by dissecting, though that soul is the immortal part of our nature and eloquence is that which gives immortality to the man. The brain is cold, the heart is still, and the tongue is silent that could express this eloquence.

No man is eloquent at all times. Owen Feltham says, "He who speaks thus cannot speak thus always." This statement applies alike to the secular and sacred orator.

In 1832 the writer heard Henry B. Bascom in Smyrna, Del. He preached on the resurrection of Christ. From the first to the last sentence it was a rushing current, not to say torrent, of magnificent speech. Figure followed figure in such quick succession that in the attempt to *catch* one we *lost* another. The late Dr. J. B. Hagany, of remarkable verbal memory, on hearing him said, he could retain no figure except the comfort of infidelity is "like a moonbeam playing upon a mountain of ice." Again we heard Mr. Bascom in 1844, during the session of the General Conference. He had gone with the late Dr. William Cooper, pastor, to attend the re-opening of Wharton Street Church, Philadelphia. There was every thing in the place, the period, and the circumstances to induce the greatest effort. The congregation was from all parts of the city, and Bascom was at the height of his fame. But the discourse presented a broad contrast to the one of 1832. The multiform and multitudinous figures of the former had faded out, and the color and substance of the thought did not compensate their absence.

That holy man and honored minister of Christ, whom the writer can never name but with profoundest reverence as having been the instrument of his conversion, the late Rev. Henry G. King, told him the following fact:

Bascom and Summerfield met in Philadelphia. They preached the same Sabbath; Bascom at St. George's, in the morning, Summerfield in the old Academy, or Union, in the afternoon. Summerfield heard Bascom, and marveled at his ability. Summerfield's home was with the Rev. Dr. Thomas F. Sargeant, who loved him as a son. While dining the Doctor said: "Well, John, what did you think of Mr. Bascom?" Summerfield answered, with bated breath, "A wonderful man, Doctor." The Doctor observing that Summerfield was not eating, said: "Help yourself, John." "I will," replied Summerfield. Again the Doctor said: "Why don't you eat, John, my boy?" In his guileless spirit he exclaimed, "I will, Doctor, for spite;" to defeat the adversary, who whispered, "How can one like you preach after such a man?" He went to fill his appointment; but the saintly Summerfield failed. The excitement of the morning, from Bascom's sermon, was too much for mind and body.

When Gavazzi made his first appearance in this country he was an orator of amazing power. The writer heard him on his chosen theme. He spoke in the largest hall in Philadelphia. He was in his physical and mental prime. He had a grand physique; his person was tall, and his movement majestic. He had a swarthy complexion, black hair, an eagle eye, a massive brow, and his features expressed intellect. His voice was full, deep, and of great compass. His spirit was buoyant and brave. His passion was like a furnace. He had a consuming earnestness. His ability for sarcasm and ridicule can hardly be conceived. His derisive smile expressed the deepest contempt, but his scowl was vengeance. The tragic and the comic were equally at his command. The platform that he occupied was deep and broad; but the space was not too great for his transitions. His attitudes and gestures knew no limits. He wore a dark heavy mantle that was as a Roman toga, which, as really as any *action*, he made to serve his purpose for impression. In a moment

17

he would gather it close to his person and stand like a
massive statue in disdain of danger. Again, throwing
it out at will he would dart across the stage to exhibit
expedition in grand achievements. And now he would
so dispose of it as to show himself like a moving tower.
Then he would spread or draw it about him so as to
appear as ludicrous as desire determined or as taste
told. He represented the Roman pontiff as an *old
woman*, disabled and disfigured and humiliated. There
was the wrinkled brow, the corrugated cheek, dishev-
eled hair and anchylosed limb, the man made toothless
by the tooth of time. Kneeling on the platform he im-
personated one, aged and broken down, crouching and
looking upward with hands clasped and eyes anxious,
asking help for her needy children, yet receiving none,
and with no device equal to the demand. We certainly
might have looked for her death before this time.

In his mood and place Gavazzi was stupendous.
Every thing was carried to the greatest height. Language seemed made for his lips, and it rang through
the vast assemblage. In voice, passion, gesture, subject, all his resources were brought out, and in the on-
rushing of a mighty soul every thing seemed swept
before him. Such was the Italian priest.

His eloquence in these efforts induced the citizens of
Philadelphia to ask a lecture on a popular subject. He
consented. Again the writer heard him. His fluency
and force, attitude, gesture, and dramatic power, every
thing that went to make him so mighty on his chosen
theme, was absent. He appeared without the toga, and,
as if his mantle was the inspiration of the man, we saw
Samson without his locks. He was like other men.
We could hardly have imagined one less likely to fail
at such time and place than he. Yet fail he certainly
did.

Dr. Durbin sometimes failed to produce the moral effect that he justly desired and that others expected. In manifest result there would be positive disparity. The most striking illustration of this that the writer has known is given in the letter of Dr. Burch. This difference none knew better than Dr. Durbin. But at such time he was one of the best examples of meek submission without nervous irritability or mental depression. The way he received the disappointment was a lesson to all ministers, as all have a like experience without like philosophy or grace. He said, " If the help does not come, I do not fret." A minister does well at such time to ask himself : " Did I make necessary preparation? Did I depend too much on what I had studied? Was my ambition sanctified? Did I look to God?" A physical or mental condition, a psychological cause for which the preacher is not responsible, or something in the subject or occasion might explain an apparent failure. Nor is it to be forgotten that sometimes the greatest visible success follows painful experiences. The soul has thus been roused to sublime effort.

It is just to say, as far as the observation of the writer extended, and it was over many years, he never knew Dr. Durbin to fail to *edify*. He had thought, language, logic, order; and in these his profiting would appear.

Dr. Durbin was remarkable for his power of *emphasis*. It was not what one in derision calls the "sledge-hammer emphasis." This excellence appeared in his reading in public worship. But its full force was seen only when he was under the strongest impulse. Then a word was a *thought*. That thought was a *photograph* of the *mind*.

His *pronunciation* of a *sentence* would sometimes produce an amazing effect. An elocutionist gave an example of this power in a speech of Senator Preston. It was in the presidential campaign of 1840. Crittenden had spoken. Webster had occupied about two hours, but the people were still attentive. Preston rose and uttered but the name " Martin Van Buren ! " This he thrice did ; the first time with the accent of incredulity. The people shouted. The second time with an accent of scorn. The people stormed. But when the third time he exclaimed, " Martin Van Buren! " with an accent of contempt, the vast assembly was wild. They clapped, they stamped, they threw their hats into the air, and were at a loss for any adequate demonstration. It was *climax* on a *word*. David Garrick, who would give so many pounds to pronounce "O" like Whitefield, understood this power. Who that ever heard him can forget the " *Ah me!* " of Dr. A. L. P. Green ?

If we were asked, was Dr. Durbin an artist ? we might answer Yes, or No, according to the meaning of the inquirer. If it is art to retrieve nature from the artificial and restore it to the easy, graceful, normal action ; if when, by study, observation, and practice the speaker has freed himself from the trammels of custom, the force of habit, and the influence of false teachers ; if when, by care and the closest attention to even minute matters he secures to *nature* self-assertion, so that it acts without restraint and assumes the attitude that gives the liberty of genuis, and by voice, gesture, language, accent, emphasis, pause, intonation, inflection, and whatever tends to his aid in the result sought, producing an impression corresponding to nature's place and power ; if this be *art*, then John P. Dubin was a *consummate artist*. If in true art there is no show of the *artificial*, he was such an artist. If art is found when, in treating with men, there is skill that compasses an unselfish and noble though difficult purpose, he was an *artist*. If it be declared "The art of the art is to conceal the art," we only say, If it is *nature* to be *natural*, he was *that*. If it is *art* to be *artificial, that* he *was not*. "Nature, not nature's journeymen, had made him."

May we not suppose this is the attainment that Schiller had in mind when he said, "I hope ultimately to advance so far that art shall become second nature, as polished manners are to well-bred men; then imagination shall regain her former freedom and submit to none but voluntary humiliations?"

He had the taste and skill that come from culture and that men associate with art. He had a quick perception of the mental if not of the moral state of those whom he addressed. He had an intellectual alertness that at once adapted itself to the *need* of the people. He was as prompt to execute as he was quick to discern. He was a master in securing attention, in holding the thought and in impressing the minds of his hearers. The means of mental arrest were always at his command. And in this his design was as undetected as in any thing he did. Without adopting the sensational, of which he was utterly free, he would give such a turn to thought, such a change to language, or voice, or manner, or by anecdote or brief narration, as at once fixed the mind of the hearer with a vivacity that compelled interest. If he saw the congregation was under the influence of the word he would not lose his hold. He makes a statement, offers an argument, thinks its full force is not felt. He would say, "I fear I am not understood." Then, like a skillful rider who reaches a chasm that the animal is unable to bound, and starts back to a greater distance to add momentum to speed, and then with a leap passes it, so did this preacher, by device to which his ingenuity was always equal, compass his end and "go on his way rejoicing." The fact was felt, the argument was clinched, and the work was done. A striking case is given by J. M. Phillips, Esq., our late Senior Book Agent. On a certain occasion Dr. Durbin was making a platform speech in Columbus, Ohio, and giving statistics that the report of missions demanded. He thought there was a listlessness that he always tried to preclude. His array of figures was not the eloquence which they wanted. There was no "fever heat." He turned to the chair, made a polite bow, and said, "When I entered this Conference two days ago I looked upon the faces of those before me and saw only two of all that were here forty and four years ago, when, a stripling, I joined the Conference. I felt lonely; I felt sad." And drawing his coat closer round him he said, "I felt like some oak riven of its branches." By this time, said our informant, the house was in tears; he then resumed his subject with the undivided attention of the people. But he "invaded the mind of the hearer." There was an intelligent order. He would be *heard, understood,* and *felt.* He preached for instruction, impression, persuasion. To this his skill, his art, were directed. In the plan of his sermons, in the conduct of his discourse, in the progress of his thought, in the climax that he reached there was the *art* of sermonizing and the *skill* of literary finish. In the *effect* he was *above art,* he was *beyond nature,* he was *a divine preacher.*

He was an elocutionist of incomparable merit. Many study it; he had it. Books are written, lectures are delivered, professors are employed, and by such attention as is given many are spoiled. He was made; he was an example of the thing itself. In his language we see the rhetorician, in his arrangement we confess the logician; but in his delivery we bend before the mighty orator.

It was a striking fact, and one of great beauty in the ministry of Dr. Durbin, that he carried his hearers with him. He did not enter regions of scholarly thought and metaphysical discussion where they could not follow him; he did not " preach over their heads." He kept both head and heart in view. Like the eagle that first rises slowly from the ground, but when fully on the wing ascends with an ease, celerity, and strength that show its power; that is never more at home than when farthest from earth, nearest the source of light, and basking in the burning splendors of a meridian sun, so did this sublime preacher rise by degrees to those celestial heights that awaken ecstasy and inspire awe; yet never transcending the vision of those to whom he showed the path of light, leaving us to rejoice more in the inspiration that he imparted than to marvel at the imperial soul that soared.

CHAPTER XV.

His Style.

AN analysis of Dr. Durbin's eloquence requires us to consider his style.

In an orator every thing should respect the end. As thought is the great means of producing conviction and of inducing action, and as language is its vehicle, it is a primary care of the speaker to secure the best medium for its conveyance. It should be presented with least fault and with the greatest force.

It is impossible to tell the influence of style as an auxiliary to eloquence. Two speakers of equal learning may address an audience upon the same subject. It is alike familiar to both. They offer the same facts, they employ the same arguments. They are anxious for the same results; but the language of one is inaccurate, parenthetical, and tangled: that of the other is clear, definite, and to the point. The words of the one are chosen, like arrows, for the mark: those of the other, if things so crooked can be called arrows, are taken at hazard, and, if shot, are let fly at random. Each has words enough, but those of the one may be uncouth and without order; those of the other show discipline and grace. The one confuses, the other clarifies. The one is heard with pleasure, the other with pain. Style makes the difference. Solomon in his wisdom as the preacher "sought out acceptable words." Wisdom still resides in like selection. The language is ample enough, the interests involved are great enough,

and the convictions that have constrained consecration
to the ministry have been profound enough to induce
necessary effort to secure the best words to commend
the truth to every man's intelligence and " conscience
in the sight of God."

Cicero named three things as essential to successful
oratory: 1. That the speaker know what to say. 2.
That his thoughts be properly arranged. 3. That he
employ the most suitable expressions. Thus he makes
ability to speak in the best way the crowning qualification. Thought is obscure or transparent, languid or
nervous, feeble or strong, as language makes it. Nor
must it be forgotten that there is a vast difference between propriety and tameness; between the bold and
the reckless; between the elegant and the affected; between the familiar and the vulgar. Dr. E. T. Channing, for thirty years professor of rhetoric and oratory
in Harvard College, and not, therefore, to be suspected
of extravagance, says, " We need not be cold to be correct, nor ostentatious to be elegant. We may be as
magnificent, as vehement as our nature will permit or
allow us to be, and all the while violate no rule of sound
criticism. Indeed, all the while we owe our success to
a careful observance of precision." Eloquence eschews
as fatal or harmful to its purpose whatever in style di-
verts or confuses the mind of the hearer. Its purpose
is not to shine, but to impress, to convince and persuade. As the finest porcelain cannot satisfy hunger,
so mere ornamentation will not avail for a live intellect
and a conscious want. Thought is the aliment of the
mind, and it craves it. Eloquence seeks by the words
employed the most perfect contact of mind with mind.
It is like the grasp of friendship with ungloved hand.
It is one nature receiving the intelligence, feeling the
warmth, and deriving some of the vitality of another

nature. It is like two hemispheres that, united, make one globe, and the circle is complete.

There is no law for grandiloquence. Sound may take the place of sense. Intellectual barrenness finds concealment in the show and spread of verbal costume. Whenever expression is stronger than the thought it is *bombast.* There is a flashy style that imposes upon the unthinking, and there are flowers that fall off with shaking. As meretricious attire gives neither symmetry to the form nor beauty to the feature, so the ornament that adds nothing is worth nothing. The shadow is sometimes *longer* and *always thinner* than the substance. A lexicon cannot make *mind*, and "the mind's the standard of the man."

Dr. Durbin was a preacher of great power in illustration.

He thought, with Thomas Fuller, that if "reasons are the pillars that sustain the temple of Christianity, illustrations are the windows to let in the light." These "windows" he sometimes made very large, and was careful not to stain them. Whatever taste might prompt in relation to "a dim light" that falls on the "long drawn aisle," he desired that the light that falls upon the intellect should be as bright as the sun, and, like that, seen without effort. His illustrations were confined to no department of thought. They might be from art or science, from history, sacred or profane, from nature, from the commonplaces of life, or from the classics. The Bible was to him a rich and never-failing supply. But knowledge of what he selected gave him skill, and he used art like an artist, science like a scientist, and history like a historian. Classics he employed as one who had traversed the ground. After his tour in Europe and Palestine they afforded such illustration as taste and time suggested.

But, whatever the source, they were to *illustrate something.* They were not substitutes for necessary matter. That was a keen criticism by an intelligent Christian lady, who, when speaking of a difference in the ministry of great preachers that she heard abroad and some that she heard at home, said, " Foreign preachers preached the Gospel and illustrated it by science, but that those alluded to at home preached science and illustrated it by the Gospel." If this were true of any, the charge did not lie against Dr. Durbin. He preached " the word," and by illustration concentrated the beams of his intelligence upon it.

We reduce his style to three descriptions that were used as best served his purpose.

1. The Plain.—This is simple, familiar, direct, and unadorned. Its aim is not so much to impress as to enlighten. It is much as men talk on ordinary affairs. The language is pure, and gives no offense to the most cultivated. Many sound discourses are preached and published that from first to last show no other style. This is what we may suppose Mr. Wesley meant when he wrote, " Only let your language be plain, proper, and clear, and it is enough; " yet in Mr. Wesley we have every style that we notice in Dr. Durbin.

2. The Animated.—Dr. Durbin showed progress in style as well as in thought. As, therefore, the magnitude and interest of a subject increased and the faculties found fuller play, his effort was to *fasten* the truth that had been only *communicated.* Style assimilated. Periods presented greater smoothness and dignity; they changed their form, were inverted, transposed; they were simple, complex, or periodic. There were variety and climax. Similes had place.

Herbert Spencer says, " To have a specific style is to be poor in speech." The gifted Henry Ware, Jr., in writing to his brother William, says, "By the way, why won't you write sermons in precisely the brief, pithy, broken dialogue style of this letter of yours? It would be prodigiously taking and lively, and it would inevitably do good to your delivery. Try it in some passage of your next sermon. We want greater variety of style; our hearers' minds want to change their positions as we proceed, and this should be a matter of calculation and effort with us, just as much as the plan of the sermon. When we always keep up the same sort of talk, always equally dignified, solemn, exact, no wonder people gape and think it a long half hour. A really excited extemporaneous actor does not do this. He changes his key, goes quick, then slow, asks questions, answers them, exclaims, reiterates, speaks by hints, by short sentences, by single words; and through this variety not only sustains but increases attention and the interest. Passages drawn up like your letter, thrown in toward the close of a sermon, would electrify."—*Life of H. Ware, Jr.*, i, 137. Thus wrote one of the most brilliant and eloquent Unitarian divines. Was there ever better illustration of the force of his remarks than was furnished in the ministry of our early Methodist preachers? By statement, by argument, by interrogation, by evolving a thought, and in repetition presenting it in different forms and various aspects, as the skilled advocate does before the jury till he has fixed it in the mind least receptive, so did the Methodist preacher sink it into the heart of the hearer. John P. Durbin grew up under the labors of such men. He was a careful observer. The Methodist preachers seemed to be "turning the world upside down," and he desired to have a hand at the lever. Quick to perceive, intelligent to appreciate, and wise to adopt the most efficient means, he imbibed the spirit and sought the power of our fathers.

He was not an inapt student of the facts, nor an unsuccessful laborer for the results.

3. The Sublime style.—Suitable and necessary as is the *plain* style for its purpose; excellent as is the *animated* for setting forth divine truth in its nature, beauty, and claim; positive and manifest as is its influence in fixing attention and winning the regard of men; exalted eloquence is never attained till such emotion is awakened and such passion is kindled as compel a higher style. As language is to express the heart as well as the intellect of the speaker, and is to reach both in the hearer, the orator should realize that he must not have the vehicle merely for his *thought*, but for his *soul*.

In the fullness of his matter, in the outgushing of his speech, in the celerity and vigor of his mental movement, in the strength of his convictions, in the intensity of his desire to compass his end impelling to every means to secure his object, he presses on irrespective of the length of sentence or of any thing but the desired result. Facts force themselves on him, and he notices them. Reasons multiply, and he gives them. Clause joined to clause and epithet added to epithet give force to the vast volume of truth; the channel widens; the current of thought goes rushing on with increasing strength and pours its fullness into the periodic sentence. The soul could allow no arrest. When such a sentence is not forced it gives grandeur to the composition and weight to the purpose. This in his highest moods was illustrated by Dr. Durbin.

According to Longinus, " the sublime is an image reflected from the inward greatness of the soul." Addison says, " The sublime is from the nobleness of the thoughts, the magnificence of the words, or the harmonious and lively turn of the phrase." Composition, therefore, that expresses exalted conceptions, profound moral yearnings, and unyielding purpose to achieve all that the good of the sinner and the glory of God demand—a composition that is alike the offspring of a burning brain and of a melting heart—must be an "image reflected from the inward greatness· of the soul." It is the soul shining on the intellect; the soul speaking from the glowing tongue; the soul subduing all to itself. In the moral world intensity is an essential condition of sublimity. The soul in ecstasy or in agony may exhibit the sublime. When the speaker feels as nearly as may be the full force of divine verities sentences assume the greatest strength, and may *fairly break* under the weight of the thought they are intended to convey, and *exclamation* takes their place. Did not Thomas feel this pressure when he exclaimed, "My Lord and my God!"

The real Durbin never appeared till he reached such eminence. Here his step was quick and firm and unerring; here he was at home; here he reveled, and thence descended with a dignity equal to the strength with which he rose. In his style there was great contrast. In the first, or *plain*, he talked and taught. In the second, or *animated*, he interested and pleased. In the third, or *sublime*, he seized, held, and made captive.

While in the first there were those who could have left without the sense of loss, in the second the same persons would have resisted an argument to go; but in the third it was impossible to make them stir. They who at the beginning were indifferent became charmed; those who were interested are now in transport. Now the pulpit is the only power. Time is nothing but as it allows the hearer to drink in the word and imbibe the spirit of the speaker. As in the seven prismatic colors we have all the diversity of light and shade—

every tinge and tint in nature and in art—so in these three styles we have the force, the finish, and the fire of the mightiest orator. As in the combination of the twenty-six letters of our alphabet we form all the words of the lexicon, and from these present the law of Sinai, the utterances of Pentecost, and the Sermon of our Lord, so from these three styles we have all the wealth of literature, whether sacred or profane.

The foundation of appropriate style is sound sense. Intelligence measures thought. Judgment weighs words. Skill adapts one to the other. Dr. Durbin's style had perspicuity and precision, beauty and elevation, variety and force. May we not assume for style as for eloquence what the philosopher says of matter: "It is capable of receiving all manner of forms?"

In Durbin there was no dead level. Now it might be close and exact, as he was calm; if he were vehement, copious and diffuse. His words expressed beauty of conception, breadth of knowledge, intensity of spirit, and grandeur of thought. He understood "how forcible are right words." He knew that they may carry frost or fire; that they may congeal or melt; that they may paralyze or electrify. He had seen words fall like snow-flakes or as the crushing aerolite. Though not lavish with language there was no paucity. He had all that rhetoric asks or eloquence demands. He had a word for every thought, and a thought for every emotion. He could address himself to every case and question, and with style suitable to each. He could be as simple, direct, and home-like as condition required. He knew the pangs of penitence, and how to describe them; the joy of pardon, and in what way to express it. He made faith easy and holiness a ready attainment, and all in language that a wayfaring man would understand and approve. With what vivid colors did he show the dying sinner! Who ever presented the departing Christian in words better calculated to induce every man to say, "Let me die the death of the righteous?"

There was sublimity in his simplicity, for it set forth great facts. There was simplicity in his sublimity, as all was natural and just.

The last century gave to English literature two men, Samuel Johnson and Joseph Addison. They were princes in their places. Johnson's style has made that of many. It has fullness and grandeur. Addison's taste has told on others, who have assimilated to his style. It has purity and precision. Each of these great writers has had his critics; both have their merits unimpaired. Fashion is found in language as in dress. Time modifies estimates. In Bascom there was more of Johnson than of Addison: in Durbin, Addison predominated; but as a rhetorician he knew all styles and could command any. He adopted for the time that which best suited his purpose, but believed, with Seneca, that "fit words are better than fine ones." But the man dwelt in his style as "Uriel in the sun."

CHAPTER XVI.

Imagination, Dramatic Power, Voice, Unction.

IN an analysis of Dr. Durbin as a sacred orator we must consider the influence of his imagination, his dramatic power, his voice, and the divine unction.

In popular and powerful address we may uniformly trace the influence of imagination. The discourse in which it predominates is wanting in moral weight, but the orator can neither doubt nor decline its advantages. A disordered imagination harms by its fantastic exhibitions; but a sound one elevates thought, imparts interest, and impresses truth. Logic is necessary for order and conviction. For instruction didactic speech is an imperative demand. Familiar narrative, facts of history, and principles of science afford lessons of wisdom. But imagination is like an added sense—a sense indeed comprehending in its use the other senses, but in its action transcending them all. It is based on observation, improved by culture and constrained by emotion. It takes in more than the eye hath seen, or the ear hath heard, or the hand hath handled. It combines and creates; it

> "Bodies forth
> The form of things unknown."

The orator, like the poet, sees the possible as well as the certain. The most logical and majestic minds give force to their reasonings and sublimity to their conceptions by the use of this faculty. Without it a speaker may argue with clearness; may communicate knowledge of

18

great value; may present conclusions that none can dispute; may obtain the reputation of a strong thinker and profound divine; and in some departments of study there may be no need of imagination. Science gives demonstrations. But the pulpit appeals to every susceptibility of man by every faculty and force at the preacher's command. It may sometimes be justly asserted that there is too much imagination in the sermon. It may likewise be said with equal truth there is too much reasoning. It is needless when things are self-evident. There is too much show of exposition; that which by a few words is made clear by many becomes cloudy.

There are those who speak of the preacher of imagination as if this were his only faculty. Was it so with Latimer, with Jeremy Taylor, with Henry Melville? Do we associate great imagination with a little mind? Do not the ablest thinkers often appear to greatest advantage, and make the profoundest impression, when imagination asserts its power? Milton is immortal in his works of imagination. But was he not one of the strongest prose writers of his age? The fathers of the Revolution were not men of small intellect. But in the most powerful words they uttered we see their imagination. James Otis exclaims, "England may as well dam up the waters of the Nile with bulrushes as fetter the steps of freedom, more proud and firm in this youthful land than when she treads the sequestered glens of Scotland or couches herself among the magnificent mountains of Switzerland."

Not less does Patrick Henry command us when he declares, "Our chains are forged; their clanking may be heard on the plains of Boston." And, when love of the whole country prompted the reply of Webster to Hayne in the American Congress — words that will be our glory while the republic lasts—the words of the constitutional lawyer, of the mighty statesman, the words that childhood will be taught to recite for coming generations and that maturity and patriotism will not cease to reproduce, were the utterances compelled by a flaming imagination. Weighty as were the principles he laid down, solid as was his reasoning, it was the climax of power in his speech as he said:

When my eyes shall be turned to behold for the last time the sun in heaven may I not see him shining on broken and dishonored fragments of a once glorious union; on States dissevered, discordant, belligerent; on a land rent with civil feuds, or drenched, it may be, in fraternal blood! Let their last feeble and lingering glance rather behold the gorgeous ensign of the republic, now known and honored throughout the earth, still full high advanced, its arms and trophies streaming in their original luster, not a stripe erased or polluted nor a single star obscured, bearing for its motto no such miserable interrogatory as, "What is all this worth?" nor those other words of delusion and folly, "Liberty first and union afterward;" but every-where, spread all over in characters of living light, blazing on all its ample folds as they float over the sea and over the land and in every wind under the whole heavens, that other sentiment, dear to every true American heart, "Liberty and union, now and ever, one and inseparable."

But nowhere do we more clearly see the use and power of this faculty than in the "lively oracles." To what part of nature do they not appeal? The floods "lift up their voice." Bel "bows." Nebo "stoops." "The mountains and the hills break forth into singing, and all the trees of the field clap their hands." The desert blossoms as the rose, and instead of the thorn comes up the fir-tree. Of the sinner God says, "The heavens shall reveal his iniquities and the earth shall rise up against him." How does imagination influence the expression of Isaiah when writing of the proud monarch of Babylon, who was about to follow and meet the kings and oppressors that had gone before him? He says: "Hell from beneath is moved for thee to meet thee at thy coming. It stirreth up the dead for thee, even all the chief ones of the earth: it hath raised from their thrones all the kings of the nations." And the Son of God makes the climax of his didactic teaching in his Sermon on the Mount in a picture of the imagination from two builders: "Whoso heareth these sayings of mine, and doeth them, I will liken him unto a wise man, which built his house upon a rock; and the rain descended, and the floods came, and the winds blew, and beat upon that house; and it fell not: for it was founded upon a rock. And every one that heareth these sayings of mine, and doeth them not, shall be likened unto a foolish man, which built his house upon the sand: and the rain descended, and the floods came, and the winds blew, and beat upon that house; and it fell: and great was the fall of it." How else could this lesson be so impressed? How could the incaution, the recklessness, and the ruin of the soul be more forcibly shown?

We can hardly conceive of the sacred orator whose mind and heart are properly influenced by the great realities of religion, and that has some realization of the powers of the world to come, without such emotion as kindles imagination and constrains the figures that most forcibly convey the absorbing and overwhelming thought of the speaker.

David Hume, judging of the eloquence of the ancients by "the noble remains and the few strokes" that have come down to us, concludes they are infinitely more sublime than English orators. As proof of this he refers to the "noble apostrophe of Demosthenes," so much celebrated by Quintilian and Longinus, when, justifying the unsuccessful battle of Chæronea, he breaks out, "No, my fellow-citizens, no; you have not erred. I swear by the names of the heroes who fought for the same cause in the plains of Marathon and Platea." Hume exclaims, "What noble art and sublime talents are requisite to arrive by just degrees at a sentiment so bold and influential." For this he thinks the English too cold. (*Moral, Political, and Literary Essays*, i, 110.)

But does this apostrophe transcend St. Paul when he would inspire moral heroism in Christians of his day? He shows the victors of faith in Hebrews xi and xii. There is Abel, the first martyr; Enoch, the translated; Noah, saved from the flood; Abraham, ready to offer his Isaac; Moses, forsaking the grandeur and prospects of an Eastern court to suffer affliction with the people of God; David, Samuel, the prophets, and other mighty men, who through faith subdued kingdoms, wrought righteousness, obtained promises, stopped the mouths of lions, quenched the violence of fire, escaped the edge of the sword, out of weakness were made strong, waxed valiant in fight, turned to flight the armies of the aliens; women received their dead raised to life again, and others were tortured, not accepting deliverance, that they might obtain a better resurrection. Did Demosthenes rise higher? What is there in vision that the apostle did not command? He lifts the curtain between two worlds and shows the cloud of witnesses, the race set before the Christian, and Jesus the inspiration and the Judge.

What a prize! What an assemblage! Seers, patriarchs, prophets—the good of all the past—looking from the heights of celestial happiness, as if incapable of perfect repose until the struggling saints are crowned. Is the Grecian orator grander than the apostle of the Gentiles? And shall the successors of Paul—men of

the same calling, conviction, spirit—shall God's ministers, in the fire of their zeal, in the subduing tenderness
of their commission, be too cold for apostrophe or vision?

Dr. Durbin had an imperial imagination, and when
he gave it the exercise it asked, nature and revelation,
every thing within the domain of thought, contributed
to its influence. It availed itself of objects of beauty,
novelty, and grandeur. It re-peopled the past, opened
the future, made the distant present and the difficult
easy. It verified and vivified its possessions and its own
creations. There were times when the boldest figures
seemed as real in what they embodied as the pulpit where
the preacher stood or the people whom he addressed.
Then imagination made the intellectual canopy shine
with the stars that his genius kindled and that his ardor
intensified.

Reason has been called "the master of the mind."
Imagination, by like authority, has been pronounced the
mistress of the intellect. The same has been said of the
powers and pleasures of the imagination that Plato declared of the soul: that they are "like the harmony of
the harp—invisible, material and divine."

In imagination Dr. Durbin saw the things he showed,
and showed them as he saw them. Who even now fails
to see Sinai as he showed it when he declared, "I have
stood on the lightning-scarred rocks?" He said, "If I
speak of a horse I see him;" and he did see him in form
and strength. It might be the war-horse of Job, his neck
clothed with thunder, his nostrils terrible, pawing in the
valley, going on to meet the armed men, turning not back
from the sword, heeding not the quiver rattling against
him, nor the glittering spear and shield, swallowing the
ground with fierceness and rage, smelling the battle afar
off—the thunder of the captains and the shouting. When
he spoke of the tabernacle in the wilderness, or the tem-

ple at Jerusalem, each appeared in its size, material, adornments, sacred emblems, and use. He made us see the person, the dress, the service of the high-priest, as compared to the appearance and functions of the great high-priest of our profession. The ark of the covenant stood before us, and there was the mercy-seat and the cherubim, and we learned much of the shekinah. For a time we were in the holy place of the tabernacle of the Most High, "beholding the glory that excelleth."

He did not make drawings on the " blackboard," but he did on the *brain*, and they were with intellectual material that time itself can hardly efface. What a moral spell bound the people as he showed the significance of the words, "See that thou make all things according to the pattern showed to thee in the mount." How imperative did he make the demand! How needful the conformity urged! It meant moral accuracy, divine resemblance, and in ourselves scriptural holiness. When he spoke of " the signs of the times " they were easily traced in states, in sovereigns, and in circumstance. It was as the " lightning coming out of the east and shining to the west." It was a blaze across the whole canopy. It was lightning, and nothing less. The signs signified that God was in them as really as shadow proves a substance. Not more truly did the Almighty direct the moon when it stood still in the valley of Ajalon, or the sun when it went back on the dial of Ahaz, than he showed the cloud in which were "showers of blessings " for the mission field that constrained the solicitude of Dr. Durbin.

In his graphic presentation of the fall of man we could see "the living temple " in moral ruins. The stately columns of holiness and happiness were thrown down. Decay had climbed over the walls and "abode within its confines." Amid the dilapidation that Isaiah describes there were the "cormorant, the bittern, the owl, and the raven," with "the satyr crying to his fellow, and the beasts of the desert meeting with the wild beasts of the island." Dr. Durbin showed this ruined temple filled with unclean spirits; yet triumphantly he assured us that the "Holy One of Israel" will "build the temple and bear the glory." It rose before us "polished after the similitude of a palace," and "all glorious within." It stood in strength, it towered in majesty. Its dome pierced the heavens, and its open door invited from the four quarters of the globe. The pillars that sustained it could not be prostrated by the convulsions of nature or impaired by the innovations of time. Into this temple he entered with reverent step and careful survey. He approached its altar, felt its fire, and flamed with the invitation for all to enter it and be saved.

The imagination of Dr. Durbin was equal to his mental demand. Whether in thought he ascended the mountains or descended the vale; beheld the ocean in its sublimity or the heavens in their grandeur; whether he pointed to paradise in its bloom or in its blight; a deluged world or the flaming cities of the plain; whether he looked upon Jerusalem as the city of the great King, or without one stone left upon another; whether he spoke of the "great white throne" or the "Lord Jesus revealed from heaven with his mighty angels in flaming fire taking vengeance upon them that know not God," or the Almighty gathering his saints for eternal recompense, he had a verbal affluence that conveyed his thought, and a judgment that kept this faculty within proper bounds and secured the desired result.

Closely associated with imagination in its highest efforts was an element that few command and none may often indulge. It was the *dramatic power*. A manifest attempt at this in the pulpit uniformly displeases and sometimes disgusts. Even gesture, when *forced*, offends. Aim at the dramatic may appear in "the start theatric," and an affectation that awakens indignation. The dramatic that is not in harmony with gravity and warmth is justly distasteful. It is a power only as the offspring of the occasion, as the exhibition of deep emotion and self-forgetting earnestness. It comes unsought, like proper gesture. It can be good only as it is true to the soul. But when a burning heart, with all the powers of the intellect, can so *project* itself, and nothing is seen but the force that impels, no one may describe the result. Tully speaks of an orator who tore open the bosom of his client to show the wounds he had received for the republic. Patrick Henry dropped on his knees at the bar of the House of Delegates when pleading for others with a power that was said to be "enough to soften rocks and bend the knotted oak."

Time would fail us to tell of this dramatic power as seen in the ministry of the logical Ezekiel Cooper, the eloquent John Strange, and of the magnetic George G. Cookman.

The Rev. J. O. Roberts, of Kansas, writes: "Mr. Durbin, when a young man, preaching at a camp-meeting on the 'Godhead of Christ' was so carried away with his theme that as he quoted, 'This is the true God and eternal life,' as only John Durbin could say it, exclaimed, 'If you deny it take the whole Bible from me.' At the same moment a small Bible flew from his hand into the congregation and fell just at the feet of an unbeliever in the deity of Christ." He says the effect was tremendous. We are sure that this would be a very unsafe thing for any man unless it might be considered involuntary. Dr. Durbin was too much of a thinker, and too close an observer of facts, not to know what folly prompts and what wisdom and the occasion permit and constrain.

The Rev. J. H. Hargis, D.D., writes: "The Hon. Willard Saulsbury, formerly member of the United States Senate, now chancellor of Delaware, was a student under Dr. Durbin at Dickinson. A score or more years thereafter to a young Dickinsonian Mr. Saulsbury told of the vividness with which President Durbin, in the pulpit of the old Methodist church in Carlisle, once set forth the unprofitable servant taken and cast into outer darkness. Said the Senator, 'So vivid was the scene depicted by Durbin as he suited the action to the word that I *saw* the fellow fall, and heard him when he dropped.'"

The writer is indebted to the Rev. Joseph Longking for an illustration of this power in Dr. Durbin's first labors in the East. It was at an anniversary of the Sunday-School Society, held in Forsyth Street Methodist Episcopal Church. Mr. Maffit had delivered a characteristic speech. Durbin followed. When well warmed with his subject he referred to the case of the young woman who was the Sunday-school teacher of the afterward world-famed Morrison, the translator of the Scriptures into the principal Chinese dialect. As he figured that young lad and his female teacher he spoke of the deep, quiet, unperceived, but not unfelt influence she had exerted on that young mind. Warming still more with his theme, he exclaimed, "She did not know what *a lion of God she was training!* His mane had not yet grown, his paws had not yet put on their strength, nor his claws their mighty grip." Then drawing himself into a crouching attitude he suddenly sprang forward, as might a lion in seizing his prey, and, grasping the Bible, and holding it aloft, exclaimed,

"*So he, Morrison, raised a nation unto God!*" The effect was wonderful. Some shouted hallelujah; some clapped their hands; some wept aloud, and others tried in vain to restrain their sobs. Dr. Longking adds, "I have seen congregations greatly moved . . . but never did I see another congregation so carried away as was that of Forsyth Street that evening by Dr. Durbin." A striking illustration of this dramatic power is given in the letter of Dr. Tiffany.

In "*Men and Measures of Half a Century*, by Hugh McCulloch, Secretary of the Treasury in the administrations of Presidents Lincoln, Johnson, and Arthur," that distinguished author speaks of Durbin as a man of not only large literary but scientific attainments, and says : "I was much impressed by one of Dr. Durbin's sermons from the text, 'We are fearfully and wonderfully made;' in which he presented, in a manner which would have done honor to one who had made the human form a life-long study, an argument in favor of divine creative power as illustrated in man's physical mechanism. One who listened to that sermon said to me that as Mr. Durbin, with a finger of his right hand upon his left wrist, described the regular but intermittent flow of blood through the system by the action of the heart, he could feel the beating of his own heart as though he had within him a steam-engine."

But in any analysis of Dr. Durbin's eloquence his voice demands particular notice. According to Cicero, in effective as well as in pleasing delivery the voice "holds the highest place." Payson thought that it is half the pulpit. With some it is more than half. Emerson says of the voice, "It sometimes of itself enchains attention, and indicates rare sensibility; that the voice, like the face, betrays the nature and disposition, and soon indicates the range of the speaker's mind." He quotes one as saying, "he learns from the first tones of his voice on Sunday morning whether he is to have a successful day." A feeble, harsh, strained, or nasal voice is a great hindrance to a speaker. This presents one of the weightiest reasons for its cultivation. From failure of the voice of Dr. Durbin in his earliest ministry the work of his life seemed brought to a close; but by care and proper use it was restored and strengthened. It had compass necessary to the greatest occasions and grandest themes. When he rose to speak it seemed to lack body, but it was clear, and audible to a large assembly. With advancing thought, and under the influence of the listening multitude, it acquired swell and fullness. The *quality* of his voice can hardly be described. We may more easily convey an idea of what it was not than what it was. At the beginning it had no oily smoothness; but it was not uncouth or disagreeable. If it did not awaken interest it did not hinder effect. In pitch, in loudness, in modulation, he was its master. Physical and psychological causes sometimes told on its exercise.

Its *expression* was more than its compass and quality. Of the power of the voice to awaken emotions corresponding to those we feel we have only to consider facts. How are we affected by the cry of "Fire," of "Murder"? The one creates *alarm*, the other *horror*. The result is according to the utterance, and this agrees with the emotion. There is a contrast between the feelings awakened by the exclamations Hallelujah and Rabboni. The one expresses *ecstasy*, the other *awe*. The voice may be cheerful or pathetic, may start a tear or heal an aching heart. At one time it may be like the sound of the bugle to the war-horse that rushes to battle, at another time like the piping of the highland shepherd when the flock gather about him as charmed by the music. He knew this cultivation of the voice in song and in the artist. If it is capable of any thing that Dr. Durbin did not understand we are unable to name it. It was trained for all parts of a discourse—the didactic, the expository, the narrative, for illustration, or for climax. This was seen in his addresses for missions as well as in preaching the Word. In a moment he could kindle a fire or extinguish a flame. In his address he was much accustomed to the *rising* inflection, which seems more spirited and intimate, while the falling inflection is more suggestive of the dogmatic and authoritative.

A teacher of the art of speaking has given three voices, that he severally distinguishes as the *English, Roman,* and *Attic.* The *English* is that employed in conversation and in good reading. This we may see in the sermons of Robert Robinson, and, from his feeble health, in John Summerfield. This makes the colloquial preacher.

The *Roman voice* is full, round, commanding. This we may assume was the voice of Otis when, in disdain of oppression, he said, "Arbitrary principles, like those against which we now contend, have cost one king of England his life, another his crown, and they may cost a third his most flourishing colonies." In this voice Bascom delivered his entire sermon.

The *Attic* is of greater compass and intensity. Such we may suppose was the voice of Patrick Henry when he uttered the memorable words, "There is no longer any room for *hope.* . . . We must fight! I repeat it, sir, we *must* fight! An appeal to arms and to the God of hosts is all that is left us. The war is inevitable, and let it come! I repeat, sir, let it come!"

Daniel Webster was *excellent* in the English, was *grand* in the Roman, but when passion carried him to the Attic, as it was apt to do in great subjects, his voice broke and the effect was unequal. Dr. Durbin began in the English, advanced to the Roman, culminated in the Attic. He was easy and familiar in the English. He was noble and commanding in the Roman ; but in his grandest thoughts and sublimest utterances, when most of the dramatic element came out, it was in the Attic voice. Here it revealed its wondrous power ; here was the man in the intellect, utterance, attitude, gesture, voice, emotion. Here was each in its fullness. Now was seen his peerless eloquence. But when the voice was under the highest pressure it showed no strain to impair either its flexibility or smoothness. It could shoot out like light to dispel doubt, or explode like a shell to accomplish its design; but, unlike the shell, it did its work without destroying its own integrity. A United States Senator from Virginia, years after the chaplaincy of Dr. Durbin, declared that he never heard a voice that so affected him, and that he could never forget its tones.

But more than imagination, dramatic power, or the voice was the unction of the Holy One in the ministry of Dr. Durbin.

No one familiar with the preaching of our fathers in Methodism can have failed to observe the prominence given to the work of the Spirit in awakening, converting, and sanctifying the soul. If it be inquired, What has been the one thought that has filled the mind of the minister? it is this: " Without me ye can do nothing."

That which distinguished our early preachers was not mental idiosyncrasy, new theological beliefs, nor physical force, whether judged by voice or gesture or forms of labor. They could not, as a rule, claim the profound learning of the schools. They were not remarkable for the exhaustive treatment of their subjects ; but whether they sang, or prayed, or exhorted, or preached—

whether they met in class, or formed a "band," or held a love-feast—their perpetual thought was, "It is the Spirit that quickeneth." The books they read, the letters they wrote, the conversations that they delighted to hold were eminently spiritual. In their conversation they claimed that the "Spirit bore witness with their spirit that they were born of God." In many cases, if they were not spiritual they were nothing. The confidence of the pulpit was in the Spirit to secure the highest success. This awoke the faculties, inspired the purpose, prompted the language, and compelled the noblest utterances of the man. The heart spoke, the tears flowed, and the joy that thrilled them animated others. The careless and the rebellious were subdued. As on Pentecost, the people were amazed, marveled, and said, "Whence this work?" The spirit in Methodism seemed to be turning the world upside down. Society showed the influence in the vices that were abandoned and in the moral purity that took their place. It was such sensational preaching as the Church might justly honor. This is a present need.

In many a minister's discourses we may have the best evidence of a richly endowed intellect, of a finely cultivated mind, of a memory stored with choicest literature ; there may be a faultless style, a polished elocution, and rare homiletic skill. In Christian apologetics, and in surveying and sustaining the outworks of Christianity, they certainly are able and may be popular men. Yet while they have the symmetry of form there may also be the coldness and the deadness of the corpse. He who vitalizes must himself be vital.

To our fathers, rhetoric, logic, elocution, even exposition, were only the stepping-stones to something higher. *Where, as a rule, other ministers left off they did execution.* Then they took firmer hold and obtained a closer grasp. When they had put the subject before the mind they tried to get it into the heart, and felt that nothing was done till the citadel gave away under the heaviest fire. It was as if, in the language of John Fletcher, "they would storm perdition and take the heavenly Jerusalem by force."

But Dr. Durbin looked to a period beyond, when an apostle spoke and said, "Paul may plant and Apollos water, but God must give the increase." This was setting truth in the strongest light. If they could not succeed without the Spirit, who can? "Who then is Paul?" He was a man of power. His mind had acuteness, compass, and vigor; his taste and tact and teachings showed superior judgment, and there was no want of imagination. He knew how to influence men by courtesy and charity. His heart was not inferior to his head, and with God as supreme in his affections he had himself under good control. He possessed great skill in reasoning, and could kindle a fire in his logic that consumed "the wood and hay and stubble" of false leaders. The intellectual Anakims of his day quailed before him.

In delivering sermons, directing councils, writing epistles, in all the work of an itinerant preacher was he not peerless? Who would not have such a minister as Paul? Would we not study his matter, commend his methods, admire his manner, and invoke his influence? Would he not fill our churches, rouse our members, convince our skeptics, revolutionize community, save men? Would we not bring the frigid that the fire of his zeal might warm them? Would we not seek the chronic complainers, that he might effect their cure? Would we not be ready to do as they did in his days, "bring the sick in beds and couches, that the shadow of an apostle might fall on them?" Grand man that he was! When Cowper would describe the "faithful preacher" it was "such as Paul." Yet what says Paul? "God must give the increase" of convictions, the "increase" of conversions; the "increase" of holiness is of God.

Besides this he says, "Apollos may water;" but then, too, "God must give the increase." In spiritual husbandry watering is as necessary to fruitfulness as planting. Apollos had high claim. He was an eloquent man and mighty in the Scriptures. That which the Bible emphasizes deserves special notice. He mightily convinced the Jews, publicly showing by the Scriptures that Jesus is the Christ. He stood in the radiance of celestial truth, and it shone all around him. Yet who is Paul, or who is Apollos, but ministers by whom ye received the word? Good in their place, and they were faithful to do *their part.*

Paul could plant in any soil. Apollos could water as the diffusive dew, as the gentle rain, or as the heavy shower. Yet clearly they saw, profoundly they felt, and candidly they confessed they could not give the "*increase.*" The very thing for which they labored they could not give. "Increase" is the only thing that the farmer wants. It is the great thing for which the minister sows beside all waters, and for want of which his head may become a "fountain of tears."

The fact remains. The preacher may excel in word-painting, attract by voice, by matter and by manner— may have the commendation that the intelligent and influential bestow, and yet find the painful lack; the "souls for whom Christ died are not saved."

It is related of Narni, an Italian bishop, that he so preached to the people that as they walked the streets they exclaimed, "Lord, have mercy!" In one week 200 crowns were spent to buy ropes for self-invented pen-

19

ance. When he preached before the pope, cardinals, and priests he so represented the evils of non-residence that forty of them went back to their cures. When in the pulpit of the University of Salamanca he induced eight hundred students to renounce the pleasures and honors of the world and betake themselves to different monasteries. But after all this the priests and the people went on as before, and Narni left the pulpit in despair. Why was this? It was the power of *human eloquence* without the proper presence and *power of the Spirit.* Without this an angel cleaving the heavens could not accomplish salvation.

It forever stands: "Without Me ye can do nothing."

John P. Durbin began and continued his ministry with the motto, worthy of the most ardent Methodism, that it is the "unction that makes the minister." This he sought with deepest solicitude. This he would illustrate in all his efforts to save the sinner and to bless the Church. In that Spirit was his highest hope and noblest triumph. He well knew that when rhetoric, logic, and eloquence had achieved their greatest results there remained the absolute necessity for the Spirit to take of the things of God and show them to those whom he sought to persuade. His divine resource was in the presence and efficiency of that Spirit that brings heavenly beauty and order out of the wreck of our moral nature. Amid the multiplied temptations of the minister to repose on human attainments and skill it must stand before him as the utterance of infinite wisdom, and therefore as an indisputable fact, "Without Me ye can do nothing."

How far the "unction of the Spirit" gave power to Dr. Durbin's ministry may be judged by the influence that rested upon him at times in public supplication.

Joseph Longking, D.D., told the writer of the first

prayer he heard John P. Durbin offer. It was in John Street. When he began he was slow and conversational. There was nothing to impress with favor except that it was reverent and sensible. But in a little time he seemed to be drawing very near to God; then he warmed; then the people warmed; then he glowed; then the people took fire; then he seemed to be talking to God, as if he was with him, face to face in the pulpit. So profoundly was Mr. Longking stirred and so filled was he with wonder that he involuntarily rose from his knees and looked at the man in audience with Deity as he had never realized with any man before or since. Other instances of his amazing power are presented in letters furnished in this volume. He had no respect to length, or loudness, or any thing but for those who awoke his solicitude. For a time these prayers awed and then whelmed the people. A moral earthquake is a tremendous thing to associate with college life in the efforts of the president in prayer. But when Dr. Durbin bent under the burden of souls it was as if the heavens bowed and the earth shook. After such seasons his physical energies required days for repair.

Dr. Durbin, when he felt the unction of the Holy One, had a nature so responsive to that power as to reveal and awaken deep emotion. They who consider emotion out of place in religion conceive quite as much as intelligence will permit. In what realm of thought, in what sphere of action, under what circumstances of our being is our emotional nature forbidden due exercise? Is it when gladness thrills? When apprehension tortures? When the irreparable loss is sustained? May the sorrowing never say, "Lover and friend hast thou put far from me, and mine acquaintance into darkness?" In the domestic circle may not joy make the eye sparkle or bereavement cause the head to bow? Then, verily, stoicism is an exalted virtue.

There are times when emotion is wisely *repressed;* when we may restrain the tear, forbid the look, discourage the action. No one knew this better than Dr. Durbin. But may it never be indulged? Is it always out of place? Is it, when the soldier leaves his family to go to war? Is it, when the prodigal comes home? Is it, when victory returns to its scabbard the sword that neccessity drew and that patriotism wielded? Who are they who are strangers to the exhibition of emotion? Why do angels rejoice when a sinner repents? Why does the Father of mercies say, "My bowels are pained within me, my repentings are kindled together?" An *emotionless* intelligence, where is it? In heaven? No! The shout of their triumph is as "the sound of many waters." Is it in hell? No! There they weep, and wail, and gnash their teeth. And shall ministers sent to warn men "that they come not into the place of torment," and when they "know not what a day will bring forth," shall preachers be cold? Who will assert that the great Teacher was emotionless? Why then did he say, "Fear him who is able to destroy both soul and body in hell?" Is fear emotionless? Why then did the knees of Belshazzar "smite one against the other?" and, under the ministry of Paul, why did Felix tremble? Is love emotionless? Then explain the tears of Jesus at Jerusalem.

This unction that rested upon Dr. Durbin spoke in melting *pathos.* This was sometimes the very soul of his sermon; but love was the soul of his *pathos.* Ganganelli says, "The preacher is to scatter the ointment of grace while he diffuses the light of truth." Fenelon declares of Chrysostom, "He entered into the hearts of his hearers." One has said, when speaking of sculpture, that "the artist ought to have two souls, in order to transfer one of them into his work." Under the *divine afflatus* the soul of Durbin was great enough to allow transfusion without harming its nature or lessening its powers. Who wonders that, when they saw the anchor cast, and were assured that it was within the vail, they wanted to lay hold of the cable and pull for the celestial shore?

The power of truth and the emotion of one kindled the emotion of many. Was it the breath of a mortal that now made dry bones stir? No! No! It was the *Breath* that came from the four winds.

CHAPTER XVII.

Extemporization.

IN any analysis that we make of a preacher's power
we are compelled to consider his communication—
whether it is read, memorized, or extemporaneous—
whether with or without notes.   Dr. Durbin is presented
as an *extemporaneous speaker.*   He was not an *extemporaneous sermonizer.*   He had his subject before him,
his plan matured, and his matter was well studied.
Though not accustomed to write sermons for delivery
he was not the "student in the pulpit," but in his
study.   In the pulpit he was the *speaker,* the messenger of God, with his message on his tongue, which,
for its purpose, he implicitly trusted.   He knew that
message in its import, design, and adaptation.   He was
far from the reproach that Owen Feltham casts upon
negligent ministers when he says, "I admire the valor
of some men, that before studying dare ascend the pulpit and there do take more pains than they have done
in the library. . . . And this makes some such fugi-
tive divines that, like cowards, they run from the text."
The preparation of Dr. Durbin for the pulpit when a
pastor was reduced to a system.   Early in the week, we
have seen, he digested his subject and had his sketch
in readiness for the pulpit.   When he began to speak
the current of his language flowed on in the channel of
previous thought, and words were extemporized as they
were wanted.   If on some occasions a text, a theme, a
division came to him as by inspiration, then every thing

was extemporized. Theme, thoughts, terms, sentences, were seized. An exigency, it may be, was thus the occasion of a most appropriate and memorable discourse. But this was not his dependence or fancied justification for neglect of proper study.

For some occasions, as is seen in Dr. Tiffany's letter, his sermons were prepared with great labor. In the early ministry of Dr. Durbin a paper sermon in a Methodist pulpit would have been like an ecclesiastical heresy—would have been regarded an invasion upon essential economy. Imagination could hardly conceive it. Read sermons in any church were construed as evidence of want in spirituality in the minister who gave such discourses and in the people who would consent to accept them. It seemed *bold* in the president of Dickinson College fifty years ago to have the skeleton of a sermon in the pulpit and hold it up before the congregation. But with us colleges were new, and we did not know how much was to be allowed to come with them.

If there are any ministers in whom we might be expected to confide as extemporaneous speakers, they are those whom Methodism has reared. Thus our fathers went forth when God bade them "*speak* to the people all the words of this life." And whether in field or forest, in barn or church, they drew listening multitudes, who heard, believed, and obeyed the Gospel. Thus, without education except in their calling, by their ardor and eloquence they attracted rich and poor, refined and rude, and other Churches were glad to have some of them for their pulpits, which, on accepting, they did not fail to honor.

Thus Dr. Durbin began, went on, and finished. It is a weighty fact, and therefore worthy of careful consideration, that in the beginning of Methodism, when we made such popular and powerful appeals—when the masses thronged our places of worship, and when many of the great of the land were awed by our influence and identified themselves with our Society—then extemporaneous preaching was all we knew; our ministers were mighty in this, our members were edified by this. By this the land shook, the Churches wondered, and it was as if the kingdom of darkness was coming to an end. This was in broad contrast to the reading practiced in the other Churches, and it drew. Philosophically considered, it might be said that the vigorous exercise of the mind in extemporaneous speaking would naturally· create earnestness of feeling and of manner. *Earnest they were.*

Dr. Thomas H. Skinner, professor of homiletics in the " Union Theological Seminary," gave as his judgment to the class that no man is prepared for the ministry who cannot extemporize, saying, Occasions will arise, and appeals must be made, when to want this ability will be construed to the serious disadvantage of the preacher. Though one may write with elegance, and memorize with ease, and have good elocution, for readiness to his work and efficiency in his labors he must be able to extemporize. But while all may commend the extemporaneous when successful, many show reasons for reluctance in adopting it·; as fear of inaccuracy and inelegance.

They think that language thus spoken is necessarily immature. If the immaturity appear only in lack of finish, and there is found greater directness and force, we may ask if the absence of the one is not more than compensated by the presence of the other; whether efficiency is not more than beauty? But is it just to assume that the extemporaneous is necessarily wanting in accuracy or elegance? Is it not the *mind* that dis-

tinguishes both pen and tongue? Is it not the cultivation of the intellect that gives choice to language
and precision to speech? And may not the speaker
as truly as the writer show culture?

From the philosophy of the case shall we conclude that
the artificial is better than the natural—that the pen,
which is man's invention, is superior to the tongue,
which is God's organ? Is the alliance between brain
and pen more intimate? Are the treasures of the intellect more fully yielded to the pen than to the
tongue? Is the composition of the one necessarily
more noble and truthful than the utterances of the
other? Will fancy afford more beauty, or imagination
take a higher range, or will invention show more skill
when the pen calls than when the tongue appeals?
Have not the readiest writers found themselves unable
to reproduce by the pen what was in the tongue during
a conversation, or in a time of seclusion and thought?

Were not the words more vital and vivid when spoken
than they were when the pen was employed? Is not the
pen of the *tongue* more naturally dipped in the ink of the
heart than the *pen of the scribe?* Is not the soul more
fully revealed when there is no paper between it and
the people—when thought, and speech, and sympathy,
seem one and instantaneous? Does not the mind
move under a higher impulse and inspiration when the
speaker is standing in the holy place amid the influences of a waiting and worshiping congregation than
when alone and writing?

We do not claim for all extemporaneous speakers
either accuracy or elegance; but can these be predicated
of all written composition? If want of time to prepare is a reason for inaccuracy, inelegance, and immaturity in the spoken word, is not lack of time for
written composition a reason why that too should be inac-

curate, inelegant, and immature? The truth is, there is much extemporaneous writing for the pulpit. There is composition of the pen as well as utterance of the tongue thrown off without careful thought.

We submit—1. How much time does it require of a man that knows grammar, and is accustomed to its use, to employ good syntax? How much time is requisite for one of a clear mind and beautiful thought to find a fitting dress? The tongue is as true as the pen, and can make as just an impression. Did any one ever detect disparity in Dr. Durbin's spoken word as compared to any thing that was written for his use?

2. But we reason from facts furnished. When Dr. Durbin was thrilling his great assemblies with extemporaneous address, there were teachers of science and professional men in the same city, outside the ministry, that were showing ability in the extemporaneous utterance of the most weighty thoughts that their position demanded them to present. Not to speak of others whom we would be glad to name, there was—

Dr. Robert E. Rogers, professor of chemistry in the medical department of the Pennsylvania University, with a class of from three hundred to five hundred students, all seeking the most accurate knowledge of that which was so necessary for their profession. He was lecturing day after day, and week after week, for nearly six months in the year, and with eloquence that held the students spell-bound. When on one occasion the writer thought he would like to have one of the grandest passages he had ever heard on the subject, he took the liberty to ask it of the professor, who assured him he would be delighted to give it, but that it was wholly *extemporaneous.*

At the same time there was in the Jefferson Medical College Robley Dunglison. He was a voluminous writer in medical science. He filled the chair of physiology, a department that demands the greatest accuracy. To him we listened in the rush and fullness of an eloquence that suggested Dr. Chalmers as no other man ever did. In the Philadelphia College of Medicine was Dr. James McClintock, the brother of Dr. John McClintock. To think of substituting written composition for his fluent, precise, and eloquent extemporaneous address would be as if one would seek for the shimmering cascade, the sluggish stream.

At the bar were David Paul Brown, Joseph R. Ingersoll, and George M. Dallas. For fluency, elegance, and eloquence, we might have searched long and diligently, and in vain, for better illustrations among readers of manuscripts. Can men of science, where there is so much terminology and such demand for precision in language, and in a profession where such momentous earthly issues are involved—can these afford to adopt extemporaneous speech if there is necessarily immaturity? If they believed that by manuscript they could more clearly, fully, and impressively inculcate their subject or make their appeal to a jury, would it be just to those concerned that they should fail to *write* and only *speak?* Surely it may not be imagined that men of science and other professions are better acquainted with what they teach, or that their minds or hearts are more in their work. Will any allow the belief that the men in these professions have better minds than those whom God calls?

3. But have not Christ's ministers special reason to expect success in extemporary speech? Are they not justified in looking for necessary help from the Spirit? Is there no "speech" that shall be given them "in that self-same hour?" Are they not permitted to make present application of an *old* promise, though no older

than revelation, that we are constantly preaching, "Open thy mouth wide and I will fill it?" Pentecost filled the mouth of Peter the fisherman, and there are still "tongues of fire" as really as pens of light. When the minister has done his part, may he not, as really and as justly as did St. Paul when shipwreck impended, say, "Sirs, I believe God?" It is no more presumption to believe God's revealed word than to accept the statement of the angel that stood by Paul and assured his deliverance. Christ appealed to his apostles: "When I sent you without purse, scrip, or shoes, lacked ye any thing?'" They replied, "Nothing."

But history has a voice to show that extemporaneous speech may be accurate and elegant while forceful and eloquent. We shall be slow to find fault with the speech of Peter on Pentecost. Who will have the temerity to accuse Paul of any deficiency in style when he was accused by the orator Tertullus, and made his defense or when he faced the philosophers of Athens? In the early Church we have Origen, the great father of pulpit oratory, at the age of sixty, when habit is so difficult to break, adopting the extemporaneous as the more appropriate style. It is said of Cyril and several of his contemporaries that they spoke to their people in extemporaneous language, and that many sermons of Chrysostom, together with his celebrated discourse upon his return from banishment, are proof not only of the existence of the custom, but that extempore compositions are not necessarily deficient either in elegance or in method.

Was not Bishop Janes an accurate speaker? Did Bishop Thomson lack elevation or beauty? We hesitate not to say that language never has greater point, precision, and power than when the extemporaneous speaker is in the right mood for its utterance.

We have the strongest testimony in favor of extemporaneous speech from some of the wisest and weightiest ministers of later times; men who are never to be questioned as to the accuracy of their thoughts or the elegance of their language. The Rev. Albert Barnes, in later life, adopted the extemporaneous address, and in power transcended the efforts of his former years.

We are familiar with the vigorous thoughts of Dr. R. S. Storrs, as conveyed in his Notes on "Extemporaneous Preaching," and we have this eloquent fact, that this commendation is from a minister who had attained the greatest eminence as a preacher before he tried what he now finds is "the more excellent way."

And are we not urged to extemporaneous preaching, from the high commendation it receives from churches long accustomed to the manuscript? And is it not a weighty fact that so many ministers with whom reading was a habit are now assiduously cultivating talent for extemporization?

But excellence in this is attained only by the effort that determination induces. Any one might fail as did those whom we have quoted. In this, as in other things of interest and magnitude, we must resolve if we would achieve, and never relinquish purpose till facts show success is impossible. Dr. Hepworth has written with eloquence of his *freedom* from the shackles of manuscript, and of his incomparable delight in the better expression of his mind and heart by the power to extemporize that he has attained. That some have more language than others admits no doubt; that by good society men may improve their speech will not be disputed. But they are greatly mistaken who think that *right* words are to roll from the lips like waves from the ocean by a necessary law; that even sentences and propositions are to be turned from the tongue in exquisite shapes for use as ornaments are turned off by ingenious machinery. · Extemporization is not the refuge of indolence.

Dr. Durbin sought no such sanctuary, and neither offered to God or the people that which "cost him nothing." Gravity does not more certainly become the pulpit than industry and earnestness. Demosthenes said he "became an orator by spending more oil than wine." And efficiency, not ease, is the craving of the gospel minister, and he knows that the sweat of the *brain* has more heat than that of the *brow*. The extemporaneous speech of Dr. Durbin had accuracy and elegance, ease and energy.

Dubious as extemporaneous speech may appear, other methods have had quite enough of failure to show that they are not without risk.

Dr. South was one of the finest minds in the English Church. He trusted his memory in delivering a sermon. It failed, and he was covered with shame. Dr. John M. Mason was one of the grandest preachers of any nation. Ex-Chancellor Ferris told the writer he was present when memory failed, and, putting his hand to his head, he said, "I am unable to say more." After this he used manuscript. Have we known no one come to grief with manuscript sermons? The light was poor, the writing was bad, the sight was failing, and the preacher had not sufficiently studied his composition, and received little sympathy.

But are cases of breaking down in extemporaneous speech common? If so, the writer has not witnessed them. Many times he has known extemporaneous speakers to be *wanting in liberty*. Fifty years ago he heard one at camp-meeting who on entering the pulpit did not give the best evidence of his trust in God, and in a short time he gave proof that he needed help.

There had been some signs of rain, and he found it convenient to say, " Brethren, I perceive a cloud arising, and I will bring my remarks to a close." The preachers thought there was a cloud that had already settled upon the speaker's intellect; but he was not speechless, and was able to say something by way of closing. The only conclusion in cases of other kinds was a *dead pause.* About the same time on a camp-ground under like circumstances the writer heard a memorable preacher. At once his memory failed. He rubbed his head, he stood, he trembled, he recovered and resumed his speech. At another time he was listening to one of the most finished preachers in the Conference. The thread of his discourse became tangled. To see a minister trusting memory for his entire composition, and in the rush of his utterance in a moment brought to a halt, though not so disastrous, reminds us of a locomotive at high speed stopped in a moment. The agony is not confined to the speaker.

Men who fail in extemporaneous speech might ask, " Why is this ? " Was the subject studied ? Was it the fear of man that brought a snare ?

Dr. Durbin once asked the writer, " How do you account for the difference in young men in public speaking ? Some will prepare a fine composition, but in delivering it will sometimes come to a dead pause and be unable to say any thing. Others will have compositions of perhaps less beauty, but from whatever difficulty they meet *they readily extricate themselves.*" The reply to his inquiry was, " No man better understands that than he who was so long president of Dickinson." but added, " one depends entirely upon memory, the other retains such freedom as always preserves him from becoming such a mortifying spectacle." This was accepted by the Doctor as the reason. We then wished to know of him which of the two young men he would prefer, the one with the better composition or him that had the reserve of power. His answer was, "By all means, the latter."

It is not denied that extemporaneous speakers sometimes lose the train of thought. In private conversation we do the same. But the extemporaneous speaker has an alertness and fruitfulness of mind that greatly lessen the risk of utter failure. When the train of his thought is broken the mental locomotion continues, and there is some idea to carry him on till the *train returns*, and then he accepts it, unless he thinks his diversion was for a good end.

The mind puts on strength and shows its treasures.

A friend asked George G. Cookman if in extemporaneous speaking he never lost the connection, and, if so, how he did. He replied, "I do sometimes lose the connection, and I just dash into an exhortation, and the people may see no difference, and the result is not spoiled."

To those who would acquire or cultivate talent for extemporization we may assume that there are essential conditions of success, and show that these met in Dr. Durbin.

1. *There should be knowledge of the theme.* The mind must have the material of thought which language is to convey. We speak not to *acquire*, but to *impart*. The tongue can no more make matter for discourse than the hand can for a globe. It is not for the eye to create objects of vision or the light by which they are seen. It would be a feat to write about nothing. It is an equal *exploit* to *extemporize* with nothing to say. In such case the pen should be still and the tongue silent. It was a sin in the task-master of Egypt to require "bricks" with no straw to make them. One

of the greatest difficulties of extemporization is that the *tongue is oppressed*—that they give it the double task of *making* and of *uttering* thought. So did not Dr. Durbin. He who complains that he cannot express *himself* may do well to ask whether it is not because he has *nothing* of *himself* to express. It is hard pumping where there is no water. Even mutes can express thought by signs, and irrational creatures have a language that makes known their suffering or their pleasure.

He who extemporizes may be far from general intelligence; but this is equally true of him that writes. Whether the young preacher is from the plow, or shop, or seminary, *knowledge of his subject is an essential demand.* He who has seen no college may know his text and treat it in the language to which he is accustomed.

As an essential condition of success,

2. *There must be sympathy with his subject.* "We believe and therefore speak." No man is fit to preach who does not accept and appreciate the truths of the Gospel that he is called to inculcate. He should have close fellowship with God. He must have deep sympathy with men. The moral wants of the world must move his soul. He must be anxious "that the word of the Lord may have free course and be glorified." The lawyer that is not concerned for his client is unworthy of a case. The physician who is not anxious for his patient is undeserving of practice. The general that does not love his country should not be trusted to fight her battles. A heart intent upon accomplishing its end would speak "though tongues were out of use." A warm heart puts a still tongue in motion and makes a cold brain burn with such thoughts as would reduce the flesh to ashes if the pent-up fires could find no outlet. Thus Jeremiah felt when he said, "His word was in mine heart as a burning fire, shut up in my bones."

20

As sympathy with the theme shows the soul in its highest powers so the soul thus awakened gives words the readiest and noblest utterance. Fancy, imagine, if we can, that such ministers would fail for words. There are streams that dry up, there are lights that expire, but we would as soon expect the Hudson to exhaust her waters or the sun to spend his beams as that the sympathy of the earliest Methodist preachers would lack language.

3. *Mental Poise.* No man can appear at his best without the control of all his faculties. That which disturbs the mind distracts thought and interferes with utterance. Hence come hesitation, inaccuracy of language, recalling words, and reconstructing sentences. Whatever composes the mind brightens and invigorates it. As the eye in an unclouded sky takes in all in the range of vision, so a serene mind apprehends according to its capabilities. And as a transparent statement comes only from a clear intellect the utterances of the tongue show a governing intelligence or lack of mental concentration and control. Mental poise is indispensable to easy, coherent, effective speaking.

In mental poise the extemporaneous speaker's inventive and constructive power are appealed to and respond. *Amplification,* so necessary to successful speech, is cultivated and disclosed. *Dr. Durbin was a perfect custodian of his endowments.* A critical observer said of John Wesley, "The most remarkable thing about him was, that while he set all in motion he was himself perfectly calm and phlegmatic. He was quiescence in turbulence." Dr. Durbin could

"Sit calm on tumult's wheel."

In the pulpit, on the platform, in the scientific or popular lecture, in the discussion of a great subject, in the vast assembly and on the floor of Conference his powers were at his command, and he seemed imperturbable. On the floor of the General Conference, when he rose to reply to Bishop Soule, though the Church was convulsed he was calm. And with the grasp of a great intellect, the appreciation of the weightiest facts, he towered in the majesty of his soul.

R. W. Emerson gives a striking illustration of the want of mental poise in Dr. Chancey, a distinguished minister of Boston, a century ago. As he was about to begin a sermon he learned that a boy had fallen into Frog Pond and was drowned. He was so disconcerted as not to be able to make a direct prayer, but went round and round. After praying for Harvard College and for the schools he implored the divine Being to—to bless to them all "the boy that was this morning drowned in the Frog Pond." Emerson says, "This was not want of talent, but of manliness." This is the man who so disliked sensational preaching—of his time—that he prayed that he might never be *eloquent*. In this Emerson says "his prayer was granted," and yet he lacked what he called manliness. Had he been more *composed*, his prayer would have shown a *sensation* better than that he evinced. There is an excitement that interest in a cause awakens. Cicero said he never lost this on rising to speak. Luther declared he never entered the pulpit without trembling. This is good.

Want of mental poise was witnessed in the late Dr. S. H. Tyng, when a young rector in Georgetown, D. C. He went to church with an intention to preach an extemporaneous discourse. "Henry Clay and other notables" entered the church. Tyng became sick with excitement and left his post. Why did Peter begin to sink in deep waters when Christ bade him come to him? Because he looked at the billows rather than at the Saviour. Looking at Clay made Tyng powerless to speak. But he did not give up his purpose to be an extemporaneous preacher, and for precision, fluency, force and eloquence, became one of the finest specimens of pulpit ability. "A too earnest desire to speak well is almost sure to make us speak ill."

A word comes to the man beginning to extemporize. It may not be the best for his purpose. He pauses; another is not at his command; he is embarrassed; he stops. Failure in such way is perfectly natural. It were innocent at such time to realize, "A bird in the hand is worth two in the bush." A word in the mouth is worth a score in the vocabulary.

We may name another essential condition,

4. *Confidence of success.* Doubt in any cause that demands energy is half defeat. Faith is half victory. If Monsieur Blondin lacked confidence in his ability to perform his feats across Niagara Falls the attempt would be more than temerity. No one admires egotism. Self-conceit causes disgust; but there is a *self-assertion* that enables one to project his powers without any display of vanity. Modesty has no merit when it hinders a just expression of what we are called to do. No one will commend the humility in a speaker that makes him distrust "the ability that God giveth."

An extemporaneous speaker, or one wishing to be such, rises to speak. What is asked of him is such a command of thought and his subject as to employ appropriate words. We will suppose he is called on for a funeral, and an address is proper. What point is there that the occasion offers that he may not present? What fact that it is right to state that he may not name? With the Scriptures in his memory what consolation that the case admits may he not urge? What exhortation to the living may he not deliver? If summoned suddenly to preach, is there no doctrine that he has so studied as to be able to explain and exhibit? Is there no history in the Bible, no hero of the Old Testament or saint of the New that can furnish him a theme? All men in their places can convey their thoughts in words that any can understand. The plowman in the field, the woodman in the forest, can each find words appropriate to his wants. Surely the mouth-piece for God can extemporize. Let him in what he attempts have confidence. When the writer, with a young friend, was beginning to exhort, there was in one of the congregations the maternal grandfather of the late Bishop Cummins, John Durborough. He was an itinerant preacher in the early administration of Bishop Asbury. To speak before him seemed too much for inexperienced youth. We told him so. He made in substance the following reply: "If you speak on a text it is fair to assume that, having just studied it, you know more about *that passage* than any one present; therefore *have confidence.* Whenever I am in the congregation be not embarrassed, but consider there is one man praying for you and *be confident.*" Nearly fifty years have closed over the grave of this venerated minister, but his memory must ever remain green in the mind of the writer. His exhortation to youth was, "Fear not, but be strong."

We know of no condition essential to successful extemporaneous speech that did not meet in Dr. Durbin. With the sensibility and spirituality that are at the foundation of pulpit eloquence there was such devotion to his purpose, such understanding of his theme, such sympathy with his subject, accompanied with mental poise, and a confidence that facts justified him in his work, that he attained his end because he employed the means. How much it cost him to become what he was we are not informed; but of this we are certain—the cost was not equal to the profit. Without wishing to disparage able ministers who pursue a different method, we are allowed to exalt that in Dr. Durbin which presents him to us as so nearly, if not fully, the ideal orator *actualized,* and as making so near an approach in his manner to the preaching of Christ and his apostles, and as affording so fine an exhibition of that style of ministry which the intelligence, the observation, and the Christian earnestness of the age are coming more and more to admire and commend.

CHAPTER XVIII.

Homiletic Taste and Skill.

OF Dr. Durbin's homiletic taste and skill, and of their influence upon sacred oratory, we may form some idea from the lessons that he impressed upon the class of young preachers that he instructed while pastor in Philadelphia, and from facts furnished as to preparation and result.

In an Introduction which he wrote to the *Short Sermons on Important Subjects*, by Jonathan Edmonson, A.M., he expresses his view of the kind of sermons the people should receive to secure the ends of able and faithful preaching. Of Edmonson's discourses he says, "His style was as varied as the topics and the occasions."

Having noticed the intellectual and moral lapse of the pulpit from the sixth to the sixteenth century, and of the strange and trifling themes that sometimes engaged the minister, as "Was Abel slain with a club? or, Of what sort of wood was it?" "Of what sort of wood was Moses's rod?" "Was the gold which the Magi offered to Christ coined or in mass?" he turns from "the Dark Ages" to the time of the Reformation and to the subjects that then engaged the preacher. These were "controversial and speculative;" the didactic had become tedious. The public mind became fatigued with the dry theological discussions, "and, having settled down upon the fundamental principles of Christianity, required that these should be adorned

and recommended by eloquence, which had become the
powerful instrument in forming and directing men's
minds. This produced a class of rhetorical sermoniz-
ers, in which may be placed Bourdaloue, Massillon,
Bossuet, Saurin, Tillotson, Atterbury, Blair, Davies,
and others.

"Of these various classes of sermons the controversial are unacceptable to the present peaceful age ;
the doctrinal are not sought after by the multitude; the
rhetorical are read chiefly for the pleasure they afford as
specimens of sacred oratory. None of them address
themselves to the multitude; and yet the characteristic
of the age is, that the multitude demand and must receive instruction in every department of knowledge.
The pulpit is required to furnish sanctified literature
for the masses," . . . in "short and plain sermons."
These he recommends in the discourses of Mr. Edmonson, who was one of the finest specimens of a sound,
devout, able, and earnest Wesleyan preacher. His sermons have excellence of style, force of logic, fullness
of matter, and are adapted to alarm the careless and
edify the Christian.

Dr. Durbin speaks of Mr. Edmonson as discussing
topics admitted by the sound portion of the Church, as
avoiding controversy, and as aiming at illustration and
application. He says, "The reader will find in this
volume, expressed in perspicuous, easy, and often forcible
and eloquent language, the opinions of a candid man,
a good scholar, nearly every topic that can interest him
in theology, morals, and experience."

Thus we have the idea of Dr. Durbin as to what a
sermon should be, and in one entitled "Christian Ministers Declare the Counsel of God" we have his forcible expression as to the duty, manners, spirit, and diverse qualifications of those who preach the word.

But we have from Dr. Durbin's own pen, while editor of *The Christian Advocate and Journal*, April 18, 1834, his clear and vigorous expression as to the great characteristics of a sermon. His remarks are founded on the question in our Discipline of the "matter and manner of preaching," and of the answers given by the book.

"1. To convince. 2. To offer Christ. 3. To invite. 4. To build up, and to do this in some measure in every sermon.

"1. *To convince*—that is, of *sin.* This is the first thing toward the conversion and salvation of sinners; till this is done nothing is done to purpose. To convince of sin is indispensable in order to repentance, and without repentance there is no salvation. In this conviction of sin two things may be noticed: 'original or birth sin,' or, in other words, as our article has it, the corruption engendered of the offspring of Adam, whereby man is very far gone from original righteousness, and of his own nature inclined to evil, and that continually." The present is no time to give up this doctrine for the speculations and doctrines of men. It is that which the Church has always held; that which the Methodists, after the Reformers, have preached with the power and demonstration of the Spirit; and a great multitude that no man can number have experimentally attested and do attest the soundness of this doctrine. So that if it be false all these are found false witnesses before God. To convince men that their moral nature is defiled is a laborious and difficult task, especially in this philosophizing age, wherein there is a strong tendency to the error of the Pharisees, the laying our own instead of the righteousness of Christ as the foundation of the hope of salvation. The minister of Christ should be clear in his views on this point, and must,

like Paul, be able to reason from the Scriptures in its
support, and, withal, to make the most pointed and
powerful appeals to the consciences of his hearers for
the truth of what he preaches.

Secondly. Actual transgression, both in respect to
things enjoined and things forbidden. Here the minister of Christ must make much use of that commandment which is exceeding broad, and is a discerner
of the thoughts and intents of the heart. The law
must be preached not only as the rule of morality in
our conduct toward men, but as the rule of piety in our
conduct toward God. When the sinner is thoroughly
convinced of his lost and wretched state and of the utter
impossibility of his helping himself, then

2. The *offer of Christ* may be made to him. In offering Christ we offer all the benefits of redemption by
him. As Christ has made an atonement for sin—that
is, as our second article expresses it, "has reconciled the
Father to us," and has obtained pardon, adoption, and
all the privileges of the children of God for us: the
whole are implied in the offer of Christ, so that if we
receive Christ we receive the whole. In the offer of
Christ is implied also the gracious *design* of God in
giving his Son and of Christ in dying for us. The *design* respects all to whom the offer is made. If God
eternally intended that any part of the human family
should absolutely perish, he could have had no merciful
design concerning them, and consequently the offer of
Christ could not be sincerely made to them. If Christ
be *offered* to us, then we must receive him in order to
be saved by him, and the necessity of receiving him is
implied in the offer. If we reject Christ we reject all
the blessings which he has procured for us. And here
it should be recollected that the object of faith—that
object which is to be received by faith, and on receiv-

ing of which the sinner is freely justified—is not what God *will do* for him, but what he *has already done.* It is true that he who cometh to God must believe that "He is, and that he is a rewarder of all them that diligently seek him." But this is not the object on which justifying faith chiefly acts, and on the receiving of which the sinner is justified. This object is *Christ crucified for us.*

3. *To invite.* To bid sinners come to Christ and to the provisions which he has made in the Gospel for them. Here it is proper to enlarge upon the love of God and the grace of our Lord Jesus Christ; to show the freeness and abundance of God's provisions; and to employ the entreaty and expostulation of the sacred Scriptures with the sinner to bring him to Christ, or to induce him to receive Christ.

4. *To build up* in grace and holiness those who have received Christ. Here is ample room for the exercise of all the skill of the minister. The believer is at first but a babe in knowledge and skill and strength. He is required to go on to perfection; but many trials and difficulties lie in his way. He still needs a guide and a sympathizing friend. The minister is to be that guide and friend, and to accomplish the object he must enter into all the circumstances of the different cases that exist in the flock over which he is appointed to watch.

If there be want of zeal and earnestness, he must admonish. If there be a sickly state of soul, the particular cause must be searched out and guarded against, whether it be temptation or sin, or want of information on some point of doctrine, duty, or privilege. When the cause is ascertained, the cure will be suggested. The minister of the Gospel is to watch over his charge and lead them on to the perfection of holiness. This he cannot do by dealing in generalities. The minister

who contents himself with saying on all occasions,
"you must be faithful," or "you must live nearer the
Lord," is like the physician who never distinguishes
the nature and cause of one disease from another, but
prescribes the same remedy in all cases.

The above are to be the general subjects of our pulpit discourses. A little different view of them is suggested by the threefold office of Christ, that of
prophet, priest, and king. A preacher may find other
subjects adapted to please the curious and philosophizing; but if he be a minister of Christ and seeks the
spiritual edification of his flock he will have little
occasion for a greater variety than the above heads
will yield him.

The end of all preaching and of all ministerial labor
is to build up the spiritual temple of God, and to bring
forth the top stone with shouting "Grace, grace unto
it." The ministers of Christ should never lose sight of
this, nor satisfy themselves with the incidental mention
of it, or occasionally teaching it more largely. Their
preaching and praying should all have a direct tendency
to this end. It should enter into their private instructions and their whole intercourse with mankind. Then,
and not till then, will both ministry and people be
imbued with the spirit of holiness. God will dwell
among men, and the whole earth shall be full of the
glory of God.

It is hardly possible to speak of this exhibition of the
duty of the pulpit in terms equal to its merit. At this
day, when men are pressed on all sides by tastes and
tendencies and innovations that touch the minister at
every point, how difficult may it seem to keep in the
plain path marked out by the Son of God; and yet the
day that sees the rigor of conscience relax as to proper
duty, as to our specific call and necessary work, the day

that sees any thing in the pulpit not in consonance with this conviction—no matter with what ingenuity and skill presented—will be a day of gloom as real, if not as painful, as was known in the "Dark Ages." The light of the pulpit is the light of truth ; that truth is to recover the lost, exalt the depressed, refine the impure, dignify the abject, and show society something of the first Paradise—the prelude to that heavenly state for which the Gospel is the only means of preparing men.

Dr. Durbin's sermons were constructed on the principles of homiletic art. There was order, progress, and climax. In all that he prepared there was implicit respect to the result. Whether he inverted a sentence or transposed a paragraph or changed the number or place of a proposition, he kept before him the sense of the sacred writer, and strove by all the means that logic and rhetoric furnished to present it in the fullest sense and with the greatest force. *Progress was an essential condition of success.* This was as really the case with his matter as with his voice and manner. His sermons were formed to instruct, impress, and move.

As in architecture there is the foundation and the "top stone"—there is the purpose, the plan and the building—so he had the place for every part necessary to the intellectual structure.

As the osseous system is essential to the human organization, so is a skeleton to a sermon. There must be something to build on. As through the entire length of the spinal column there runs what may be called brain matter, so in every well constructed discourse there must run the matter that shows a sound and disciplined mind. The part of an oration that mind does not influence fails to show the orator. Passion is not enough. Thought must kindle passion, as passion awakened emotions. This Dr. Durbin realized. His respect to result expresses itself in strongest language.

The introductions to Dr. Durbin's sermons were varied by subjects and circumstances. One might be formed from a scriptural fact or from the occasion of the passage; another from a philosophical principle or an event of history. Pertinence was the governing law. As a rule it was brief and direct. One thing bore upon another and there was nothing useless. He had none of the abruptness of Sterne, who began with "that I deny;" nor the elaboration that Richard Winter Hamilton shows, especially as we see him in a sermon on the Last Judgment, from the text Rev. xx, 11-13: "I saw a great white throne and Him that sat on it." After a most vivid exhibition of Bishop Massillon, on the occasion of a royal funeral, closing with the expression "there is nothing great but God," Hamilton says, "There is nothing solemn but the judgment." Then he declares: "The thunder-storm is solemn, when lightnings as arrows shoot abroad, when the peals startle up the nations, when the dread artillery rushes along the sky. But what is it to that far-resounding crash, louder than the roar and bellow of ten thousand thousands, which shall pierce the deepest channels and which all the dead shall hear?

"The ocean tempest is solemn when the huge billows lift up their crests, when mighty armaments are wrecked by their fury, when the proudest barks are shattered, broken as the foam, scattered as the spray. But what is this to that commotion of the deep when its proud waves 'shall no more be stayed,' its ancient barriers be no more observed, the largest channels be emptied, and the deepest abyss be dried?

"The earthquake is solemn when, without warning, cities totter and kingdoms and islands flee away. But what is it to that tremor which shall convulse our globe, dissolving every law of attraction, severing every principle of aggregation, heaving all into chaos, and heaping all into ruin? The volcano is solemn when its cone of fire shoots to the heavens, crimsoning the zenith with its portentous blaze, while from its burning entrails lava rushes to overspread distant plains and to overtake flying peoples. But what is that to the conflagration in which all the palaces and the temples and citadels of the earth shall be consumed?"

Of the merits of that composition, of its terrific grandeur, we need say nothing; but are we not justified in asserting this ought not to be an example for an introduction? In all the sermon there is not such another passage. Was this the place for it? Dr. Durbin's purpose would not allow such an introduction. It is said of Dr. John M. Mason that on one occasion he began a sermon with rapping three times upon the pulpit and saying, "A voice from the eternal world addresses you," and then announced the text, and at once the congregation showed emotion. Yet, as a remarkable fact, he held the closest attention of the people to the close of the sermon. Few men could accomplish such a result. Certainly this was not his habit. We never saw it in Dr. Durbin. In his sermon in the *Methodist Preacher*, founded on John i, 1, " In the beginning was the Word, and the Word was with God, and the Word was God," the theme is the "Character and Mission of Jesus Christ." He begins this simply: "By consulting the fourteenth and eighteenth verses we learn how the text regards the Lord Jesus Christ, and the whole is predicated of him." This was one of his great sermons preached while he was at Augusta College, Kentucky. On the same theme he preached for two hours at Vincentown, N. J., and such was the influence against the error of Elias Hicks as to keep the sermon in perpetual memory. Six lines comprehend his introduction.

His sermon on the " Omnipresence of God " is from the text, 2 Chron. vi, 18, "Will God in very deed dwell with men on the earth ?   Behold heaven and the heaven of heavens cannot contain thee; how much less this house which I have built."   The introduction covers a half page.

With a sermon so introduced he would raise his proposition or divide his text.   Then he began an exposition that was usually calm, clear, and luminous; not permitting himself to impair his purpose by consuming too much time in the earlier parts of his discourse.

Arguments, narratives, illustrations came in natural order.   But *application*—what our fathers called the " life of preaching "—was to Dr. Durbin a strong hope for the moral effect and permanent result of the discourse.   His peroration was the place of concentrated thought and power.

He expresses caution against being "too diffuse and minute in the first part of the discussion, leaving but little time for the latter part, which is generally the most important."   He says, "Probably the preacher ought never to exhaust himself on his subject ; certainly not in the first part of his discourse.   His matter ought to increase in interest and importance to the close, and the expenditure of his strength and energy ought to increase with the increase of his matter.   In this way the services terminate with a powerful and abiding impression, under the influence of which the people depart to their homes.   Such a sermon on ordinary occasions need rarely exceed three quarters of an hour.   This leaves time for hymns and suitable prayer.   If there be any two things of the prudential and discretionary kind more important than others to the success of the preacher of the word of God they are these :

"1. Judgment and discretion in the selection of a subject. Recollect the *subject* is the object of the selection rather than the text ; the text is the occasion generally to discuss the subject.

"2. So arrange the matter that it will not make your sermon too long, seizing upon the strong and practical points in it and not attempting to exhaust every point, and in doing this, if possible, and it generally is, throw the most interesting part or parts of it toward the close, and often dispose of one division of the subject by way of application if it be copious."

In studying Dr. Durbin's power as a preacher we may consider :

1. The general character of his sermons. In the specimens of the discourses furnished we can see his skill in treating subjects in the various departments of homiletic teaching. They were expositions, illustrations, and divine orations. His themes corresponded with his purpose and his plans were suited to his design. His texts presented ample matter for discussion and declamation, for philosophy, poetry, and the highest Christian eloquence. They sometimes permitted speculation, which he was quick to perceive and careful to guard.

Evremont advises the minister to "make choice of such subjects as are susceptible of ornament and energy." To a nature capable of apprehending or appreciating things according to their claim a great theme induces great thoughts, and these in turn compel vigorous and elevated language. Genius asks scope, and eloquence will have fullness and freedom.

Sublime artists and poets give proof of this demand. Rubens sought immortality in the "Crucifixion;" Ra-

21

phael, in the "Transfiguration;" Michael Angelo, in the "Last Judgment;" our own West, in "Death on the Pale Horse." Homer lives in the "Illiad;" Milton, in "Paradise Lost;" and Dante, in "The Vision." This includes paradise, purgatory, and perdition. Great sermons are associated with great subjects. Thus we have Bourdaloue in "The Passion;" Barrow on "The Resurrection of Christ;" and Massillon on "The Small Number of the Elect;" Howe on "The Redeemer's Tears over Lost Souls;" McLaurin on "Glorying in the cross;" Edwards on "Sinners in the Hands of an Angry God." Amid the great number of sermons that we read from Hugh Blair, with high admiration of the beauty of his rhetoric, where is there one that for its grandeur makes such an appeal as that on "Father, the hour is come"—the death of Christ?

Great subjects are found in every department of Christian teaching. They may be doctrinal, experimental, or practical. They may be expository, textual, or topical. Types and parables, biography and history offer themes to interest the mind, to touch the conscience, and to subdue the heart. Dr. Durbin employed all.

He presented symmetry in the body of truth. Every doctrine had its place and purpose. *Essential truth* gave him *great themes*, such as "The Omnipresence of God," "The Incarnation," "The Character and Mission of Jesus Christ," "The Atonement," "The Conversion of Saul of Tarsus," "The Resurrection," "The Word of God Abiding in Us," "The Signs of the Times," and "Divine Providence." These subjects induced sublime thoughts. As he who would rear a majestic structure must have a strong foundation, or as the tree that is exposed to storm and tempest can only war with the elements and retain its place by having sufficient soil, and sending down and out its roots, so his ministry respected the means of stability and support.

His preaching looked to the conviction, conversion, and profiting of men. To fell the forest requires a robust woodman; but he has honor who cultivates the grounds so cleared. The psalmist, speaking of building the temple, says, "A man was famous according as he had lifted up axes upon the thick trees." Thick trees fell under the stroke of Dr. Durbin. But he knew and improved the soil and gathered of the fruits.

His ministry was not weakened by dangerous theological *speculation*. He did not add to or take from the words of the book, nor mystify the manifest. He had an active mind and an inventive genius. It was quite common with him to suggest an inquiry that philosophy might prompt in relation to things not revealed. Then he showed vigor of reasoning and plausibility of conjecture. It imparted the interest that novelty gives, and served to enlarge, if it did not brighten, the realm of thought. But it was in profound submission to the written word. This was calculated to exalt rather than depress faith. He well knew our perpetual tendency and multiplied temptations to lean to our own understanding; that a cultivated mind is prone to depart from the simplicity that is in Christ. He was not a stranger to the lures that offer and the diversions that are so easy and frequent. He would consider a weak faith one of the saddest things in its effect upon the ministry. It compels weak utterances. He cannot be called a "preacher of the word" who does not know the word to preach. The language of his labor was, "The prophet that hath a dream, let him tell a dream; and he that hath my word, let him speak my word faithfully." While he acknowledged there is much that is unknown in relation to the future, as there certainly is in regard to the present, he felt, as does the true scientist, that the unknown is not to impair the power of the known, or to lessen the effort of securing from it all that it offers. He who knows God, and Jesus Christ whom he hath sent—he who knows that he is born of God, and possesses the peace that he gives—knows something; knows that he has not followed fables. Dr. Durbin spoke with authority.

His preaching was not distinguished as polemical. He had a creed and he preached it. In some instances he encountered an error with directness and vigor, as when in his early ministry he delivered his famous sermon in the West on the "Deity of Christ." He was not ostentatious of his ability as a logician in seeking to show how he could demolish a difficulty or annihilate an adversary. He rather *projected truth* than *fought error.* He expelled the one by making place for the other. His treatment was systemic. He was like the physician who builds up the constitution to overcome the infirmity, and by moral means secures natural ends.

Christian apologetics had only due place in his ministry. With him the pulpit was not the professor's chair. He could defend the Scriptures in the evidences furnished by their necessity, inspiration and benefits. But his custom was "to preach the word." He had less rubbish to remove than truth to offer. He did not make fruitless attempts to convince men's minds, when he knew that their *hearts* presented the *citadel* to attack. It was wittily said by a great statesman, when Bishop Watson wrote his *Apology for the Bible,* that the Bible needs no apology. Of Dr. Durbin we may say the Scriptures commanded his reason, inspired his confidence, and satisfied his noblest aspiration. He found Scripture history sustained by facts, Bible doctrines the necessity of the race, and showed the influence of its moral precepts in exalting a nation and in purifying and honoring men.

He was pre-eminently a preacher of fundamental truths. To this he was called; in this he delighted; and the results of this that he witnessed satisfied him that to this no merely æsthetical or metaphysical preaching bears any comparison. He sought to "make the tree good that the fruit might be good also." He insisted, therefore, that neither circumcision nor uncircumcision avails any thing, but a new creature, and that without holiness no man shall see the Lord. Dr. Durbin knew that in Christianity Jesus Christ is "all in all;" that he is our rock of stability and defense.

Some of his discourses were highly expository. He loved the logical, and frequently made his sermons on a theme before selecting his text.

Analysis was the habit of his mind, yet the synthetical found large place in his preaching. He was fond of the psychological treatment of subjects. This he used to achieve the best results. He looked at principles that, though unconsciously to ourselves, influence conduct—principles that are as real, though not recognized, as the intuitions. By close observation, by natural tendency, by rational processes, he detected and exposed the springs of moral action.

As the astute statesman by broader observation and deeper insight foretells results of legislation or government, and the course of events that astonishes the less acute, so he, by discussing "mind-nature," revealed to men facts in their own bosom that they had failed to recognize, but that, being now made manifest, they were compelled to acknowledge in the obligations that they involved. Such reasoning is to our consciousness what introspection in the Christian is to the *heart*. It gives to conscience the greater grip, and compels conviction to assert itself. But we are not to suppose that he indulged in terminology that perplexed the hearer, or that he dealt in the abstruse or recondite, that true oratory forbids. Metaphysical labyrinths were condemned alike by his intelligence and his purpose. It was only as people followed him here that he obtained the desired response.

Thus to an enlightened conscience he held up the mirror and compelled men to see themselves, or presented scales the accuracy of which was accepted and constrained men to weigh themselves, and acknowledge they were "found wanting."

His sermon in *Pulpit Eloquence of the Nineteenth Century* shows this character of preaching. "Will God in very deed dwell with men on the earth?" 2 Chron. vi, 18. He sees in "the constitution of men, the nature of reason, the observation of every day, the consciousness of each pure heart, the mission and testimony of the Holy Scriptures, that a sense of continual personal omnipresence of Jehovah is the most powerful restraint on vice and the most efficient encouragement to virtue." F. V. Reinhard, the illustrious "Court Preacher" at Dresden, furnishes a fine example of such preaching in his sermon on John the Baptist, as given by Professor Edwards A. Park in the sixth volume of *Bibliotheca Sacra.*

Saurin's sermon on "the Passions" was pronounced by John Foster one of the best specimens of such discourse in the language. Bishop Butler's sermon on "Human Nature" illustrates the highest skill in this kind of pulpit appeal.

Of the same class is the celebrated sermon of Dr. Chalmers on the "Expulsive Power of a New Affection;" of like nature is Bushnell's admirable discourse on "Unconscious Influence." In this grand category we place the eloquent sermon of Dr. McClintock in

Pulpit Eloquence of the Nineteenth Century. The subject is "the ground of man's love to God."

It requires a high order of intellect to produce its proper power; but here Dr. Durbin was a master. He reasoned like Paley; he searched like Butler; he warmed like Massillon; he subdued and conquered like Wesley. Shall we call this psychological probing? The rather let us say, *Moral vivisection.* Only the soul can certify the scrutiny. It was like Nathan's parable to David to impress the sin of the sovereign.

With what delicacy and deference did he prepare the case and address the king! How perfectly did he conduct the parable to awaken the indignation of a man by an appeal to moral *consciousness!* In all the concealment of his design how fairly and fully did he obtain a verdict of an inward but now outspoken conviction of moral right! Thus is it in the kind of preaching of which we now write. Truth is exhibited; her claim is so clearly shown, the evil of the sin is so manifest, that the man pronounces sentence upon himself. This *is* individualizing. It is thus that God says, "Out of thy own mouth will I judge thee." This is tremendous preaching. It is moral consciousness that has become the preacher. The pulpit has fired on the fortress, and there is war within.

But Dr. Durbin knew how men become Christians indeed, and he struck at the conscience, that "main pillar of the soul," which amid all the ruins of the fall gives evidence of the original grandeur of the moral temple. Before the highest tribunal on earth he arraigned the sinner and made him tremble, and when conscience failed in its functions he caused the truth of God to flash into the darkest corners of the heart, and showed the chamber of images with all kinds of idolatry and odious objects.

Did ever any mere man possess the power to make a bold and startling statement of the most weighty truth greater than he sometimes did, when his soul was full of his subject and the end for which he labored made the demand?

The writer is indebted to Edward Sargent, Esq., of Cincinnati, for the following illustration. He says: "Dr. Durbin was preaching a sermon on the general judgment, and in the course of it said the general judgment might last an indefinite length of time, 'perhaps ten thousand years,' and then, with a flash in his eye, said, 'the damnation of the sinner would then come soon enough.'"

CHAPTER XIX.

The Lord's Call to the Ministry.

A CONSCIOUS call to the ministry is both an inspiration to duty and a guard against discouragement in the work.

In secular pursuits men justly make their choice. Their future is at their disposal, and they are responsible for its results. Having freedom of action they may consult their tastes, their talents, and their opportunities. Their supposed interests influence their conclusions, and excellence and success may be anticipated where the widest doors open and aptitudes and preferences are indulged. But a call to the ministry is of God. He who from the beginning has had a cause in the earth has had his own way of sustaining and advancing it. Moses saw God in the burning bush and heard his voice from the flame. The tribe of Levi was separated for the tabernacle, and he inspired the prophets. Isaiah responded to his appeal amid the glory that filled the temple and awed the six-winged seraphim, when his tongue was touched with a "live coal from off the altar." To Jeremiah God said, " Whatsoever I command thee thou shalt speak." Paul was a chosen vessel to bear his name to the Gentiles and to the kings and to the children of Israel. To his apostles he said, " Go ye into all the world and preach the Gospel to every creature." The commission to preach remains with the divine head, and " no man taketh this honor to himself but he that is called of God, as was Aaron." Greatly as he has honored the Church in her labors to extend his kingdom, positive as is the aid that his people often render the student in preparing for his work, and manifest as is the power of the faithful in sustaining him when in the field, the *authority* to *preach* is from a higher source. This the Church recognizes when she asks the candidate, "Do you trust that you are *inwardly moved* by the *Holy Ghost* to take upon you the office of ministration ?"

Respect for the offices, the functions, and usefulness of the minister might induce an *earnest Christian* to desire the place, and one might reason from his natural endowments, his educational advantages, his mother's prayers, and his father's wishes, and ask himself whether it is not his duty to preach? If after the careful searching of his heart, rigorous analysis of his motives, and humble prayer to know the will of God, the impression is made, and stirs the soul to such effort, he may accept it as the *inward call.* If then in attempting to speak he has the help of the Holy Spirit, and the Church witnesses his " gifts, grace, and usefulness "— if providence opens the way and seems to point out this path—if in following those indications the mind settles in the belief that God calls, we say this is enough to justify conviction of duty. *This is the outward call.* This ends anxiety. He discriminates between a *conception* and a *consciousness,* between a *wish* and an *obligation.* He then acts on *divine authority,* which feeling is one of the greatest forces that he ever experiences in delivering his message.

It is not himself speaking ; it is not merely the church that licensed him ; it is not the ecclesiastical economy that directs him, but it is God that speaks through him. It is not too much to assume that a man may be *conscious* of such call. If God by his " Spirit bears witness with our spirit" as to our *conversion*—if the "Spirit help our infirmities" so that we know the things we ought to pray for," surely it is not presumption to suppose in desiring men for the greatest work on earth he should *satisfy them* concerning his will. He who called Samuel by a *vocal utterance* can now speak by the *inward voice* of his Spirit, and thus make an indelible impression upon the mind.

It was for such *consciousness* that young Durbin waited. The taste of his childhood, the wish of his mother, his respect for the ministry, and the exercises of his mind were not sufficient. The mental struggle continued till facts compelled conviction. The searching question as to his duty, coming from his saintly grandfather, went through his soul with such power that it shook all secular purposes out of his heart. The observing church expressed its judgment, and the presiding elder sought his service; such concurrent evidence and the influence of the Spirit satisfied his mind, and he modestly but earnestly entered upon his work.

Consciousness of a *call* from God, and the felt presence of the Holy Spirit, are the highest inspiration that the *preacher* needs. It causes the obedient servant to spring forward with a noble alacrity and with necessary determination. The soul rises into a moral realm, where earthly ambitions and prospects have no influence. Gold has lost its glitter, fame its lure, and the richest possessions fail to deter or divert from duty. A holy passion subordinates all things to its control. With the obligation comes the impulse to its discharge. He says, "This work shall make my heart rejoice." Not *less is this consciousness a guard against all discouragements.* Profound as are the convictions that impel to action, powerful as is the influence that urged on the young preacher, he will become familiar with trials which this *consciousness* alone will overcome.

(*a.*) There may be physical suffering that will test devotion to the work. He who reads the journal of Freeborn Garrettson in the earliest ministry of Methodism in this country well knows what it is to suffer in this calling. Even in Maryland, his native State, he was beaten by his persecutors and left *unconscious* on the road, and Mr. Hartley was imprisoned.

Who can read without tears the narrative of ministers of later years? In the biographical sketches edited by Dr. T. O. Summers we have two, written by Bishop H. N. McTyeire. They were the first laborers in Louisiana. The Bishop says, "Louisiana has been the Macedonia of the Methodist Episcopal Church." As an example of suffering he quotes from Elisha Bowman, the pioneer, January 29, 1806. "Every day that I travel I have to swim through creeks or swamps, and I am wet from my head to my feet, and some days from morning till night I am dripping with water. . . . I have given you a faint idea of my travels. . . . What I have suffered in body and mind my pen is not able to communicate to you; but this I can say: while my body is wet with water and chilled with cold my soul is filled with heavenly fire. . . . And while these periods drop from my pen my soul is ready to leave this earthly house and fly to endless rest." What but *consciousness of his call* held this man in such a work? He was a writer of beauty, tenderness, and force. The next case is that of Richard Nolley, of whom we have a sketch also in Sprague's *Annals of the Methodist Pulpit.* He was a preacher of whom the late Daniel De Vinne, of the New York East Conference, used to make devout mention. In self-denial and in holiness Mr. Nolley would compare with Thomas Walsh. Of

South-western Louisiana it was said "the gospel plow-share never struck into a harder soil," but this saint essayed to break it. Omitting his almost unexampled difficulties, shameful persecution, and the great revivals that marked his short history, we view him in his closing suffering and triumph. He had finished a journey of three hundred and fifty miles through the wilderness, swimming deep creeks and lying out eleven nights, and had reached his appointment. He passed a village of Indians, and in attempting to cross a swift stream he and his horse were parted. He escaped drowning, but, chilled and exhausted, the cold and darkness every moment becoming intenser, he sank down and seemed conscious of his approaching end. On Friday, his fast-day, amid the gloom of the place and period, the Bishop says, " he met the shining ones." Thus in his divine vocation, when only thirty-four years of age, perished one of the best men out of heaven. " His knees were muddy, and the prints of them were on the ground, showing what his last exercise had been. . . . A traveler the next day about four o'clock found the corpse . . . and the neighbors bore the frozen form to the house where it was supposed he aimed to go." Died he not as a martyr? Received he not a martyr's crown? May it not be written of him as of Saint Paul, " In perils of waters . . . in perils in the wilderness . . . in weariness and painfulness, in watchings often, in hunger and thirst, in fastings often, in cold and nakedness?"

Such cases are not common, but they show us the necessity—at least for our fathers to know they were moved by the Holy Ghost to take upon them this ministry. How much was *comprehended* in J. P. Durbin's case has never had a full record, but we have seen sufficient to justify our joy that he was *conscious* that

God separated him to this work. Few preachers of the present day have the same kind of *trials* or so much of such difficulty. But we shall see that they have enough to make it desirable that they should realize how imperative is their duty.

(*b.*) He has the depression that arises from felt inadequacy to his work. An apostle exclaimed, "Who is sufficient for these things?" Flushed as the young preacher sometimes is with the results of his first efforts, encouraged as he has been by the kind expression of devoted friends, there are few, if any, who do not experience a mental depression that their failures to meet their wishes have induced. Criticisms may be heard, sometimes doubts are expressed; his painful want of knowledge, his need of more of the Holy Spirit, and his exalted ideal of a sermon, may awaken strong temptations to despair in the prosecution of his work. He is not unwilling to deny himself. He shrinks from no part of his labor because of its difficulties, but he is oppressed with the thought that he is unequal to the place. Nor has this been the experience alone of those not educated nor distinguished for talent. Preachers who have been most admired have had this trial. Robert Hall was a great orator, but he called together his vestry to resign his pastorate because of the thought of his inadequacy. It was not because Lawrence Laurenson, of the Philadelphia Conference, was not one of the most eloquent men of that body that he rolled on the floor and protested that he could not preach. We have seen what were the reasonings of J. P. Durbin in relation to his first efforts, and of the kindness that he thought was necessary upon the part of the people to receive and treat him so well.

(*c*) The preacher needs the consciousness of a divine call to guard him against discouragement.

According to the Methodist Discipline, the *sole* business of a preacher is to save souls. It says, "You have nothing to do but save souls." For this he studies, prays, and weeps between the porch and the altar, but, like the disciples, he sometimes says, "we have toiled all night and taken nothing." What, then, will satisfy ? Will the hospitalities that have been received, the courtesies extended, the commendation bestowed, the friendships formed, or the salary promptly and liberally paid ? Will the largeness of the congregation or the intellectual make-up of the assembly ? Will these satisfy him ? If they will he is out of his place or is out of the right state of mind and heart. A Methodist preacher without souls is like a glorified saint without a crown. What is our hope, our joy, our crown of rejoicing ? Are not even ye, in the presence of our Lord Jesus Christ at his coming ?

The preacher *considers the import and difficulty of his work.* To operate upon matter is one thing, to influence mind is another. To span the East River with a single arch, to bridge the distance and to open a highway of travel and commerce between New York and Brooklyn, is a work that intelligence, energy, time, and necessary means could accomplish. By civil engineering, by scientific knowledge, by mechanical skill, by a wise calculation of the forces of nature, all this has been done, and millions in a single year chose this as a highway without apprehension of harm. To this the genius of a Roebling is equal; but who shall close up the moral distance between an offended God and an unforgiven sinner? One Mediator bridged the chasm of the fall by the cross of Calvary, that opens a "highway and the redeemed pass over it." But what unrepenting soul experiences its advantages? Who shall conquer rebellion ? By what power shall we make the alien a real child ? To move the mind in the right direction, when taste, and habit, and a depraved heart are behind it, is such labor as even the Holy Ghost does not accomplish without the sinner's consent. God asks, "How shall I put thee among the children ?" It is not in man to do it. The vastness of the interest at stake, the authority on which the minister speaks, the ardor of his spirit, the earnestness of his effort, and the efficacy of his prayers, together with the force of his arguments and the power of his appeal, will not secure the end. A church in tears, a revival in progress, and angels in waiting to carry the intelligence of a sinner's repenting are not enough to save one soul, who will not have this man to reign over him. This almost breaks a preacher's heart. ·

He may feel that his skirts are clear, but he knows that the skirts of others are crimsoned with "blood-guiltiness." How felt the holy Rutherford when he said, "My witness is in heaven ; your heaven would be two heavens to me and your salvation two salvations ?"

Richard Cecil declares a country minister fighting the devil in his parish has a higher idea than Julius Cæsar or Napoleon ever dreamed of. All ministers may say, " We wrestle not against flesh and blood, but against principalities, against powers, against spiritual wickedness in high places."

The *obstacles that are sometimes encountered in the state of the Church demand the guard and support afforded by consciousness of a call to the place.* God. says, "I would that you were cold or hot." Paul declares it is good to be zealously affected always in a good thing.

Zeal for God in the Church is the pastor's hope, want of it his fear. If there be inertness, it matters not what else there is, there is real grief. The learning, the wealth, the social position, the numbers may all be readily and gladly acknowledged ; but what are these if conscience is obtuse or energy sleeps; if they know not that they are poor and miserable and blind and naked ?

Not to help is bad, but it is worse to hinder.

In the Evangelical Alliance held in New York, in 1873, no essay moved that vast assembly like the one delivered by Dr. T. Christlieb, professor of theology and university preacher at Bonn, Prussia. It was on "Modern Infidelity." But the utterance of greatest power was to the effect that modern infidels do not read the Scriptures. They study the Bible in those who profess to follow its teaching. If they are not right they condemn this book. Thus religion is judged not by what it is, but by what our example makes it. If they see in the life of a professor even apocryphal conduct, the charge is upon religion—that it does not make us just and good. It has often been found that the church that is not a hot-bed for the fruits of the Spirit is one of noxious weeds, and that roots of bitterness springing up trouble it. There are those who "walk disorderly and will not be reproved." Thence come dissensions and every evil work, and the minister is compelled to resort to the discipline of the Church. Inaction is construed into connivance or cowardice, and administration may be regarded by others as unnecessary or severe. This is the most painful, and sometimes the most perplexing duty of a pastor, and he may ask, "Did my call mean this ?" "Besides those things that are without, that which cometh upon me daily, the care of all the churches. Who is weak and I am not weak? Who is offended and I burn not ?"

Young Durbin knew the import of what we have thus stated. But as our ministry sometimes involves physical sufferings, and even death, so it comprehends such

22

trials that we justly deplore. Who would not shun such a fold?

Financial embarrassments may add to the facts already named. When one gives himself to the itinerancy his first care is to make full proof of his ministry. He may have but himself to support. Whether his salary is less or more than $50 a year is a minor matter. The trade of young Durbin might yield more in a month than his preaching would in a year. But what of that? He lived among the people and his wants were met. Yet the man who has a family, and for five or six years receives about $100 a year, as was the case with one clergyman, is in a different case. He can bear privations, but his wife and children must have support. To add to the trial, he sees men in business rising to wealth, and that with no more talents, energy, and enterprise than are demanded of a preacher in order to success.

He sees, moreover, that riches gained are enabling men in secular life to accomplish for the Church and society what the minister is unable to do —planting missions, establishing Sunday-schools, endowing professorships, building hospitals, and contributing largely to the support of the Church, whereby they obtain an influence to which the minister can never rise. It may not astonish us that he is tempted to think he would be justified in departing from the work.

When Sir Matthew Hale meditated the ministry and the law, and thought of the influence that he might exert in adopting the legal profession, he reasoned thus: The same acts that the love of God prompts in an earnest Christian exert more power when coming from a layman than from a minister. In a lawyer it would be attributed to zeal for usefulness, in a minister it would be regarded as a part of his profession. In the law he certainly made himself useful as a Christian.

But the minister ponders his call and what it involves. With something like a just appreciation of his case he says:

"I am a 'shepherd' of Christ's sheep, and must fold and feed, must guide and guard the flock. Shall the sheep perish for whom Christ died?

"I am a 'steward,' and it is required of him that he be found faithful. Shall I be derelict to duty?

"I am a 'watchman.' Will I see the sword and give no alarm?

"I am an 'ambassador.' Shall I not entreat men to be reconciled to God?

"Shall I leave my post? If dignity be judged by the authority that confers it—if his intelligence and skill and loyalty are equal to his charge—then earth and heaven meet in the ministrations of him who negotiates between God and man."

Who shall describe his responsibility? The shepherd must go into the wilderness after the lost sheep. That is what Garrettson, Bowman, and Nolley were doing.

The steward must give to every one his portion in due season. The watchman lifts up his voice like a trumpet, and the ambassador in Christ's stead asks, implores, and exhausts his resources that this war with God may come to an immediate end. All this was recognized by John P. Durbin.

Such relationships do not allow these spiritual functions to be neglected. In the life of Robert S. McAll, LL.D., we have an illustration of the liability to discouragement in a minister of pre-eminent ability and of the power that held him in his place. He was called "the Cicero of Nonconformity;" yet he declared that such was his sense of responsibility that nothing could induce him to continue his labors but the most absolute conviction of duty, and that he dared not retire, else he should have done so long since, adding emphatically these words, " O, sir, frequently have I come home Sabbath morning when, under the agonizing feeling, I have thrown myself on the sofa, and had it not been a sin to commit suicide I should have done it rather than preach again in the evening."

This language is too strong; but it came from one of keen sensibility, who allowed the tempter too much power; but it gives those who do not know it some view of the mental sufferings of which a faithful minister may be the subject.

Such are some of the trials that ministers meet, and that make a clear sense of duty an imperative demand. When a weak mortal feels the confluence of so many streams, and some of them of such volume—when such bitter waters rise and rage around him, could it be expected that he will stand firm if he has nothing behind him but his own tastes, a college education, a theological training, or his past preparations of whatever sort— nothing but those things that are from the human to keep him firm? If there was ever a tinge of romance in the life it is gone. If there was ever experiment, it is over. If it was to reach a certain reputation, that matter is settled with joy or grief. But there is something higher. He pauses, he prays, he weeps. His mind reverts to his mental processes and his moral conclusions. He thinks of the books he read to help his thoughts of duty. He remembers that then, if ever, his devotion to God was pure; then, if ever, his eye was single; then, if ever, he had God's work at heart, and he asks with an agonized mind, " Shall such a man as I flee? Shall a standard-bearer faint? Is the necessity absolute? Then only may I feel my call for this work at this time is out." He sees his way is not fully shut up. Now he would retire but for the conscious call.

With one who once was an evangelical power in this land, he says, "Die on the field of battle."

Before once fleeing, welcome a thousand deaths. We honor the soldier whom danger makes more brave. We laud the physician whom pestilence does not drive from duty; but worldly ambition may prompt the one, while lucrative practice may influence the other. But God's minister looks at his commission, and says it is from a higher power, is for a nobler end, and is governed by *celestial motives*. What if the depressed Elijah was under the juniper-tree—what if Jeremiah said, "I will not speak any more in his name." I live under the dispensation of the Holy Ghost, and mine may be the tongue of fire. "He that walketh in the midst of the seven golden candlesticks holds the seven stars in his right hand."

Of the trials of Dr. Durbin in the ministry we may not adequately speak. He was not accustomed to recount or to dwell upon them. He saw the end rather than the difficulties in his way. Time and trial were less than duty and destiny. But we have seen his aspirations and the obstacles in his path. We have seen him with a salary that it shames our present Methodism to remember. We have seen him with loss of voice at the end of his first six months, a fact well calculated to crush hope and extinguish every fire of sanctified ambition. We heard him tell of painful failure in preaching the word, but he had heard God. He had heard the Church. He had not gone without being sent. He knew the exercises of his own mind, and the experiences of his heart, and he could calmly say, "None of these things move me." And his life was made grand. What like such consciousness of a call makes a man courageous and eloquent as a preacher of the word.

CHAPTER XX.

Eloquence a Worthy Study.

ELOQUENCE is a reality. Nothing more certainly affects individuals or masses of men. In war and in peace it makes appeals that compel response, and if it is truthfully said "the pen is mightier than the sword," he who knows the full power of speech will confess the tongue is mightier than the pen. The fathers of the Revolution did well to consider the statements and the arguments of Jefferson's pen; but what roused the colonies like the utterances of Adams, of Otis, and of Patrick Henry?

In classic Greece and ancient Rome eloquence was the highest study for power and fame. It was a remark of Henry Clay that "there is no power like the power of oratory. Cæsar conquered men by exciting their fears; Cicero by captivating their affections and swaying their passions. The influence of the one perished with its author, while that of the other continues to this day." It is said, "Julius Cæsar was subdued by the eloquence of Cicero, and absolved the criminal whom he had determined to punish."

But this very power has been made an argument against the cultivation of eloquence. It has been said, "it may influence the simple, but not the wise." There may be those who can make the worse appear the better reason. But eloquence is not sophistry. Eloquence has been pronounced a "virtue." This, like any other power, may be used for good or evil. The sun

that warms the soil for the seed may burn up vegetation and cause famine. And the rains of heaven that
the farmer asks may flood his fields. The very strength
that God gave to Samson made him the sport of fools
that " make a mock at sin."

We are even cautioned against " receiving the grace
of God in vain." There is no faculty with which we
are endowed, and there is no acquisition in learning
that we can make, that may not be turned to ill account.
As really from the printing press that gives us Bibles
at so cheap a rate comes polluting literature at prices
that any may pay. Men do not refuse money because
there are misers; and even Christians labor for its possession, though " the love of money is the root of all evil."

But what is there in the eloquence of speech to justify opposition to its cultivation? It is the clothing of
our thoughts in such language and expressing them in
such manner as are adapted to produce conviction and
persuasion. It is the art of speaking to effect our purpose. Quintilian says, " It is in the heart, in the genius,
and in the thoughts, that eloquence properly consists,"
and surely a *wise* man will not refuse these. It will
hardly be assumed that Benjamin Franklin was a weak
man, or that David Hume or Lord Chesterfield were to
be pronounced simple as to their judgments of the
works of men. Yet the eloquence of Whitefield made
Franklin, despite his former purpose, empty his purse
for a collection, and caused Chesterfield to say he would
go twenty miles to hear him and captivated Hume.

Emerson says: " The orator is he whom every man
is seeking when he goes into court, into conventions,
into any popular assembly. His speech is the electricity
of action." Hervey declares, " When Secker preaches
or when Murray pleads, the church is crowded and the
bar is thronged."

Eloquence is oratory in its highest perfection. "It is successful, triumphant oratory." It impresses others as the speaker is impressed. It is touching a chord in another's heart responsive to his own. It may be eloquence of *thought*, and strike like a missile. It may be eloquence of *language* that goes through men like a sword. It may be eloquence of *passion* that wraps us like a flame. It may be found in massing the weightiest truths and in projecting them with greatest force. It is intensity intensified. It seeks no pomp of diction, assumes no airs of importance. The orator is not to be gazed at or admired, but to be felt. Ostentation is fatal to its purpose, and seeming design is certain defeat. But eloquence respects taste, conciliates prejudice, and studies the avenues to the heart. It accepts and appropriates any means of moral power. By a happy phrase, by an intonation of the voice, by a glance of the eye, by an undesigned gesture, it will achieve results to which it might have been deemed utterly inadequate. The stage is for *acting:* the pulpit is for divine sincerity. It is for showing the truth of God. Real eloquence seems so natural and easy that many are ready to say, "Why can't I do that?" It is not merely what many call elocution. That may mean good voice, fine articulation, graceful attitudes and gestures, and pleasant accent. There may be nothing to offend and yet be no better approach to real eloquence than a statue is to a man. It is cold marble in the one; it is animated flesh and flowing blood in the other. It is as much eloquence as Adam was man before God breathed into him the breath of life, and he became a living soul.

The elements of eloquence inhere in every man's nature, and there is no one who is not at some time eloquent. Let but the subject be presented and the appeal made that wake the soul, and in his way the slave may be as eloquent as the senator. The eloquence may not be in a *stream*, but it is in a *jet*. It is stronger or weaker, longer or shorter, as facts influence. Eloquence is popular as moving the rude as well as re-fined. As the susceptibilities of eloquence are in all, the response to eloquence is from all.

But there is difference both in the kind and degree. All eloquence moves, but not to the same degree or in the same manner. Orators made after one model are artificial and powerless. To be eloquent one must be himself. David would not have been a greater failure as an adversary in the armor of Saul than he would have been as speaker in the style of Jonathan. Imitation in an orator is apt to be detected even by those who never heard the original. For popular or power-ful effect no one is required to conform to any pattern. Bascom, Summerfield, and Durbin were all eloquent. All had admirers, and enough of them for fame. A distinctive impression was produced by each. *Tastes* in hearers, as really as *talent* in speakers, differ.

How far eloquence may be cultivated, and *whether it will compensate the efforts for its attainment*, are questions that should command the devoutest thought of him who would neglect nothing that adds to usefulness.

It may be cultivated: That some have a genius for eloquence that others do not possess admits of no questioning. That all who have the genius do not reach equal excellence is alike certain; but such facts do not justify discouragement. One person has an aptitude and fondness for languages, another for mathematics, another for metaphysics; some for poetry and others for general literature.

Are men endowed for positions? Are specialists thus directed? Minds, like bodies, differ in complexion;

yet vitality is more than color. But as the place of our birth, notwithstanding love of locality that it induces, does not forbid emigration if found to our advantage, so our tastes should not prevent the exercise of our talents in the direction where they can accomplish most. As like genius does not always reach equal eminence, so like effort may not invariably reap the same fruit. One may do with difficulty what another does with ease. But ease and difficulty are not the question to govern one intent on a worthy object. Genius is not to be disparaged, but industry must not be ignored. In some things the impulse of genius will do what hard study will not effect. But he who conceives of genius as that which makes men wise without study, or illustrious without effort, conceives of something that no sensible man should covet.

Dr. Johnson says, "Men have sometimes appeared of such transcendent abilities that their slightest and most cursory performance excel all that labor and study can enable meaner intellects to compose, as there are regions of which the spontaneous products cannot be equaled in other soils by care and culture. But it is not less dangerous for any man to place *himself* in this rank, and fancy that he is born to be illustrious without labor, than to omit the cares of husbandry and expect from the ground the blossoms of Arabia." Because Providence gave the church such young preachers as Spencer and Summerfield is no reason for youthful presumption. Genius does much, but let no one presume.

The counterpart of Napoleon's genius for war may not appear in a century. We may in vain read all history to find another Julius Cæsar, and many years may elapse before our "military academy" will give us another Grant. But this is no proof that "the sword has become a plowshare, or that the spear has been converted into a pruning-hook." Nor would it be deemed wise for our nation to close West Point, or for our young men to decline to study the science and art of war. Ages have passed without producing another Demosthenes or Cicero. Yet England boasts her Sheridan, her Canning, and her Fox; and America points to her mighty orators in Patrick Henry, Fisher Ames. and Henry Clay. And the names of Gladstone and Webster will live in history for their eloquence as well as for their wisdom.

Another John P. Durbin may be sought for in vain among the pulpit orators of the land; but the influence of his example survives him, and the lessons and labors of his life will go on blessing the world. Other men have learned eloquence from his utterances, and some of his characteristics have been and may yet be reproduced in those who heard his discourse or study his life. We wisely aim at what we may not fully reach. The effort is both a discipline and an advantage. We are *endowed for labor*, and the minister may not only cherish a sanctified ambition, but indulge an animating hope.

When Rubenstein heard a distinguished preacher say, "A man must not be expected to do better than he can," he declared he did not like the sermon, because, said the great pianist, "It is false; for men must do the impossible. I tell my pupils if they do not try to compose better than Beethoven they must never come to my tuition." The Greek adage is, "The gods sell every thing to labor." Eloquent speaking may be assumed to be largely the result of study and practice. Much that is almost forgotten may have been learned in childhood at school when the mind and the organs of speech might readily receive some of the best aids to the end meditated. "In former ages the opinion was held that the talent for eloquence was pre-eminently one of discipline, and it is one of the maxims that has descended to the present time that "men must be born to poetry, but bred to eloquence;" that the "bard is always a child of nature and the orator always the issue of instruction." (John Q. Adams's *Lectures on Rhetoric and Oratory*, vol. i, 25.)

Temperament, sympathy, grace of person, compass and sweetness of voice, together with readiness of utterance, make their contribution to the speaker. But which of these may not be improved by use or impaired by disuse? By reading, by conversation, by study of models, one may imbibe the spirit and find the secret that we seek. Eloquence spurns idleness and disowns the self-sufficient. If to be public speakers men study grammar, rhetoric, and logic, why not eloquence in its best manifestations? One may have grammar, rhetoric, and logic; yet lack of ability to speak makes all unavailing. If to be a scholar, to acquire useful arts, we pursue study, and adopt the best means to fit ourselves for positions of responsibility and honor, surely it is not unworthy our best effort to prepare for the calling of a minister of Christ. Galen says, "An unskillful sculptor spoils only a block of marble, but an unskillful physician spoils a man." But a more painful thought is, the unskillful minister may at least fail to save a soul from death.

Men not influenced by the high motives of the Christian have deemed no cost too great if they might acquire eloquence. We are familiar with the narrative of Demosthenes—the impediment in his speech and awkwardness of gesture; that to overcome his faults, under the shame of his defeats he sought seclusion for careful study; then harangued the ocean that he might be superior to the tumult of a great assembly, and put pebbles in his mouth, that if with them he could manage to speak he might find ease in their absence; and to correct the shrug of the shoulder placed a sword to pierce him. His reward was greater than his expenditure of time and effort.

Cicero failed in the beginning "through weakness of lungs and excessive vehemence of manner, which wearied his hearers and defeated his purpose." Study conquered, but it was not till he had traveled in various lands, secured the aid of instructors and critics, that he reached his mark. He passed no day without exercise in his art. The end justified all the means employed.

When Fox first rose in the House of Commons he blundered, stammered, and at last "sat down in discomfiture." But success followed failure, and diligence raised him to the first place of an English orator. When Richard Brinsley Sheridan began his course as a speaker his painful failures induced a friend to say, "Speaking is not your calling." With an emphasis of more vigor than refinement he exclaimed, "It is in me, and I will bring it out." In that reply we have the elements of a mighty orator. There was intensity, determination, and consciousness of his own capability, and all his labor was in faith. It has been stated on good authority that Patrick Henry owed more to the study of the art of eloquence than many have supposed. In early life he had one habit besides that of indolence; it was that of watching the working of the passions and of detecting the motives of human conduct. For these purposes he drew around him groups of companions and engaged them in conversation on excellent subjects.

If there be enough in eloquence to justify such efforts and reward such toil in men of the world is there any labor too great for him whose highest ambition is to reach the minds and hearts of men to save them from "going down to the pit?" Can the minister of the

Son of God allow men of any calling to do more for their purpose than he will do to accomplish the end of his mission? What are crowns on earth, though studded with diamonds, compared with the honor of him that is faithful to his divine vocation, when every soul that he saves by his speech shall be " a star " to shine in the crown of his rejoicing forever and forever? Eloquence is eloquence whether at the bar, in the senate, or the pulpit. If in eloquence there is enough to inspire an army when on the fiery edge of battle; enough to rouse the patriot's soul when death looks him in the face; enough to kindle the fire that no waters of adversity can quench; enough to make the men who heard Demosthenes say, "Let us march against Philip;" if there is enough to cause Burke to say of the speech of Sheridan, " Such a display of powers is unparalleled in the annals of oratory—such a display that reflects the highest honor upon himself, luster upon letters, renown upon the patriot and glory upon the country "—then surely there is enough in eloquence to make the minister do what he can to command it.

What like the eloquence of reason, of conscience—and that the Spirit gives—makes men feel their obligation to rise superior to all the enemies in their path? At such time it is not so much a question as to what a man *knows* as a student as what he *feels* and expresses as the mouth-piece for God. With half the human *knowledge* of another he exerts double his power and secures tenfold the benefit. He carries his cause because he is in it and makes others feel it is in them. Who, then, shall ask, *Is there enough in eloquence to justify a minister in using the means for its attainment?* Are not the means of acquiring eloquence as really at his command as of any other person? Are his faculties and susceptibilities inferior? Will it cost him any more than it does others of like condition but with dissimilar sphere; or can any motives be more powerful to impel than those that influence one of his vocation? Is there not as much in his calling to demand and reveal the highest style of oratory? Has he not greater aids to his pursuit of this power in the fact of God's presence and influence? If he hear God saying, "Go, stand in the temple and speak all the words of this life," is he not then under obligation to employ every auxiliary and improve every opportunity to his usefulness? In the imposed duty to speak there is the implied obligation to speak the best he can. But who has not marked the disparity between able men in relation to eloquence? What makes the difference in many cases between two ministers as to their fields of labor and their opportunities of success? At this day what numbers of excellent preachers are scattered through the country with few to hear them and little to encourage labor! At college and in the theological seminary, or in the places of their preparation, they were the equals of and even superior to those who now fill positions that afford them every encouragement in the work. What is the difference between these men? Piety? No! Learning? No! Unfitness by training for the best society? No! It is solely as to the "art of speaking." In this the difference is sometimes slight, but it is real, which, added to some other minor matter, gives the disparity. In other instances the contrast between preachers is very broad. This calls for the greater effort. We have seen a theological student, about to graduate from one of the noblest institutions of the land, after all the advantages of a college course attempting to deliver a sermon from manuscript in a way that no congregation would endure. We have listened to another, from one of the first schools of theology, standing with his manuscript before a large audience with no more apparent knowledge of what was written than if another had just sent it to him and he was trying for the first time to make out the subject, yet in a manner so irreverent as to excite the derision rather than the pity of the people. Any one of taste for divine things would infinitely prefer the rustic from the plow, without knowledge of a rule in grammar, provided his heart glowed and he "just spoke right on." Ralph Waldo Emerson relates that the Persian poet Saadi heard a person with a disagreeable voice reading the *Koran* aloud, when a holy man passing by asked what was his monthly stipend. He answered, "Nothing at all." "But why do you take so much trouble?" He replied, "I read for the sake of God." The other rejoined, "For God's sake, do not read; for if you read the *Koran* in this manner you will destroy the splendor of Islamism."

If any have need of an audience for the work and for a worthy end it is he who speaks for God. Martin Luther, in naming the qualifications for the preacher for the word, says, "He should be eloquent." It is recorded of Chrysostom, "the golden-mouthed," "that he studied the Greek orators." It is stated that George Whitefield took lessons of Garrick. It is certain that John Wesley advised "all who could to study the art of speaking." He names particular "faults and vices" to be corrected, and impresses rules that secure ease and efficiency in public address. To remedy bad gesture he suggests even a "large looking-glass," that there may be seen reflected in a mirror what the people see in our action before them. He gives Demosthenes as an example of benefit by such means. He says, "There is but one way better than this, which is to have some excellent pattern as often as may be before your eyes."

The Methodist Discipline, in receiving preachers for

the itinerancy, asks, "Do they speak justly, readily, clearly?" Here is the foundation for eloquence, and no Church has a broader, firmer, better one.

Longinus says, "The works of the great masters are like so many sacred sources, where the most frigid kindle and take fire." It is said that Rubens loved to have some one read to him while he delineated his pictures, asserting that the finest imagination needed warming. No one who seeks eloquence has greater helps to its attainment than the gospel minister.

The Father of languages has inspired one Book that is a study and authority and an inspiration to the preacher. Its themes are diverse and its reasonings conclusive. Its light is so perfect and pervading that all may walk in its brightness. For mental elevation, for verbal grandeur, for exalted spirit, for the material and examples of eloquence, the Bible has no equal. The greatest statesmen, the sublimest orators, as well as the most illustrious ministers of Christ, have sought its aid and showed its impress. What book like the Bible quickens thought, broadens intellect, incites and increases mental penetration? In its study we rise to the vastness of eternal verities.

"I have often observed," says Addison, "that whenever the Roman orator, in his philosophical discourses, is led by his argument to the mention of immortality, he seems like one awakened out of sleep; roused and alarmed at the dignity of the subject he stretches his imagination to conceive something uncommon, and with the greatness of his thoughts casts, as it were, a glory round the sentence. Uncertain and unsettled as he was, he seems fired with the contemplation of it."

What God thinks of the power of language and of speech may be judged by the facts that he has furnished. The eloquence of Scripture speaks for itself;

23

and when the lawgiver of Israel thought his lack of ability to speak would be a hinderance to his work the Almighty gave him Aaron, saying, "I know him, that he can speak well.'

But did not St. Paul say he "came not with excellency of speech," and that he "determined not to know any thing among them but Jesus Christ, and him crucified?" Yes, he said this. What did he mean? That he ignored rhetoric? That there was no passion in his utterance? That he did not try to persuade men? Study his life, analyze his speeches, and tell why Felix trembled and Agrippa was almost persuaded to be a Christian, and how it came to pass that he made such an impression in Athens.

St. Paul speaks of himself as less than the least of all saints. Was he? He spoke as it seemed to him rather than as it was. Why did the people of Lystra do him such honor? Longinus, in his work on the sublime as it comes to us, in giving the list of great orators, adds, "And Saul of Tarsus, the chief supporter of an opinion not yet established."

It is justly asked, Where is there a writer that can vie with St. Paul in sublime and pathetic eloquence? Demosthenes could rouse up the Athenians against Philip, and Cicero strike shame and confusion into the heart of Anthony or Catiline. And did not the eloquence of St. Paul, though he was bound in degrading fetters, produce equal effects?

But Peter was the preacher of Pentecost. He says, "Ye men of Israel, hear the words of Jesus of Nazareth, a man approved of God among you by miracles and wonders and signs, which God did by him in the midst of you, as ye yourselves also know: him, being delivered by the determinate counsel and foreknowledge of God, ye have taken, and by wicked hands have crucified and slain." His words cut like cimeters; his sentences were like battering-rams. The people were pricked in their hearts, and said, "What shall we do?" Was it the Holy Ghost that made Peter so eloquent? Then that is a high commendation of eloquence. Judging from the narration, did his speech have any power with men in producing great results? Then eloquence is to be desired for such good. Who shall tell the power that Apollos exerted when he "mightily convinced the Jews?" But we come to a higher source—to Christ himself.

As if to give dignity and weight to the ministry, "Jesus began to preach," and the officers said, "Never man spake like this man." The truths that he presented were pure, majestic, and necessary. The style that he employed was simple, direct, and appropriate, and "the common people heard him gladly." He knew what he spoke. He had come from heaven and was familiar with its glories. The fires of hell had flamed on his vision, and he could tell their intensity. He knew the enormity of the sin for which he died, and the "beauty of the holiness" that he came to exhibit and impart. His words were things, his figures were facts, and his ministry was life. The seed he scattered was from his heart. Archbishop Leighton says, "He is fittest to preach who is most like his message." When the Sun of Righteousness rose the benighted saw his beams and came to the light. His intellect and heart, his voice and manner, blended in his presentations of truth. He put his whole self into his subjects. If he was not a sensational preacher he was a preacher to produce a sensation. He took every subject by the right handle, and handled every subject that he took in the right way, and "they came to hear him from every quarter." He hallowed the pulpit by his presence, taught it by his doctrines, and inspired it by his spirit. Yes, yes; he once stood where we stand. Marvelous, peerless honor of our vocation! The physician can boast his Galen, the jurist his Justinian, the soldier his Leonidas, but the pulpit can boast the majesty of Him that was "God manifest in the flesh." When John Newton would actualize his ideal orator he took the virtues of many and united them in one. But in this Preacher we have all the rays of light, all the forces of life, and all the blessing of speech centered in and emanating from one. For all time the "Prince of the kings of the earth" is the Prince of preachers.

Is there enough, then, in eloquence to justify the effort demanded for its attainment?

If sought as an auxiliary to usefulness, then to the extent of our concern to do good should be our desire for this means. If sought for selfish ends, we may backslide while we study it. If it is the eloquence of *sound*, not of *soul*, it is no more than " sounding brass or a tinkling cymbal."

Though it has been asserted that there are few great orators in any age, it may be said without presumption the pulpit has in every period had its share. No country has been without some of which they might justly boast. From the days of Apollos and Austin and Cyprian and Chrysostom there have been eloquent men and " mighty in the Scriptures."

Albert Barnes, than whom perhaps we have had no better judge, remarks in his *Life of President Davis*, " It is one of the honors of our country, young though we are, that we do not lack for examples of the highest order of preaching; and even now, when we look through the great library for the best models, we instinctively fix on some that have been produced on this side the ocean. The purest models of preaching are to be found undoubtedly in the discourses of the apostles and of the great Preacher; but after leaving those times we shall find no land, probably, where there have been exhibited more correct specimens of pure classic style, of sober thought, of instructive discourses, of appeals adapted to rouse the conscience of a sinner or to warm the heart of a child of God, than have been furnished in our own land. The American pulpit, imperfect as it is, is more elevated in its influence and power than that of any other nation, and in no other country is its influence so justly appreciated or so deeply felt on the public mind. Much as we may revere the memory of the past, much as we may learn from the wisdom of other generations, and much as we may honor those who have been or are distinguished for eminent usefulness across the waters, yet if we wish to see the power of preaching exemplified in the history of men, and derive instruction from the lives and success of those of other times, we cannot find a more appropriate place than to sit down at the feet of such men as may be named."

Have we not reason to believe, from the eminence that some of them attained as speakers, that the fathers of Methodism, both in this and in the old country, made sacred oratory a careful study? To this day the Wesleyans speak of Samuel Bradburn, one of their first preachers, as the Demosthenes of their history. Quickly after him came Robert Newton, whom George G. Cookman called the "Apollos of Wesleyan Methodism." To show the appreciation of sacred eloquence by the holy William Bramwell, he at an early period revised and reproduced from the French an old work on the subject, and gave it the name of *The Earnest Preacher*. Miles Martindale translated from the French another eminent author on the *Eloquence of the Pulpit.* And such was Dr. Durbin's conviction of the importance of cultivating eloquence in our ministry, that, while in the pastorate of a large charge, as we have seen, he formed a class that he personally taught. Mr. Wesley wrote on "Voice and Delivery," both with regard to pronunciation and action, and says, " They are far more acquirable than has been commonly imagined. A remarkably weak voice has by steady application become strong and agreeable. Those who stammered at almost every word have learned to speak clearly and plainly. And many who were eminently ungraceful in their pronunciation and awkward in their gesture have in some time, by art and labor, not only corrected that awkwardness of action and ungracefulness of utterance, but have become excellent in both, and in these respects likewise the ornaments of their profession."— *Wesley's Works,* vi, 220. So wrote the founder of Methodism for the benefit of his preachers.

How great may be the force of the felt want of eloquence in some instances may be judged by a case. " A worthy gentleman listening to the debates in the General Assembly of the Scottish Kirk in Edinburgh, and eager to speak to the question, but utterly failing in his qualification, and delighted with the talent shown by Dr. Hugh Blair, went to him and offered him one thousand pounds sterling if he would teach him to speak with propriety in public."

" In much labor there is profit."

It has been stated that Dr. Durbin took lessons in eloquence from the best teachers. It is certain from his attention to the great speakers when chaplain of the Senate, and his remarks on such an orator as Henry Clay, that he had a critical taste and a high ideal. That he had a genius for it must account for some of his earliest efforts. For, though we have heard of doubts expressed as to his having "much in him," we have it on good authority that he gave positive promise, and "that he held his audiences by a strange spell and thrilled them with his electric bursts of surpassing eloquence." Yet he was a constant student of the power of speech, and used what he believed to be the best means to secure the highest eloquence.

A discriminating writer and great admirer of the eloquence of Dr. Chalmers, of its effect, of his holding his audience "spell-bound," and as advancing with a speed and strength that none could withstand, pauses to ask, "What was the secret of this amazing power?" Was it the importance of the subject, the loftiness or vigor of his thoughts, the originality or splendor of the composition? He then says: "All these have existed in equal completeness, perhaps, in other preachers who have yet failed to make any particularly strong impression on their hearers; who, at least, have never been run after as men of commanding and extraordinary eloquence. With a dull, tame delivery, the discourses of Chalmers would read as well as they now do, but their fame as preached would never have been achieved." He adds, "There is something potent, then, about delivery. The greatest of ancient orators assigned to this the first, second, and third rank in the order of qualities requisite for eloquence."

We abate nothing of our estimate of the excellence of his style, the soundness of his exposition, the fullness of his matter, the force of his reasoning, or the skillful construction of his discourse, when we say the pre-eminence of Dr. Durbin as a preacher was in his imperial imagination, the dramatic power of which he was master, his voice that obeyed all his mandates, the divine unction that attended his presentation of the word, and in his *peerless delivery.* Well as the sermons he has left us *read,* it was *eloquence* that gave them power. If any thing is better than the best thing we have to say it is—the best way of saying it.

In introducing the eloquence of Dr. Durbin we made allusion to the three men who formed the triumvirate of eloquence in the Methodist Episcopal Church. The benign Providence that permitted the sainted Summerfield to burst forth as a light to shine over a continent, in his twenty-seventh year extinguished his beams. How much brighter would have been his light had he been allowed to attain his meridian we may conjecture rather than predict. But Henry B. Bascom and John P. Durbin lived long enough to reveal their full powers. These two men were for many years moving in the same circles and commanding vast audiences by the charms of their eloquence. Each had those that admired him the more, while the high merits of both were confessed by all. They were Henry Biddleman Bascom and John Price Durbin. They both rose in the West; they both began their ministry with about equal disadvantages as to education. In a few years they were professors in Augusta College, Kentucky; they both traveled at large as agents—Durbin for Augusta College, Bascom for colonization. Near the same period they each served as chaplain to the American Congress. Durbin was editor of *The Christian Advocate and Journal,* Bascom of the *Southern Quarterly Review.* At a later time they were presidents of different colleges—Durbin of Dickinson, Bascom of Transylvania. They met as Delegates in the General Conference of 1844. Bascom wrote " the protest " to its action. Durbin wrote the reply. In 1850 Bascom was made Bishop of the Church, South. In 1852 Durbin declined to be a candidate for the episcopacy, preferring missionary service.

Bascom died when fifty-four years of age, Durbin at seventy-six.

As when they lived many things were said of their eloquence, so now we hear inquiry as to the two. As there may be comparison without disparagement, the writer, having heard them both, may suggest some contrasts as well as some resemblances.

In some things few men could compare with Bascom, and in some things Durbin stood alone. In port and person Bascom was a prince. Durbin had no external attraction except in refined taste and manly bearing. Bascom's style was gorgeous; Durbin's luminous. Only the personality of Bascom broke the charge of bombast. Durbin's language is its own vindication. Bascom labored as if the body was the engine to give power to the soul, Durbin as if the soul only used the body to show *itself* in its intensity and ardor. The first paragraph of Bascom was a burst of eloquence. With an electrifying shock Durbin closed. Bascom began as if five minutes were to do the work, Durbin as if preparing a foundation for a pyramid. Under Bascom infidels hid for very shame; under Durbin they threw down their weapons and sued for pardon. From first to last Bascom was vehement; Durbin restrained his vehemence for cumulative force. Bascom was Niagara, with the rapids behind it; Durbin was the Hudson, with mountains and vale, with highlands and palisades crowned with villas and pediments gleaming like diamonds upon crests of beauty. But as amid the charms of that noble river there is the strength of a West Point so amid the attractions of Durbin there was the power of moral conquest. The effect of the preaching of these two men on a minister was dissimilar. On listening to Bascom one felt as did the musician when he exclaimed, listening to one more skilled, " I will bury my instrument." On hearing Durbin he would say, "I will dig it up, for now I have learned how to play better." If we should attempt to convey an idea of these men by authors, let Robert Montgomery and Richard Winter Hamilton represent Bascom, Bishop Atterbury and Archbishop Tillotson, Durbin. They were alike men of rare qualities, endowments, and successes. They are still great in the influence as well as reputation that follows them. For either to have attempted the other would have been to mar the economy of God. As in the works of creation, there was unity in diversity.

CHAPTER XXI.

Conclusion.

IN the General Conference of 1872 Dr. Durbin, as we have seen, declined re-election as Corresponding Secretary of the Missionary Society. Then he whose life had been so full of labor, and whose labor had been so full of grand results, withdrew from the active services that had so long been his delight. Needful as rest had seemed to him, it was soon found that, out of his accustomed work, the powers of his mind and body more rapidly failed. He rarely appeared on the platform or in the pulpit, and after a serene and happy old age he was stricken with paralysis, and on October 18, 1876, at his residence in New York city, surrounded by his children and grandchildren, he saw the last of earth and first of heaven. The Church rendered him appropriate honor, and he was buried at Laurel Hill Cemetery, Philadelphia.

In his life of the Rev. John Ryland, Sr., Dr. Newman when speaking of his death says : "Well do I remember the awful stillness of that evening. I felt as if all the world was dead." Strong language this, but the language of the heart is always strong. Kindred to this was the feeling of the writer when John P. Durbin ceased from among men. But as "mists and vapors, when exhaled, descend in rains, as fountains and rivers pour their fullness into the ocean, as every morning sun rises but to decline, by the same necessity, the same inviolable order of nature, every man is born to die."

"I said, Ye are gods" by the loftiness of your intellect, by the dignity of your station, and by the glory of your achievements; "but ye shall die like men, and fall like one of the princes." Mortality shall shoot its shaft, and neither majesty nor merit shall change its aim or impair its power.

But who can think of the removal of such a moral force from the earth as John P. Durbin exerted without feeling this world has sustained a loss? That life is long enough for our highest interest when it reaches life's great end. But who that contemplates the departure of one who has caused the blessing of so many ready to perish to come upon him without thinking of loss to the race? We are accustomed to say "God buries his workman, but carries on his work." He does. No one doubts this when he knows that the mantle of Elijah rests upon Elisha. But when the leader and lawgiver of Israel died the Almighty said, "Moses, my servant, is dead." This is pathos above the human; and it is as if God thought more about a bereaved world than of the reward of the saint.

But beams from the Sun of Righteousness form the rainbow of hope in the falling tears of Christian affection. The inexperienced youth of eighteen years who "girded on the harness," ere "his hands had been taught to war or his fingers to fight"—that in his early manhood showed such discipline and skill, and that in advanced life could look back upon victories gained in perilous conflicts—he surely could illustrate the Scripture, "Let not him that girdeth on the harness boast himself as he that putteth it off." He girded it on with uncertainty as to the issue; he put it off with the recognition of the nature of the victories won; he that girded it on with trembling put it off in triumph. And it was fitting that he who had been the means of bringing so many sons to glory should himself at three score and sixteen hear the voice of the great Commander saying :

> "Servant of God, well done!
> Thy glorious warfare's past.
> The battle's fought, the race is won,
> And thou art crowned at last."

As we have endeavored to make an analysis of the powers that distinguished Dr. Durbin as a preacher, so we may notice him as he appears before us and in his various relations as a man.

He was twice married, in each instance to a daughter of Alexander Cook, Esq., of Philadelphia. By his first wife he had three sons and two daughters. She entered into rest in 1836, while the Doctor was at Dickinson College. Only one of the sons survives, Alexander C. Durbin, Esq., of Montclair, N. J. One of his daughters was married to William Whitaker, Esq., of Philadelphia; the other daughter was married to Fletcher Harper, Jr., of New York. But a short time has elapsed since the tears of the Church and of humanity fell upon her grave.

All the wealth of Dr. Durbin came through his marriage. It is doubtful if his salary ever more than supported him. In domestic life Dr. Durbin showed the love of the companion, the devotion of the father, the kindness of a friend; and affection and reverence were rendered him as the head of the family and the priest of the household. Even in his home he was not without the impress that public duties made upon his spirit. He was thoughtful and weighty, but was observant of those attentions that go so far toward imparting happiness and dignity to domestic life. He trained his children in useful study, while he impressed the duty of remembering the Creator in the days of their youth. His table was not made a snare to conscience by indulging conversation that would violate "the golden rule," or be likely to impair the proper influence of the minister or the man. In extending, as in receiving, hospitality, he was without display. He was accustomed to say, "when a friend calls in we just set one more plate, and it is no trouble." *His friendships were real and tenacious.* We can see the heart of the man in the grateful memory that he maintained of those who in his comparative youth rendered him great kindness. The following is a glance at a correspondence of fifty years. It was his custom to send his New Year salutations. Even when his domestic bereavement was exerting its depressing power he adhered to this habit.

Writing to one whom he had known from her childhood, and at whose father's house he had received great sympathy in his early struggles, he speaks of "your dear mother and mine" and says: "She is to me half natural mother and half Christian sister; therefore I have double pleasure in loving her." To the same he writes when she was in deep sorrow from the death of her husband, who had been an honor to the Church and an example of Christian uprightness and purity in the community, Philadelphia, April 4, 1853: "Grace, mercy and peace from God our heavenly Father, be given unto you all, through our Lord Jesus Christ, to sustain and comfort you under your sore bereavement. Out of my immediate family circle I could not have lost a friend whose death I do so sincerely regret and so deeply feel; my early, warm, fast friend."

We see the father's heart in a letter dated New York, May 13, 1859. It relates to the death of his son Willie. "I write to say that not all the light has gone out in our house, but one of the most pleasant and promising is extinguished. It is strange. When I suddenly think of him it seems that he cannot be dead, that he is only asleep and must awake. Alas! He is dead. But he died in peace; his death was beautiful, triumphant; he was sensible to the last, spoke to us within five minutes of his death; his last words were heard on the subject of religion, and just before he died they were, 'I go to Jesus just as I am.'" Writing of early years in 1861, he says, "I am too old to create other such friendships again. With your dear mother and myself the journey has been a long one and not yet ended, but we are so near to Jordan that we ought now to see over, to the promised land." In the fullness of Christian hope he writes, "Our next dwelling together, *all* will be in heaven" but adds, "I must not preach, nor is it needed."

In 1866, amid the cares that crowded him, when about to sail for Europe, he wrote with the devotion of ardent friendship; when abroad amid the interests of travel and the responsibilities of office as Corresponding Secretary of the Missionary Society he kept before him the helpers of his early joys.

July 4, 1866 he writes to a friend: "Mrs. Durbin has just handed me a letter she has written to Elizabeth, and requests me to send or forward it. . . . God, whose work made us friends, and whose mercy and goodness have kept us friends for many years, will, I trust, spare us yet to see each other in the flesh; you now seem to me to be the only link that binds me to my early ministry in the old stone church in Cincinnati. Those were bright days, and I never can forget them. I say you are the only link in my ministry in the old stone church; perhaps I ought to add, Lizzie and Hester and Mary. They were children, and link me back to my youth rather than to my ministry. God bless them for your sake and for my sake; for they know that I love them. . . . Let us strive so to live that we may meet in heaven." This letter was written amid the mountains of Switzerland.

Again he writes from Biel, Switzerland, July 16, 1866: "The evening of life is drawing on in both of our cases, but we have been many years preparing for it, and I hope it will close on both of us without a cloud. Let us take care that this shall be the case. I have thought that you and the children might be pleased to see the inclosed photographs, taken in Germany. The vignette one does not look like the boy preacher that used to live with you in Sycamore Street nearly forty years ago. We are all quite well and have been quite well since we left home. We have seen the most interesting places and objects in Germany and Switzerland, and I have visited nearly all of our missions in those countries. The war in Germany prevented my seeing our missions in Saxony and Hamburg, and in Denmark and Norway and Sweden. But I propose to visit there while Margaret remains in England. We go to Geneva and on to Paris this week, where Margaret and John will remain two or three weeks, and then go over to London. We expect to return to New York in the first half of October.

"I do not expect you to be at the trouble of reading this, much less of answering it. But Hester or Lizzie can do both, for your and my benefit. A letter written on receipt of this and inclosed to the office in New York, to Brother Terry, would reach me in London, whither Brother Terry will forward it. Let Mary and Edward share this letter. Adieu; may you yet live many days. Margaret bids me give her love to you all. She wrote to Lizzie a few days ago."

To the same friend he writes, New York, September 24, 1870: "I cannot tell you and your dear mother how much we are grieved by the death of John. Although it was expected, it came so suddenly that we could scarcely realize it. He was struck down Saturday morning, some time before day, in his room, and he was insensible to his end. It occurred at Saratoga, among strangers. I arrived two hours before he died, but he knew me not. He died easily." . . . He adds, " Your dear mother will feel as I do, somewhat. We feel like pilgrims standing on the bank of a river waiting to cross, while the young and beautiful cross over before us; but when we do cross we shall find them on the other side." Again writing of the same painful event, the death of his son John, he says : " He died from apoplexy. . . . For three or four years his mind had been almost entirely on recovering his health and saving his soul. I believe he escaped into the bosom of his heavenly Father. It is my earnest purpose to join him there." In the midst of his own sorrows he thinks of another's anxiety, and writes, November 26, 1870: "If you see Edward tell him I sympathize with him in Mary's ill-health, and do earnestly pray that she may be spared to him and his children." God permitted this honored servant to be visited with stroke upon stroke. His heart bleeds at the death of his grandson, named after him. He says : " Affliction makes us remember our faults and our friends. Our dear little Durbin is no more. He died last Saturday morning without a struggle or a sigh. He was sensible to the last, and spoke to his mother not more than five minutes before he died. He said : 'Mamma, is that you?' She answered, 'Yes.' He said, 'I cannot see you.' He was then laid down on his pillow and died in a minute." The gloom of Dr. Durbin's mind again caused him to say, "I feel tempted sometimes to complain of Providence, but I still strive to say, 'Thy will be

24

done.'" But in the midst of his sorrow he writes : " I might as well send my New Year's salutations to you all. How little did I dream that my only grandson would be taken from us! He was with us in New York last New Year full of life and hope. Now he is gone—I trust, to the heavenly world, to grow up there free from danger and sorrow."

We may speak of Dr. Durbin's personal appearance. He was of medium size. His head was not large; his forehead was low, narrow and receding. His eye was hazel and was sometimes sleepy. In repose it suggested no genius. It was, in size and show, what circumstances made it. It was capable of an indefinable expression. His hair in early life was light and soft. Time gave it a darkish hue. His mouth was that of an orator. His dress was faultless. His senses were unimpaired, even when his body and mind showed the effects of age, if not of labor.

Bishop Wiley says of the likeness contained in this volume :

The portrait we consider the greatest success that has yet been attained in getting the physiognomy of Dr. Durbin on paper.   He is one of the impracticable men for all kinds of artists; the photographer dreads such a man, so much of whose facial appearance and character depends upon his moods, and whose appearance differs so widely as you look upon him alive, and with his animated countenance aglow with feeling and inspiration, or as he sits down in quiet repose to have his face caught up in the camera. The same facts make him the dread of portrait artists and of engravers. We remember his leading us at one time to look at a very finely-painted portrait hanging in a room of his son-in-law's house. The picture was an admirably-executed one, but we were mortified at our blunder in not for a moment supposing it had been intended for himself; but were saved by his genial laugh when we innocently asked whose portrait it was. Several attempts have been made to put him on wood, but the failure has been complete. Years ago Dr. Stevens, then editor of the *National Magazine,* made a desperate effort to secure his likeness, but unmercifully threw the block under the table. A few years ago the Doctor visited Europe for the purpose of studying more closely our European missions. The Germans caught him, led him to a gallery in Berlin, and in a moment the sun fixed him on the plate in one of his best moods. From this photograph our engraver has produced the excellent likeness that embellishes this book.

The manners of Dr. Durbin were such as would indicate a born gentleman. It cost him no effort to be what he was. Dr. McClintock said of him, "He was always a gentleman through and through." In personal intercourse he had a quiet dignity, and, though never austere, rarely relaxed. While he was everywhere recognized in his superior talents and position, in no instance did we ever know him to indicate the existence of vanity. On going into a company there was a reserve that might be construed to shyness or to pride. There was the business rather than the social air. But contact and conversation drew him out, and he mingled with the company and in sympathy with the occasion. With personal friends he could even become sportive, and one remarks that at such time he had a smile full of benignity and delight and could indulge a hearty laugh. Under no circumstances would he make himself the hero of the company. He was never the monopolist of conversation. Nor did he fail to give respectful attention to the opinions of those least in harmony with his own. He entered into no cabal, and was a stranger to cliques and cunning. He sought not by indirection what open honesty would spurn. Jealousies, envies, rivalries were not indulged, when the greatest freedom prevailed. Though not remarkable for fluency, wit, or humor, he had enough of each, which with the salt of wisdom made all savory, and imparted the raciness that is remembered without a pang. The positions that he filled were thrust upon him, and such were the responsibilities that he felt, and such his devotion to his work, as to leave little time for rest, for amusement, or relaxation. So intent was he on discharging the obligations that his place imposed, and such were his habits of reserve, that though while in Europe multiplied opportunities were afforded him for mingling in the society of distinguished men, he avoided rather than sought such intercourse.

Dr. Durbin's position in his Church and in community for fifty years gave him power. But who ever knew him to be arrogant with the weak or supple with the strong? If at any time he was subjected as a writer, or in any way, to criticism, he let it pass, and it was a rule with him to allow no concerns for the result of duty.

The same charateristics that marked his intercourse in society *distinguished him in his Conference relations.* He was transferred to the Philadelphia Conference in 1836. It was a Conference of strong men.

The princely Pitman was in his prime. The sublime Lybrand was exerting his attractions, the majestic Sorin was never greater, and Henry White was melting his congregation by his pathos. The late Bishops Janes and Scott, and T. J. Thompson and Solomon Higgins and William Cooper were known as distinguished in the business of the Conference. Among such men J. P. Durbin received the honor that his station would suggest and his talents command. But he showed the deference that his association prompted, and by real affiliation secured the confidence, the affection, and admiration of his brethren.

His identity with the Conference was not *nominal* but *real.* He observed its doings and took part in its debates. As a rule, he spoke only when others had expressed their convictions or thoughts and the subject was fully before them. Then, with a modesty and suggestiveness that gave weight to his words, he would express a judgment that was often like the conclusion of the matter. When, as in some instances, there was a slight abrasion, he was even remarkable for the urbanity of his manners and for the control of language.

He who should have accepted Dr. Durbin as an example of "clerical manners" in debate might never find cause to criticise his conclusion. Seven times successively was he elected a delegate to the General Conference, and his Conference never ceased thus to honor him till the infirmities of age forbade the compliment.

The Christian character of Dr. Durbin re-enforced his ministerial influence. Though not accustomed to expressions of spiritual rapture he had the fruits of the Spirit, and the consciousness of divine approval.

He had the same kind of reasoning in regard to his spiritual character that many of the most conscientious and consistent Christians have indulged. So far are such from the *presumption* too common in the Church that they fail even to rest as fully on the *foundations of faith* as facts justify and the word commands. No one that did not know the youthful Durbin can tell the tendencies that he recognized, fought against, and overcame. As we saw him in his quiet reserve and caution, we would not suspect that his *temper* ever required particular guard. But he knew the struggle that it cost him; that he had attained so perfect a *mastery* is one of the evidences of the reign of grace in his heart. The brief extracts that we have made from the letters of friendship show the devout spirit of the

man.   Nor can we think of his demeanor in the
house of worship, the care with which he guarded the
divine service from the interruptions and intrusions so
common in some of the churches, the instructive and
edifying manner in which he read his hymns, and the
devout rendering of the lessons from the Holy Scriptures, his profound reverence in prayer, and the outflow-
ing of his heart in his comprehensive supplications,
without thinking of him as an example in his place.
His prayers might vary in length and ardor, but not
in becoming humility or in the simplicity of language.
He was a child speaking to or pleading with his Father.
But there were times when he seemed to open heaven
to the penitents at the altar and to hold back the arm
of the Almighty in providence.   No one can conceive
of such prayer without recognizing the grasp of his faith
and the firmness of his trust.   Illustrations of this power
have been furnished in the narrative of Dr. Joseph
Longking and in the letter of Dr. O. H. Tiffany.   We
give one in this place from Dr. Spottswood.   It was
at a camp-meeting.   He says of Dr. Durbin:

He talks with God as one talketh with his friend.
He tells his heavenly Father the simple story of the
people's trouble and expense in coming there, of the
purity of their motives, to get good and to do good,
and of the constant and excessive rain that had in-
terfered with his children's holy plans.   "Now, Lord,"
he prays, "If it be thy will, give us clear weather
from this time to the end of the meeting."   Here he
lingers, wrestles, asks, pleads, and importunes.   At last,
in an exclamation, nay, in a triumphant shout, he declares "It shall be done; we shall have clear skies from
this time forth!"   Never can the teller of this incident
forget his feeling at that moment.   It was a cold shud-
der as the thought rushed into his brain, What if the
preacher's prediction should prove a false prophecy?
But it did not; that "prayer of a righteous man" was

no doubt directly inwrought in his soul by the Holy Ghost. It was an effectual, fervent prayer, and might by a sublime faith, to which all things are possible, accomplish its end. It verified the divine affirmation — it availed much; for the rain ceased, the clouds departed, and God gave clear weather from that time to the close of the camp-meeting! He that had such access to the Almighty, that so clearly told inquiring souls how to find the heart of God, was not without the comforts and strength of successful prayer. Sometimes in his sermons he bore his grand testimony of his personal experience of the "powers of the world to come."

In a conversation with the Rev. A. Lowry, D.D., when dining at the residence of his son-in-law, Mr. Whitaker, of Philadelphia, in 1876, Dr. Durbin in substance said, "In my experience as a Christian I have never been impulsive, but I have a steady peace with God and am resting in the truth of his word." A short time before his death Bishop Janes, the Missionary Secretaries, and the Book Agents, called on him to present a resolution passed by the Bishops at their last meeting. On hearing it read he replied, " he could recollect but one paper of the sort in all his life that was not distasteful to him," adding, "this paper was so evidently sincere and was expressed in such terms that he received it with gladness, and would cherish it among his pleasant memories." He alluded to his Christian experience. At first he said, "The fact that he had not the joys which other Christians had gave rise to questioning doubts. But he afterward had learned better, and though he had never been demonstrative, his experience as a Christian had been and still was satisfactory to his heart."

But in considering the elements of Dr. Durbin's strength *there should be a steady recognition of his sterling common sense.* Amid his multiplied, diverse, and brilliant endowments this in many cases was a basal fact in accounting for his success in his varied labors and in enterprises of great moment. It did what nothing else could do.

Want of this power, besides subjecting the individual to humiliating criticisms, is sometimes attended with worse consequences than result from deficiency of education. Was it not this in St. Paul that caught some with guile? Was it not this in Dr. Durbin that caused the management of difficult cases in college to end in peace and honor? Common sense is sometimes called "mother-wit," as if inherited from the mother. It is a gift of nature, but may appear, like other mental faculties, in various degrees. It may be improved by observation and exercise or impaired by indifference to its value or neglect of its dictates.

Some have conceived the idea that remarkable geniuses and profound scholars are as a rule wanting in this power. If so, the fault is not in genius or scholarship. Common sense is exercised before learning is acquired. It is one of the earliest, as it is one of the most necessary, exercises of the mind. It may be called common sense, as that which we may expect in every well-organized human being. We therefore look for it in men much as we do for intuition and conscience. It is not what is sometimes seen in absence of mind. This may be found in the greatest intellects, and is the result of mental absorption. Roused to its exercise it is found in its force.

One of the infelicities of the lack of common sense is seen when he who is deficient cannot be persuaded of its absence or its need, and so gives no hope of improvement. Was it this that many years ago induced a theological professor to say to his class, what others have since thought, "If you want Hebrew, we can teach it; if you seek Greek, we can impart it; if you come for theology, we can give you necessary instruction; but if you have not common sense, the Lord help you, for we cannot?" Thomas Adams says, "An old man that is not made wiser by his experience is like a bolter, that lets all the fine flour go through and catches only the bran." But there are those to whom the lesson of one day is nothing for the next. By the same processes the same bitter experience is kept up. Thus they go stumbling and falling, then rising up with a *bruise* and again·falling with *greater injury*, now inviting and now encountering an opposition that is as real, if not as hard, as adamant; yet reposing in their own strength they show an inflexibility of purpose in matters of indifference that is justified only where principle is involved. No man more certainly needs common sense than the Christian pastor. To be wise in preaching the word, in suiting his sermons to the people, in the labors of the altar and the Sunday-school, in the leaders' meeting and quarterly conferences, when in all these places we have so many facts to consult, here is indeed a loud call for the exercise first of grace and then of common sense. Lack of this shows what we call imprudence. A word improperly spoken in some of these relations may kindle a fire that no waters can extinguish and that hardly any time will cause to die out. Such incaution has made many a minister pass sleepless nights and weeks of uncertainty as to result. But the discomfort to his own mind may not be the worst of it. A generation has not removed from a community the difficulty that the lack of common sense in administration has created.

Strife about minor matters has blasted all hope of success in things of greatest moment. "The mint, anise and cumin" have destroyed the weightier matters of the law, and the preacher is powerless.

The writer once heard one of the wisest professors in a theological seminary say to his class, with great tenderness, "Brethren, more men in the ministry lose their positions and are kept out of places from want of discretion than from want of talent and learning." They are scarcely in a charge before some novel thing of questionable utility is proposed, suspicion is roused, prejudice is awakened, and opposition starts, a schism is made, and the pastor is gone. He enters another parish; he begins on the same course; the people now inquire of his history and find he is reproducing the past, and for like reasons he has to leave. The facts are carried to other churches. In vain is it said he is a good man, that he is educated, that he is eloquent, he is young, and therefore allowance is to be made. He has lost his place, and there is no prospect of another, and this when he should be in the height of ministerial power.

It may sometimes excite our marvel that the *cause* seems so slight that renders high merit unavailable. But as a fly may spoil the apothecary's ointment, so "doth a little folly him that is of great reputation for wisdom."

Common sense does not forbid an issue when principle demands it. He is a *craven* who will not meet responsibility. There were times when Dr. Durbin encountered difficulty with a courage that no fear could daunt. The narrative of his life has set forth some such occasions. It is not the fear of man, but the fear of God, that gives caution to the wise.

If common sense could not be *taught* as well as improved it were vain to speak or write of it. Like some faculties of the mind, it may be of difficult development, but by close observation, by past mistakes, by careful guard against those tendencies whence greatest danger arises, even the obtuse will reveal new characteristics. By studying theories, indulging speculations, allowing unhealthy trains of thought and habit, the wise may become foolish, and by *ignoring* common sense fanaticism may take the place of discretion. Is it not a high tribute paid to such decision when we say in *ordinary* affairs "our first thought is generally the best." Common sense seems like a law within us—determining the questions of which it is capable.

In the face of the assumption that great geniuses and scholars are apt to be lacking in common sense we present John P. Durbin. Will any doubt his genius? Was he not an example of the excellence of common sense even from youth to age? Guardianship of his younger brothers; the care with which he sought and the fidelity with which he observed the counsel of his friends in his early ministry; his manly recognition of the need of study and education for the highest usefulness that he desired; his administration of affairs in the various departments of his work, and nowhere more than in his conduct as Corresponding Secretary of the Missionary Society, all manifest the possession of this faculty in an uncommon degree. Let any one read his articles in *The Christian Advocate and Journal* when he was editor, and especially the one on "Worship," and tell us when as a preacher, debater, writer, he failed, with all his genius, to show his common sense. Let those who consider the exercise of this faculty after he became learned say whether fine education impairs its exercise. Was it not like the background in the picture of his life, that showed all his other powers to greatest advantage?

It was remarked of the Rev. Albert Barnes that

his clear, strong, honest, practical good *sense* was the secret of his power and the source of his success. But, while showing this sense what honor did he bring to the Church! What benefit by his writings did he confer upon the world! Was it not the sterling common sense of Dr. Durbin that showed his administration in every place that he filled to such advantage? Is it not permitted ministers still to say, with St. Paul to his son in the Gospel, " God has not given us the spirit of fear, but of power, of love, and of a *sound mind?* " 2 Tim. i, 7.

But while we justly emphasize the common sense of Dr. Durbin we *must not fail to consider those powers that impress us with his high capabilities.* He had a mental penetration, a clear and comprehensive view of matters of magnitude to the Church of Christ; a recognition of the tendency of events. He well understood the workings of human nature; the influence of the varying conditions of society; he had accuracy in estimating the forces that it is necessary to compute in the anticipation of desired results. His self-control in the midst of strong excitements kept him from the mental disturbance that impairs energy and destroys faith, and so unfits men for a great crisis or important changes. These facts marked him as a controlling spirit in any association, and fitted him for the highest ecclesiastical statesmanship, while his elevation of character, his utter freedom from sinister or selfish motives, gave weight to his reasoning and made his conclusions next to moral demonstrations.

The greatness of a man may not be traced to its origin except in God. One who is truly great lives rather in posterity than in ancestry. Like Abel, " he being dead yet speaketh."

One has beautifully said that " The beginnings of

many a successful career, like those of the **river Nile**, are unseen." And Mahaffy declares, "The intellectual kings of the world are, like Melchisedec, without father, without mother, without descent, having neither beginning of days nor end of life."

Dr. Durbin is one of whom it is difficult to write with fairness and fullness without seeming to exaggerate; and yet not to describe him as he was is to do injustice to his memory. The writer knows no motive for adulation, and the biographer of an extraordinary man should not write of him as of one of ordinary powers.

David said, "In thine hand it is to make great." Whatever of intellectual or moral susceptibility Dr. Durbin had he received from God, and recognized it as a divine gift, and improved it as one who must give account. He as truly as St. Paul could say, "By the grace of God I am what I am." If we consider the powers of Dr. Durbin's mind in the departments of study to which he devoted his attention, and remember the embarrassments under which he in so short a time accomplished so much, we have no reason to doubt that his aptitudes were equal to his aspirations—that he could have achieved any other purpose that he might have cherished. He who at the age of twenty-five had risen so far as to be the skillful professor of ancient languages, at the age of thirty to be elected to the professorship in natural science in our first university, that at thirty-two could edit *The Christian Advocate and Journal* with such ability, that at thirty-four could fill with highest reputation the presidency of a college that had failed under the greatest talents and strongest denominational influences; he who could honor all these positions and at last give twenty-two years of his mature life to such a work as Corresponding Secre-

tary of the Missionary Society and advance it to such
a power; he who showed himself a master in skill, an
oracle in wisdom, and a pillar of strength in the cause
of his advocacy, he surely may be accepted as "a
prince and a great man in Israel." Might not the
words that were considered an appropriate epitaph for
Wordsworth be applied with equal justice to Dr. Durbin, "Here lies a man who did what he intended?"

To one who carefully observed the life and labors of
Dr. Durbin it would be just to conclude that from his
conversion to his death he was influenced by the conviction that human existence implies real, stern, abiding responsibility; that talents are for improvement
and time for a wise appropriation, and that opportunities impose obligations. We cannot better convey the
estimate of Dr. Durbin as to his true position than in
the language of Albert Barnes on another occasion:
"It has been comparatively rare in this world that
any individual has embarked on life, or on any enterprise, with a determined purpose to see how much
could be done by the utmost efforts of which the
mind and the body could be made capable. Occasionally such an individual has appeared, and appeared to
astonish us no less by the vastness and the success of
his own efforts than by the proof which he has thus
furnished of the imbecility and indolence and wasted
talents of the great mass of mankind. Such a man
was Howard—living to make full proof 'of how much
could be done in a single object of benevolence.' The
energy of his determination, it has been said, 'was the
calmness of an intensity kept uniform by the nature of
the human mind forbidding it to be more and by the
character of the individual forbidding it to be less.'
The habitual passion of his mind was a measure of
feeling almost equal to the temporary extremes and

paroxysms of common minds, as a great river in its customary state is equal to a small and moderate one when swollen to a torrent.' Such a man, in a far different department, was Napoleon, living to illustrate the power of great talents concentrated on a single object, and making 'full proof' of the terrible energy of the single passion of ambition. Such a man, too, was the short-lived Alexander; and, in a different sphere, such a man was Paul; and, to a considerable extent, such a a man was Whitefield. But, compared with the immense multitude of minds which have existed on the earth, such instances, for good or for evil, have been rare. A part has been sunk in indolence from which no motives would rouse them. Part have been wholly unconscious of their own powers. Part have never been placed in circumstances to call forth their energies, or have not been endowed with original power to create such circumstances or to start a plan that should require such concentrated efforts to complete it. Part have never been under the right influence, in the process of training, to make 'full proof' of the powers of the soul. Part have wasted their talents in wild and visionary schemes, unconscious of the waste or of the main error of their life till life was too far gone to attempt to repair the loss; some are thwarted by a rival; some meet with discouragements, are early disheartened, and give up all effort in despair. Most reach the close of life feeling, if they have any right feeling, that they have accomplished almost nothing; the good usually with the reflection that if they ever accomplish much it must now be in a higher state of being." Dr. Durbin felt he was God's property, and that he must make the most of the divine investment in him. To show the benign influence of a life of such labor and success in the cause of God and the results of the efforts of an arch-infidel upon the world, whatever may be his learning or eloquence, we adopt the language of Dr. Southey in his contrast of the lives of Voltaire and Wesley. He says: "While the one was scattering with pestilent activity the seeds of immorality and unbelief, the other, with equal unweariable zeal, labored in the cause of religious enthusiasm. The works of Voltaire have found their way wherever the French language is read, the disciples of Wesley wherever the English is spoken. The principles of the arch-infidel were more rapid in their operation; he who aimed at no such evil as that which he contributed so greatly to bring about was himself startled at their progress. In his latter days he trembled at the consequences which he then foresaw, and, indeed, his remains had scarcely moldered in the grave before those consequences brought down the whole fabric of government in France, overturned her altars, subverted her throne, carried guilt, devastation, and misery into every part of his own country, and shook the rest of Europe like an earthquake. Wesley's doctrines, meantime, were slowly and gradually winning their way; but they advanced every succeeding year with accelerated force, and their effect must ultimately be more extensive, more powerful, and more permanent, for he has set mightiest principles at work." Nor can any one calculate the influence for good that went forth from Dr. Durbin, in the various positions that he filled in the Church, upon our own country and upon the globe: while he who rejects the claims of the Almighty, of whatever power of tongue or pen, must be regarded as an enemy to the human race.

More than thirty years ago Dr. Abel Stevens, the historian of Methodism, pronounced Dr. Durbin "the most interesting preacher in the Methodist pulpit." Learned men we may have had of a more accurate, if not a broader scholarship; writers of a more fruitful, if not of a more facile pen; but where one whose mind was better disciplined, whose faculties were better directed, or whose resources were more fully at the Church's command, or by whom more was accomplished in the divers and responsible positions that he filled? When was learning, genius, culture, devotion to duty, turned to better account? American Methodism has always had men adapted to her stations, but who from her origin has occupied so many distinguished places, and for so long a time? Is there one of all those various positions that he did not exalt by his talents and his skill and moral worth? If as a Church we can boast a greater name than John Price Durbin, then indeed we are honored! In the senate, cabinet, diplomatic corps, judiciary, or chair of the executive, he might have filled the first place in the nation.

To the glory of Christ's kingdom, he laid his talents at the foot of the cross and gave his life to the duties of the ministry. To the young Methodist preacher the life of John P. Durbin is a vast folio for study, but in its title-page is the motto that formed the theme of one of his first baccalaureate discourses at Dickinson College: "The High Purpose and Firm Resolve." This is the key to his greatness, and Grace furnishes that key.

25

THE END.